GOODNESS

D1570535

GOODNESS

MARTHA ROTH

Spinsters Ink
Duluth, Minnesota

First edition
10-9-8-7-6-5-4-3-2

Spinsters Ink
32 E. First St., #330
Duluth, MN 55802-2002

Cover Design & Illustration by Lois Stanfield, LightSource Images, with images from ©1996 PhotoDisc Inc.

Production:

Helen Dooley	Lou Ann Matossian
Joan Drury	Jami Snyder
Emily Gould	Amy Strasheim
Claire Kirch	Liz Tufte
Lori Loughney	Nancy Walker

Library of Congress Cataloging-in-Publication Data
Roth, Martha.
    Goodness / Martha Roth.
      p.   cm.
    ISBN 1-883523-11-7 (alk. paper)
    1. Peace movements—Minnesota—Minneapolis—Fiction.
    2. Friendship—Minnesota—Minneapolis—Fiction.
    3. Feminists—Minnesota—Minneapolis—Fiction.
    4. Women—Minnesota—Minneapolis—Fiction.
    5. Minneapolis (Minn.)—Fiction. I. Title.
PS3568.O8542G66   1966
813'.54—dc20
                     96-7105
                      CIP

ACKNOWLEDGMENTS

(This page is an extension of the copyright page)

For everyone who was there and everyone who will be

TABLE OF CONTENTS

PART 1

PART 2

PART 3

GOODNESS

CHAPTER 1

CORA

Don't know why I showered this morning. Seems silly to shower and then stand outside with the temperature at twenty-seven below zero. If I hadn't washed, I wouldn't have felt the lump, the little lump like a lima bean on the outside of my left breast. I imagine I can feel it rubbing against my bra when I bob the sign up and down. *No More Bombs,* mine says. We stand in a sequence like the old Burma Shave signs: first me, then Maureen's sign says *No More War,* then Dinah's says *U.S. Out of Nicaragua & El Salvador,* and Persimmon's says *And South Africa, Guatemala, Honduras, Costa Rica, Persian Gulf, Asia Minor, Middle East, Western Europe,* in smaller and smaller letters until you can hardly read the word Europe.

"Where are your kids?" I ask Persimmon. Sometimes she brings them with her and carries the baby on her back.

"James is home for a week, so I let them stay warm."

She's too young to remember Burma Shave signs, with their little homilies on safety and personal grooming, but Dinah and Maureen and I are old enough. Maybe there is an America where they still bloom under hot sunny skies, family cars whizzing past full of little kids jamming their heads and arms out of the windows, while Dad drives and Mom tries to keep order with license-plate poker and an occasional swat.

"I'm warning you!"

The metal of the window frame got so hot you had to be careful to touch only the furry strip that protected the glass.

"Mom! Peter pushed me and I got *burned!* I have a *red mark!*"

"Peter! I'm warning you!"

The turnpikes were new in the late forties, and those old heaps went sixty, seventy, eighty miles an hour.

"Mom! Cora pinched me!"

"Anyone I can reach gets hit!"

"Look—Burma Shave!" And everyone would go quiet for a moment while we read the signs:

> *Harry's dead*
> *Impatient fellow*
> *Tried to pass*

"On a double yellow, I bet. I bet it is—"

"No fair! You spoiled it—"

"Where the heck's the sign?"

Whizz, whizz. "Oh, Paul's right." Then, in chorus: "Burma Shave!"

> *Susie met Billy, Billy had a beard*
> *Away from Billy Susie veered*
> *Billy shaved, and the following week*
> *Bill and Sue dance cheek to cheek*
> *Burma Shave*

with the little pennant flair underneath. After that breather, Mom could stand even another chorus of "A Hundred Bottles of Beer on the Wall." Brahms wrote that, or somebody.

Goodness, it's cold. My theatrical friend Dinah, over there in her lumpy down coat, is always calling up sense memories, but I can't really feel how hot it was in the car, the smell of the upholstery, that bristly gray-brown Chevrolet velour. Mom and Dad both smoked, not much, but the upholstery soaked up the smell of tobacco.

We have to be crazy to stand here with our signs, freezing our buns, our feet, our faces. Even with a scarf over my nose and mouth, I can feel my sinuses freezing stiff. I hope these people enjoy us crazy women. These people aren't on vacation, of course. They're going to work. Where else would they be going at seven o'clock on a winter weekday morning, at a freeway entrance?

About a third of the cars that pass are Mercedes, Volvos, Saabs, or BMWs. I don't even count the Audis. People have money, they don't want to think about where it comes from. I wonder how many of them work for some company that makes weapons. Or for some other defense contractor. Even the food companies, the big conglomerates, a lot of their business comes from the Department of Defense. Department of War. The armed services buy huge quantities of baking mixes, instant mashed potatoes, underwear, shoe leather, beans. Beans. I know that little bean in my breast is a disease, it's a messenger of disease. But at the same time, I know it's probably nothing at all. Thousands of women find lumps in their breasts every day, and most of them are benign.

Benign, like the sun's rays, clear and well-intentioned. Only some are not bean-ign. They are opaque, they stop the X-rays, and they're malignant as the sun on the roof of a Chevrolet. Worse. They send out malignant emissaries in the blood, in the lymph, they're like an evil empire. That's what our idiot president calls the Soviet Union. Communism as cancer.

My moon boots kept the cold out for a while, but now

3

they have surrendered. I try to keep warm thinking about the sun, but that gets me into Cancer, the sun in Cancer, July, smells of the upholstery in my parents' old Chevrolet, and Peter and Paul's sweat. I still don't like the smell of my brothers' sweat, not that I smell it so often, investment bankers don't sweat much, and when they play tennis they splash themselves with stuff, Gentleman or Pour Homme. Scottie and M. J. give them expensive cologne for their anniversaries every year, and they go to a nice inn and drink champagne and make love in the shower. In the shower. Hands gliding over breasts, lingering, finding lumps. Breasts that gave up their bloom in the cause of infant nourishment. Sagging breasts with lumps in them.

All feeling has left my fingers. I'm going to hold the sign with one hand and stick the other in my pocket. Oh good, the darkness is lightening a bit, we're going to have another day. This will be the day when I call my doctor, the minute I get home, I promise myself, I promise Jerry and Maureen and Dinah and Persimmon. Our breath looks like smoke, like dragons' breath. What was that terrible weapon they had in Vietnam? Puff the Magic Dragon they called it, a machine gun that fired some unbelievable number of rounds per minute. They mounted them in helicopters, we did, the Americans, and flew low over villages and fired on people, incredible rapid bursts of death.

The blue dawn gives a pretty light, the snow sparkles under the streetlamps, a bright, soft blue. Stamping my feet gets the blood going but it doesn't do much for the toes.

"Maureen!" I have to push my scarf down so she can hear me.

"Yeah?" She does too.

"Let's yell."

So we yell together. "No more bombs, no more war, in Nicaragua or El Salvador, no more bombs, no more—"

I know they can't hear us, everybody's got their windows

rolled up tight against the cold, but if we bob up and down they'll see us easier, four women in thick coats and boots and heavy gloves, holding signs lettered on posterboard and stapled to pieces of raw lath.

The cars stream past us, about half of them taking a right turn onto the freeway to the University or St. Paul, the other half going straight to downtown Minneapolis or the western suburbs. Oh, here's the guy in the white Mercedes who always—yes, he's giving us the finger again, very vigorous today, jabbing straight up toward the roof, ducking his head low over the steering wheel. Oh! Making eye contact! Goodness! And a very good morning to *you*, sir.

Maureen pulls down her scarf again and shouts, "What a jerk!"

"Love him."

Persimmon smiles broadly and gestures back, but as she's wearing mittens the point is lost. It's good to return hostility with a smile—that way you diffuse it, instead of hanging onto it, building it, the way we used to in the car.

"He hit me first!"

"I did not!"

"You did, too. The very first. You started it!"

"Did not, liar!"

"First one I can reach gets hit."

Most people keep their eyes on the road, they're drinking their coffee, it's early, they have the radio on, listening for the weather, is there going to be a blizzard? We dread knowing a bad storm's on the way, but there's a secret glee: we won't be able to drive anywhere. Maybe the schools will close. Jerry has to get to the clinic, that's why his car has four-wheel drive, doctors can't let themselves feel it, but I can, the gleeful dread. Snowbound!

What if I were a homeless person—what if I slept in a public shelter that I had to leave every morning at seven-thirty with a bellyful of instant oatmeal and weak coffee, charity food? How would that be, to spend a whole day on the street during a blizzard, when even the shabbiest coffee shop is closed, even the place where on a nice day they let me sit for a couple of hours over one cup of something that I've panhandled the money for? How would that be? At eight we can go over to Ragamuffin's and get some sugar and caffeine.

Maureen believes all these people can see us, but I'm not so sure, especially in the misty blue dawn with the street-lights on. When you're driving a car you look for signs, not human beings, they're pretty indistinct. Maureen doesn't drive; she doesn't have that sense. You look at the road, really, not the pavement—except to see signs. Well, maybe she's right, maybe they pick up our signs subliminally:

Yield.
Slower Traffic Keep Right.
No More Bombs.
Freeway Entrance. No Stopping.
No More War.
30 MPH Ramp Speed.
U.S. Out of Nicaragua & El Salvador.

But I'm afraid we're invisible, in a hole. What was that other song we used to sing in the car? "There's a Hole in the Bottom of the Sea," Pauly screaming with laughter when we got to

> *There's a hair on the flea on the fly on the*
> *wart on the frog on the twig on the branch*
> *of the tree in the hole in the bottom of the*
> *sea—*

and then Peter would always go on to

> *There's a nit on the hair on the flea on the*
> *fly on the the wart on the frog—*

and Pauly would scream louder, and then once he sang

There's a dingleberry on the hair on the flea
on the fly—

And Mom said, *That's enough.*

There's a lump in the breast of the woman with a sign on the corner of the street by the entrance to the freeway—it doesn't sing.

🍃

We had our first street demos in 1963, against the strontium in the milk, and we went on marching—against nuclear power, for school desegregation, and then against the War. We were deadly serious but we were—speaking for myself, *I* was—exhilarated to be on the street. We gathered to celebrate being alive even more than to protest the government's plans for making people dead. We shouted out our fellowship with draftees, with resisters, with the Vietnamese, not one of whom we had ever seen in person. We flouted city ordinances, we painted our faces and sang. Being together in the street, marching and shouting, felt like summer vacation— joyous, lawless, peaceful, like having a dirty face and not caring, like dropping your peach in the sand and eating it anyway.

Some people carried signs, and we chanted things like *Hey, hey, LBJ, How many kids didja kill today,* and *One, two, three, four, We don't want your fucking war,* but there was no harm in us, no violence. We felt we were liberating ourselves from some strictures, and we discovered what they were as we freed little bits at a time. *Pop!* my ears. *Snap!* my eyes. *Boing!* my uterus.

Uterus. You-tear-us, you-truss. When I was little and first heard that word I visualized a bulky leather sort of pouch, a bag with many folds. Uterus was something big ladies had, women who wore stockings and garter belts like my mother,

7

women who smelled of scented powder and sweat from the thighs and crotch. Her dresses hanging in the closet held that same faint smell of cunt overlaid with powder. Her underwear drawer was neatly filled with slips, rayon they must have been, peach or "flesh" color, she had one navy-blue one, and rolled stockings neat as sticky buns, and big brassieres, engineering marvels, did she have to iron her rayon brassieres? Ordinary women like my mother probably couldn't afford silk underwear, so they wore rayon—or cotton in summer. Rayon, spun from coal tar, a lumber product—another development of military technology, like nylon, like polymers, and ersatz coffee that became instant coffee. War is such a spur to industry.

Under their lady clothes, the dresses of rayon crepe or faille, or the good wool suits and nice blouses, under the modest slips and the wide-legged panties trimmed with lace, under the soft flesh of their bellies, puckered and cross-stitched where the appendix came out, or the ovarian cyst, under all of this they carried the big bag, the uterus.

Women of my mother's generation seemed to me clothed in impenetrable decorum even naked, and I imagined they were correct beneath their skins as well. For married love, they stuck a little rubber hat on the bag, smearing it first with jelly or cream. They only left off the little hat when they planned to get pregnant, and then the leather folds opened decorously to let the babies out. Did the bag contort riotously when she Achieved Her Climax? Did the bag ever convulse, stand on its head, kick off the diaphragm, flip and flop and let in some of that dangerous seminal fluid when she hadn't planned to?

Mine's not a leather shopping bag, it's a silk purse. Mother never told me I had one too, a satin doll of a uterus, supple and glistening, and ovary rosettes with tiny eggs, the delicate necessities embroidered inside me, waiting inside me for love, for Jerry, for Serena and Seth. They really brought me into the peace movement, my gorgeous little kids.

My satin doll is shrinking, but I'm still marching, still shouting.

🍂

I wake up all at once. Saturday morning, the clock says six. Jerry's asleep. In our room, the darkness has a silvery graphite look, snow light.

I feel good, expectant. Then it hits me like a screech of brakes, yes, the lump's still there. Monday I go for a biopsy.

I always wake up with a sense of promise. Great things might happen today, tomorrow, next month—dogs might learn human speech, the State Department might declare peace, justice might break out in the street. If that lump is cancerous and if I die, I'll miss Ronald Reagan announcing the end of the Cold War. I'll miss the signs on the Pentagon: *Everything Must Go! Make Your Own Plowshares and Pruning Hooks!* New schools, universal health insurance, a floor under incomes, taxes on corporate profits, incentives for small co-ops, CIA out of the drug business, open-door prisons, happy anarchy, peace.

I dive into my old flannel robe and come down to the cold kitchen. The thermostat ignites the furnace—the Gladdwin thermostat, I always mark it. I put on water for tea and let Jean Harlow out into the back yard, where she goes right into the tunnels she made weeks ago. Golden retrievers are so patient. She was Seth's puppy when he turned eight, when Serena broke her collarbone and got so much attention. That's when she decided to be a doctor. She'll be here in six weeks, to start her residency at University Hospital.

It's wonderful how the light comes a little earlier every day. I love to welcome the dawn on Fridays with my friends, Dinah, Maureen, Persimmon. Dinah came to Minneapolis in 1963 with her first husband, a shrink named Reuben Berns. Stuck in a suburban house with two little kids, she went part crazy from loneliness before she found the peace movement. She should have been a strolling player, a cheerful vagabond; she had the soul of a hippie trapped in the living room of a doctor's wife. If the lump is cancer, how many more dawns do we have?

I've seen Dinah through the bust-up of two marriages and through casual affairs and serious affairs, with men, with women. My neighbor, Max, once screamed at Dinah when she changed lovers. *You use people,* she yelled, *like, like, like hand cream! You rub them on your body and then forget about them!*

Jean Harlow barks, and when I let her in, I see clear pale violet light in the sky and smoke rising straight from all the chimneys: another cold, still day.

I love my clean, quiet kitchen, lavender light peeking through the windows. All my pots and pans hanging neatly from their hooks, my knives and spoons lying orderly in their drawers.

Good girl, Jean Harlow. You want some more water in your bowl? Thump your tail, that's right. Can you talk yet?

Persimmon adopted me six or seven years ago, when Serena went off to college. Her name was Jodi Ann, then, and she was pregnant. She came to a meeting and looked at me with eyes the color of seedless grapes. *You are Kore, my other aspect,* she said, and promptly changed her name to a fruit. She is like a daughter I don't have to worry about— another flower of my dreams.

Jean Harlow groans and thumps her tail. The house creaks. My big, round, red plastic clock ticks, and my knives wait in their drawer. I could take the boning knife, with its thin flexible blade, and tunnel the lump out myself. It's in my left breast. I'm right-handed. What a piece of luck. Couple of twists of the wrist: in deep, turn, scoop, and out before I know what hit me, before I lose consciousness—

I hear a solid sound from upstairs, Jerry's feet encountering the floor, and I flip the coffeemaker switch. It'll be nice to see my old darling.

*

"Dreamed about the goddamn dog." He pours out a mug of coffee and sits down across from me. His hair is all riled up on one side of his head. "You doing okay?"

I get another flash of the boning knife, this time in his long, loved hand. "Pretty much. What did you dream?"

He makes a fist and touches my jaw with his knuckles, softly as a thought. "She was in a cage like a lab animal. I wanted to get her out, but there was nothing I could do."

"How come?"

"Wasn't my lab."

Jean Harlow sticks her muzzle in his hand, and he squeezes her dewlaps. She makes a sound between a whine and a snarl and backs away. She's been doing this all her life, sticking her wet muzzle into his hand, and all her life he has responded by squeezing her thin jowls to show he doesn't like it. What is it that she hopes will happen for the first time?

"You're cute, but I can't sit here all morning watching you wake up," I tell him. "I've got things to do. Mailing party here this afternoon."

"What's it for, again?"

"You know. Max is going to run for school board. We're mailing the flyer for coffee parties. She's doing fifteen, all over town."

He combs through his hair with his fingers. "You really want to do that today?"

"You bet I do. Get my mind off my troubles."

He wraps his long arms around me and holds me against his warm, familiar body. "I know. Me, too."

*

Will I ever not want to hear Jerry snore? Such a safe

sound. We both felt funny going to bed tonight. *This might be your last chance at two boobies,* I told him, but he just wanted to hold me. We held each other for a long time.

Can't keep my fingers away from the spot. Where is it? Is it gone? No. No such luck. Feels like a wad of bubble gum. No. Feels like a cloth-covered button, one of those little round metal shank buttons covered with something woolly, let's see, dark red wool crepe. Bright red wool jersey. Get your fingers off it, you numskull. Stop, stop, you're spreading it, every time you press the button you're sending evil messages. Creep cells. Why do you want to flood your body with poisons? Ay-yi-yi, poison. Every cigarette, every joint I ever smoked. Not so many, really. Every fast-food burger, every drink of liquor, every pill. I'm glad I was such a chickenshit. I never did drugs. Never. No—I lie, cocaine when Jerry was a medical student and morphine for pain, when my stitches got infected after Serena was born.

Every breath of polluted air—every sip of water, every mouthful of food—everything, everything is poisonous. But poison is just too much of something: Too many chloride ions, too much sulfur or nitrogen, and the air divides against itself, it sears the lungs it was meant to nourish.

And there's too much of everything. Mercury. Bromates. Pesticides. Fertilizers. Ions that hang around too long. Those substances were meant to have specific short-term effects, only nobody told their chemical bonds. Benzene rings. Detergents. Solvents. Workers in paper factories along the Gulf Coast wear rubber suits, masks, and gloves, and the chemicals in the pulp eat right through the rubber, I saw those photographs of Black workers' hands, they looked like flank steak.

When Serena was a baby, I used to tell her a story about her shit. Every day before her nap we'd go through the saga of what happens to it after it leaves her little tushie, how it goes down into the sewer system and gets taken apart into its simple components, and then it goes into the river and it flows downstream, past the pig farms of Iowa and the corn-fields of Illinois, and finally into the big salted ocean, and everywhere along the way a part of her shit nourishes the snails and fishes, the weeds, the grass on the riverbank, the corn and wheat, the hogs, it feeds the birds that follow the river and finally some part of that nourishment returns to her, in sardines or cornmeal or spinach or apples or–

She would say it along with me, chiming in on the words she liked: *Iowa,* she'd say, her eyes soft and faraway, *apples.* She'd clap her busy hands together, flat palm to palm the way babies do, lying on her back gently kicking her legs on the madras bedspread of our big bed, I can see the stripes of blue and green against her amber head. And I'd change her diaper and dump the shit into the toilet and flush it, clean her up and put on doubles for her nap. But I didn't tell her about poisons. I never mentioned the strontium in the milk, or the weed-killers from nice Mr. Nelson's beautiful lawn, or the out-and-out crooks who flush their dyes and slurry and acid baths down the same sewers as her innocent shit, all the poisonous residues that wash along, carried by the rain. Of course, now the rain is poisoned, too.

Seth never liked that story.

I didn't tell her about the poisons because I didn't know. And when I found out, I did something. We started Women Strike for Peace, Max and I. I hope she gets on the school board, she knows a lot about schools. Jerry says her flyers should read, *Don't Raise Tax, Vote for Max!* But she's not afraid to raise money and spend it on children. She'll feed them breakfast. We picketed the supermarkets and the dairies. We baked cookies and sold them to pay for mimeo-graphed leaflets. That's how I met dear Dinah, at a bake sale. But I didn't know I'd be lying here twenty years later with my hand on a button of evil disease in my breast, the breast that fed my babies.

And who's to say it came from those poisons? Maybe poly-chlorinated biphenyls and benzene had nothing to do with it. Maybe it's part of my genetic program: the cells on this side of my breast have been planning to lump up all along. Lump readiness, I've had the condition for years, a latent lump's been there since I first got breasts, maybe even before. Most girls wait and wait. Dinah told me she was fourteen before she had anything to put into the cups of a bra. Me, I could have waited a little longer, thanks very much.

Maybe it's my own wickedness, collected there on the outside of my breast, too close for comfort to the lymph drainage system under my arm. My own little sewer system, my own evil thoughts, judgments, refusals. Everything I ever repressed, and now it's backing up on me.

Hey, wait a minute, repression's good. You've got to have repression to keep the strong from tyrannizing the weak. Repression lets us have the idea of justice. No, I'm for repression. We need laws.

But when we repress our own desires, we turn ourselves into police. Why let The Man into our heads? I can't help it. I don't know how to free myself. The snap and pop of breaking chains in the sixties, that liberation was temporary. The shackles slipped back on, some time after Watergate. What have I repressed, what's coming back? Is it bad enough to kill me?

I really hate Jerry's snoring.

But I love Jerry, so I put up with it.

I used to feel frantic with rage at Seth and Serena, not when they were babies, not even the three months when Seth had colic. I was never angry at them. I was angry at myself, at the gods, maybe at Jerry a couple of times. But when they were older, toddlers, playing with each other, she was so cruel to him, poor little guy, and he adored her so. Swena, he called her.

Swena push me, he'd say proudly when I came running after one of those lingering crashes.

He wouldn't cry much. Is that because she didn't hurt him, or was he repressing the pain and sorrow, poor little mannikin? Is some lump gathering to lurk in his well-loved body even now, one in the morning, two where he is, Eastern time? Is he in bed, Seth, are you sleeping? Are you alone? O Seth, Seth, I was so amazed to give birth to your little pecker.

Seth fell, she would say calmly when he fell down the stairs, that dull, soft lumpety-lumpety-*lump.*

He would cry, briefly, then he'd smile like an angel and say *Swena push me,* and shoulder his way out of my arms and crawl back up the stairs.

Once I picked her up and shook her until her hair flew and her eyes rolled like marbles, my hands were numb with anger. I scared myself. *Don't push him, Serena,* I seethed at her. *Keep your hands and feet away from Seth.*

She cried then, and of course I felt shitty. So what did I repress? I felt the anger, I felt close to hating one of my children because she was hurting the other. What should I have done—kill her? Let her kill him?

I want another chance to do it right.

Now Serena's going to start her residency in pediatric reconstructive surgery, helping to mend the world we broke. She spent a summer in Managua after her third year of medical school, working with a team of Cuban doctors to put kids back together after Contra attacks.

When Jerry was a resident, he used to come home with terrible stories, kids with multiple fractures, babies bruised or scalded, one little boy I've never forgotten who had second-degree burns, in stripes, in a pattern of radiator coils, on his tush and his legs.

"The mother says the babysitter told her he fell against the radiator." Wearily he turned his coffee mug around in his hands. "But the clinical signs aren't consistent with that story.

The tissue damage indicates there was prolonged contact with the source of heat, and so forth. Finally she admitted she makes him sit on the radiator when he wets his pants. Chrissakes, this is a two-year-old! And she said—"

He put down the mug, I can see him, and he rubbed his forehead with one hand and his eyes with the other, as though he could rub out the sight or the memory. "She said, 'It worked with the other kids. And it worked with me and my brothers. This kid's just *stubborn.*'"

In this country, we torture our own children. In other countries, when children are harmed it's a hideous technique of war, it's terrorism, *la represión,* they make you watch while they hurt your kids so that you'll tell them things.

How is it that we do it to our own?

The night is so quiet, around the edges of his snoring. Don't know if I'll ever get used to a quiet house, not listening for the kids—Serena and her pack coming in late to drink coffee and spin plots in the kitchen; Seth dancing around in his room with his headphones on. First she left, then he left. Now I only feel real when they come home, Christmas holidays or summer vacation. The rest of the time there's no one who shouts for me, no one who comes in late, no one for me to answer to. Kids are such jealous lovers. I wish I had another one.

Jerry's stories obsessed me—children smacked, broken, terrorized, the violence in their ordinary parents that caused them to do these things. They obsessed him, too. I think that's why he likes working with Indian people, even though most of his patients are so poor. They mostly don't do those things to their kids. Neglect, maybe; brutality, not. I believe that violence exists in me, and I've repressed it, and now it's gathered itself into this lump in my body.

Goodness, do I really believe that? I'm never going to get to sleep. Tomorrow when I have to go to the hospital, I'll be a wreck, whatever they have to do to me will go badly. When I close my eyes I see bruised flesh, I see the faces of children who've been beaten and know they'll be beaten again—children of violence who'll grow up to hit their own kids, an endless spiral of terror and *represión*. We teach ourselves to inflict pain and to call it something else.

I haven't done these things. But I'm capable of them. No, I'm not. I could never break my baby's arm, no matter how desperate I felt.

But I could smother it.

If I were a seventeen-year-old mom with a colicky baby, like Seth, and no husband and no money, or even let's say the baby's father lives with me, and it's hot, it's summer and the baby cries all the time, or it's now, it's the dead of winter, I can't go anyplace, my apartment's crummy and overheated, or drafty, they turn the heat off at eleven even though it's too hot during the day. I have to get up with my baby in the middle of the night, and I can see our breath in the room. The windows leak cold air, so I can't put the baby on the floor. There's no place to go. I haven't got a car. The baby cries all the time. Sometimes it falls asleep, and I open a can of pop and sit down or—if the baby's dad is there—we have a couple of beers and try to get it on, but then the baby wakes up and cries. I have to walk the baby so it won't cry, or rock it, sometimes it'll go to sleep on my shoulder and I can watch TV, but if I try to put it down, it wakes up and cries. I feed it, and then it spits up and cries, writhing as though the milk from my tit or from a bottle hurts it inside, crying and arching its back, everything I own smells of sour milk or baby shit, I have to go to the laundromat every day, and I can't get anyone to stay with the baby, and I haven't had a full night's sleep in six weeks, the baby has diaper rash and cradle cap, and it cries all the time, yes, I might try to shut it up forever. Forever. Tomorrow.

CHAPTER 2

CORA, LATER

I never really went under. I felt the tube go down and heard them muttering while they draped and cut me, heard the snicker of the anesthetist's plastic gloves, heard an instrument drop on the tile floor. I felt every turn of the wheels when they took me into the recovery room.

I can't move my hand. When I wiggle the fingers, turns out it's imprisoned in Jerry's. The world's behind bars, I'm seeing things in strips, like through a Venetian blind.

"So what's the word?"

"It's a primary carcinoma, baby."

Shit, I knew it, I'm going to have to lose that breast. Goddamn it. I can taste the meds they dripped into me, my throat's sore behind my nose where the tube went in. Tears trickle out of my eyes and nose, over my hair and the pillow, and Jerry's crying too. Tears crawl down the gullies of his face and I'm crying like a baby for its mother's tit, only this is my own tit I'm weeping for. *Jerry, I'm so scared.*

Gradually the tears clear my head. I wake up all the way and it's the same Monday morning. Winter sun streams into the hospital room. Thank goodness no one's in the other beds; I always love to see the sun getting strong in February. We hold each other awkwardly, favoring my wounded breast which has a big dressing on it. We wrap our arms around each other and nuzzle and as the anesthetic fades my breast starts to throb, a dull sensation at first, but I know it will get stronger, like a police siren getting closer with every pulse-beat. I stare past his shoulder at the shiny floor, waxed asphalt tile. They caught me this time. There's no escaping now.

After a while an aide pokes her head in the door and says something chirpy.

"In a minute," says Jerry. "My wife has just come out of the anesthetic."

She drops her brisk manner to come in and pat my shoulder, the good one. They give me fruit juice to drink, and they load me into a chair and wheel me into the elevator and down to Sydney's office. We discuss options, a treatment plan. *Yes, I want you to go ahead with the mastectomy, a modified radical, please, don't mutilate me any more than you have to.* In the old technique, the Halstead procedure, they not only cut off your breast and stripped most of the muscles from your chest wall but also excavated the lymph nodes in your armpit, hollowing you out so you looked like a Picasso painting, with one breast and a concave gouge in the place of the other. Negative space.

But Sydney's not a ghoul, he is considerate of our feelings and he schedules surgery for the day after tomorrow, Wednesday. "After you're healed we'll talk about radiation or chemo," he says. "They might not even be indicated. We won't know until we get in there and see what's what."

In the car I have to squint against the crashing brilliance of sun on snow. Jerry whistles a Monk tune. As we head for home, I start to feel longing, like hunger. I long for a child. Not for a child I have. Not for Serena or Seth. For a new baby. I imagine saying, *How would you like to have another baby?*

I imagine Jerry looking at me from under his eyebrows, a say-*what?* look.

Jerry walks me into the house, and I tell him to go to work. I want to dwell with this longing for a while, this new conceptual baby. Light slowly drains out of the afternoon, then I call Dinah and tell her about the carcinoma.

"Oh Cory," she says. "Oh Cory. You are the last person. Are you going to call Serena and Seth? Oh Cory, let me come with you on Wednesday, I want to be there when you wake up. I'll go get stuff for you."

"Don't you go to pieces on me now, Dinah. I need for you to be okay. Listen, what do you think about–" But I don't say anything just yet. The baby is my secret. If I go ahead with it– and I know I will–I'm going to need a lot of help.

"What about what?" she asks, and I say, "Oh, nothing. You'll help me fight this, right? We're scrappers."

"Hey. Don't mess with us."

Jean Harlow comes into the kitchen, wagging her tail and whining in her old-dog voice. Good dog, you're going to outlive me, Jean Harlow, ain't that a bitch?

We call the kids that night. "Bum-mer," says Seth quietly. "Do you want us home, mom?" I tell him no, it's more important for him to stay where he is. "Think of me, but not too much, honey,"

"I'm coming in," says Serena. "My residency starts in six weeks anyway, don't you think they'll let me come early? Cook County can get along without me. Daddy's got to work, and you need someone there."

"Really," I tell her, "I've got lots of volunteers."

"I'll bet you do," she says. "You're so popular, mom."

Maureen and Persimmon both call to tell me they're praying for me. It's weird to sit in ordinary lamplight and hear my friends invoke their Powers. Maureen will make a devotion to Marymotheragod, but Persimmon worships an eclectic batch of spirits she calls *loas*. I suppose Max prays to

Krupskaya. Dinah used to call herself a priestess of Isis when she had young men eager to stretch themselves across her altar.

For supper, Jerry buys Middle Eastern takeout, pita bread sandwiches, and garlic burns my throat, still sore from this morning. Ordinary life goes on, but now my life has this stuff in it that is not ordinary. I may be nonviolent, but I'm going to fight this one.

It could be a chance. Another chance. For me, for a baby too. What's happening right now in Salvador? In Nicaragua? There are children there who need families, babies whose parents have been killed. Maybe my baby is already born, brown and squirming and hungry for me.

*

Cancer brings the thought of death, like Jean Harlow dragging her rawhide bone into the room.

"It would be a good thing to just accept death, wouldn't it?" I ask Jerry. "After all, it's part of life."

"Cut it out," he says. "People live for years with all sorts of cancers, it's a chronic disease, for shit's sake, like—like—diabetes. Anyway, you're too tough to die. Don't you accept anything too fast. Maybe you should get mad, boiling mad."

I'm tired early, and Jerry comes to bed too, about ten. We reach for each other, and catch fire. *Nothing like a good scare, eh?* He licks me and strokes me, and my pleasure comes fast and very strong. Then he moves in me slow and deep and it comes again. Both my breasts feel sore and precious, my nipples sharp as jewels. He is exquisitely careful of the place where they took the biopsy sample, where pain is gnawing.

Touch me, Jerry, and he does, and when I feel his tongue on my nipple I start to come again, helplessly, as though our loving under threat of death reached up inside of me, turned me inside out and released a flood of feeling that had been dammed by health, by my ordinary life.

We lie on our sides looking at each other, Jerry's face—every bump, every wrinkle, every gray hair, I know them all, I knew them when. His hands trace my face and I kiss them, his wonderful hands, and when he comes the first time he groans the way he did when he was young, deep and heartfelt, pulsing in me. Then he lies quietly, but I feel him still partly hard inside me and I'm still contracting, and we start to move again together. Moisture pours out of me, I haven't been so wet in years, and I slither on top of him. He reaches for my breasts, his fingers rolling my nipples tenderly, and I start to cry, bucking and rocking, gripping and twisting, the core of me melting and running out. He holds on for a long time, moving his hands over my body and kissing and sucking all the old familiar places, some of whose days are numbered, and then he comes again with a long low moan while I hold his balls, and we fall asleep in our puddle of desperate love.

Next morning I startle awake, as though a baby were crying.

*

Anesthesia binds your bowels, puts thick walls between you and your feelings. Wednesday. Sydney suits up in his greens and cuts off my breast, and this time I'm not even there. When I wake up, I know right away where I am and what has happened because the pain is godawful, nothing they can give you does any good. I'm glad the cancer's gone, but it looks like they've filleted out quite a lot of other stuff besides my breast; the dressing goes clear to my elbow.

Then Jerry comes in, then Sydney comes in, and the news is not good. There were cancer cells in most of the lymph nodes they took out. They think I've probably got other little cancers growing in places they can't see. It spreads easily through the lymph. I don't know much about the lymphatic system, but it's always sounded like a subversive organization.

Sydney smiles and says, "Nobody knows much about it."

They're going to shoot the works on me: chemotherapy, radiation, everything. We need to discuss a treatment plan, he says, after I've healed from the surgery. Healing is important; resistance is important. I'm going to need a lot of strength for the baby.

*

Jerry's brows draw down. I grab his hand. "So many families have been destroyed, in Salvador, in Guatemala, as well as Nicaragua—"

"Baby, I know you're tough. But chemo's going to knock you on your ass, you won't be in any shape to take care of a *niñita.*"

"The treatment won't go on forever! And you said yourself, I'm tough. We could start working on the adoption at least. Remember those friends of Max and Einar's? It took a year and a half for them to get a child. Think about all the destruction our money's paying for—all the guns, the uniforms, the training. Wouldn't we like to pull out something positive—like another little Bookbinder?"

He looks me deep in the eyes. "Baby, I know you want this, I can smell it. But I think it's your fear talking. I think you're shoving away the negative feelings about the surgery, and chemo, and radiation, and concentrating on this new—"

"Is that so bad?"

He smiles, but the worry lines don't smooth out.

*

Serena comes home early to start her surgical residency, and I tell her about the new baby. "God, mom, are you sure? I think it's a hassle to try to get a Central American kid. Besides—"

"What?"

"Well, the politics is kind of screwy, isn't it? Adopting a baby from another culture? I don't know—"

"Carl Kjellstrom's living in Guatemala, you remember him. I'm writing him today."

Fifteen years ago, Carl was Dinah's lover, and he went to jail because he wouldn't register for the draft. He's a good friend of ours, a good man. I would trust him to find my baby.

"I think you have to deal with all sorts of lawyers and officials," Serena says. "Didn't Max and Einar know some people?"

Max brings her friend, Letricia, to talk to me about Central American adoptions, a sad-looking woman with tan teeth. Her son, Samuel, is in junior high.

"It was a hassle," she says, "and we couldn't believe how much it cost. Americans think of Costa Rica as a democracy, but it's a client state of the U.S. You wouldn't believe it. We went down to San José and stayed in a hotel, and this lawyer came to see us every day, and *every day* he needed more money for another bribe. We couldn't believe it. Five hundred here, three hundred there, plus the costs for the mother's care, the baby's passport, the lawyer's fee."

"Why did you want to do it?" I have to ask.

She flushes a dark rose color, quite becoming. "We wanted a child, and we didn't think we had the right to breed one of our own. I mean, every American baby uses up resources that could keep thirty children alive in the developing countries, you wouldn't believe how much. So we wanted to help one of those children. We wanted a street kid from Rio de Janeiro, but it was just beyond us to travel there."

"So what's your advice?"

She snorts and glances at Max, who nods. "Bring *mucho dinero*. And you wouldn't believe how committed you have to be, or you won't survive the process."

After they leave, I'm anxious, restless. It must have been worth it? Samy looks like a nice, friendly kid in the photos. Of course, they must love him.

Serena is always in a hurry. I crave the sight of her, her beautiful eyes, her tall sturdy body, the reassuring heft of her hands, but she can't spend enough time—we can't finish our talk because she's rushing off to a lecture on immunosuppression. I want her to see how right I am, how right the new baby will be. How well we will cope.

"I want you to promise me something," she says.

"What?"

"Don't want that Central American baby too much. Seth and I will be jealous."

I'm shocked. I can't believe it. "Darling, darling, I could never—"

"Seriously, mom. I'm kidding about jealous, but I don't want you to get your hopes up. You write to Carl, fine. Then just wait to see what he says. Promise?"

"Okay, Doctor."

Serena is on a seventy-two-hour rotation, three solid days on call, cutting and sewing human flesh sometimes without sleep, then three days of ordinary twelve-hour days, then a day off, then it starts again. At home, when she is not sleeping, she gives me wonderful massages. I don't mind her touching the puckered scar across my chest with her sturdy, delicate fingers. Sometimes I worry that she has no social life. Then I remember the years when I hardly saw Jerry.

She plays the dragon when my friends want to come, but after a couple of weeks I get lonely. *You're supposed to rest,* she says.

I beg her to let me have my friends, my lifeline. So one by two, she admits them to the house. My brother Paul's wife, M. J., has sent me a raw silk caftan in teal blue with a tapestried border of purple and green. Serena lowers it gently over my head so I can receive in style.

Dinah is the first, her hands full of flowers. "God, you look beautiful. I'm so glad Serena's here—thank god she's a doctor—she can look after you—I'll only stay a couple minutes—I don't want to tire you out, but oh, Cory, I miss you. We all miss you—I'm so jealous of Serena but thank god you've got such good care—"

That night Serena tells Jerry that Dinah's grateful I've got a doctor looking after me and he snorts, *What am I, chopped liver?*

Persimmon stops in one day with all her kids. So beautiful, their smooth little bodies. "So you're Serena," she says. "Your mom talks a lot about you." They smile at each other cautiously.

"I really like your caftan," says Shawana, like a grown-up. Shaman goes after Jean Harlow, pulling and petting her. Abdul-Aziz crawls toward them, drooling. I want to smell them, taste them, the sight of them hits me like an ocean wave, and I get that swelling feeling, I want one of my own. I'm aching to tell her.

"We can't stay," shouts Shaman. "We have to buy some shoes. Please, mama, can we stay? This old dog likes me."

"We really can't stay, Cory, but I wanted to lay my eyes on you." She kisses me tenderly. "Be well."

Shawana stares with round eyes and as they are leaving she whispers, "Can I see your scar?"

Maureen calls every few days. She is a nun. Or an ex-nun. I don't understand the fine degrees of religious life. In the sixties and seventies, while Dinah and I were cooking dinner and answering phones and copying names and going to meetings and writing leaflets and marching and dying-in, Maureen worked as a missioner in Central America. She ran an orphanage first in Guatemala, then El Salvador, then Nicaragua. The Army kicked her out of Guatemala when they resettled her entire village; then the Salvadoran army kicked her out of El Salvador, very polite but pointing their rifles: *Please, Hermana Maurina, you are not safe, and we cannot protect you from the rebels. You must leave.* And all the time the Army making new *huérfanos.*

So she went to Nicaragua, opened another orphanage, and enjoyed the Triumph of the Revolution, in '79. *Everything really seemed possible then,* she says, *hope spread like mumps.* And then, in '82, the Contras blew up her house. She came back one day after taking the children on a visit to a nearby village to see her walls chopped open, roof tiles blasted into fragments lying thirty yards around, dead chickens, feathers everywhere, broken eggs leaking into straw, and, when she walked into the kitchen, she found her housekeeper dead on the dirt floor, and in one bedroom the housekeeper's two young brothers lying like logs, their blood drained into the dust. She says she had to be thankful none of the children was hurt, and it pained her to give thanks.

After the Contra attack, Maureen came back to the States, here to Minnesota, and went to work at Isis House, the women's shelter we started in the seventies. She runs it now, and it's called St. Savior's. I've only known her these few years, but I love Maureen. She still knows people in Central America, missioners. I could ask her—

I love my women friends, but I don't want them to touch me, to see my wounds. Sometimes I can't bear to be with Dinah, the pressure of her need is so great. *You're too good,* she tells me, *how can such goodness die from the world? I will be lost without you.*

She wants me to console her for the loss of myself.

"You know what I'll regret the most?" I ask Jerry one night when I can't sleep.

"Yeah," he says, "that you didn't end war on the planet."

"You're a jerk."

I say that a lot. I used to say it in fun, but now I say it like a crab. I'm ungrateful and full of self-pity. Never knew I was such a fair-weather friend, all it takes is cancer to blow my cool.

"No, you jerk, two things: that I didn't have friends who were women of color, and that I didn't treat the friends I did have better."

"Not to mention your ever-lovin'."

"Him, too."

The chemotherapy tastes of death. They tranquilize you when you go to be perfused, but afterward you know the poison's in your body. My hair falls out, I dread waking up in the morning. When I look at the pillow the crater made by my head is lined with my hair, like a nest. Carl hasn't answered my letter.

One beautiful spring day, Serena says, "You know about focus therapy, mother? Meditation, relaxation, you pick a prayer or a phrase to repeat over and over in your mind so that your consciousness is occupied."

"Honey, don't you remember mantras? People are so fickle. We knew about that in the sixties. You get your ego out of the way and the universal truth kicks in."

Of course, the sixties was more than that—liberation from ordinary thought, a door into another sunlit reality. Possibility, the richness you glimpse when you're young. I could be anything—you could be anything—

"Well, science withholds an opinion on the universal truth," says Serena, kneading my muscles, "but it works something like that. Only now you add visualization. Sort of like a video game, only the video is your brain, you visualize the cellular events taking place inside you. Your immune system is fighting your cancer."

April sun fills the window, followed by April cloud, then a sprinkling of rain. This is important; I want to use it. "But if I understand what Sydney told me, the cancer cells aren't invaders, they're my own cells, only they've picked up the wrong instructions somehow. They've lost track of their function in my little commonwealth."

"That's it, that's a good way to look at it."

Before my eyes Serena turns into Doctor Bookbinder, the big cuddly lady who can make you feel better after she has cut you up and sewn you back together.

I spend a lot of time in bed these days. Our bedroom has become almost like a hospital room. In fact, it's my room; Jerry sleeps in Seth's room. He has moved the belly telly in there, leaving me with the big foot-of-the-bed TV. Sometimes he watches it with me.

Some days, I don't feel well enough to get up; the clutter of trays and pitchers, plastic cups and glass straws and paper tissues almost comforts me. My brother Pete's wife, Scottie, sends me a box of terribly expensive powders and creams, Chanel, and I don't even open them. Now I know the worst, this squalor of sickness has been my fate all along. Cancer is like a secret I was keeping from myself, but now it's out. Well, we're going to heal it. When I remember the baby, my baby, health flushes me. I'll get well for her.

"That's a good way to look at it," Serena encourages me. "How will you visualize the cancer cells and the helping cells, the T lymphocytes and the others?"

Jean Harlow thumps her tail. Or is that some kid throwing a basketball through the hoop on the garage? Tulips and crocus must be pushing up through the grimy crust of city earth, eager for the space we grudge them. Pale satin leaves, smooth as babies, craving the sun. The scramble of spring begins again, for air, for water, a place, a chance.

"I'm going to impose a Cultural Revolution on them. I'm going to send them to re-education camps in the countryside where they can learn from the peasants."

Serena bursts out laughing and singing. "Only you, mother.

Only you can make this change in me
For it's true, you are my destiny—

Only you can do it, you know. Seriously. We need some serious visualization metaphors, here."

"This isn't frivolous, honey. I don't want to think about combat. I'd rather think of transformation."

"Okay. But we need details. *How* are they going to be transformed? What's the motivation, as Dinah would say?"

My clever child. Tulips and crocus and scilla and grass push upward, drawn by the sun as water is drawn by the moon. How can I change the hectic life inside me? "Change the rewards."

"How?"

"Look—soldiers are conditioned to fight, to be brave instead of kind. My cancer cells are like that, attacking their neighbors. I need to train them better."

"Good. How did they get that way in the first place?"

Behind Serena's shoulder, I see my old wooden waste-basket brimming with used tissues. A pile of newspapers lies under last week's *TV Guide,* waiting for someone to find time to haul it to the recycling center. Will I ever have the energy to do such things again? Sure I will; there'll be the baby to feed and change.

"Let me get this right. Most soldiers are poor boys with no prospects. They join up because recruiters lie to them about what war is, about what the future is."

"So," she prompts me, "what can you do to change them?"

"So—I—try to—to show them they can change the conditions that keep them poor. Make life better for everyone."

"How? This is really going to help the chemo, but you need to visualize it totally."

"Serena, you're pitiless. I have to think."

But I fall asleep. Then, late at night, she brings me some diluted apple juice, and I get back in the groove. "My poor soldier-boy cancer cells need to take back their power. They've given themselves to death—to the large institutions—

corporate, educational, governmental. *That's* where the malignancy is. Instead, they need to control their own wealth. Invest in their own communities. Educate their own children. Provide for their own needs. They need to learn to cooperate instead of competing."

"Terrific," she whispers. "That should work just fine." And she gets out the sweet almond oil and rubs my poor back, sore with lying down.

Serena helps me write a script, and for fifteen minutes every day, I do a little guided visualization. We tell Seth on the phone, and he draws us a storyboard, with cancer cells in jungle camouflage fatigues like Contras and lymphocytes and T cells in bright-colored blouses and white trousers.

In the first panel, the cancer cells wear bandoliers of ammunition and carry assault weapons, big ugly rifles and grenade launchers, flamethrowers, things I don't even have names for. The helping cells hide in the brilliant green undergrowth. In the next panel the helpers emerge from their thickets, holding machetes, flowers, fruits and vegetables in soft colors: peach, watermelon, and orchid purple.

In the next series of drawings, the helpers are leading bullocks by their bridles. One by one, they offer to exchange agricultural tools, books, food, and flowers for the weapons, which they discard out of the cartoon frame (Seth draws them dribbling off the edge of the board), and one by one the Contras are transformed.

In the last series of drawings, the Contras change their uniforms for the pretty clothes of the helping cells.

"Cell membranes have to become stronger, less permeable," Serena tells me. "Seth understands how it works."

"If only Congress would," I say.

We are in my room with the air-conditioner on, because it is one of Minnesota's rare hot spring nights. Serena's knowing fingers press me lightly, drily. "Time to focus."

I don't know what time it is, day or night. I drowse at all

hours, sleeping without fatigue, waking without energy. "Okay, mother. Visualize. They're ugly, they're disorganized, they're destructive. They totally don't know how to live, they only work together to destroy others, not for the good of the community."

I see their faces, half-grown men with empty eyes. I see their bodies that no one has touched in love. They are filled with hate because they are wretched. They know they have been ripped off, but they don't know how or by whom, so they are angry. Can I turn their anger so it will work for them, not against them? Gently, gently, I want to let them learn, to let them turn. I want them to learn enough about their condition so they can change, to save their lives, and mine, and my baby's.

*

After the course of chemo, I feel a lot better, and they schedule me for radiation therapy beginning in June. The heat breaks, too. I get up, get dressed, make my bed. I go for little walks with Jean Harlow and dear Dinah. Life seems like a possible project again. My friends come over often, sometimes together, bringing human warmth and abrasion.

They act as if they can't come without flowers or fruit. "Don't bring me things," I tell them.

"Don't be ridiculous," says Dinah. "You're always giving people things. It's time you were on the receiving end."

"She's right, mom," says Serena.

"Oh well, if you're going to gang up on me."

"Serena is such a pretty name," says Persimmon. Sun pours in the windows. She has set her children to coloring at the dining-room table, while Abdul-Aziz practices pulling himself up on their chairs, drooling on his own knuckles and humming that determined-baby buzz. "How come you say Ser*enn*a instead of Ser*eena*?"

I don't remember, and Serena herself isn't here at the

moment, but Dinah gives a big whoop of laughter. "You remember, Cory. The short E? The long I?"

Short E, long I. I remember our friend Susan wrote a poem once . . . Except Serena was a teenager by then. She's named for my mother's mother, who died when I was a baby. Her middle name is Rose, for one of Jerry's grandmothers.

"What about the short E and the long I?"

"Oh," says Dinah, "there's this wonderful book. You'd love it, Persimmon. It's called *Adam's Rib,* written by this amazing poet. She took the words *clitoris* and *penis* and she looked at their Greek and Latin roots and she said—"

Dinah's hooting with laughter and it's infectious, I start to laugh and so does Persimmon.

"—she said *clitoris* should have the strong sound, *kleitoris,* and penis should have the short E, *pennis.*"

"I love it, I love it, revolutionary," says Persimmon.

"I have a clitoris," says Shawana. "What are you talking about?"

"I have a penis," says Shaman. "You don't say it right."

"Revolutionary. And then this woman, Susan Sloan, who was in our group, she's in the State Legislature now—"

"She was really the one who started the women's group. Susan. She used to go with one of the draft resisters, one of the heroic guys—"

"Well, so did I," says Dinah.

"I know," says Persimmon. "His name was Carl Kjellstrom. I heard all about you when I was just a kid, you guys were Movement Mythicals. Go on, go on."

"Well, Susan wrote this little poem. Can you remember it, Cory?"

Of course I can:

> *Call me hetero*clite *or iso*gamous
> *If I protect old Isis from young Tammuz*
> *Though fearsome enemies may crowd the field*
> *At times the* pen *is stronger than the shield.*

"Wow," says Persimmon. "Wow. I don't think I under-stand it—"

"I don't really think it means anything," says Dinah, "but it's cute. And that's where we got the name for Isis House."

"Sure. And now it's called St. Savior's?"

"Maureen changed it. God, Susan's in the Legislature now. I wonder if she still writes poetry?"

Then weeks later, after my longing has subsided to a dull ache, a letter comes from Carl:

> Dear Cora, great to hear from you tho not about your illness. I think about you a lot and all our friends in Minneapolis. I'm so sorry you are sick. Did you know my sister Sarah died about six weeks ago. I was glad I could be with her at the end and say goodbye. But I miss her a lot.
>
> Life here in Quetzaltenango probably hasn't changed too much in three or four hundred years, except that there are trucks and buses now on the mountain roads that used to be just for donkeys.
>
> Families are more important here than anywhere I know. Tho the Army has resettled people from other villages, there are no chil-dren without families. So I can't think of how you could adopt a child from here. Maybe things are different in the cities. I have asked Karen, one of the Mennonite missioners if she can find out. They have a workshop here but Karen goes to Guate every few months.
>
> Tell everybody hello, Jerry and your kids and everybody. I hope the treatment works and you get well. Love, Carl.

CHAPTER 3

CORA, LATER STILL

When the school year ends, Seth comes to visit. Probably to his third-grade class he looks like a grown-up, but I'm still shocked to see him with a man's Adam's apple. He hugs like Jerry, hard.

We tell him how wonderful his drawings are. "Do you really like them?" His hair is thick and lush, like Jerry's at that age.

"She thinks they're great art," says Serena, "but it's better than that—they're helping."

I keep a mental calendar, marking off the weeks until I think Carl's friend Karen might have gone to the city and come back. There is so much we could give a child. I can see her tottering through the door, little feet bare, toes clutching the rug pile. She should be here to smell the spring. When the lakes are thawing, there's a wild wet scent to the air. The geese come quacking and honking over the black water, and babies blink in the strong sun. Next spring I'll be taking her to the lake, to the wildflower garden.

One day Persimmon stops by with her kids. I used to fear for her; she had her kids so early, and all of them with Black or Brown fathers; but Persimmon knows what she is doing. She is not ashamed to receive Aid to Families with Dependent Children.

"After all the taxes my parents have paid," she says, "it's the least the government can do, buy some rice and beans for their grandkids." They are beautiful children: Shawana, Shaman, and the baby, Abdul-Aziz.

Seth knew who she was in a vague way when he was in high school, One of Mom's Friends, but now. . . . She wears thrift-shop rags, her long light hair is greasy, Shawana is in a pissy mood, Shaman has an ear infection, and Abdul-Aziz is cranky, but when she and my son meet, they could be Juliet and Romeo at the Capulets' ball. His eyes and face flaming, Seth invents a reason to leave when she does.

Dinah notices too and asks me, "How would you like some instant grandkids?"

That night Seth asks, "So, is she married to the baby's father? Was she married to the other guy? She ever finish school? She still dancing?"

Persimmon knows more than we do because she's younger—the way we know more because we're older—and I trust her. For instance, she never heard that men are doctors and women are nurses. She never read novels written by men who think women climax from a penis.

"She's never read anything," Dinah said to me once, in awe. "Do you think that's the secret? Could you raise perfect people if you never taught them to read?"

I get a pang. I want my new baby to be a perfect person, but of course I want her to read *everything*.

Seth goes out late and comes in mid-morning the next day.

I'm growing stronger. Most days I get dressed, I can sweep the floor, make the bed, do a little laundry. Our senators vote for increased aid to the Contras, and I write passionate letters, trying to be respectful although I despise their lack of judgment. Max's campaign for school board goes well; I do a little phoning for her and get very positive comments.

Maureen visits me on a break from duty at St. Savior's, full of good works and cheer. "We've got two new families," she tells me, "Hmong and Vietnamese. The courage of those people is amazing, both of them were—"

She spots Seth's storyboards leaning against the living room wall and lets out a yip. "*¡Ay mamita!* That's the reredos from the chapel of Bataola del sur in Managua! You were there, Serena, right? Do you remember the painting?"

Serena looks uncomfortable. "I might have seen it. I don't remember. I don't pay much attention to churches."

"Oh, but this church is different. I'm sure you'd remember. It's a chapel in one of the first housing developments that was built after the Triumph of the Revolution. Shame on you, Serena! This is a mural that the whole community pitched in for, they painted Sandino into it and Carlos Fonseca, Che Guevara, and the martyred Oscar Romero. You must have seen it."

"Hey, Maureen, I was working hard in Managua, remember? I didn't do much sightseeing."

"Seth! You must have seen photographs. Bataola del sur, no? Some of the young people from the community went off into the Army, they were killed fighting the Contra and the community painted their likenesses into the mural. No? You don't remember?"

Seth shakes his head. "I don't ever remember seeing it, Maureen, and I've never been in Managua. I thought I was being original this time. Persimmon says—"

"Well." She sits still and important, gathering our attention. "It's a powerful image of health for your mother, and I suspect God's hand."

Seth and Serena indicate they are grossed out, but politely. Jean Harlow wedges her nose firmly in Maureen's crotch.

"Don't you still have friends in Central America?" I ask her.

"The woman I worked with in Nicaragua is in Honduras now, but I know some women in Guate, Guatemala City. They try to keep a soup kitchen open, but they have to move it around or the Army trashes it. They're not supposed to feed undocumented persons. Oh, Cory, it's fearsome! Peasants stream into the city constantly, they have no money and no job skills, and they live in shantytowns on the outskirts, without sewers or electricity."

"I have this fantasy—" I start to say, and Serena says, "C'mon, bro, we don't need to eavesdrop."

"—this dream of adopting a baby from one of those places, some abandoned or orphaned child. Do you think it might be possible?"

"Bless you, Cory, there are so many kids sleeping on the streets of Guate and San Salvador. . .and probably Teguce. . . . I'm not sure how you could adopt one, though." Her forehead wrinkles and she pats the dog's nose. "You want an infant. That might be possible. Listen, let me see if I can telex. Mail is hopeless, and the phone is chancy, but we stay in touch by telex. Must go," she says jumping up. "All goodness to you."

"Never did I think I'd have to protect my mother from missionaries," says Seth later. "Persimmon says Maureen is really a closet goddess-worshipper."

"She probably thinks that about everybody," says Serena.

"Give Maureen a break," says Jerry. "She's a nun, for Christ's sake."

"Ra-*ther*," says Seth.

Maureen has set my heart racing. One of her friends could find my baby! If she is right about Seth's paintings, it is a miraculous coincidence, a sign. I've had some twinges in my uterus, almost as if—

Jerry notices that Seth has fallen for Persimmon. "Doesn't she have someone? The baby's father, what's his name?"

"James is his name. He seems like a reasonable guy. She told me they had a little chat about civil disobedience. He doesn't do it himself, but he'd never interfere with her doing it. You know what happens to Black people when the police get hold of them. Why should he get beat up? She said, 'I mean he's as much for peace as I am, but deliberately breaking the law is a whole, like, different *thing* for a Black person, you know.'"

"So? What does he do?"

"He's a musician, he's on tour a lot. He sends her money, and I think he plans to move back with her and the kids in the winter."

"Christ, three kids. And she's what—five years older than Seth?"

"It's their life, Jerry."

Jerry moves back into our bed, and we get rid of some of the sickroom clutter. We make love again. The miracle of love, the miracle of the painting, are no more wonderful to me than simply waking up in the morning and feeling well.

*

In ten days Maureen has a reply from Gloria, her friend in Guate.

"You have to do this privately, through an attorney," she tells me. "Gloria says it's risky. Everything in that country is hard. You have to go down there, find the child, appear before a magistrate. She says it can be done, and she knows a lawyer with the right connections, but it takes a lot of money."

Joy surges in my throat. "Any idea how much?"

"No. And Cory—maybe it's not such a great idea. Rich gringos taking babies away from their people. You know?"

Et tu, Maureen? Whoa. Wo. Woe. I don't know.

From mid-June to mid-July, I go and lie down in the radiology department while the linear accelerator shoots death rays at my ex-breast and armpit. Ionizing radiation. The skin gets red and tight over the stump of my breast, then it peels off. The new skin burns and peels.

I never see a doctor, of course, although the radiologist strolled through on the first day as a courtesy. I just see the technicians, cheerful women. "We want to zap all the bad stuff," they say heartily, and they give me cream to put on my burns.

I try to visualize the radiation not as a blast of death to my poor-boy cells, my poor wrong-headed soldiers, but as new information, a wind of change wafting into their blighted lives.

One night, Jerry asks me if I want strong drugs, LSD or heroin.

"Lotta people are administering 'em to cancer patients. We could probably get you some, and we don't have to tell Sydney."

"You mean if it gets bad again, like after the chemo? I'll take them if you take them with me."

When Jerry and I met, back in 1952, he was a hipster: tall, dark, dangerous-looking. He and his friends hung out in a drugstore coffee shop near the University of Chicago, where I was an undergraduate, and he was a pre-med student who cut most of his classes but got all As anyway. He couldn't cut Organic Chemistry because of the lab work; he used to haul himself up from the formica table in the drugstore and cock his cap forward. "Gotta split," he'd say, and his friend Lothar would mime the action of a cyclotron splitting an atom, or what he thought was its action. We were all very sophisticated about nuclear things in Chicago in the fifties.

My roommate's brother was one of his friends, and I

asked her to introduce me to Jerry. Such a mouth on him; he looked me up and down and said, "Solid, a tough chick."

"A jerk," I said. He made me angry, but there was something. . . . He called my dorm, and we went for a walk. He rolled a joint, offered it to me, and I pulled on it and coughed.

"Easy, baby," he said. Nobody had ever called me "baby."

"You ever dig the bubbling place?" he asked, and I hadn't. The bubbling place was a plaque on a chain-link fence around the laboratories where, just a few years earlier, Enrico Fermi and the others had worked on the Manhattan Project. Jerry called it the bubbling place because if you stood by the fence and looked at the plaque you could hear a low-pitched burble, a sound like–

"Like, bubbling, man, it's the world's first self-sustaining chain reaction sustaining itself. Man, it's gonna go on till all these atoms are split." He gestured around at the buildings, the sidewalk, the fence, the grass, a hydrant, a streetlamp. "Don't wanna be here when it gets to us."

I loved it that he was tall, that his voice was deep and rough, that he joked about terror. His shadowed eyes seemed tragic, mysterious. He was going to be a psychoanalyst–or he was going to do pharmaceutical research and find drugs that would revolutionize psychoanalysis–or he was going to go mad himself.

"Some cats think schizophrenia's a chemical imbalance, like diabetes," he told me.

"What do you think?"

"Could be," he said, humming softly. "Could be you treat a wig with drugs. Maybe you get a solid cat, maybe you get a stoned wig."

He loved Lester Young. "You know what Billie Holiday calls him? The President, Prez. And he calls her Lady Day. He calls everybody Lady, he calls Charlie Parker Lady Bird, cat's too cool, man, he's insane." And he'd whistle a sixteen-bar solo for me, "I Cover the Waterfront" or "Down 'n' Adam."

Lester Young sometimes played in our neighborhood, at a dingy bar on Fifty-fifth Street called the Beehive. Jerry would scrounge the money so we could go hear him. Jerry turned out to be a phony hipster: he worked hard. He had a scholarship but his parents in Jamaica, Queens, didn't send him any money.

"I wouldn't take it if they did, man. It's too humiliating. They know that, they dig it."

The drugs part was real. He gobbled Benzedrine to keep himself going, then he'd take a sedative or something to come down the next day.

I went with him to hear Lester Young because I was curious, but I didn't really understand the little man with the big saxophone. I sang madrigals: *Fine knacks for ladies, cheap, choice, brave an-nd new.* I liked counterpoint, Gerry Mulligan or Dave Brubeck, but Prez's notes sounded tight and flat to me.

"Just listen, listen," Jerry would say urgently, taking my hand in his two. "He's taming the beast, man, he makes it sit up and roll over."

Jerry worked the night shift in a funeral home. "Man, you would not believe the scene, what people do with dead bodies. These old chicks are always asking can they be alone with their old man, well, we can't do that because, you know, they cop their joints. Like, right *off*, they take 'em *home*. What would you do with your old man's dick, man? Stick it in an urn, next to Aunt Maude's ashes? Man, it's *morr*bid."

"I can't understand you," I'd giggle primly. "Speak English. And don't call me 'man.'"

"I have a limited vocabulary," he'd say, "but a rich syntax. Just listen, listen to me: We made the scene last night, right? And it was a groove, you're a groovy chick, man, I dig you the most, you make it. So then I split and made it over to the popsicle factory, and there was this rich chick, man, grooving on her old man, but he's a stiff, you dig, she wants me to let her in to the icebox so she can make it with a stiff, man. Most ungroovy. You pickin' up what I'm puttin' down?"

Whatever it was that drew me to Jerry, I still feel it, the elegance of his character. He always understood, he was always with me, even pale and shaking, wired or stoned. He wanted me, with my sweater sets and my *round-a-bout, round-a-bout, in a fair ring-a, trip and trip and go, to and fro and fro,* and I lusted for him, his long legs, his lips, his delicate thumbs.

"I have big eyes for you, man, let's ball," is how he put it, but I wouldn't change my virtue in a morgue, so he quit the mortuary and got a job as night clerk in a hotel.

"I trust you don't object to hotel rooms, man," and what could I say? We learned our lessons on a series of sagging beds in a fleabag hotel, where at least we could lock the doors.

We had candle stubs in a wine bottle and jazz on the radio. I remember lying with him, the sweat cooling between my breasts, and listening to the music while right outside our door the hookers and their johns trooped up and down, wrangling and laughing. "What you expect for a twenty, sad sack?" "I thought you'd show me a good time." "You got to make your own good time, sucker, it ain't none of mine. And you can take that to the *bank.*"

It's a comfort to me now, remembering those rooms. "What was the name of that hotel, Jerry?"

"The Parkside, baby. How can you forget?"

He sometimes brought drugs, but—after sniffing cocaine once—I didn't take them with him. I couldn't get to sleep after the coke, so I stayed up all night studying and I thought, *This is great,* but the next day I crashed in a Nat. Sci. III lab and almost cut my head open on a faucet.

I used to ride a taxi back to the dorm. Sometimes his rinkydink cabdriver friend Lothar, pronounced low-tar, took me for free, but sometimes we had to scrape up the two-fifty for a real cab. "Can't have you walking around the South Side alone at night, nice suboiban goil like you."

That winter, he started stealing drugs from the hospital pharmacy, morphine, Dolophine, cocaine. He supplied his friends.

"Pharmaceutical grade cocaine, man, this is too much."

"Aren't they going to suspect you?"

He wouldn't answer. "I can't see you any more," I told him. "I think I really love you, but junk scares me too much. I'm not ready for it."

He called me up high and sang Prez solos, *"Sca-weetn deetn doolia-datn reebop, shebop.* Come on the scene, baby, there's some cool cats I want you to meet." But I wouldn't. I couldn't explain it. I didn't tell him he was ruining his future, I just couldn't see him.

He worked two nights a week as a substitute orderly, besides his hotel job five nights a week, so he couldn't go to the clubs, he wasn't sleeping, just gunning his engine with amphetamines and cocaine and hanging out with musicians in the early mornings at the tail end of their after-work jam sessions. Then he'd shoot some shit to come down, heroin or Dilaudid, sleep for a few hours, pop some pills to get back up and make the scene at the drugstore until it was time for Organic Chemistry lab. "I did all that, seems unbelievable. I'm such a straight arrow now."

"It was because Lothar died in your arms, remember? That scared you straight."

"Nah, baby, I quit junk for you. Love of a good woman."

But it really was having his friend die, seeing him nod off and then start frothing, going into convulsions. I pictured the scene many times: *Lothar, talk to me, man,* gently slapping his face, Jerry fighting the drug in his own veins, trying to get Lothar up and walking and the others staring, shaking their heads, *It's no use, man. He's bought the farm.*

"He bought it, poor bastard. But he was truly fucked-up,

you know, Lothar. Brilliant guy but socially retarded, totally hung up on his beagle bitch, Johnette. Only female he ever loved. You're right, you know? Seeing him just die like that did scare me straight."

He stopped hanging out in the drugstore, he started going to class. He finished the year with a 4.0 grade-point average and was accepted into medical school. I graduated. The Dean of Rockefeller Chapel married us in his study, with our parents there and everything, and we never told our kids what we used to do, at least I never told them. Some day, maybe they should know their daddy was a junkie.

"Do I want heroin? LSD? I'll take anything if you take it with me. I don't want to go on a trip alone."

When he smiles, I feel caught up and rocked in the laugh wrinkles around his eyes. "This would be medicine, baby, for your condition, for your pain. Therapeutic, not recreational."

*

Radiation's finished. I have no nausea at all, I feel almost normal. I'll go to the clinic for monthly checkups, but otherwise I can live like a normal person with one breast and a stripped-out armpit who has lost most of her hair. M. J. and Scottie and Serena and Jerry all give me lovely scarves to wrap around my baldness, paisley chiffon and beautiful creamy colors of china silk. I don't have the strength to picket at the freeway entrance, but I can put a meal together and take the newspapers to the recycling center and walk around the lake with Dinah.

At the end of the summer I kiss my baby Seth and send him back to his third-graders in Boston.

"I'm crazy about Persimmon, mom," he tells me, "and I love her kids. I just wish she was free."

"No one is free," I tell him. "Everyone is expensive."

I read the papers and write letters to my congresspeople and senators and president and anybody else I can think of about Nicaragua, about El Salvador.

Maureen is probably right, but I'm right, too. I want my baby.

How could it be wrong to take her out of extreme poverty, a baby that no one from her own culture can raise? If I were a Central American woman, I might be angry; I might think rich Americans are just ripping off another natural resource, taking babies. But I would be grateful, too, knowing someone wants to share the goodness of life with my child.

I can't really talk about this with Jerry; he just says, "It's your fear talking, baby." So I go to Dinah.

"You need me to go down there?" is the first thing she asks. "I've never been, but I can go. I have to renew my passport anyway, what's it going to cost?"

"Sweetie. Thanks. We're not at that point yet. Jerry doesn't want us to do it. Maureen tells me I'm an imperialist exploiter of women in developing countries."

"I don't see that. I don't see that at all. I think it's wonderful."

"Seriously?"

"Seriously. I would be the perfect person. I even speak pretty good Spanish, I've been to Belize, I've been to Mexico and Guatemala, not the cities but the ruins—"

"So you don't agree with Maureen, that it's wrong to take a kid out of its culture?"

"How could it be wrong, when cultural authenticity means starvation? Listen: if you want me to do it, I'd be so proud to go."

This baby could have two mothers. I'm not up to traveling right now, and I don't feel like battling with Jerry. She really wants to do this for me. By next year I'll be good as new—maybe better.

Jerry says I want a baby to substitute for my breast. Serena won't talk about it, and I can't bring it up with Seth on the phone—he's too remote.

Our old house has settled, the light comes in kindly. The floors are mellow, the rugs are clean. A baby born in poverty could thrive here. Poor old Jean Harlow would lick her; we would feed her vegetables from the garden. She would bang on her high-chair tray with the old silver spoon my mother put in Serena's little fist. We would learn about her culture—Quiché or Cakchikel or whatever it might be—and raise her to be proud, to know her heritage and her people. We could learn Spanish well enough to speak it at home. We would go to Guatemala with her, when she was older.

But Dinah will eat me up with her need to help. "Cory, if you want this, it must be right. Let me talk to Maureen. I'm serious. I'm pretty mobile. Leaf can get along without me for a while. Let's just say I'm going to Guatemala."

If she goes there, she might have to do the actual, formal adoption. She would be the baby's legal mother. Then she would bring it back for us.

"Whatever. Just let me know."

"My goodness, Dinah, do you understand what's involved here? Lawyers, judges—you might have to bribe people—"

"I heard you. Relax, I'm good at lawyers."

At our next appointment, Sydney looks worried. After they've taken pictures and blood and I have my clothes back on, he says the disease isn't halted. My kind of tumor was estrogen-dependent. Because I'm still menstruating, it gets a hit of estrogen in every cycle that encourages it to grow. He wants to talk about cutting out my ovaries.

My beautiful ovaries that made the eggs that grew into Serena and Seth—I could weep, my poor little ovaries curled like fiddleheads, big bad doc wants to take them away, they're nothing to him. Who will protect them? I'm the only valiant goosegirl.

Most ob-gyns believe there's no reason for women to hang onto our sexual organs after we've had our kids. That's one of the first things we learned in our women's group, fifteen years ago. What if I told Sydney, *But I'm attached to my ovaries*? What if he laughs, ho-ho: *Sheer sentimentality, dear girl. You're not going to use them, why not lose them?*

They don't feel the same way about their testicles. I plead with him, *They're mine and I love them. I loved my breast and you took her away from me. Can you promise that if you cut them out of me, my curly ferns, my ovaries, I'll get better?* Jerry can't promise; Sydney can't promise.

Serena says, "It's like everything else, mom. You have to have faith."

I don't believe I will get better.

Sydney talks about clinical guesses and successful series. A series is a group of women with breast cancer. Half of them have their ovaries carved out, shrinking, horrified, *No, no!* in ladylike shrieks, and half get to keep them. The ones without ovaries die slower than the ones with; that is a successful clinical series. You never hear their names: LaVonne, Rita, Judy, Elaine. You never find out how many children they had, or whether they worked for a military contractor.

I didn't use to think I had a right to details like names and faces. *Women take things so personally,* men said, and I felt embarrassed by my friendly curiosity—before the women's movement. But then we changed. Some time between the late sixties and the mid-seventies.

The way I remember it is that the draft lottery changed the work at the Military Information Center. The eighteen-year-old boys literally drew numbers, like in a raffle, one for every day in the year, from 1 to 366, and then local draft boards called them up in order. But by then, the war was staggering to a halt like a brain-dead ogre, and fewer men were called up. In the anti-draft movement, we took some credit. *Nixon's scared of us,* we told each other, *Kissinger's scared. They don't dare start another draft. We've made it too expensive for them to go on with this war.*

Because of the lottery and slower call-ups, fewer boys came looking for help to stay out of the draft. The phones sat silent on the scarred desks. Fewer young men called the office for help from inside the military, too; the GI coffee-houses were organizing opposition to the war from inside.

One of the draft counselors, Jonathan, told me, "They've started letting them out easier, on 4-A discharges. It's a neutral discharge."

When I came in for my volunteer shift, I had more free time. After sweeping the gummy floor and dusting the perfo-rated metal bookshelves, I would chat with the young women on the staff. Susan Sloan was the only woman draft counselor, but I remember two others particularly, Carol and Rebecca, who had been girlfriends of Jonathan and Miles, two of the counselor-organizers.

Rebecca was sturdy and square, with dark-brown hair and heavy eyebrows, and she spoke in a voice that creaked with disuse. Carol had light hair and narrow bones and whispered. Around the time of the lottery, these gentle girls fell in love with each other and discovered lovemaking, something they had not experienced in several years of sexual activity with the boys. They proposed that we—the women associated with MIC—start to meet as a women's peace collective.

"Peace has a different meaning for us," they said, "because women don't go into combat. Still, if we don't resist militarism, we are complicit. We need to pay attention to the difference."

The second great movement of my lifetime was beginning.

I called my radical neighbor Max and invited her to the first meeting of the women's peace group. Max and her husband Einar are mainstays of the Soviet-American Friendship Society. They go to the Soviet Union every couple of years, and on the off-years, they entertain Russian visitors. They have cruised the Dnieper and the Don, toured the factories of Zaparozhe and the farms of the Ukraine. Max and Einar never miss a chance to tell us that most Soviet doctors are women. Their kids, Ilya and Kaia, went to school with Serena and Seth.

"It's high time American women did something like this," Max said, "but I don't know what we'll *do*. We don't have enough in common to accomplish anything."

"You and I have been disagreeing for ten years," I said. "For instance, Soviet doctors may be women, but most of the specialists are men, isn't that right?"

"Honestly, Cora. What are you saying?"

"I'm saying you and I understand how to struggle together."

"You mean, because we've been in some meetings and demonstrations together, that makes us *sisters?* Wait, wait, wait. I think separate women's organizing is a bad idea. You can't secede from society. You have to struggle together with men."

This was my own position until Susan and Carol and Rebecca educated me.

"There are some power issues here," said Susan, looking at the floor. "We don't start on the same level as the men. Women are socialized differently."

I didn't understand. I thought I'd always met men head-on, face-to; if Jerry and I had an argument—rare—I usually won.

"*You* may feel that you're able to struggle with men as an equal," said Carol and Rebecca, "but *we* know we're not."

"When I went South in the summer of '65," Susan said, "I spent my time making iced tea and typing letters for the guys in the office. They did all the fun stuff, all the dangerous stuff."

"I trained as a draft counselor," said Rebecca, in her gritty voice, "but the guys never schedule me."

"She never has any clients," Carol said softly, "and then they use that as an excuse to cut out her hours."

"Who does this?" I asked, righteous and wrathful.

They sighed. "All of them. Miles. Carl. Jonathan. Ian."

"Can't you talk to them about it?"

"No! That's just what we're saying. When we start to talk about how they treat us, they get that look, and we get angry or we start to cry! Or else we nag. We need to thrash this out with other women."

"Me, I'm scared of other women," said Dinah when I called her. "I always get a better deal from men."

"I know what you mean. But isn't that a little fishy?"

"Hell, no. Women compete with each other. Men cooperate."

"Dinah! Men *invented* competition."

"I mean with me. Men cooperate with me."

"Men cooperate with you for sexual reasons. What happens when you take away sex?"

"Why should I *take away* sex? I like sex."

"What you're saying, basically, is that you get what you want from men by manipulating them sexually."

"Sure." Her leather vest creaked, and I could see her lounging with the phone, fondling a cigarette, bare legs propped against a wall, long skirt pushed back to her thighs. "What's wrong with that?"

I scratched around for my reasons. There was no way to tell her except to tell her. "Well, it's kind of like whoring. I can't do it. Susan and Carol and Rebecca can't do it. Max can't do it. The point is, you have to be pretty and sexy to do it, which just leaves most women out completely."

"Cory, what are you talking about? You're gorgeous!"

"Come to this meeting," I begged her. "We need you."

And I was thinking, maybe you need us.

I announced to Jerry and the kids that a women's group was going to meet at our house.

Serena wanted to know if she could come, and I told her we would welcome her as soon as she finished high school, and she said, "Mo-om," on that downward couplet, the call of the junior-high bird.

"What will you talk about?" Jerry asked. "Will you tell terrible secrets about us?"

"I don't have any terrible secrets," I said.

"Oh, yeah," he said, "all those times I've chained you to the stove, the ironing board."

"Don't be a smart-ass," I told him. "The most terrible thing will be if we don't talk about you at all."

I gave Seth and Serena grilled cheese sandwiches and navy bean soup. Had a cup myself. Seth fidgeted. "Quit that," said Serena superbly.

"Okay, Serena-Sir-Enema."

There were times when his teasing drove her to hysterics, but that night she rose above it, and I was grateful. After supper, they were occupied with homework and the telephone. My house felt unnaturally calm and clean. Jean Harlow picked up some of my anxiety and, yes, dogged my footsteps. I decided to put out fruit and cheese, then not to put out fruit and cheese because that's what women always do. I changed into a dress, then put my jeans back on, then put on a pantsuit. Then the jeans again. Combed my hair. Mussed it up. Lie down, Jean Harlow. Stay.

I remember that first meeting so vividly it's like an ache in my side, only these days my side aches all the time. Then I felt well and strong; it was consciousness that pierced me with a clarity like pain. I hear our voices—solos, duets, a chorus. Carol and Rebecca sat side by side on the sofa like Spirit and Body, wearing jeans and sweatshirts. Dinah, in tie-dyed harem pants, sprawled in an armchair. Max wore a pantsuit. A jug of California wine eased us into the meeting, although Susan, very task-oriented in her rugby shirt, wanted us to stick to an agenda.

Braces gleaming, she asked, "What are our goals, what do we want to take away with us?"

"How about we just try hanging out with each other? We need to establish a level of trust," said Dinah, gesturing with her cigarette. "Talk about stuff like our issues with men."

Carol and Rebecca moaned. Max snorted.

"Or our issues with women," Dinah said. Then we sat silently. Susan's hair covered her face. I thought twice about crossing my legs, clearing my throat.

"I have trouble trusting other women," said Susan from behind her hair.

I was so grateful to her for breaking the silence, as we did not yet call it, that I gushed. "Me, too. It's one of those big secrets. Women are supposed to confide in each other, but I don't think I've confided in another woman since—since—"

"Since high school, I bet." Rebecca's voice rasped as though every word cost her, but when she was Miles's girl-friend she hardly said anything at all, so this was what Max and I called a Great Leap Forward.

"It's true, high school was the last time I had a really best friend."

Her name was Judy Gardner. All we ever talked about was boys and clothes, but we called each other every day, several times, and in the school lunchroom as well as at parties and dances we gave each other a place of refuge. I would have died for her, yet I knew almost nothing about her. Yet I knew everything, and she knew everything about me. Our secrets nested in our bureau drawers along with sachet-filled satin hearts, the slightly fetid perfume of excitement, of shame. I remember her telling me the first time a boy named Alan Mohrbacher put his hand inside her panties, the sound of her breathing on the phone.

"I have trouble trusting straight women," said Carol, who

until very recently had been Jonathan's girlfriend. "I trust lesbians."

"Well *I* don't," said Max explosively. Max tries to look tough, keeps her hair short, wears no makeup. "I don't trust anybody who puts me down for being a *breeder.*"

I laughed, I couldn't help it. "Who calls you a breeder, Max?" And she told us about going to a women's meeting in New York where a group of angry lesbians walked out.

"But I know *you're* not like that," she said to Carol and Rebecca, a little uncertainly, and Carol and Rebecca looked at each other, and Carol's face turned a bright pink, and they both said they felt ostracized. Dinah said she felt ostracized too, by both lesbians and straight women.

"According to Eleanor Roosevelt," said Max, "no one can put you in your place unless you agree to go there."

"What about Black people?" croaked Rebecca.

"Well, exactly," answered Max. "Look at Fannie Lou Hamer."

"It took *years* of organizing to lead up to her action. You have to be ready to make *huge* sacrifices," said Rebecca.

"Oppressed people don't agree to their oppression," murmured Carol.

"What? Look, look, look," said Max, wagging her finger. "They're all oppressed, men and women too. But women can be on the receiving end of abuse from their oppressed husbands, so Black and Brown women are even worse oppressed than White women, because Black and Brown men are lower on the scale than White men. The economic system exploits them all."

"Did you see that article, 'Does Jackie Onassis Oppress Her Garbageman?'" asked Dinah.

"I thought it was 'Is Jackie Onassis Oppressed by Her Garbageman?'" said Susan. "The other way it's too easy—of course she does."

"I don't see it," said Rebecca. "How does she oppress him?"

"She's part of the ruling elite of a system that—"

"But that's not *her* fault. *She* doesn't, like, personally hold him down. Whereas he—"

"—has absolutely no power over her. Ruling-class women are insulated from the ordinary kinds of male chauvinist piggishness, she doesn't even have to walk down the street, for god's sake, she has a limo to schlep her wherever she needs to go."

"I don't buy it," said Carol. "She's still physically prey to any man that wants to knock her down—grab her purse—rape her—"

"Are you *kidding?*" cried Susan. "She's got *Secret Service* men on her ass."

We went on meeting all through the seventies.

"I just wish there were some Black or Native American women meeting with them," said Max after our first meeting.

"You've been saying that as long as I've known you," I told her.

"Well, I wish it especially now. I don't think a feminist group should start out being elitist, and they're elitist."

"We're not elitist! Who are we keeping out?"

"That's not the point. The point is, who are they not including?"

But all the Black and Native activists in the Twin Cities that we knew were men. Sometime in there I started to wonder why Max called women *they*. Wasn't she one?

I did mention the women's group to a Black man who sat on the co-op board with me. "Maybe your wife would be interested?"

"I'll tell her," he said, but nothing ever came of it. For all I knew, she was White.

◢

The second course of radiation makes me weaker and more nauseous. I imagine the beam they shoot at me saps my strength; I can't help it, I have a terrible time visualizing my poor bad-guy cells being changed for the good. Some science-fiction image pops up in my head, people exposed to a beam of light that shrivels them, turns them into slaves. I try to tell Serena and Jerry about this new trouble, and they listen, but what can they do?

"People respond differently to the radiation," Jerry says. "It seems to depend on how many vital organs get a dose. Oh, baby, it's all over you."

All over you like a cheap suit, Seth says. I feel so sick, it's hard to hold the image of my baby, my new baby in a Guatemalan shantytown whose young mother can't feed her. She won't get fed and loved, unless by me. Dinah gets her new passport, and she comes over, and we give her a cashier's check for ten thousand dollars, borrowed on Jerry's life insurance. I know it's right for her to try and get my new baby. I'm so tired.

Finally my old friend Thelma Kjellstrom calls. I call her a friend, but it's years since I've seen her—not since Carl joined his sister Sarah in Guatemala. She has two daughters besides Sarah (everyone always called her Sister), and her sons are Carl, Ian, and Duke. I tell her about Carl's letter and how sorry I am that Sarah has died. I ask about Ian, who lives in northern Wisconsin—but I can't talk for long. And I can't bear to ask about Duke, who lives on the street. Life exhausts me. More and more I spend the time remembering.

CHAPTER 4

DINAH'S TRAVEL JOURNAL

*G*uate, *Aug. 1*—Finally. Tropical storm Justine delayed our flight out of Miami, and we had a twenty-eight-hour layover. Had to spend some of Cora & Jerry's money on an airport motel & terrible dinner. Hung around airport until they cleared our Aviateca flight for Guate.

The Guate airport is just a huge shed full of Indian-looking people selling pathetic chatchkas, yarn bracelets, cornhusk dolls, long sashes woven on backstrap looms. Barefoot women and children swarm around the paleface gringos coming off the plane. They look up at you beseeching, determined.

Waiting to go through *aduana & immigración* I met two other couples who are down here looking for babies to adopt. When the *aduana* finish with you and you walk outside, the mountains loom all around, huge wedges of purple, blue, and gray. The five of us were booked into the same hotel, so we shared a taxi.

Aug. 2—Street life never stops in this place. We took a walk after dinner and saw women in rebozos or whatever they call them here, setting up for market at midnight. They lay out their little bundles of vegetables on their blankets—army blankets; I'll bet they're U.S. issue—and sit down cross-legged with their babies to wait for the first customers. Shoppers come out between four and five, if this morning's typical. The street lighting and the shop lights are all fluorescent, so everything has a flat greenish cast.

Soldiers with guns are everywhere. They look like little boys of fourteen and fifteen with great big assault rifles standing in doorways, strolling on the street, hanging out in the hotel lobby and the bus stop. The air is gray and foul; Guatemala City sits in a bowl in the mountains, like Denver or Mexico City, and everybody rides the buses, red or blue and silver and belching smoke. The wide streets are choked with cars, little Mexican-made Fords or Toyotas. I'm terrified. I can't eat. I have the *abogado's* name and number written in my address book and on a slip in my wallet and pinned into the lining of my purple silk jacket. He could make this trip a success or a failure.

Aug. 3—Today I go to meet Sr. Rogelio Vasquez de Flores. I keep counting my traveler's checks, wondering if we'll have enough.

Dinner last night with the other Americans, the Earmanns, pronounced Ermines, and the O'Donnells. They're both Catholic and working through some church agency. We didn't even think of that. Jerry and Cora Bookbinder—what kind of name is that for a nice Central American family? Ermines are okay, tall, nice-looking, childless, a little uptight. Looked funny when I said my husband was too busy to come down.

O'Donnells are hilarious. They already have five kids; Katy says she gets nervous without someone in diapers. I mentioned money, and they both said they'd been warned about extra expenses. "You gotta grease the baby's whole family," said Jim O'Donnell, "and the lawyer's whole family and the priest's whole family and the whole government." Then Katy said, "Since there are these twenty-three families that run the country, at least you know it's gotta end some time." Ermines live in Massachusetts, O'Donnells in New Jersey, and both go to churches that have contacts here. I can't worry about the Catholic thing, I just have to get through this meeting with Vasquez de Flores. Basket of Flowers.

The streets of this city fill me with dread, and I've forgotten how to sleep. The air burns my nose, even though it rains every afternoon, the boy soldiers scare me, the street children kill me. They have red eyes and smeary noses, the Ermines said last night that glue-sniffing is a big problem. Soldiers and sniffers seem almost the same age: who goes through neighborhoods and sorts them out, here's a gun, here's a tube of Resistol? Two streets over we passed a basement video-game parlor full of little boys. They earn centavos and spend them on glue and video games, the Ermines said. Lots of them live out in the *colónias,* ghastly slums on the sides of those beautiful mountains we saw from the airport.

Aug. 4—Basket of Flowers was brusque but not uncivil. Yes, it might be possible for a generous American family to adopt one of Guatemala's many orphaned children. He formally asked after Maureen, and I felt better because, of course, I do have a church connection. The problem, I must understand, is that usually people want an infant, and the children in most need are long past infancy. I offered him money, but he raised his broad hand. Not yet: when negotiations are further along it will be appropriate for payments to be made in certain quarters.

I thanked him and his eyes slid down to my breasts. Would I fuck this dude if it meant getting Cory's baby? You bet I would.

Aug. 7—The hardest thing is waiting. I was never good at it. I didn't bring enough books, of course, and I can't really concentrate on what I'm reading. You can't masturbate all the time. The rain brings me down. To talk to Leaf I have to make an appointment for a call, and then sometimes it doesn't go through, or she's not home. We didn't think about things like phone dates. I talked to her two days ago, and she says Cory's not doing so hot. I can't think about that. I should write letters to her in this journal—it's hopeless to try to get mail to the States—but would I 'fess up about Basket of Flowers?... maybe not . . . Carl is in this country. Has he ever forgiven me? Should I try to go to Quetzaltenango, try to see him? For all I know he's with someone, can't picture Carl without a woman. That friend, Karen, must be a lover. Does he do our same things with her, a missionary? I do them with Leaf, I love to play those games with her.

I could start writing my memoirs. Hah.

Aug. 8—Dear Leaf, the Basket called late yesterday to say he has located a baby whose mother has died and whose grandparents are willing to discuss the possibility, etc., etc. Let me describe him to you: He is short, like most of the men I have seen in Guatemala, but strong-looking, with lots of glossy black hair and small clever black eyes, lots of moles on his forehead, cheeks, and chin. He dresses beautifully in three-piece suits of glen plaid or discreet checks, with pastel shirts that have white collars and cuffs, and a modest amount of gold jewelry.

The baby's name is Rosalia. I hope this is Cory's baby; I

hope she is healthy; I hope her grandparents really will let her go with me. The Basket looked at my ringless hand and asked if I was married. I described Jerry; my husband is a *médico,* I said, *demasiado occupado* to come with me, but he is a good husband, a fine provider. He nodded and smoothed his hair. He smelled of strong cologne.

I look at Katy O'Donnell and Linda Earmann and I try to imitate a model Catholic mother. They each wear a gold cross on a fine chain. Linda's clothes are strictly Ann Taylor, Katy's look like J.C. Penney, but they both wear nylons and pumps with small heels. Modest and unassertive but not dumb, that's how I want to look; no leather, nothing too bright. Today I went to a chic store with Katy and spent some more of Jerry and Cory's money on a gray suit of thin French wool. Guatemalan women are shorter than Americans, and their breasts are bigger for their size, more like you than me, but the suit will look fine with a silk shirt and I will look respectable. Why didn't I think of a wedding ring? I had to tell the Basket that I lost it, I've lost weight, I said, and it slipped off. Do you want to get matching rings?

All for now, love, Dinah

Aug. 9—I can't stand to think about Cory's illness. I know I'm a terrible coward but there you are, as my stupid husband number two used to say. Number Two is right: his name was King, but he was a shit, full of small lies and betrayals. My first husband had a small soul, but King's could have been removed with a tweezers, probably was.

Cory is like light and air for me; without her I'll suffocate. If I don't see her for a week, my petals droop. She was the first person who made Minnesota bearable to me, and I can't imagine living there without her. I'm here in this tacky room for love of her, but I can't stand to think about the real reason. So why not start my memoirs?

I grew up in Milwaukee, and I went to the University of Wisconsin, in Madison. In those days Madison was full of smart bratty Jewish kids from New York, maybe it still is. They were nothing like the kids I grew up with. One guy told me every city flavors people with its own dominant ethnic group—like everybody from New York is Jewish, he said, quoting our hero Lenny Bruce, the way everyone from Chicago is Polish, even the Jews. Everyone from San Francisco is Chinese: the Jews, the Blacks, the Japanese. From New Orleans, everyone's Black. From Philadelphia, Italian. From Boston, Irish. So I guess maybe everyone from Milwaukee is German.

At Washington High School, if you were smart and a girl, you kept it a secret. In Madison, the New Yorkers thought it was cool to be smart, and they were all lefties. They invented the New Left, right there on campus. I could come out as a smart person, as a left-wing person, and the high point of my freshman year was when someone asked where in New York I was from.

Madison was sorted into tribes, and every tribe lived in its own co-op house, a big, bare, shabby old place where the bathtubs had feet, no one ever cleaned the oven, and everybody slept on mattresses on the floor. In the Poli. Sci. house, all there was in the fridge was peanut butter and vaginal jelly. I lived with the theater brats, in our fridge we had recording tapes and dry, black, faded roses.

I was a theater major, and mostly I acted in plays. Senior year I got scared. I'd had an abortion, had the clap, had a disgusting case of crabs, and I said to myself, *If you go to New York and try to make it in the theater, you can expect years more of this.* On a blind date I met Reuben Berns, little skinny medical student, thickly furred and horny. When he found out I was Jewish, he wanted to get married. I thought I could handle it. I didn't fuck women then.

My parents had moved to the suburbs by this time, and

my mother insisted I get married at her house in Whitefish Bay. White Folks' Bay, my college friends called it. She made herself crazy with architects and decorators and florists, but the wedding was pretty nice. Reuben's parents flew in from New York, and they hit it off okay with mine. They gave us ten thousand dollars for a wedding present. We went to Door County for a week of nonstop fucking, lots of fun, but immediately afterward Reuben turned into a *husband* and a *doctor;* he told me we were moving to Minneapolis so he could take a family-practice residency. Did not *ask* me, *told* me I was moving to Minnesota, several hundred miles further away from New York.

"But honey," I said, "it's all Scandinavians up there. What'll I do?"

He could care.

We got to Minneapolis, and he planted us in an ugly suburb, in a house with yellow fake-brick siding. We went to a furniture store in a shed and bought ugly sofas and dressers on credit. I would have lost my mind except that I was pregnant again, only this time I was going to have the baby. I loved being pregnant, and I loved having Joel, who was born the summer the three civil-rights workers disappeared. I was still nursing Joel during the standoff at the Edmund Pettus bridge that next spring, when I found out I was pregnant again. I carried that baby through the summer of the Watts riots. Amos was born in the winter of '65, and I nursed him through the next summer's riots, in Chicago, Detroit, Newark, even a small one on the north side of Minneapolis.

Father James Groppi was leading marches for open housing and fair employment in Milwaukee, and when my parents drove up to see the boys, my father bad-mouthed the marchers. We would get into shouting fights. Reuben always took his side.

So now we had these two adorable boys. I realize that Reuben wanted to have children fast so he couldn't be drafted, but it was okay with me at the time. I had my babies like a cat—carried small, labored hard, snarled and bit, and out they came. They took the tit right away. The kids were my real friends.

Reuben had said he wanted to do a three-year family practice residency in Minnesota because it had such a good rating. He wanted to be a GP, a family doctor, where you can really do some good. What bullshit. Eight months into it, he says he made a mistake and he's going into psychiatry. The lazy doc's choice, Derm or Psych—you work an eight-hour day, and your patients? They never die, and they never get well.

To change his specialty, Reuben had to take loads more clinical work, a bunch of practicums, and go through incredible bureaucratic rickytick. I didn't see him in daylight for two years, during which I was a single parent, you bet. Then he joined a practice and started *coining* money. We moved to a ritzier suburb.

"Why don't you get some draperies made, matching bedspreads, valances, that stuff?" he said. "We can afford it. And you should buy yourself some clothes, go to Harold's or someplace where the doctors' wives shop."

"I like my clothes," I told him. "There's nothing wrong with the way I look."

He snickered and said I looked like Grace Slick.

"You used to like my look."

"I was a student," he said. "I'm in practice now. You're Dr. Berns's wife; we have a position in the community. I really think you should act like an adult."

I couldn't believe our tax returns; of course, he had huge student loans to repay, but still.

"I should have gone into the Indian Health Service," he said once. "They forgive your loans."

On a reservation, I might have had someone to talk to, unlike our suburb where the moms all left the house as soon as the kids did, driving off in their woodies to play golf or drink coffee to support the symphony or some goddamn thing. All I had to do in life was shop, clean, cook, do the wash, take care of the yard, and look after Amos and Joel. An Indian woman named Arlette Thibodeau came in once a week to help with cleaning, and a retired man in the neighborhood trimmed the shrubs and mulched the chrysanthemums, so it really boiled down to me and the kids.

I was alone so much I thought I was going crazy, just me and my vacuum cleaner and washing machine and two small people that didn't talk English so hot but owned millions of toys with tiny parts that got lost and broken and hundreds of miniature socks that divorced their mates as soon as they hit detergent. I'd catch sight of myself in plate-glass windows when I wheeled the kids through the shopping mall in their collapsible twin stroller, and I'd wonder who was the madwoman wearing my coat.

Women Strike for Peace saved my sanity. I saw a sign advertising a bake sale, and I went because I hated the war, also I needed something for dessert; it was a place to take the kids; and it had a nice *Lysistrata* ring to it, women striking for peace. Not that Reuben and I got together much—sex starvation was a big part of my problem.

"How do you join?" I ask the the first person I meet, a tall goddessy creature with red-gold hair pinned on top of her head in a wonderful chignon, looking like the sun with little shining hairs like rays escaping from the pins. She takes in my beads and fringe, my hair and eyes and nose, and smiles. "The Land o'Lakes must be kinda tough for you," she says, and I fall in love. That's how I met Cora, over a pan of lemon bars.

I joined WSP, took my kids to meetings, hooked up with the angry moms of the Twin Cities who marched and leafletted and agitated because they—because we—were pissed about all the strontium 90 in the milk. Without asking, the military-industrial complex had sneaked into our children's bodies and loaded their precious fluids with a radioisotope that would belong to the family for the next hundred thousand years, and we were going to do something about it.

"You gals and your ideas," Reuben snickered. "What happens when women go on strike? The laundry piles up, hnh hnh."

I always hated the way he laughs in back of his nose. I stood it for as long as I could, but when Amos was two, I left my crystal and china and silver and I walked away from the doctor's split-level house with the horizontal picture over the sofa and the vertical picture over the fireplace. I headed straight into the Sixties, and I brought my little pals along.

Ten years later I made the same mistake again, only worse. And that's enough for now.

Aug. 10—Dear Leaf, I miss you. I wish I was going to the movies with you right now, sitting in the balcony at the Uptown with a big box of popcorn. When the movie gets boring, I would eat up all the popcorn you've spilled down your front, stick my tongue between your breasts, nibble it off your stomach, and then find the ones in your crotch. I want to smell you and taste you along with the popcorn. Then I want you to . . .

I want you to be missing me.

Yesterday the Basket summoned me to his office to meet with the grandparents, tiny, wizened old people, and when I asked him how old they are, he shrugged and said, "Could be fifty, fifty-five."

They are Isaco and Maria Arcano, and they are *evangelistas,* Protestants, living in a shack in the oldest of the unofficial settlements. I might be older than Maria; she has maybe five teeth in her head. Their shack has electricity to run a TV and a tiny fridge, but they have to queue for water at a community tap. Their daughter, Luz Maria, was a good girl, they told me over and over. Her husband was so saddened by her death that he has gone away, and they can't find him.

The old woman's eye kept running, and she wiped it with a corner of her dress, and the old man simpered, but hey, Cory's not adopting them. After they left, I asked the Basket if there was some way the adoption could go through their church, and he told me they aren't devout, the old man drinks, the daughter probably never married, the baby has *parásitos.* His manner sharpened, and he fussed with his papers.

Was something wrong, I asked. Had he incurred expenses? He must tell me if there were expenses.

"*Dos mil dólares,*" he said, turning dark red.

"I understand," I said. "I was prepared to spend money. But what do we have for the two thousand?"

"We have the probability," he said, "that the grandparents will make no objection when we come before a magistrate." So I peeled the money off my roll with a beatific smile.

God only knows when this will get to you, honey. I miss you, I miss your mouth, I miss your body. I'm scared. All for love, now, Dinah

Aug. 12—Nearly two weeks since I've been here. Don and Linda Earmann left yesterday for Antigua, the old colonial city, where a chambermaid in one of the fashionable hotels is about to give birth. They found this young woman through personal contacts, but of course they're hooked up with an *abogado* and have been shelling out *dólares* like mad. We had a lot of Chilean wine at dinner, and Katy got weepy.

"God bless you," she said to them, "and your blessed baby. And you too, darling," she said to me.

Today I have a headache, and it's raining more than usual.

At least Reuben was smart. King was dishonest and dumb—he'd lose or break something and blame the cats or one of the boys. Like what he did with the gas gauge. The gas gauge on our car was broken, and I kept track by setting the trip meter. Every two hundred miles or so, I'd know we needed gas, and I'd fill it up. King would put in a dollar's worth whenever he thought it was low, and reset the trip meter anyway. I don't know how often he stranded me.

If I can get on my anger at King, I won't have to feel sad about Cory. King said he was an artist, but he was really an artisan, an engraver. He made prints from other people's drawings. He taught art in Amos's high school, that's how we met. Amos was one of those kids who's good at everything but academic work—art, music, sports, lunch—and King was his art teacher and advisor.

I had started fucking women, and I was sort of on the rebound from my first woman lover, Annie. There was something *elastic* about King that appealed to me. Annie and I were good together. I really loved her, and she calmed my whole life down. But I always missed something, making love with her—I missed cock, the hot live flesh. Also, Reuben was threatening to sue me for custody of the kids because I was living with a woman, and he said it was damaging to the boys. Amos got along fine with Annie, but Joel never looked her in the face or said her name.

It's funny about the man-woman thing. Carl Kjellstrom, my true love, was like a foreign country to me, strange landscape, new language, a place of constant discovery. His wacky brother Duke, too. Whereas life with Annie felt familiar and comfortable, we spoke the same language and moved in the same space.

Carl once said I was really in love with his mother, Thelma. "You're just using me to get close to her," he said, like it was a joke, but later, when I did have women lovers, I thought maybe he was right. Annie had been Carl's girlfriend once. Weird, huh? After we split, a low-intensity parting compared to some I've had, I sniffed around for a man. I got cock, all right; it was what came along with it that was the problem.

King was fastidious about his work and his grooming, an attentive and enthusiastic lover, and a total shit. He belonged to some strange religion, half Christian fundamentalist and half Far Eastern mystic, the worst parts of each: it encouraged him to be judgmental and vague at the same time, intolerant of other people and vastly forgiving of himself. That smile and "There you are!" I mean, this is someone who never took a phone message in his life.

We were married in 1978. The only good thing about King's religion was they had very short weddings, lots of people, food, and flowers but almost no ceremony. Joel hated him. Amos laughed at him. A couple years later I finally told him to leave, I wanted a divorce on grounds of total incompatibility, but getting rid of him was like scraping shit off your shoe. He kept coming back to the house, saying he couldn't find his things. Then he wanted to rent a room from me. He told me he needed me, he admired me for my peace work, he hated the military. How had he stayed out of Vietnam, by the way? He convinced an Army shrink he was crazy. When he first told me I thought it was funny, but by the time I kicked him out I agreed with the shrink. You *are* a loony, I told him, no acting talent required.

Maybe I'll sleep tonight.

Aug. 15—I'm sick. The Basket took me to see Rosalia yesterday, finally, and the stench, the squalor was too much. I waited up half the night to call Leaf, and then I sort of collapsed talking to her.

I don't think I can bring this baby home for Cory; she is tiny, puny, listless, her scalp and her little weak arms and hands are covered with scabs. The grandparents live in a hellish *colónia* where the mud streets swarm with sickly looking children who constantly ask for gum, *chicle*. Then they pose for you, whether you have a camera or not. Jim and Katy O'Donnell have been to the temporary settlements, and they looked very doubtful when I said that was the source of the baby the Basket found for me. "I wouldn't do it," said Jim. "God only knows what you'd be bringing back with you."

Katy punched him in the ribs and said he was mean, but I noticed she didn't express any great enthusiasm. They visited the settlements with a priest, but the baby they're negotiating for comes from a peasant family. Of course, Isaco and Maria were peasants too, before they came to the hideous *colónia*.

Leaf understood when I said how scared I was of that terrible place, the kids have very red lips and rotten teeth from sucking all day on cheap candy. On every mud street there is a *bodeguita* that sells soft drinks and candy but no fresh food, I don't even know where you would have to go to buy a piece of fruit. Their eyes are cloudy and their noses run, their bellies stick out like the starving Biafran kids in the magazine photos, and their bare arms and legs are covered with gray dust from the dirt streets. Dust or mud.

Men lie around, toothless, playing cards or just staring. Women stand in line for water or hang out wash. Families seem to stick to their terrible shacks, four poles stuck in the bare ground with corrugated paper walls and plastic sheeting or tin for a roof. The sewer ditch runs through the settlement.

This whole camp has been here for twenty years, the Basket says, perched on the side of this hill. Down the other side is the Guate garbage dump. Enterprising members of the community pick over garbage all day. I didn't vomit, but I felt like it.

The Basket got impatient and tried to tell me how much better off they are now that the city has electrified the settlement. He thinks I am a stupid, squeamish *gringa*. Well, I am.

I've been poor; I've had to feed my kids on peanut butter.

But this poverty is violent; it makes people into vermin. I would be bringing Rosalia back like a rat in a cage.

Aug. 18—After extracting another *mil dólares,* the Basket told me this morning that Rosalia has died. My god, what a nightmare. Did I want to go to the funeral? No, I did not. Did I want to discuss plans for finding another *niña?* When he asked me this, something snapped, and I started to cry.

His manner changed, he got all courtly. This must be a great shock. He understands my disappointment. Would I like to go for a drive in the country? To calm my nerves.

This operator has three thousand bucks of Jerry and Cora's money. I sniffled and said yes. He began to breathe loudly through his nose, shuffled papers, gave staccato instructions to his secretary, took my arm. Today's lustrous shirt is lavender, and under his perfume I smell mansweat, hairy armpits, balls.

He drives a yellow Lincoln convertible, old but well kept. For the first half hour, he keeps the top up because we are twisting through Guate traffic, stinky with exhaust and loud with horns. He turns on the air and plays a tape of some sexy female singer. We're on the outskirts of the city, where there are fewer buses, dusty used car lots, *jugo de frutas* stands, or brown men with Mayan faces standing around. Every so often I see another adolescent with a high-powered rifle slung over his back.

The streets twist and climb. We're in the hills now, or maybe the mountains. Truck farms, flowers, some nice houses. Basket touches a button and the top goes down, with a creak of hinges. He floors the accelerator and starts singing along with his tape: *"No me olvidas, querida . . . tu cuerpo junto a mi . . . ."* The air conditioning is still on, cold streams gushing through the vents as the sun beats down.

We pull up to what looks like a country club, with a white

gate across the road. Basket tootles his horn and a small man in tan work clothes comes running, opens the gate. Basket tips him a lordly nod, and we drive in. The grass and flowering bushes have been carefully planted, carefully tended. Except for the music, we could be in Kentucky or North Carolina.

Basket turns left, drives down to a small pond with manicured edges, stops the car. "You like? Yes? To calm the nerves?" And he reaches for me.

I knew this was coming. He pulls me into his arms and starts to knead my upper back and shoulders. When I don't resist, he gets bolder and sticks one hand inside the neck of my shirt and gently squeezes one tit, as if he was a stroke patient and it was one of those foam exercise balls. It's not unpleasant, but this person does not turn me on. He has failed miserably at the only thing I asked of him. How will I tell Cory?

"*Mañanita* we will start again," he breathes, and he sticks his other hand up the skirt of my expensive gray suit and finds the crotch of my pantyhose. Lyndon Johnson was supposed to have said that something-or-other was "the worst thing since pantyhose ruined finger-fucking." I sprawl there, feeling nothing. How can he want to do this? There's not going to be any *mañana*.

"Darling," he murmurs, taking off his dark glasses. "Let me make love to you."

"Love?" I say and burst out laughing. Of course, he is deeply offended, unhands my vulva and breast and puts his shades back on. "Why do you mock me?" he says sternly. "My desire for you is a beautiful thing. You are a beautiful woman." His nostrils flare. "The love of a man and a woman—"

"I'm not mocking you," I tell him, "but love is *lejos de mis pensamientos* right now. Besides, I am a married woman. The poor baby—the money—please take me back to Guate."

He shrugs and turns on the engine but punishes me on

the drive back by not playing music and by turning off the air. Of course, we hit hideous rush-hour traffic, and by the time he pulls up in front of my hotel, his beautiful glen plaid suit has uneven half-moons of darkness under each arm.

Muy correcto he sits behind the wheel while I get out. I thank him for the ride. He nods, then with a growl of gears pulls out into traffic before I'm even on the pavement. Oh Cory, I fucked this one up for sure. How can I tell you?

Aug. 19–The hotel has got me on tomorrow's Miami flight, leaving at seven in the morning. I said goodbye to the O'Donnells tonight; they know "my" baby died, and they were sympathetic. "Let me tell you, this ain't for everybody," said Jim. "Don't think badly of yourself. You did your best."

CHAPTER 5

DINAH'S MEMOIR

The two moments I hate worst on a plane are takeoff and landing, because Reuben once told me they're the most dangerous. I always think I'm going to die, so every time I quick tick off my debts and debtors, make a sleazy peace, consign my soul. This flight stops in Mexico City, then I change planes in Miami. I feel horrible but glad to get out of Ghastly Guate. Wish I could have seen Carl. Has he ever forgiven me? It doesn't matter. Right now I miss him so much I could cry, the beautiful boy from the Military Information Center.

When was it—sixteen years ago? Seventeen? Cora cooked dinner for the staff once a week; I answered the phones two afternoons. Miles was my lover at the beginning, but I soon relinquished him to a stocky grad student named Rebecca. Miles and an actor named Crater, one of my exes, both were living in my house and it got to be a little creepy, so I wasn't altogether sad when Miles took his skeleton suit and moved in with Rebecca. Carl's old lady at the time, Annie, was a nurse in a Pilot City clinic on the North Side.

God, the MIC. The guys probably did good work, and we

were heavily into servicing them—we were girls who said yes to boys who said no, cleaning, cooking, screening, screwing.

There was only one woman draft counselor, Susan Sloan, a graduate student from the suburbs. Tentative as a grasshopper, Susan never challenged the men, though she complained mildly to us other women that they only scheduled her for duty no one else wanted.

"You don't need to take that kind of treatment," I told her. If I'd been in her shoes, they would have heard from me.

Susan always came fifteen minutes early for her shift, and she sometimes brought flowers or a pretty bunch of leaves.

"I thought . . ." she'd say, gesturing at the shabby room, and then she'd dust and straighten, re-shelving literature, swatting flies, making a new urn of coffee. She'd sweep the floor next. I'd be in my hippie drag, a flowered caftan or my precious ancient embroidered bluejeans, and here she'd be wearing a neat pants suit or a dress, just like for a straight job. Sometimes she worked through dinner without any phone-answerer.

"I'd stay to help you if I could, Susan, but I have to get dinner for my kids."

"It's okay, I can manage." Susan had braces on her teeth and pretty bad acne. She was in love with a jerk called Eli, who played Irish music with a local ceilidh band and was 4F because of something called Crohn's disease. Eli came sniffing around when he was drunk, but mostly he acted as if he didn't know her.

"Have I got many appointments?" she'd ask, flapping lightly over my shoulder. "Oh, they've given me another suicidal one," she'd say, when she recognized the name of some ROTC kid who just discovered he was gay or a pacifist or a gay pacifist. Boys were always threatening to kill themselves.

Sometimes Susan had a problem client, one who'd already been seen by one or two of the male draft counselors. "What are 'problems,' Susan? Aren't these guys all problems?"

"Well, sure.... But—you know, you want them to feel good about coming here...."

"Their problem is they don't want to be drafted, right? Can't you help keep them out?"

"Sometimes...."

Once, passing a hand across her forehead, she said, "I really like it when they come here before they are absolutely ordered to report for induction, you know.... It gives us a little more ... a little more scope for ... "

"You mean then you have a snowball's chance in hell of helping them stay out."

"Yes. See, they should start thinking about the draft early, before they have to register. Sometimes they do; there's some that come while they're still in school and ask you how to start to be a C.O. Then you can sometimes help...." She sighed and folded the damp cheesecloth she'd been using to dust the desk. "But usually..."

"What are you saying, Susan? These guys don't come in until it's too late? So what can they do? I mean, Joel and Amos are little guys, but this fucking war could go on forever. I sure want to know how to keep them out."

"Oh, Dinah, your kids would never even register for the draft."

"Hey. It happens."

"Well ... " She gave me a rare smile, exposing all her shiny plating and wiring. "The surest way to get to be a C.O. is for some member of the clergy to speak for them. The draft boards almost always believe clergy."

"For our family, maybe a nice warlock."

"See, Dinah, your kids aren't ever going to fall for the old patriotic lie. They're not going to go charging off to shoot and be shot for the sake of some old oil fields or fruit merchants. They'll understand that wars are fought for markets, not ideals—that old men send young men to die, and women buy the whole crock of shit because that's how women get along in the patriarchy. Women acquire status when they send their sons off to war, no question about it. And a lot of women will value that kind of status over no status at all. The masters of war ask us to believe they're making the world safe for democracy instead of just for Coca-Cola. Like that Bobby Dylan song."

She sat on the corner of my desk and swung her leg, her tentative manner shearing away. "The corporations that get the contracts to make the weapons—Dow, McDonnell-Douglas, Boeing, Honeywell, Gladdwin—they're all controlled by the same small ruling class. *Ramparts* did a terrific piece on Bechtel Corporation."

"What's that? I never heard of it."

"Most people never heard of Bechtel, but it's tremendously influential. I had no idea how many people in the cabinet are, or were, on the board of directors. It's a construction firm, but they get contracts for, like, airports, military installations. Have you read *Who Rules America?* Did you know that about one percent of the population controls about ninety-five percent of the wealth in this country? And all their boards of directors interlock with each other and with the big banks, Bank of America, Chase Manhattan, Continental Illinois. And with the big newspaper publishing companies. And the major airlines. Even the computer companies. War is good for business. Very bad for people, especially young men, but good for business."

"Jesus, Susan, is that the kind of stuff you tell your clients? They should be lining up to refuse induction!"

"Oh . . . most of them aren't ready to hear this stuff. They don't have much understanding of economics. They just want to stay out of the military. It isn't even about peace, for them. Like, it's a negative thing, *not* going in, *not* getting drafted, rather than a positive thing, *resisting*. . . or just, like, taking a stand. . . . "

By god, if I were a man, I'd be ready. I hoped that when

Joel and Amos needed to hear this, she'd still be around to tell them. But the men didn't quite see it my way.

"Susan's good, sure, but the young guys aren't too comfortable with her," said Miles.

"Susan kind of puts guys uptight," said Ian.

"You have to fit the counselor to the client sometimes," said Carl.

The men counselors fitted the good clients to themselves: the smart, steady guys who could carry through on their C.O. applications or the heroes-and-martyrs who were ready to resist. Then, when they evaluated each other's performance at the end of the quarter, Susan, because she'd been counseling the problem cases—the skittish, suicidal guys who had a couple of counseling sessions and then went down to their friendly local recruiting office and volunteered just to end the suspense—always had the lowest rates of success.

All that long, dirty spring I hugged my little sons morning and night, except when they went to stay with their father and I could hug someone scratchier, and I tried to whip Susan into shape.

"You've got to stand up for yourself. The guys are not fair to you. You have to tell them what you've done."

Cora tried, too, with better tact. "The men may not realize what's happening," she said, "but you seem to be the only counselor who is acquiring the skills to work with really difficult cases."

Susan wouldn't confront her colleagues. "It's all right," she said. "They have enough on their minds."

Some of the men were heroes-and-martyrs themselves, nonregistrants, noncooperators. I wondered what it would be like to know you were going to prison. Mornings and evenings I said to my sons, "And stay out of prison."

"They have no power over me if I don't acknowledge their authority," said Carl. "Let them come and arrest me."

Which they did, later.

The guys all gave talks in high schools and churches all over Minnesota. The brothers, Carl and Ian, had relatives in a couple of western counties, and they'd ride a bus out to the farm for the weekend, eat a big pot roast dinner maybe with prunes, go to church with the family, and give a homily. Or give a high school assembly on Monday, with their jug-eared cousins acting proud and embarrassed.

"Bet they never saw hair like ours," Ian would say, when they told us of their adventures.

One spring day, I turned up for my shift and Carl showed me an item clipped from a rural weekly.

> Thorfin Holdseth and his son Arlon of Two Mile Creek Township pleaded no contest at their arraignment in district court on Thursday. They were charged with dumping animal and human excrement on files in the offices of Selective Service at Cedar River, seat of Muskellunge County, on March 20, 1969. Judge Liljeblad ordered the Holdseths released on their own recognizance.

"Shit!" Carl whistled. "They dumped their own shit on the files!"

"Do you know these guys? Where'd you get the clipping?"

"Not by name. But they could have heard me at the high school in Cedar River, I talked there last winter."

"Someone sent us the clipping," said Ian. "No return address."

"There's a strong pacifist tradition in some of those places," said Jonathan. "Those old Norwegians, y'know. Some of 'em are almost like Mennonites."

"So what'd you tell them, to shit on the Selective Service System?"

"No," said Ian. "We just told 'em about it in terms they could easily understand. Told 'em that according to the Selective Service Act, their bodies don't belong to them, and so forth. Told 'em the government has serious plans for their future. Told 'em how much tax money leaves rural Minnesota, and how little comes back. No one's built a helicopter factory in Cedar River lately. Or a tank factory. Just told 'em stuff like that."

"The shit was their own idea," grinned Carl.

Carl had almost graduated from college when he left to start MIC. Miles and Jonathan were dropouts, and Ian had just finished high school. Carl said he was taking a furlough. "It's a peace furlough," he'd say importantly. "I'm doing government work." And then he'd laugh.

The sight of his strong white teeth flooded me with warmth and curiosity. What would happen if I flirted with Carl?

"Say, uh, Dinah," Susan mumbled one day in June. "You know, uh, Carl's going with Annie."

"I know."

"I, uh, sort of hoped you didn't know. I mean . . . I know he's attractive and everything, but . . . "

"Susan, we're not in high school. If he's committed to her, he should tell me himself."

I saw her braces again. "Oh, you know guys. Any mail?"

Dammit, what business is it of hers if I want to flirt with Carl? Or even ball him? He's been painting houses and already his skin is burned a dark, smooth brown, his hair has bleached to silver, and his eyes shine like blue topaz, clear and hot. I'm a good parent to my boys, I deserve some rest and recreation.

When she finished opening the mail, I started to bully Susan. "Exclusive relationships are bourgeois. No one owns anybody. We're all free to decide what we do with our bodies, isn't that right? What if Carl and I do become lovers? It doesn't take anything away from Annie. She didn't *have* him before."

Susan got pink and turned away, her hair falling over her face. "I don't want to get involved, okay?"

Feeling brutal, I left early. Susan had lots of experience holding down the fort alone.

*

God, coming down into Mexico City looks like heading into a swamp. We have fucked up this planet royally. My arms hurt and my chest feels like Basket stomped on it. Please don't make me get off the plane, oh, *grácias,* I'll just close my eyes and go on dreaming about the past and hope we really do go up in the air again *a las nueve.* Maybe the Goddess will send me a vision of how I'm going to tell Cory.

*

Carl and Ian, whose name was really Ingvar, came from a farm family named Kjellstrom in western Wisconsin, about two hours from Minneapolis on old Highway 12. The Military Information Center staff held a retreat there in the summer of 1969.

"Sure, bring your kids," Carl said. "There'll be child care."

"There's chickens and horses and a neat old barn," Ian said. "They'll have a great time."

So I notified Reuben that I was transporting our children to Roy and Thelma Kjellstrom's farm, across a state line, for the weekend, and he warned me about insect bites and poison ivy, deep water, barbed wire, dogs, cats, skunks, nettles, leeches, snapping turtles, pollen, poison oak, poison sumac, poisonous mushrooms, rattlesnakes, and dry rot. I said "Yes" into the phone every eight seconds or so, and eventually he ran out of hazards.

We drove to the farm in my old VW bug along with Susan and Eli, her fella. Amos had to sit in the little well under the rear window, and Joel sat up front with me. "Let's sing," he said, the moment we hit Highway 12. We sang "We All Live in a Yellow Submarine" and "We Shall Overcome" and "Old McDonald Had a Farm."

Susan asked Eli to play for the boys, and he snarled, "Not enough room, stupid."

"Is your name Eli?" Joel asked. "Eli, Eli, Yo! Old McDonald had a farm, Eli, Eli, Yo!"

"Yeah, well, don't get carried away, kid."

"What instrument do you play, Eli?"

"Fartophone," said Eli.

Joel stared at him in fascination. Susan said, "Not really. He plays the panpipes and the pennywhistle."

"I can fistle," said Amos.

"Quiet or I'll teach you how to smoke," said Eli.

"Do you moke? You're a dope," said Amos bravely, repeating one of Reuben's wisdoms.

"Blow it out your ass," said Eli. "Anyway, it takes one to know one."

Roy and Thelma's farmhouse overlooked a small twisty river, more of a creek. The Kjellstroms kept a lot of their property wild, so lavender harebells, yellow lady's slipper, bluets, Queen Anne's lace, purple loosestrife, and wild raspberry canes pushed through the long grass on the river bank. They owned the other side of the river, too, a limestone bluff left by the glacier when it chunked out the creek valley. Ferns and little mauve flowers grew in crevices of the rock, and morning sun spattered through the leaves of birch trees clinging lightly to the bluff. In this dappled light the little river ran swiftly away from the house, angling out of sight fifty yards downstream, but we could hear it gabbling and chuckling as it ran around rocks and beaver dams and sandbars fringed with reeds and cattails.

Insects buzzed the water's surface in squadrons, but the ones we could see best were electric blue dragonflies. "Mom!" said Joel. "Darning needles! And they're stacked up!"

"I think that's how they make love, honey." The flies glided ecstatically in tandem, light striking blue glints from their wings. My heart ached at such perfection.

Roy and Thelma's house featured aluminum siding and combination windows. A hundred yards away across a dirt road stood another house, dark and tumbledown among the weeds, and this house they turned over to us for our dormitory. Huge wooden cable spools stood in the yard for us to use as picnic tables and chairs, and in back someone had dug a rough fire pit and surrounded it with logs. Tall elms and pines kept the house in shadow. We heard the cries of young blackbirds and their parents' reassuring trills.

"It's a antique," Roy told us when he brought us over. "In one o' th'upstairs bedrooms you can see where somebody wrote the date, 1869. It's a hundred-year-old house, th'original farmhouse on this prop'ty. 'Course, it's got no foundation, that's the way they did then, just a dugout cellar. And no water or electric. We don't use it no more except to have people to stay, like this weekend, or if one of the kids has a pajama party, why, we turn it over to 'em."

"Why don't they tear it down?" mumbled Eli.

"Cost too much to tear it down," said Roy cheerily. "And then where would you folks stay? There's a three-seater outhouse over by them lilac bushes, you can go in shifts."

An old range stood in the big bare kitchen, hooked to a canister of white gas outside the window. All the windows had spring pegs in their frames that fitted into holes in the molding. If you needed to raise or lower the window, first you had to release the pegs. *"That's* a dopey window," said Joel.

The empty rooms of the old house buzzed and hummed with flies and yellowjackets. Ian and Carl were busy with a roll of wire mesh and a staple gun, tacking rough rectangles of screening to the outside window frames where the paint had worn off generations ago.

"Hi, Dinah. Hi, Dinah's kids. You know, your mom talks about you all the time."

"That's dumb," muttered Joel, and his ears got red.

I asked Ian where we should put our stuff, and he took the nails out of his mouth and told me to claim a room. There were about eleven bedrooms, each one shabbier than the next. Some had vast iron bedsteads, and some just a roll of foam rubber against the wall. Along the stairwell and in some of the rooms, bare lath showed where the plaster had crumbled to the floor. Sheaves of wallpaper thick as catalogs furled off the scabby walls, and in the cracks and crevices nested many flying, crawling, fluttering creatures.

The corners looked dark and cobwebby. The floorboards creaked, and our footsteps raised a heavy white dust. A choking smell of mold and must, age and disuse filled the old place, but it felt cool and safe, too, a house that could stand up to any kind of treatment.

"I'm fightened," said Amos solidly, clutching his square of bankie.

"It's strange, but it's not bad, honey. This is an old, old house. If it was a person we'd say it was sick, maybe."

"I'm not scared," said Joel, picking some dry mortar off the naked lath.

"Don't make it any worse, Jojo."

"Don't, Jojo!"

"Shut up, scaredy-cat."

Cora's station wagon turned up the dirt track, bearing Jonathan, Carol, Cory, her son Seth, who was just enough older than Joel to fascinate both of them, and her daughter Serena, a tall strong girl of twelve. Of course, there was no one to look after our kids except us, but we had a terrific time. We jumped in the hayloft and picked berries, looked for fresh-water mussels and special rocks, and missed all the heavy-duty political meetings, meaning I missed talking to

87

Carl. He promised the three older kids he'd take them fishing tomorrow.

Saturday night, Roy and Thelma had us over for barbecued hamburgers and chicken, and we drank beer and horsed around with Ian's older sisters and his baby brother, Donald, who was very cute and said, "You can call me Duke," in a John Wayne voice. The vegetarians made do with corn on the cob and three-bean salad.

Summer twilight lasts forever. Sweet smells rose from the fields, stars came out by twos and threes, the sky shaded from pale blue lit by the dying sun in the west to deep night, delicate as the glaze on fine porcelain. Pallets of mist hung knee-high above the ground. Joel chased a few fireflies winking under the overgrown lilac trees.

"Gol, when I was a kid they was everywhere. Remember, Thel?" said Roy, and I told them I remembered fireflies in Milwaukee when I was a kid.

Cory and I went back to the old house to put our children to bed, and when we came outside the others were kindling a fire in the pit. I had brought some dope to share, and so had Miles, and we all got nicely stoned sitting on logs under the stars.

"Okay," said Carl, "I've got something you're going to thank me for."

The last joint was making its way around the circle, and as it reached me, Joel's voice called "Mom?" from an upstairs window. Carl went to tell him I'd be right there, and they had a little confab through the window while I toked up, then I left the circle too.

In darkness heavy with the scent of meadow rue and dope, I leaned in toward Carl, trailing my hand up his arm through the soft hairs, and spoke to the dark window above our heads.

"You okay, Jojo?"

"Yes." Carl stroked me back, soft as milkweed silk.

"Mom?" came Joel's voice again.

"What is it, honey?"

"What if I have t'goat the bathroom?"

"No problem, Jojo. I'll take you to the outhouse."

"But what if you're asleep?"

"You can wake me up." Lightly, lightly I felt Carl's muscles under his shirt, long ropes along his shoulder blades, strong cushions below his collarbone. His body radiated heat through his thin dark shirt. All I could see of him by starlight was a fall of hair and pale eyes gleaming.

Joel said something muffled. Carl's fingers brushed the front of my shirt and my nipples flickered. "What is it, Jojo?"

"I said, what if I *can't* wake you up?" Carl leaned forward and touched my neck so lightly with his lips that I felt his breath.

"You can give him a pot," Carl murmured in my ear, sending arpeggios cascading through me.

I caught my breath. "You want a pot to pee in, Jojo?"

He chuckled. "Yeah, mom, that'd be good. I don't want to be without a pot to pee in."

I floated away from Carl's touch and went into the house, dreaming he might follow me, and found an old enameled basin in the kitchen, took it upstairs and held Joel's little penis while he pissed. When I went back out to the circle by the fire, Carl had dug from his pack the treat he'd promised us, something in a plastic yogurt jar. He made room for me on the log next to him, on the other side from Annie, sort of like a pasha with his two favorites.

The cornfields surrounding the old house exhaled coolness. Stoned as I was, the tall rows of corn could have been palisades, stockades, the reed walls of a hut, the tapestried walls of a castle. I smiled across at Cora but I felt attached to Carl by threads as subtle as the touch of his fingertips, threads from my nipples, my earholes, the palms of my hands, my thighs, my clit, the tender soles of my feet. My insteps.

"What is it?" I asked, when the plastic jar reached me. The others were smacking their lips, falling over with pleasure.

"Dopers' Delight," said Carl, beatifically. "There isn't much left."

It was the best thing I ever ate, and I said so, thinking, Oho, but I haven't had *you* in my mouth, you big toasty beauty.

Miles said softly, "I want to smear it all over my body."

"I want to lick it off you," said Rebecca.

"No, me!"

"Me!"

"Carl, like, what's in it?"

"Almond butter. . . "

We all moaned a little, ecstatically. "Cashew butter. . . "

Miles fell over and buried his head in Rebecca's lap.

"Tahini . . . "

Ian picked up the empty container and stuck it over his nose.

"Crunchy peanut butter, of course. . . . "

"Of course!"

"But *the best* . . . "

"Nothing but the best. . . . "

"And honey. Basswood honey." Carl's voice spoke these words in dark amber, the color of the honey. His voice purled through the darkness under the stars and penetrated my perfect ears, intimately and wonderfully, swimming into me through some viscous medium like honey.

"But mixing it up is a bitch."

"You bet it is," said Annie, who didn't seem too concerned that Carl and I were, like, joined at the hip.

"Then I cut it with a little yogurt. Stretch it, you know."

"How much of each thing?" Susan asked.

"Mmmm, good question." My whole body vibrated with his dark golden voice, for a long moment of darkness, and as it faded I yearned for it to come rumbling back and set me going again.

"Equal quantities."

We all collapsed in ecstasy, all but Eli.

The Milky Way cut the sky like a spangled sash. I lay with my head in the grass, feeling Carl's leg against mine, his hard thigh and knee. If I lie here, sooner or later I'll see a falling star, I thought, breathing in the wet scent of the grass. At that perfect moment, there was no war. I had no children. There were no other people, only the blood glittering through my veins and the fine threads linking me with Carl.

I heard what was going on around me, my friends laughing, breathing, muttering, coughing, and underneath them a million bugs busy with bug business, traveling their bug routes, making secret bug deals, building bug empires, waging bug wars. Maybe some of them were negotiating bug peace, flitting here and there with their little bug briefcases from bug Dulles to bug Hanoi, looking for new methods of conflict resolution, shit, I thought, here even the goddamn *bugs* are doing it and Nixon and Kissinger don't know how.

"Stuff tastes all right," said Eli nasally, "but it has the consistency of wet cement."

"Yeah, well, that's another reason to cut it with the yogurt."

"You could plaster up the walls with it," Eli snickered. Susan snuggled against him. Annie sat straight, but the other couples sank in to each other as the stars jingled and jangled through the sky like bells on a merry-go-round pony's bridle.

Eli and Susan had the room next to where I slept with the boys. I don't know where Carl and Annie slept, but I heard the whine of bedsprings everywhere. You know how when you're stoned, a sound can go on indefinitely. The bedsprings sang "The Solomon Song," from *Threepenny Opera:*

Remember good old Solomon
Recall his history
He was the wisest man on earth
And so he cursed the day of his birth
He knew that all was vanity.
So not much fun
Had Solomon . . .

over and over. I'd try to lose it and I'd think I had succeeded
but then from somewhere in my head the soft groaning of
springs, the hurdy-gurdy of the song would unwind,

So not much fun
Had Solomon . . .

for hours it seemed. Probably only about ten minutes. I didn't
have memorable dreams.

*

Never thought I'd be grateful for Florida, but I am. And
for U.S. Customs and for the smell of good old U.S. frying
grease. Let's see if I can get myself on a nonstop to the Twin
Cities, then I'll call Leaf and tell her to lurk on the baggage
level. I won't tell her about the baby, not until I figure out
how I'm going to break it to Cory.

*

The boys woke up early and whined because there was
no TV. They demanded cereal and wouldn't eat granola like
Seth and Serena, so we got in the car and drove five miles to
the nearest town, Prairie Farm, no kidding. Realizing they had
me in a sort of behavioral full nelson, they caused me to buy
Oreo cookies as well as Wheaties and sliced American cheese.

When we got back, Jonathan was brushing his teeth in the kitchen with water he'd hauled from Roy and Thelma's.

"You shouldn't let them eat that stuff," he said. "I mean, like, here's your chance to bring up Americans with really healthy eating habits."

I should have told him to butt out, but I rose to the bait. "I know, I know. But every other weekend they visit their dad, and he feeds them pretty much everything they ask for. Besides, feeding your family healthy food means a lot of extra work."

"What do you mean?" He rinsed his mouth and spat into a glass, then took off his pajama top and stretched. Carl came up behind him and tickled his skinny, pearly white ribs. Two alpha males engaging in play after successful mating. Jonathan jumped, then whirled as Carl went into a crouch and grabbed him. They tussled like puppies, the pale body and the dark.

"Left-wing deviationist!"

"Anarcho-syndicalist!"

"Power to the people!"

"Power to the working class!"

"Smash the dying forces of bourgeois decay!"

Amos shrieked and threw himself on top of Carl.

"Hey, hey, hey, Joel," said Jonathan. "Don't hurt me."

"That's Amos," said Joel and I at the same time.

So our conversation about healthy eating got dropped, but I continued it in my head—lazily, a little stretched out like you are the morning after—and then later with Cory as we took Amos down the road to an old gravel quarry.

"If we're going to get all our amino acids from non-meat sources, that's a lot of corn and beans or peas and rice," I said. "Somebody has to plant and thin and harvest the beans and peas, hull them and dry them, soak and sort them."

"Yes," she said, "and somebody has to plant and harvest and thresh and grind the grain. Somebody has to catch the fish, find the sea vegetables, feed the chickens, gather the eggs, milk the cows, make the cheese, the yogurt. Nutritionally, feedlot beef is a convenience food."

"Potatoes are good, especially when you eat the skins."

Joel, Seth, and Serena were fishing with Carl, and the others set up a softball game. As we walked toward the quarry pool, the landscape changed every few hundred feet, from the deep cool shade of the riverbank to waving cornfields to the hot glare of the road as we trudged along the shoulder, our swimming towels around our necks.

Amos kept stepping out of his flip-flops, so I bundled him up into my arms, hot and heavy, dusty and teary.

Gravel crunched under our feet and the scent of wild roses blew up from the ditch. A little ground squirrel darted across the hot surface of the road. Red-winged blackbirds sang their cracked trilling song.

"I'm hot, mom."

We turned off the road and onto a rutted track that sloped downward through a grove of pine trees, cool and fresh-smelling. Plush fat bees hummed on the lacy blooms of wild carrot, and milkweed and Queen Anne's lace frothed up to the edge of the trees. "Hey, Ame, you know who lives in there?"

Amos tightened his arms around my neck. "I'm fightened."

"Deer! I'll bet."

"Goodness!" said Cory. "Think we'll see 'em?"

"No. I think they mostly come out in the evening. They're probably asleep right now."

Amos yawned. "Weal deeuw?"

"Yup." I shifted his weight and asked him how he'd like to do his own walking. But I knew the answer to that one.

The trees ended, and the track sloped up between two more cornfields. The sun seemed to concentrate its force on us, on our shoulders and noses, as if we were under some huge glass. The whole world around us shimmered in the light, brighter than city sunlight, clearer, more intense. We are like bugs, I thought, remembering my stoned bug vision of the night before.

"Baby bug," I murmured against my baby's damp hair.

"I'm no bug," he protested.

"Roy doesn't use any chemical fertilizers," Ian had told us, "or pesticides or herbicides. He and Thelma try to keep their land organic with natural repellents like tansy, garlic, onion, nasturtiums."

The pinky-puce milkweed blossoms crawled with lady-birds. Gnats and flies swarmed around us, grasshoppers the color of dust raised tiny clouds at our feet. Clover's sweetness and the mild stench of cow manure came from the fields, and the air zinged with the songs of flying creatures.

Organic was the new word. It sounded good to me but naive, as if the people who believed in *organic* believed that your life could be a seamless whole, like Cora: as if you could be one thing inside and out, your beliefs, your acts, and your desires all pointing in one and the same direction. If you were a pacifist, you could find ways to end small wars in your life—stop your children hitting each other, stop manipulating your lovers or lying to your ex. Your sexuality could flow through your life, a source of energy, not shame.

But maybe all they meant was small fields, sweet smells, dragonflies, birds, ground squirrels, and clean water.

We found the quarry pool, and I set Amos down and slipped off my caftan. "Race you in, guys"! And I ran naked through the duckweed into the shallow water where frogs thunked and sunfish darted and nibbled our legs. As I floated on my back, I looked up into the sky where the color dark-ened almost to indigo next to the sun, and my heart was full and stilled.

Amos whined for a minute, but then he got interested in some fish-egg slime, sieving the water through his fat fingers to see what stayed behind on his palm. I had to be careful not to bliss out, because I know a kid can drown even in shallow water. What cranky, fragile things kids are. They look so sturdy, they sound like the horn section of a really big orchestra, with the destructive capability of a tornado, and you have to struggle to keep them alive. You haul them on your lifeline from birthday to birthday, and it's hard to find time for ecstasy.

Amos loved to swim between my legs and Cory's, of course he did. And the water felt so good, and his smooth pelt felt so fine against mine, we had a little be-in just the three of us there in the pond, ducking underwater and then rising in a spray of clear drops, snorting and laughing. He was born again and again from between our thighs. He held onto our legs and floated his body out at full length so we could admire the downy fork of hair just above his buttocks.

His skinny little cock waggled in the water, and sometimes he got stiff against my body when he climbed over and through me, but then he'd go wiggly again. I carried him on my back over the deepest dark-green water to the other side of the quarry where cattails grew. Amos shrieked with joy and kicked his legs, and when we got back to the duckweed I saw his lips were purple.

"Out for a while," I said, and stretched out on my caftan while he looked for neat rocks. But I knew I couldn't fall asleep.

Toward dusk, as we were putting our things together to leave, Carl stopped me in the upstairs hall. I felt smooth and perfect, although my hair was wild as if I'd been fucking all afternoon. I had him in my nostrils, on my skin, the awareness of him. Sure, I admit it, I dawdled packing up.

"Dinah," he said, and kissed me, and again his lips were as soft as his muscles were hard. "I was thinkin' about you."

"I thought about you, too."

"Oh yeah? What'd you think?"

"I thought, 'I'd love to ball Carl.'" I leaned forward and nibbled his earlobe.

"Oh, wow. That's kinda what I was thinkin', too." We kissed again, and I felt him grow hard against me. "Come in here for a minute," and he pulled me inside the room he had shared with Annie.

"Carl," I said, "my kids, I can't, we can't...." But I wanted to, he wanted to, and we did. We didn't take our clothes off; we didn't dare get on the noisy bed; we just fucked there on the floor, very, very hot and urgent.

"Mom!" shouted Joel, pounding up the stairs as I lay gasping across Carl's chest. "When are we gonna go?"

In the seconds between his voice and his flinging open the door, my new lover and I stood up, brushed off, and picked up our bundles.

When we left, Carl murmured to me through the open window of my car, "First requisite of a revolutionary."

All the way home, while Susan tried to talk to my sons about war and the draft, and Eli made snide comments, I wondered what he meant. I asked Cora a few years later, when I got my feminist consciousness raised, and she thought maybe he meant revolutionary comrades should be lovers. "Bullshit," I said, "he means women should stay in the kitchen and the bedroom, fucking and feeding."

Now that years have passed and my life is simpler, I think he was talking about clandestinity and passion, about how to keep the pieces of your life separate. That way, they make a satisfying pattern. Mix them up, and they're unmanageable. Look what happened when I tried to pull this little scam for Cora. Like in the Solomon song, *She trusted me and was undone.* I hope Leaf got my message.

CHAPTER 6

CORA & DINAH

On good days I know I'll get well. On bad days I just have to try harder.

Dinah's back, finally. She comes over and tells us there was no baby for her this time, but she's in close touch with this lawyer she met, and he is hopeful of finding one soon. I'm disappointed, of course, but in a way relieved; I do need more time to recover from these heroic interventions in my health.

When Dinah looks at me, I can see in her face that she thinks I've gone down in the weeks since she saw me.

"I don't want to hear about it," I tell her. "I'm getting stronger all the time."

She helps me get dressed and we walk down to the lake. "Let's take Jean Harlow," she says, but the old dog just wags her tail.

I love late-summer air, its thick perfumes, even the greasy green goose shit on the path next to the water.

"Can we sit here? Put your arm around me, Dinah."

Cottonwoods rustle in the breeze. A man and a woman

jog past, I smell their sharp cologne. If I let my eyes slip out of focus, the sun glittering on the water doesn't hurt.

She tells me little bits about her trip. She was surprised to find she misses Carl.

"I was crazy in love with him," she says, "and now I can hardly remember what he looks like. Maybe I was really in love with his mother. I was so deluded...."

"Youth is delusion, that's the secret of life," I tell her. "When we're born we're wrapped in it, thick stuff they have to siphon out of our ears and eyes. We get less and less deluded until we finally achieve utter clarity. And then we die."

"My god! You talk as if delusion was some kind of ozone layer. When it gets so thin it doesn't protect us any more, poof!"

That's my pal. "You want to live forever?"

A fish leaps in the water, making a series of widening rings. A couple of teenagers stroll past, with a ferret on a string. They're dressed in black with metal studs, rings in their ears and noses, magenta hair. The beast zigzags, twitching its nose. They've put a little harness on it.

A man and two children armed with fishing rods and plastic pails walk over to the storm-sewer culvert. The man bends down and comes up with a handful of writhing live bait, holding it out to each kid.

"It's not safe to eat fish out of these lakes," says Dinah softly.

The kids bait their hooks and the family disperses, with a few words in an Asian language. They might be Hmong. They're beautiful. People look beautiful. Their pets are beautiful, the ducks and geese are beautiful. The little black muskrat steering with its tail and holding its snout out of the water just won the Miss Muskrat contest. The world's most beautiful jay lets out a scream over our heads. I squeeze Dinah's hand and she squeezes back, a little too hard. "Rosalia is a nice name, but I'm hoping for a newborn—someone we can name ourselves."

"What do you know about whole-body warming?" she asks. "I mean as therapy."

"I hear it's effective in some cases. You're getting to be such a *clinician,* sweetie."

"What I really mean is, can you have it?"

Jerry and I talked to Sydney about it a couple months ago. "They think it's not appropriate in my case. I need madder music, stronger wine."

"Stop me if I'm out of line. I read everything I can find, Cory."

"I feel how much you care about me, honey, that's never out of line. Who else went all the way to Guatemala? And will go again?" She shudders, then she laughs. "Tell me what you did down there. Tell me about the babies you saw. Did you meet people? Go places, see things?"

"I started writing my memoirs."

Wow. I lived through some of them, but I'd buy the book. "Pretty hot?"

"Pretty dumb. It's almost time for your meds. Let's get you back."

Memoirs—now there's an idea.

CORA'S MEMOIR— What makes one person conscious and not another? I will never understand this. Or how you can be conscious of some things and not others—like Dinah, loving and giving in some ways and cold in others.

I feel I have always known how evil war is, how perverted. We as a species don't need to hurt each other, but I don't know how to say this. Children learn to inflict hurt when they suffer hurt, and all children suffer—we can't help hurting them. Life is a gift but an injury, too.

I dedicate this memoir to my children, Serena the doctor

and Seth the teacher and the new one, niñita sin nombre.
*Serena, my dear, I know you will be a wonderful doctor
and a happy woman. You don't talk to me about your
personal life any more, but I trust you.*

*Seth, if you make a life with Persimmon it will be a rich
one. She is as full of possibility as you, and I love her children already as though they were my—*

"Hey, Cory, cut it out. We've got to keep you in the
present tense, here."

"Who says?"

She shakes me gently. "It scares me when you slip away
like that. Don't you have to focus your mind on healing, or am
I missing something?"

"You're right. But I get so tired. Besides, I didn't really go
away."

"What were you doing?"

"I was starting my memoirs."

Slowly we walk back to the house. My bare arms are
lapped by the warm air. I knew this was going to be a good
day.

DINAH'S MEMOIR

Breasts! Breasts! How old was I when I first rubbed my
nipples and got an answering tingle down below? "Tongues
of fire," one of my classmates called it, in a creative writing
seminar. She was a tall, horsey girl, and she surprised us with
an erotic poem. "They talk to each other in tongues of fire."

You think you'll never be able to feed your baby that way,
and you nearly die when it first fastens onto you, soft tiny

bundle with a lamprey mouth. In high school I went out with a boy named Gene Lovett, who used to suck my breasts for hours in the front seat of his dad's car. We'd come back from the movies and park down the street from my house, and he'd pull up my sweater and unhook my bra. Then he'd bend his big dark curly head and start sucking. When we finally kissed goodnight, I'd rush into my bedroom and rub myself raw.

All the men who have kissed them. The women who have kissed them. My sons who sucked from me. The pain when they were engorged with milk—once I left Amos at home with a babysitter while I took Joel to a demo, and we got hung up, the cops closed the street and we couldn't get back to our car. Joel was three, and I had him on my back in a Gerry carrier. I'd left a bottle of breast milk with the sitter to take care of the baby, but I'd forgotten that I'd need to be milked. It was early days in Vietnam, maybe 1966 or '67. The straps of the carrier dug into my shoulders with the weight of the big boy on my back, my breasts got hard as stones against my chest, and I made Joel suck me.

That was the first big street demo in Minneapolis against the war and the draft. When we sang "We Shall Overcome," my milk let down, and I felt it flooding the front of my shirt. I felt sexy all the time while I was nursing a baby, and when Reuben and I made love, my milk would let down and flood over his chest, over the sheets. He was disgusted at first, but then he let himself taste the stuff and he kind of got into it, not suckling, exactly, but he'd lick it up after I came and the milk let down. Poor Reuben! He tried to change. He really tried, for my sake, to be something different: a radical, a pacifist, an alternative kinda guy. For the sake of my beautiful breasts.

They shine like stars, and when they're full of milk they are solid as the finest, most satiny marble. I only have two. Some lucky witches have three or more. Imagine three nipples! I love them as much as I love my fingers, they're part of my belonging, they say myself to me. Don't hold them in contempt: hold them in love, in awe. You may look at them, smell their perfume, taste them, touch them, listen to their high sweet humming.

When I was eleven, I used to rub cologne on my nipples. It stung and excited me. I dreamed of knowing someone who would reach up under my peasant blouse and feel my breasts, but I knew no such person, and I barely had breasts to feel—I had to wait until I was fourteen for a lanky lovely boy who didn't talk but kissed and kissed with chapped eager lips and reached and stroked and squeezed with calloused hands. My breasts remember him. If ever I lost one, would I forget . . . ?

*

I learned to lie when I was a little girl, as soon as I realized I had things to hide. What things? Comic books; masturbating; playing with kids my mother didn't want me to, like the pale hillbillies who lived in tenements on the other side of my school, whose mothers dosed them with kerosene when they had worms; going to the movies during the week—Cornel Wilde, Yvonne DeCarlo.

Sanitary napkins. Tampons. Lipstick, mascara, cigarettes, beer, boys. Dope. Sneaking into the dorm. Staying out all night. Marxism. Abortions. I loved my secrets.

After I got married, I kept my whole life a secret, and the habit persisted after the divorce. It's actually easier to live in pieces, especially when you have kids: The mom piece stays separate from the hippie, the actress, the sex goddess, the peace activist, the friend. The mom protects her kids from her own bad habits. The friend can listen to sad stories the politico would put down. The hippie loves everyone but knows when to come home.

Cora is different. "I want to live without secrets," she says. "The great social movement of my lifetime is about love and acceptance, the opening of our hearts. We're learning to love each other, we're breaking down barriers. We want to be whole people."

This seems like real goodness to me, and I hold her in awe. Right now, she is sicker than she knows. My little lie of omission is a kindness. She'll realize soon enough that she can't take care of a baby. Better she should come to this decision by herself. Sometimes I feel bad because I can't measure up to her. Sometimes.

When I was in college, in the early sixties, I thought maybe I should be an actress because I liked to take my clothes off.

Nowadays the energy is in rock, all the kids do music, my son Amos is in some desperate garage band. Then, we all did theater. We did Shakespeare, we did Shaw, Brecht, Pirandello, Lorca, we did the Second Shepherd's Play, we wrote our own plays. We called them plays, but they were mostly attitude.

After I took the boys and left Reuben, I realized I had been a theater person all along, so I joined a company called the Icehouse. I kissed goodbye to the bourgeois life, the upholstery and appliances, and my little house was bare but lovely. We all decorated the walls; my lover Crater and his buddies painted the outside green in the spring. I threw Indian-print spreads over Salvation Army furniture and hung my beads on the walls, stuck fat candles into the old wall sconces where a previous owner had ripped out the gas mantles without wiring them for electricity. Every night I went to some communal occasion—a meeting, party, or rehearsal—and my boys slept on floors, couches, in bureau drawers like Kayo in "Gasoline Alley," always with some good person looking out for them.

New things went on at the Icehouse—improvisations, audience challenge, company-created work. We shared the work—we all learned to run the light board and the sound. We learned to tumble. We practiced juggling.

Marcus Inchloe was our leader, the producer-director and, incidentally, the guy whose money kept the Icehouse cool. Inchloe thought the real political frontiers were sex and art. "We need to de-privatize erotic relationships," he'd say, sliding a long, juicy look at me. "We need to personalize revolutionary change. Experientially, we must change ourselves, and then confront our audiences."

Of course we were all against the war, but Inchloe didn't think we should be directly political in our performances.

One day in 1967, I'm at Cora's house folding WSP leaflets, my boys playing peacefully for once with Seth's puppy that I named Jean Harlow, because she is a shrewd dumb blonde, and I'm telling her about the latest flap at the Icehouse.

She says, "Don't you think audience confrontation is sort of boring?"

I always feel like a waif at Cora's house. She wears soft, old clothes, sweaters and pants and baggy skirts and long socks, but she and Jerry are real grownups with their own washer and dryer, a cabinet for their hi-fi components, kitchen canisters full of flour and rice. Sometimes I wish they would adopt me and my kids.

"Boring! According to Inchloe, it's the hottest thing since jalapeño jelly."

"But you *know*," she said, "in a theater, nothing's ever really going to happen."

After my three-week affair with Inchloe, things became tense at the Icehouse. We were not well suited sexually; he was mainly interested in seeing how long he could keep from coming.

The theater held workshops four nights a week where we played improvisational games and practiced our tumbling and juggling. We were working on a scenario by a new playwright who had written in a beat where the actors confront the audience. We had started confronting our audiences when we did a version of *Woyzeck,* starring Crater. After he kills his lover, he turns and faces the audience and says "Isn't that what you want from me?"

"Hold that moment," Inchloe told him. Five of us were onstage with him, me as the murdered lover and four others. "You get up and face the audience," he said to me. "Everybody face the audience. Hold it. Long silence. Initiate eye contact, maintain it. Prolong . . . prolong."

At this point, I started to giggle because Prolong is the name of a stay-hard cream, but Inchloe ignored me. "Now," he said, "one by one, everybody say, *'Isn't that what you want from him?'* Move your lips but not your eyes. Stare them down. Prolong. Prolong. Stare. Confront. *'Isn't that what you want from him?'*

Inchloe wore dark turtlenecks, and his long face floated before us in the darkness. I lay where Crater had pushed me, breathing in the smell of old dust. I was glad to get up. We stared, we accused.

"Good," said Inchloe. "You will force them to confront their own violence, the criminal voyeur inside each one of them. You will force them to see that this criminal kills whatever it touches, kills what it loves. You interrupt their synapses, you de-habitualize them of their customary responses. Neurologically speaking, you carve new pathways, almost as though you were giving them acid."

"Why don't we just give them acid?" asked Crater.

"Yeah," we all said, "put it in Kool-Aid, pass it around like grape juice in church."

Inchloe nodded judiciously. "We could give them acid."

Only we never did. He dropped the subject. So that day at her house, Cora said, "In *Woyzeck,* it was exciting, but only for a moment. The thing is, for that moment, no one knows what to do, how to act. There are these actors staring at you in silence. It's thrilling, it's uncomfortable. But after that first shock, you find yourself playing by the same rules. Oh, you say to yourself, it's part of the performance. I wonder what they'll do next. You see? You don't really get out of that audience mind-set, except for that moment."

"Don't let this get back to Marcus," I told her. "It would kill him."

"It's like getting stuck in an elevator. You make the best of the situation. Seriously, were you ever stuck in an elevator? First you panic; you think all bets are off. Civilization has no script to cover this. Then you realize it does. People sort themselves out. The ones who are dominant, the alpha males, assert their dominance. The calm ones stay calm. The troublemakers make trouble. The jittery ones go to pieces and give the rest of us something to do. Artificial crises are boring. I don't think you can change people by manipulating them, not in any good way."

Amos started screaming at that moment, and ran in and fastened himself to my leg. Jean Harlow yelped once or twice. Joel called from the living room that it wasn't him, Ame bumped his head. I picked up Amos and fed him half a banana, and we finished our pile of leaflets, which announced a meeting with U.S. Representative Don Fraser, one of the few congressmen opposed to further involvement in Vietnam, and one of our favorite anti-war university professors. WSP had been urging the Minnesota state legislature to introduce a resolution against the war.

"Maybe the Icehouse should do this as a play," I said, bouncing Amos and waving a leaflet. "Brechtian, you know: *The People of Minnesota Offer Legislation Against the War in Vietnam.*"

Cory looked worried. "Do you think the war is too remote? Do you think people will feel it's their issue?"

"I don't know. As Marcus says, it's really hard to get through to people, to break the crust of everyday habit, convention. Like with the audience challenge, interrupting the habitual response. How can we make them feel the urgency?"

"Especially when other things in their lives are urgent too. How about some juice?" she said to Amos, and Joel heard that and swarmed in with his hands full of little trucks.

She made tea, in an earth-colored Japanese pot, and we drank it. I loved to sit with her, basking in her light, watching the golden hairs on her arms. The puppy loped in, all ears and tongue, and buried its nose in my crotch. I hate it when dogs do that. Hard to believe that puppy's now an old dog with white hairs on her muzzle and arthritis in her hips.

"See, at the Icehouse, we all believe we're really doing something new and important. Jesus, Cory, I thought we were, until you said that."

"Just smack her on the nose if you don't want her smelling your privates. She belongs to Seth, and he doesn't really train her."

"Where's Seth?" whined Joel. "I want to see Seth."

"Maybe he'll be here before you have to go home." She smiled sadly. "This war is hard on men, you know? I guess all wars are. They have to think about terrible things. I remember the Korean vets who came to Chicago on the GI Bill. They weren't just older than the rest of us, they had a terrible moral gravity. I used to ask them questions, but they didn't want to talk. War is hard on the ones who don't go, too. Maybe you could think of the work at the Icehouse as Inchloe's personal heroism."

"All that manhood stuff."

Inchloe definitely was into manhood stuff, sort of Zen macho. He not only rationed his semen, he followed a strict diet with the goal of reducing his bowel movements to one per week. What he saved, he spent on words. I started to wonder about Cora's husband Jerry Bookbinder, a Jewish doctor, tall and rangy, ugly-attractive, the kind I thought I was marrying when I took up with Reuben: He worked at a clinic in a poor neighborhood. Not that I ever thought Reuben was tall.

"Manhood stuff," she said. "I'm so thankful I don't have to deal with that. You fellas want some more juice?"

"Jewish men say a prayer every morning thanking God they're not a woman," I told her. Cora's not Jewish.

"I'm not a girl," said Joel.

"I not guru," said Amos.

"Yes you are," said Joel.

"They do? I never heard that. I'm sure Jerry doesn't."

"Well, of course, I mean Orthodox Jewish men. Jerry's just not a pious Jew. I never heard it either, but it's in the *shulhan aruch,* Reuben told me."

"Maybe we could start a religion where women give thanks for not being men," said Cory.

"Of course you're not a girl, and neither are you," I scolded my sons. "But there's nothing wrong with girls, don't say those things around me. Boys are glad to be boys, girls are glad to be girls."

I looked around Cora's kitchen at her butcher-block cabinets, her hanging plants in their macramé slings, her neat pegboard hung with copper-bottom pans and blue enamel strainers, Seth's drawings stuck up on the cupboards. Dear Cory's got everything she wants: nice house, nice kids, a husband who digs her, golden retriever. But what about me? What about most women?

We're supposed to keep the kids in line *and* do the housework *and* most of us have to take a lousy job to make ends meet, so we can see that men get paid more money for exactly the same work. Our husbands ignore us—or they get drunk and slap us around. Most of us are not going to give thanks for the breasts and uterus that amount to a life sentence at hard labor.

But I didn't say what I was thinking; instead, I asked her how Jerry copes with the manhood stuff.

"Oh, heroism," she said, "you know—they get it fed to them all their lives, 'Terry and the Pirates,' Beowulf, for goodness' sake, Homer. Jerry's a pacifist, but he's got violence inside him, you can't grow up without that. He works hard to turn it into righteous anger. Doctors get off on the heroism stuff, you know. I'm sure they're not going to draft him, he's too old, but I don't know what he'd do. He was too young for Korea. He might go for a C.O. Or noncooperation."

Of course, that wasn't an answer. "God, would they draft him with two kids?"

"I don't think so. But we need to be thinking about it, about the military, and what it means for men to know that they're all supposed to be potential killers. Or if they're doctors, they're supposed to patch up wounded men, men who've been hurt worse than they ever imagined, and send them out again."

Our tea got cold, and Seth came home, and then Serena, and Cora probably fed us, and then it was time for me to cart my sons back to whoever was staying with them that night, so I could go to rehearsal.

The play I'm remembering was called *The Recruiting Officer,* adapted from a seventeenth-century Italian comedy, with stock characters from the *commedia* repertoire, updated to Vietnam. The braggart soldier/recruiting officer wore black pajamas and carried a swagger stick, like Nguyen Cao Ky; the rest of us wore karate clothes and straw coolie hats, and we limped across the stage or moved in giant steps and dips or prances to let the audience know we were jealous fathers, young lovers, scheming valets, or bawdy duennas.

"The costumes emblematize what roles we are playing vis-à-vis the war," announced Inchloe. "Our moment of confrontation should occur in silence. Maybe we should conceal our visages, masque ourselves. Confronted with masques, the audience will be forced to conceptualize. They will create our personae from their own animus or anima, from their own shadow self."

"No, no," we said, "no masks. If we're not going to give them acid, let's shove it in their faces."

"Sheesh," said Inchloe, "I'm talking about archetypal conceptualizations here. Whatever happened to subtlety? Suggestion?"

Crater and some of the others rumbled. I wanted to take it to the streets: the play, the audience, everything. Crater and his faction agreed. One of them was a draft resister named Miles Lofton who owned a skeleton suit.

"What you are proposing is anti-theatrical," said Inchloe.

"Look at Brecht," said Miles.

"Brecht was a genius, and he came out of a specific historical moment," decreed Inchloe, who, after all, paid the bills. "Once we forfeit the spectators' attention, we have failed. We will have abandoned the theater for the lecture hall."

So Crater, Miles and I, and three or four others left the Icehouse, which was located in a district of warehouses and equipment yards, so that even if we had taken our play onto the streets no one would have seen it. We founded a street theater called Drop Dead Company and performed street plays in which we all died and Miles triumphed over our bodies wearing his skeleton suit and holding a scythe. Inchloe went ahead and did the play his way, and the Twin Cities newspaper critics loved it. *Boffo anti-war antics,* they said, *Subtle but scathing.*

Minnesota is really too cold to support a radical street theater; you don't get much street life when the temp hits thirty below. We tried to pay our expenses by passing the hat. Most of the actors lived in my house at some time. I left Crater for Miles, and he was my old man until I met Carl.

When the weather warmed up, we took our clothes off and painted our faces, walked barefoot on our calluses, wore our real hair. After years of perms, of teasing and setting, ironing and rinsing, I finally got my real coarse hair back in 1967. We all became pagans, even the Minnesota Lutherans learned to drum and to chant, and Joel and Amos had long hair, they were beautiful hippie children, except they did get their shots because their father was a very straight doctor. A girl named Sunsparrow who lived in my house for a while acted shocked.

"You *really* want them injected with poisons? You know how many kids get sick from those shots?"

Lots of people stayed in my little green house in south Minneapolis—my theater buddies, draft resisters, assorted hippies and musicians, and their women, which is what we called each other in those days. I didn't mind being some-body's woman, it sounded earthy. We took our shows on the road to college towns wherever there were anti-war groups—Saint Cloud, Mankato, Eau Claire, even down to Madison—and of course I schlepped the kids along, although Reuben never failed to give me a hard time, usually on the phone. Did he offer to take them? No. He just gave me a hard time.

"How do I know what you're doing, Dinah? What you're exposing them to?"

"Get hip, Reuben. I'm their mom."

"Well, I'm their dad. How do I know what you're feeding them, where they're sleeping. This filthy hippie life breeds incredible parasitic diseases, *scabies,* for god's sake. People haven't had scabies since the Middle Ages."

The alimony and child-support checks came regularly, I'll give him that, so I didn't have to work at a lousy keypunch job and pay some woman down the street to babysit my boys. I had time to raise them properly and to educate myself. Miles became a draft counselor at the Military Information Center, and Cora and I volunteered there along with the organizing work we were doing for Women Strike for Peace, and guess what? There was Carl, waiting for me.

*

One of the bad things about divorce—and I'm a fan of divorce, I think it's a big improvement on marriage—but one of the bad things about it is that when you have kids, you do have to talk to your ex. The wonderful space and time you acquire with your decree disappear when the phone rings and it's Reuben wanting to talk about the boys' religious upbringing.

"This is not a question, Dinah, it's a statement. I want them to know they're Jews."

This was in the year of the murders: Martin Luther King, Bobby Kennedy. Reality had big holes in it. "Reuben, a new world is coming into being from the ashes of the old. We're on the threshold of a cataclysm that will bring about a new world of peace and understanding, and you want these kids to wear yarmulkes and *payis*?"

"I didn't say that. I just want them to be aware of their people, their heritage. We would be depriving them if we didn't make this available."

"Tell you what, Reuben: *you* believe in it, *you* do it."

And he did. Instead of taking them every other weekend, he rearranged his schedule so he could take them every weekend, and he started them at a Reform temple Sunday school. I mean, neither of us had grown up in a particularly observant home: temple was a social thing for me, I got confirmed because all my friends did, same reason I streaked my hair. I didn't even want my boys to be circumcised when they were born. Someone told me it cuts down on sexual pleasure because the head of the cock loses sensitivity, so I said to Reuben, "Let's do something nice for them and leave the foreskins on." You would have thought I said, "Let's raise them as dogs."

I hardly ever even thought much about being Jewish except when other people reminded me. Sometimes at MIC they'd get this ecumenical glow and talk about me and about Jonathan and Susan, who were exotic blooms, native Minnesota Jews, as though we were integrating them, saving them from being white.

Once Miles said, "No, but seriously, have you noticed that in any volunteer group, Jewish people are disproportionately represented? Look at us here in this room—one-quarter of us are Jewish. Now, the percent of Jewish people in the Upper Midwest is a lot less than that."

If that was the kind of heritage Reuben meant, I had no objection. But I suspected it had more to do with naked cocks and planting trees in Israel.

PART 2

PART 2

CHAPTER 7

DINAH'S MEMOIR

That first summer I was with Carl, the boys spent every weekend with Reuben. I'd drop them off, then pick him up in my VW, and we'd go out to the old house on Roy and Thelma's farm. As soon as we left Highway 12, we'd start to sing and clown, groping each other like high-school kids, and when we got there we'd head straight for the deep grass out back. Afterward, we'd be covered with insect bites, and the grass looked like what Winnie-the-Pooh calls a Large Animal Lying-Down Place, and Carl's little half-brother Duke would shamble across the road as though he'd been waiting from the time he saw the car until the moaning stopped.

At first I thought Duke was cute, then I thought he was creepy, but Carl always shared our dope with him, poured him a glass of wine, and along about eleven o'clock at night I'd have to tell him we wanted to be alone.

"How come you never tell Duke to get lost?" I'd say, biting Carl's neck and ear. "Don't you like to be alone with me?"

"He doesn't have too many friends. He's *differnt.*"

"Your mom's crazy about him."

Laugh. "Yah, well."

In the morning, Duke would turn up again. Sometimes I'd leave the two of them and go hang out in Thelma's kitchen. If she'd had a letter from one of her daughters, she'd read it to me, and she'd put me to work.

I can date our conversations by the work we did—early in the summer, we'd be chopping weeds, picking rhubarb, or hulling strawberries. Then when her daughter Monette went on a week-long canoe trip, we were thinning beets and carrots and picking peas. The week Sister was called in by the Area Director of the Peace Corps who told her to stop making waves at the Ministry of Agriculture, we were tying up toma-toes, spraying them with garlic water, picking squash blos-soms, and topping-and-tailing green beans. While her daughter Holly was traveling through Europe on her way home from Germany, we blanched the early tomatoes and peaches and skinned them for putting up. "Roy always says when he was a boy, the good peaches come from Michigan. But now they come from California, Arizona, Texas. Not so fresh. Says he can taste it."

"What happened to the Michigan peaches?"

"Same thing happened to the Michigan cherries, blueber-ries, plums, nectarines, Roy says. All the fruit farms got bought up and subdivided. Them developers. Thank good-ness there ain't nothing they want to develop around here yet," and she gazed out of her kitchen window toward the bluff where the delicate birch trees rooted themselves in crumbling rock and made a curtain of pale leaves all spring and summer. When the leaves turned yellow and began to fall, the staghorn sumac blazed red.

Roy thought people ought to eat what grows locally: corn, soybeans, peas and beans, cheese, eggs, quail, venison, trout, pike, bass.

"What about tomatoes?" I'd argue. "They're not exactly *native* to the *region.*"

"Everything comes from somewhere," she'd argue back, "and tomatoes sure have took hold here—like peppers, eggplant, muskmelon."

We talked recipes, and we talked about our children and our pregnancies—personal but impersonal. It was easy to talk while our hands were busy. Endlessly we talked about our kids. She had so many.

"When they're real close together, how do you get them not to fight?"

That must have been in July, we were sorting wild raspberries and gooseberries. "Some of 'em just naturally have less fight in 'em. You take Sister—she always shared with Carl, never hit him, used to protect him from the other big kids. Where Holly and Monette fought over every scrap of soap in the bathtub, what to watch on the TV. They slept in these bunk beds, and they fought over who got to sleep on the top bunk. I made rules and made sure they followed 'em: Monday night Holly sleeps on top, Tuesday Monette, or whatever. Ingvar and Donny never fought, but those girls!"

I tried to do that with Joel and Amos, I told her, but then when they were at Reuben's, he'd have different rules—or they said he did.

"Maybe you and him should get together—on this, anyways."

"Oh, Thelma. If we could get together on this stuff, we'd still be married."

She cut me a look. "I don't think you would, it's more than that. Tell yourself it's for the little guys, and you can talk to him. Now save out these green gooseberries, they're sour. We'll put them up and make a cobbler with the purple ones."

It rained that day, a soft, steady summer patter. Funny how the sound of rain brings back your childhood, mine I mean, pressing my nose against the dining-room window of our brick house in Milwaukee, watching the rain drop onto the ruffly white and yellow petunias in the back yard. The light was a soft greenish grey, and my breath made a cloudy patch on the glass, where I could draw with my fingernails. I drew the letters of my name on my breath and flowers and little girls.

In the soft green light, our dining-room table gleamed. My mother's silver coffee service sat on a crocheted runner on top of the gleaming sideboard, and I could just make out the glints of gold on the rims of her coffee-cup collection, behind the glass doors of the matching breakfront: bone china, Chinese porcelain, Irish Belleek. I didn't hear her come up behind me, and I jumped when she scolded me for drawing on the window.

My mother always wore stockings and high-heeled shoes at home, and she wore her old good dresses around the house. Once a week, she had a manicure that renewed the deep red polish on her nails. In those days, she wore her dark hair in a roll, like the rolled edge on my father's favorite almond coffeecake that we always ate for brunch on Sunday. "Don't *do* that," she snapped. "You'll smear the glass."

Only the Jewish kids ever had coffeecake or ate brunch. I never dreamed there were mothers like Thelma, proud of their kids and trusting them.

Sister Sarah and Carl were Thelma's children from her first husband, before she married Roy. Carl wasn't sure his father was even alive. When we'd go out on Saturday nights to drink beer in the little bars around Prairie Farm, I'd point out lean guys in their forties. "Maybe it's him." You wouldn't want to be sired by most of the gents we ran across, National Rifle Association badges on their windbreakers, feed caps with Legion insignia, beer bellies, and the rest of it.

Thelma and Roy had four children besides: Holly, Monette, Ingvar, whom I knew as Ian at the MIC, and Donald, who called himself Duke. "I had to switch vets to get myself some more boys," Thelma used to say. She and Roy always called doctors vets.

Sarah was a nurse in the Peace Corps in Guatemala. She sent bright woven things back to Wisconsin, along with letters about the hard lives of rural women and how no one in authority paid any attention to the water supply in her village. The people knew they should boil their water, but they couldn't spare the fuel, and the children got sick. Many died. *There is no safe water in most of Guatemala,* she wrote. *No one from the provincial capital will take it up with the Ministry of Health.* Thelma's eyes clouded when she read the letters.

"Don't you wish all the young people would go down there, Dinah? Fix things up, dig a sewer system—"

Holly and Monette studied at Stout State University over in Menomonie. That summer Holly had gone to Germany to learn the language, living with a family and looking after their children.

"She's a hired girl, just like my grandmaw when she come from Norway," Thelma explained. "She's pretty quick, though, where grandmaw was dumb, married the first Norskie farmer that asked her. Holly's gonna get a extra year's credit, and no husband."

Monette had a summer job as a camp counselor in the Superior National Forest. "She was a junior counselor last year, and then she got her Water Safety badge and that. She was always a outdoors girl." Duke had finished high school in June after only three years. "He's too young to go to college, only sixteen." She told me all these things right away. Must be lonely, I decided, with her daughters gone. Roy probably doesn't talk to her much.

"So tell me about your little guys," she said, cutting exact parallel slices off a dense-looking loaf of bread.

"Joel's the older one. He's pretty neat. But Amos is my baby." I was careful to spread margarine all the way out to the edge of each slice of bread as it lay like a dark continent on the blue oilcloth counter.

"Well, sure. I feel the same about Donny—Duke. Always have. Tell me, though: is it hard bringing them up alone? I always wondered about that. So many people get divorced these days, seems like hardly anybody stays married. My own sister-in-law up and left my brother with a six-week-old calf. 'Course, they didn't have no children. It's different for her. But you wonder. He had to sell off forty acres of woods to pay for the divorce.

"Think we want some preserves? I got apple butter, rhubarb butter, and some of that peach butter I put up last year. You know, at the end of the season, they sell you a lug of peaches for about four dollars; well, in our family no one cares too much for just plain canned peaches, but the boys love to put preserves on their pancakes, Roy included, so that's what I do with 'em," and she chattered on so I didn't have to answer.

"You know, Thelma, you were absolutely right about talking to Reuben," I told her later in the summer, when we were pickling peppers.

"The curvy yellow ones go here, they're not so hot, but these little red guys'll raise blisters—you want rubber gloves, here, I'll get you a spare pair. Glad it worked out with you and him."

"It's just like you said—the boys come first. There's so much hurt feelings between me and Reuben, we sometimes lose it."

After a minute she said, "You been with a lot of men, Dinah?"

"Tons. Battalions."

She blushed. "I ain't had so much experience, but it's always seemed to me my kids are one thing, and the man-woman thing is something else."

In September, when Holly and Monette were back at college in Menomonie, we shelled beans for drying. In October, we made the new peach butter, sliding skins off the slippery fat peaches behind kitchen windows veiled in steam. For Hallowe'en, Thelma made a heap of her prettiest squash, gray with gold stripes and dots and deep orange with green tiger markings, and arranged them in her front yard with some pumpkins against a bundle of hay.

*

The one subject I couldn't talk about with Thelma was Carl. I hoped some day my sons would make their lovers feel the way I felt with him, but probably I wouldn't want to hear the details.

I used to wash his long hair, heavy and bright as cornsilk, in water I hauled from Thelma's kitchen and heated on the gas stove. He sat in a straight chair backed up to the counter, and I poured the water into a deep enameled tin canning kettle, midnight blue with white speckles. *Now lean back*, I'd say, and he'd slide forward in the chair and his beautiful hair would fan out in the water. I used a baby shampoo, and I'd throw the rinse water out the door under the white lilac bush where I dumped our eggshells and carrot tops. He loved to have his head scratched or fondled, and I loved touching him like that, like a mother and a lover.

We made love in the sun, on the grass, on the edge of the quarry pool, in the loud beds of the old house. I sucked his beautiful cock on the riverbank; he spread my legs and kissed my cunt in the shallow water of the pond right there with the frogs. When the wild raspberries ripened, we brought a bowl of them to bed with us and took turns falling asleep while the waking one—just barely awake—tucked raspberries into the sleepy one's mouth, bursting the little cells with our sleepy tongues, pressing the juice out and sucking it from each other's lips, sliding into sleep on these kisses.

I felt like a child, all the love I poured over my sons came back to me with Carl. The dumb silky feel of his hair, his smooth hide, his breath warm in my ears, against my belly. He sucked my nipples like a ravenous baby, and when I took his cock in my mouth and rubbed it against my lips, and played with his foreskin and licked the underside until he shivered and sighed, I had a woman's mouth pleasure and a baby's, too. I loved to drink him, warm, salty, slightly sour. "Like *schav*," I told him. "You know what *schav* is? Sour grass soup—sorrel? You don't? I'll make it for you some time."

The smell of his darkened skin mingled with the breath of meadowsweet, then coneflowers, then goldenrod as summer sashayed on toward fall. *You're obsessed, girl,* I told myself, but I was too happy to stop. *Who was I hurting?* I asked Cory. He was breaking up with Annie when I found him; Annie left him because she didn't like the way they were together. I loved everything we did.

Cory blushed and shrugged and said *Goodness, Dinah, you're grown up. Just be careful of your kids.*

Starting in late September, we built fires in the wood-stove. Carl's dark tan faded, and his hair smelled of smoke. We mostly stayed inside on the clear frosty nights, laced together under old blankets and sleeping bags. After the peach butter was done, Thelma and I shelled butternuts from the trees on the ridge across the river, their leaves yellow now and slick on the ground where puffball mushrooms poked their swollen heads. Carl and Duke turned over the gardens and spread them with mulch. Roy would be out with the haying crews if it was dry but on wet days he was around, mending machinery or cleaning guns.

"Come November, you won't want to be comin' out so much," said Thelma. "Nights get real cold. I'm going to miss you, lady—miss your bright eyes and sweet smile."

"Come and see me in the city," I said, and she said she just might do that. "Or I'll see you next spring."

🌢

That fall, Carl moved in with me and the boys. "Is Carl going to live here all the time?" asked Joel.

"He is for now," I said. "Would you like that?"

"I don't know."

"Carl feep in mama bed," said Amos.

"That's right. Carl and mama are lovers."

"Ame feep in mama bed."

"You slept in my bed sometimes when you were little. You can come in bed with me and Carl sometimes, but you sleep in your own bed."

I braced for a fight with Reuben, but *surprise!* He tells me he is thinking of getting married. Suddenly the boys have to deal with two complete sets of ap-parents; the contemplated stepmama and Reuben buy them little suits and try to teach them table manners, while Carl's idea of table talk runs thus:

"Where did your hockey sticks come from?"

"From the store!" Joel answers triumphantly.

"Where did the store get them?"

"From a warehouse."

"How did they get to the warehouse?"

"On a tuck!" Amos knows this from earlier catechisms.

"And where do you s'pose they got loaded onto the truck?"

"Maybe at the factory where they got made?"

"Yeah, maybe so. And who d'you think made 'em?"

"Workers, I know that."

"Do we know what workers? Were they Americans? Did they belong to a union?"

"We don't know."

"Does it matter?"

Eventually the hockey sticks would be shown to come from Canada, where Miles was going to emigrate. The peace community held fund-raisers for him and my old sweetheart Crater, and they scrounged and borrowed until they had the ten thousand dollars apiece they needed for landed-immigrant status.

"Miles says most of the Canadian workers belong to unions, and they get paid better than most workers here. So this factory is probably a good place to work, and the price is probably fair. We'd buy this hockey stick again."

"What about this shirt?" and he turns out the label at Amos' neck and blows down his back. "Can you read it?"

Joel peers at the label while Amos twists and giggles, "Do it again!"

"Tay-wan?"

"Tie-wan. Do we know where that is?" Blowing some more.

Joel shakes his head.

"It's an island near China where the people used to be farmers. But some rich guys bought up the farmers' land, so they had to go to work in factories. The rich guys own the factories. The men make machines, and the women make clothes, like this shirt, and toys and stuff."

Joel is silent for a moment. Then he says thoughtfully, "But if the daddies make machines and the mommies make shirts, who takes care of their kids?"

My god, my boys had such a wonderful education. Why didn't it take? Carl excited me. In his kiss, I felt the wind lifting.

Always before when I was in love, I had the feeling of playing a scene called *Lovers lost in each other's gaze,* lit with amber gels, while just behind the set, a stage manager stands waiting in harsh white light to strike our scene and get on to the next. So after a certain amount of time, always, the fiery sexy spirit that had enchanted me turned out to be housed in an ordinary guy, just another guy with underpants caught in the crack of his ass.

That never happened with Carl. Maybe because we did a kind of acid that was called Clear Light.

*

My politics changed. Carl was really an anarchist. "Why should I risk my life for my country? What good can I do for it dead? And why should I pay taxes—what do I get for them, besides a bunch of bombs I don't want? Gimme sex and drugs and rock 'n' roll."

I used to argue with him about welfare and civil rights, and he'd always get me by saying that the government created the problem in the first place. "Look at the Constitution: Slaves are valued at three-fifths of a person. Women aren't citizens at all. If there was no constitution, all our revolutions could be peaceful ones."

"But we never had a real revolution," I'd say, and I'd talk about the stuff I learned from radical boyfriends in Madison: how states' rights is always a screen for racism, and how we need laws to curb the rich and protect the poor, and then he'd start talking tariffs and proving to me that the laws just made this country safe for business.

After we'd been together more than a year, in the fall of 1970, Carl was indicted for Noncooperation with Selective Service. He started meeting with lawyers, figuring out his defense. Cory and Thelma and I organized a support committee. We thought maybe his trial could be a real test case on the war.

"I never slept with an important criminal," I told him.

"Maybe you did and didn't know it." His hands played on my back gently as a breeze, stroking my shoulders and flooding my spine with cataracts of pleasure that ran down along the insides of my thighs and made me bloom. "I was a criminal before they indicted me. It's just words."

We made love every night, then we'd get up in the morning like any man and woman and listen to the radio while we made breakfast for the boys. Garrison Keillor had a morning show from St. Cloud, and his humor tickled Carl, the stuff he made up about Lake Wobegon and this mythical store called Jack's Auto Repair. Jack was always marketing improbable services. Once he advertised "The Jack's Auto Repair Course in Speed Living—some people who've completed this course are already an entire season ahead and living in the middle of next winter."

"Do we want to send away for that?" I asked Carl. We always took Jack's Auto Repair seriously, that was the best part.

"Well, I'll probably be in the joint."

"Yeah, but if we keep it up, you'll be out in no time flat."

"Okay. Let's do it."

We'd send Joel off to kindergarten and Amos to nursery school in their little windbreakers or their yellow slickers if it was raining, then we'd zip them into their snowsuits, then new jackets in the spring, just our little family living in the house.

Without rent from any housemates, we were basically living on my alimony plus the tiny salary Carl paid himself out of the pledges that kept the MIC going, and the little bits of money we collected for his defense committee. On weekends, when Reuben had the kids, we sometimes went out to Roy and Thelma's, or we sometimes took a trip. That's a nice thing to do on a cold Minnesota weekend: lay in your supplies, your music, your Dopers' Delight, bake some cookies, buy a jug of wine and some tabs of acid or hits of mescaline, pull the curtains, and fly. Next day you're kind of washed out, but not as bad as the hangovers we used to earn in Madison.

🍃

Weaving through the west side of Minneapolis on our way to the lake, the snow falling thickly and softening the angles of streets and houses. No cars out, only a few intrepid dogwalkers, but as can happen when you're on acid, all the dogs just happened to be Chinese temple dogs, ornate beasts of brilliant blue or jade green with rococo features, that spoke to us in dog-Russian. *"Bozhe moi?"* *"Lobachevsky?"* *"Nyet, Rimsky."* *"Da, Korsakov."* Then it got so late, no one was out except us.

We lay down in the snow and made angels and angels and angels and tasted the snow on our skin. Snow crystals sweet-talked their way up my cuffs and down my boots. I got into feeling like a tall cake, my slopes frosted with sugar. And not the only one: the refraction of light in each and every snow crystal let me see millions of cakewomen, one in each snow-flake, different sizes, all delicious.

Then, if I looked up into the black and blazing sky, it opened and there were angels in their mustard and saffron robes whirling handfuls of snow down upon us. The snow-flakes looked like big fragile wafers, fish food, like what I guessed Communion wafers were. As each one fell I saw its cakewoman and saw precisely how she was engineered and understood, for that moment, how she fitted into the vast mosaic of snow constructing itself around us.

"Female energy runs the world!" I told Carl. Looking up again, I saw the curtain pulled aside and the silent dance of snowflingers, gorgeously robed beings with hands the size of planets shooting out at the ends of their elastic arms to bestow on us the snowblessing. *"Snowblesse oblige."*

"Snowblesse snowblige." I took off my jacket, and my skin understood the cold. I took off my sweaters and rubbed some snow against my breasts. "Hey, meltski. Meltskovitch."

"Bozhe moi." We stood near the middle of a lake. A reddish glow from street lights far away tinged the darkness. Carl helped me put my clothes back on. Chords of music, organ diapasons rang in my head, and I understood that in that moment of wanting to merge with the snow, I had made myself ill. Deep inside my chest, a warning uncurled: you're going to be sick tomorrow. No chiding, no guilt, just the information. And I was.

"This stuff will tell you everything," I said to Carl, my body throbbing with knowledge.

"Yes," he said, "if you let it."

When Marcus Inchloe from the Icehouse Theater got an
induction notice in the winter of 1970, he decided to refuse.
Several other local draft resisters had been sent to prison with
two-year sentences. No one had been tried yet for nonregistration; Carl had been indicted but no date had been given for
his trial.

"I could probably obtain an exemption," said Inchloe.
"I've got asthma. And my family exercises some influence in
this state. But I would rather use the opportunity to generate
drama and to educate the people."

We planned a big demo for him on the steps of the
Federal Building in downtown Minneapolis, a Greek Revival
square of pale gray limestone. Selective Service always called
men to report for induction at six a.m., to discourage family
members from coming along, so of course everyone came to
our house and stayed up all night. Carl and I and Crater and
Miles, who were on their way to Canada, and Crater's new
lady—was she Sunsparrow? I can't even remember; Rebecca
wasn't there because she had become a lesbian and broken
off with Miles—dropped some Clear Light and lay around for a
while having visions.

Carl's sister Holly came in from Wisconsin to stay with
Joel and Amos. She was in her last year at Stout State, majoring
in education with a minor in German, a Future Farmer of
America and vice-president of her class. We weren't sure what
would happen at the induction-refusal demo, if we would be
arrested or not. We had Iron Butterfly on the stereo, then the
Stones, and Crater and I danced hard. About four, I put out the
candles, and we danced in the light of the amplifier. My kids
slept through it all. Carl was meditating. Miles played his
guitar, sometimes weird counterpoint to Keith and Ron,
sometimes all his own, and Crater's woman danced with us.

About five I woke Holly. "Joel likes raisins on his oatmeal.

Amos likes honey. Joel eats a peanut-butter-and-apple-butter sandwich for lunch. We'll call you if we get busted."

"We'll be fine," she yawned. "The boys can talk, they'll tell me what they want. So how do you feel, Carl, like a hero?"

"Hey, I'm not the hero here."

But we all knew that nonregistration was a felony violation of the Selective Service Act, and if we were busted, things could get ugly for him.

Crater's lady had her radio tuned to an AM station. "It's two below," she said.

"We're hardened," said Miles. "Remember to bring your tambourine."

I spent some time making up my face and body while Carl got his shit together. I wasn't sure what I was going to do for Inchloe, but I knew it would be silent. The Têt offensive had put the war into a new phase, Carl said, that called for a new response from the U.S. peace movement. I wanted to be naked for him, a naked priestess, and I had bought this beautiful big turban squash, bigger than a man's head and slathered with color, gold and red and green.

"Think you'll get arrested?" Holly was wide awake now.

No, we told her. This is going to be like a happening. Marcus is the only one who's breaking the law. We're nonviolent. I grabbed the biggest knife in the house and put it in my bag, along with the squash and my I.D. "No drugs, just in case." We all emptied our pockets, but I popped a Dexamyl to help me with the transition.

"Sure that was acid, not speed?" asked Miles. "I'm so *wired.*" We all were, electric currents whining in our brains. Then we were ready, wrapped in our cloaks of many colors, Miles in his skeleton suit, me in a hooded velvet cape. The five of us squeezed into the Volkswagen bug with our bags, guitar, and tambourine. The windows clouded completely.

"Nobody breathe, okay?" said Carl, yanking the car into first, and we set off through the frozen streets.

"Where are all these other guys going?" Crater asked in amazement. "They all refusing induction?"

"There's a whole straight world out there," Miles answered. *"And there's doctors and lawyers, / And business executives, / And they're all made out of ticky tacky / And they all look just the same."*

On the broad steps of the old Federal Building, Marcus stood in the center of his friends, all the actors who had stayed with the Icehouse, most of them in costume from last year's big hit, *The Recruiting Officer.* Inchloe had his arm around his chick of the moment, a Korean dancer named Su-Li. Orange light surrounded them, and I felt their rhythm pulsing toward us as if they were in the warmth of a brightly lighted cave, but I knew it was really cold and dark. Two tall men in hats and trench coats stood near the far wall of the building. "Eff bee eye," growled Crater. Our breath made fragile vapor trails in the light of the streetlamps.

"Ah, the prodigals return," said Marcus. "To solemnize the occasion."

A good-sized crowd had gathered on the steps. Jerry and Cora were there, bless them. I would like to remember Cora always the way she was that morning, tall and full with her beautiful hair shining like a torch.

Trust Inchloe to bring the light and sound, it was the best-produced draft refusal of the sixties. The Icehouse band struck up a song Marcus had written for the occasion, a little "Induction Refusal Blues":

> *When you get your induction notice, gotta*
> > *refuse that call*
> *Whether you live in Minneapolis or in Saint Paul,*
> *Got those Twin Cities blues, blue is what I am*
> *Cause I ain't gonna do no fightin' over in*
> > *Viet Nam.*

This war is evil, it's too evil for me
If they want some killin', better start with
Nixon and Ky.

Our early-morning voices rose in white puffs, and I saw with extreme clarity, as though I were looking into a view-finder. Marcus made his little speech, studded with long pretentious words, and then he burned his draft card, which made a tiny, terrible smell. We all cheered, and an actor named Roger Sorenson, who wore a torn tee shirt and liked to be called Bubba, gave a mock military briefing as though downtown Minneapolis were under attack. Su-Li sang a high-pitched Korean song she said was for peace. Miles did his death number. And I performed a ritual murder of the beautiful turban squash, raising my knife and stabbing it twelve times on the steps of the Federal Building, like a victim on an altar, as pale blue light sneaked across the eastern sky. The shell finally broke open and seeds and pulp spilled down the steps.

The FBI men and marshals just watched. They didn't arrest anybody, although I was naked under my midnight-blue velvet cape. We went for breakfast to the all-night restaurant near my house, and then we crashed. The next month Inchloe got re-classified 4 F, because of his asthma and his father's money.

🌱

The following year, while Carl was still under indictment but untried, Duke moved up to the Twin Cities to be with him. He was just seventeen, and—although his test scores were in a genius range and all his teachers at Prairie Farm Consolidated High School told him he could be a National Merit Scholar—he decided he didn't want to go to college. Basically, he hung around with me and the boys; I was glad for the company, especially after the trial, when Carl was sent up.

Joel loved him because he had a five-year-old's maniac

concentration; they played pick-up-sticks with Cuisenaire rods for hours on end. Duke was full of theories about how children learned math and physics naturally, and my boys were his laboratory.

"What weighs more," he'd ask them, "a pound of wood or a pound of feathers?"

"Wood," says Joel promptly.

"Fezzers," says Amos.

"But they both weigh a pound. How can one be heavier?"

"The feathers can blow off," says Joel after some thought. "The wood you can pick up in your hand."

"So it's like the wood is a better weight, more compact."

"I like fezzers."

"Yeah," said Joel. "More weight in a smaller bunch."

"More compact, you could say."

"What's compacked?"

"More dense."

"What's dense?"

"Dense is more stuff in a smaller bunch. Now, if you have a piece of stone the same size as that piece of wood, does it weigh the same?"

"Yes," says Amos.

"No," says Joel superbly. "The stone is more heavy. More—what is that word?"

"Dense. More dense. Denser."

He could keep it up as long as Joel paid attention. Amos would get bored and stick his thumb in his mouth, and Duke would pick him up in his rangy arms and swing him gently while he chatted with Joel about density, mass, area, volume, compression, expansion, dimension, transformation.

"If we filled this whole downstairs with water, what would happen?"

"We'd be wet!"

"And what else?"

"Would we float?"

"Well, would we?"

"I can fim," says Amos around his thumb. Duke tickles him.

"What if we filled it with Jell-O?"

"What slavor Jell-O?" Amos giggles.

"Well, what if we filled it with air? Would it float like a balloon?"

"But it *is* filled with air!"

"That's right. So why doesn't it float like a balloon?"

"Gravity, stupid! The walls keep it down!" Duke never minded when they called him names.

He was a great support for me, he ate everything I cooked and praised it, he helped me bathe the boys and read them bedtime stories, and then one evening, after Carl had been in Sandstone Federal Penitentiary for about six weeks, he leaned over me as I leaned over sleeping Amos to kiss his forehead, and he licked me lightly behind the ear. The boys slept in separate rooms by this time, Joel clinging to a night light and Amos claiming it kept him from feeping. Heavy darkness filled Amos' room. I smelled Duke's young body, and I shuddered at his tongue. He stepped back.

"What did you do that for?" I whispered out in the hall.

"I wanted to." He giggled.

"I'm Carl's lover."

"I know. He doesn't own you, though."

"I'm too old for you. Get a girl your own age."

"Does he?"

"Duke!"

"Well, does he?"

"You know better. No one owns anybody."

"So you can do what you want."

"I don't want to be lovers with you."

"Oh, yes, I think you do," and he started to dance slowly, unbuttoning his shirt and shaking out his long blond hair. The prison barber had cut Carl's hair off, shaved his beard and moustache. Duke's body was thin, more delicate than Carl's. I stood there while he unwrapped himself for me like a birthday gift, swaying in the dim hall light, and I felt myself get hot.

"I think you do. I sure want you, Dinah, I've wanted you since last summer, since you used to come out to the farm and flatten the weeds with my big brother Carl," and he took my wrist in his finger and thumb and led me slowly into the living room, walking backward with his cock standing up and waving and his hair flowing down his shoulders. Like Joel's little nightlight, his white body seemed lit from inside. I was charmed, like a snake; I followed him onto the couch. And that was how that started.

CHAPTER 8

CARL

Letter from Cora tells me she's sick. No news in years, now this. I could get really depressed thinking about the people in my life who've gotten sick or died or just disappeared. Maybe she won't die. It's breast cancer. Sometimes they can just cut that out, I think, not like leukemia. My sister had leukemia.

I don't think too much about the past these days. I don't think too much in English. I've been living in a workers' hostel here in San Onofrio Milpas Altas for nearly nine years. The light is so different here in the mountains, it's hard to see myself back home. My work is here now, but I guess a lot of the important people are still back in *los estados unidos.* We have a workshop where we make composting toilets, it's a project Sister started when she was in the Peace Corps, and it's doing pretty well.

Cora's letter made me think of the letters she wrote me when I was in the slammer, and that makes me think of Dinah. She always knew I was headed there.

I never registered for the draft, and I got indicted in 1970 and sent to prison in 1971, Sandstone Federal Penitentiary in upstate Minnesota, near the Kettle River, where I went canoeing once or twice. I spent two and a half years in Sandstone.

Back when I was in high school, the reserve lieutenant who headed up the JROTC was always after me to join, but I hated the uniforms and the ideas. All the while I was growing up, my mother and my stepfather Roy talked peace at the dinner table—not Christian pacifism, just how stupid wars were.

"My great-grandparents were forty-eighters," Roy said. "They come to America to escape service in the armies of the superpowers of that day. If Carl don't want to register, why, he's just carrying on a family tradition."

Your family, not mine, I'd think to myself, but out loud I'd say, "Thanks, Roy."

American Legion's strong in those little towns. Lots of them have the cannon on the courthouse lawn with the bronze plaque, names of Those Who Gave Their Lives 1914–1918, 1941–1945. Roy always said something when he drove past the cannon. "Dumb farmers don't know enough to let the rich man fight his own wars." The ROTC lieutenant served on the county draft board along with a bunch of Legionnaires, insurance salesmen mostly.

When they busted me for Noncooperation with Selective Service, I was working with the Military Information Center in Minneapolis, a draft-counseling office I started with my brother Ian and some other guys. I went up to the Cities to go to college, but I dropped out after a while. It seemed like such a waste of time to be studying calculus, chemistry, *me llamo Carlo,* when your whole generation was threatened with the draft.

At that time, there was no such thing as an atheist conscientious objector. If you were religious, you might get some minister or priest to wangle you a C.O., although some of those cloth-covered guys were bloodthirsty. To be fair, a lot of clergy opposed the war, and some of them counseled draft-age guys to help them stay out. But if you were just a peaceful anarchist atheist like me, you had to violate yourself somehow in order to stay out of military service. Either you made yourself into one of the elite and got a 2-S, a student deferment, or you got some poor dumb woman pregnant and married her so you could get a 3-A. Or else you shot off a toe or made yourself crazy with drugs so you could get a 4-F. You had those creative options for self-mutilation, and if you didn't exercise one of them, you'd be drafted and very likely sent overseas to kill guys your own age who were Vietnamese.

I thought it over when I had my eighteenth birthday: if you registered for the draft, you stayed in the power of the Selective Service System, and you had only the choices they gave you; if you didn't cooperate, they could put you in the slammer, but your head still belonged to you.

So I didn't register. But after me and Ian and our friends Miles and Jonathan organized the Military Information Center in a storefront near the University of Minnesota, on the banks of the Mississippi River—Mother of Waters, Dinah called it—people in the U.S. Attorney's office began to call me up, asking me where I came from and when I was going to report to my draft board. I changed my residence legally from Wisconsin to Minnesota, and for a couple of months they lost track of me. But then the calls started again, along with unfriendly letters from the Selective Service System. Finally they indicted me on a bunch of charges: conspiracy to commit a felony, aiding and abetting others to commit a felony, and finally the felony itself, *dum-de-dum-dum*— noncooperation.

At the indictment, they pretty much ignored me, and when my lawyer asked for me to be released on my personal recognizance, there was no trouble. Except they told me I wasn't supposed to leave the state, which meant I couldn't go home to see my mom, Thelma.

At the trial, I was glad to see a lot of the peace community in the Twin Cities, my friends from the MIC, my family and other friends like Jerry and Cora Bookbinder, the lawyers who had taken my case pro bono, and some of the guys who had been clients at MIC. Dinah was there with her children Joel and Amos, and so was my old girlfriend Annie. I winked at Joel and Amos, but they just stared back like they were watching me on TV. The courtroom was shabby, with some plaster missing from the walls and dirty windows too high to see out of.

Not a single person stood up for the judge. When the bailiff said *All rise* again, louder, the judge just waved his hand, peered through his granny glasses, and said, "Let's get on with it." My main defense lawyer, Arne Tuma, made an introductory motion to have the case dismissed on the grounds that war had never been declared and therefore the Selective Service System had no basis in law. The U.S. Attorney objected on grounds that that was beyond the jurisdiction of this court, and the judge sustained the objection. It was just downhill from there.

For starters, the U.S. Attorney announced that they, the state, had dropped the two big charges, conspiracy and aiding and abetting.

"What?" said Arne Tuma. "Objection."

"Approach the bench," said the judge, and everybody got to look at the lawyers' backs for three or four minutes, Arne's rumpled cheap suit and the prosecutor's tailored ass, while they talked to hizzoner. Arne kept shaking his head, and when the huddle broke he came back to the table and pressed my shoulder.

"They're ganging up on us," he whispered. "They're supposed to tell us if they drop charges, but the judge is going to let it go."

The spectators in the courtroom rumbled, sounding like a far-off waterfall. *Order!* yelled the bailiff, and the judge banged his gavel. *Objection,* Arne kept saying, and the judge kept saying *Overruled,* in a bored voice.

Of course, I'd been preparing for this day for months, meeting with Arne and the other lawyers, talking with Dinah and with the other draft counselors. We put together a really eloquent defense.

"This is our chance," said my brother Ian. "You get to talk about the war, how it was never declared. It's a civil war among the Vietnamese, and the U.S. has no business in it."

"The president is lying to the people," said my buddy Jonathan, "and none of the major media are telling the truth. You got a chance to sock it to 'em."

Arne bragged. "We got a list of expert witnesses as long as your hair, pacifist clergy and professors from the university who can talk about the background, U.S. imperialist adventures in Asia, our permanent war economy. They've had you under surveillance, which is clearly illegal, and we get to say that."

But now that those two charges had been dropped, it looked like the defense wasn't allowed to call any witnesses and the trial was cut and dried. Had I registered for the draft? No, I hadn't. Then let's proceed.

Arne's going to be so disappointed, I said to myself, *he really thought we had a chance to be heard this time.*

"Objection, your honor! Our testimony bears directly on..."

"Overruled."

The only thing I got to say all morning was my closing statement. I put in all the stuff I had talked about with Arne, about how I sincerely believed the war was wrong and about how my family supported my nonviolent resistance. I finished up with "I believe I'm serving my country best by trying to correct her mistakes," and everybody clapped until the bailiff threatened to clear the courtroom, and then they twinkled. You know how you can twinkle in silence, hold your hands up and shimmer your fingers like a cheerleader. My stomach was rumbling to remind me that I hadn't eaten any breakfast. Hell, if I'd known my trial was going to be such shucking and jiving, I'd have taken the time for some pancakes.

The judge tried to shame me when he read the sentence. "A strong young man like you," he said in an angry voice, like I'd been wasting *his* time. "You should be serving your country gladly, grateful for your family and your opportunities, instead of flouting the law and urging others to flout it. You are worse than those who strike at others' property, for you strike at the root of government itself."

All of which just corroborated my sense that what they *really* want is to own you. That judge was pissed off because I wasn't going to let him and his cronies design my life for me.

The judge gave me four years, twice as long as any other Twin Cities resister had gotten. You'd think one of them, one judge somewhere, would see what's going on. We're not just *hippies,* we are young men acting on our beliefs, the way they tell you in civics class. Wouldn't you think *one* federal judge could turn out to be sympathetic to a pacifist world-view? But no. They take this really short-ass attitude, a fucked-up syllogism: you broke the law; the law says you go to jail; therefore you go to jail. Not seeing the right or wrong of the behavior.

Arne Tuma said he would appeal, of course. "This judge has got a bug up his ass."

My mother Thelma asked what kind of bug.

"He's got a son," said Arne, "just about Carl's age. Been in trouble with the law—DWI, petty theft, that kind of thing. And here he sees this strong, good-looking kid who stands up for what he believes. I think maybe we can get it thrown out on prejudice."

Annie's new woman lover, Brenda, asked if anyone else noticed that in my statement I called the country "she." "That's really sexist."

"I told you," Annie said. "In some ways he's really a pig."

Those were the last words I heard before the marshals led me away.

*

The lawyers did appeal, and it went all the way up to the Supreme Court, which agreed to hear the case, *U.S. vs. Kjell- strom,* but the Supremes upheld the Appeals Court position that I had been fairly tried and fairly sentenced. I didn't even get to go to Washington. They trucked me off to prison with no notice at five o'clock one winter morning, so no one was there to say goodbye. Dinah told me she thought about that a lot in the weeks afterward, how her lover had to ride out of town alone.

She told me about a conversation she had with my brother Duke. "That's the way the Man does it," Duke said, "rips you out of the garden like you was a volunteer cornstalk. It leaves a raw place for awhile, but then the grass grows back."

"What about when you get out?" Dinah had asked him.

"That's just it—the grass grows back, no place for you, women don't wait, your friends gone on to other things. Lots of guys, gettin' out's harder than bein' in, so they hurry back through that revolvin' door."

Duke had been shoveling snow in front of the Military Information Center while Dinah swept the steps, on a blue- and-gold February day with a soft east wind that she said smelled like a postcard from spring. Every afternoon, the sun thawed more of the snow, then it froze solid again in the black winter night.

"So it's sorta like the army," Dinah said.

"Yeah," said Duke. "Just like the army." Dinah repeated all this to me like Duke knew what he was talking about.

*

There was a gap of two weeks while they processed me into the prison population, then Dinah could apply to go on the visitor list. Even relatives had to apply: Roy and Thelma, Duke and Ian, my sisters Holly and Monette. I could have only four visitors on the list at any one time, and Dinah and the family took turns going off the roster so I could rotate other people in, like Cora.

I liked to have Cora visit because she made me laugh, and sometimes she sang to me, softly so the guards wouldn't tell us to cut it out. Once she brought her daughter Serena, a nice kid, serious. Serena asked her mom about the children in the visitors' room, how did they get along without their dads? You should ask Carl, said Cora, but Serena was shy. They sang "Dona Nobis Pacem" in a round, and it sounded so pretty I wanted to burrow my head in Cora's lap, but I didn't.

When she was on the roster, Dinah drove up to see me every week. For the first months, it was really hard. We'd whisper things and get all hot, I could tell by the way her mouth fell open, but the kids would be there, Joel and Amos, hanging on to her or whining at me to look at something.

That's when you really notice the difference between the guards. This one Black guard was mellow, never hassled you. Some of the inmates got it on, right there in the visitors' room.

"You want to try?" I asked her, only half serious: you joke a lot with your visitors because it's such an artificial situation. You don't have the time or space to talk seriously. But she said no, not with the kids.

The visitors' room looked like a bus station, only not so dirty and no pinball. Most of the guards were rotten, most of the Black guards and all of the White ones. They made you sit so they could see daylight between you. You could have a kid on your lap for five minutes, no more. You could kiss your lover once when you came in and once when you went out.

At first, Dinah wanted to know what life was like in prison, and I tried to tell her, but I'd just start laughing at the absurdity of the place. It was cruel, but so mickeymouse you had to laugh to keep from crying. "You have to keep your feelings hidden or else they'll really hurt you," I told her. "Everything about the place is just calculated to hurt you. There's no privacy, constant humiliation, petty rules, boredom—little pinpricks of hurt and no comfort except what you can give yourself. Some of these prisoners—bourgeois criminals who are in the joint for things like mail fraud—they don't have it so bad. They bribe the other prisoners to do their work, and the guards leave them alone. But the other prisoners hate us because we question the system, they call us 'politicals.'"

"How many of you are there?" she asked.

"About twenty in the prison. But we can't all get together at one time. Usually only about four or five at once."

"Don't any of the other prisoners agree with you? About the war? Or the guards?"

"Sure, a lot of them. But they think we're fools. They tell us we're making it harder on them because we don't play the game. It's a *stone drag* being around people all the time who think you're a fool."

Thelma never asked questions, just told me news about the farm, how Roy was trying sorghum in one field, how she bought three setting ducks and a drake, and she'd read me her latest letter from Sister. Roy acted uneasy when he came, grinned and fidgeted in his chair and asked me did I need anything, like a cake with a file baked in it. He only came twice. Thelma brought old clothes for me to wear for outdoor work.

My brother Duke decided not to register when he turned seventeen, and after his eighteenth birthday, I was in the joint. I thought maybe there was something going on with him and Dinah, but I wasn't going to be the one to say it.

When he came to see me he asked, "So, can you get dope?"

"Sure," I told him. "Want to take some back with you?"

147

"What do you mean?"

"Sandstone-grown. Federal gold, Dinah calls it. Get you anything you want besides—reds, blues, hash, skag, speed. For a price. For cartons of cigarettes. You bring cigarettes next time, and you can leave here a walking pharmacy."

"Can you get acid?"

"No problem." But I was half kidding, and Duke knew it. I didn't want him staying stoned the whole time. "You're too smart, kid. You can offer some leadership in the movement if you don't fry your brains up with that shit. A mind like yours— you could be a historian, a theorist like Chomsky. You could strategize, hell, you could be an American Chou En-lai. Me, I'm just doing time, as easy as I can make it. But you got to stay cool."

Between visitors, I lived through the days: working, reading, getting stoned. You really do need discipline in the joint. I'm fairly big, so I didn't have to fight, but once or twice it came close. Some half-crazy guy would bump me in the hall or come up tight against me in the dining room and ask for drugs, but I'd just say, "You're not going to get what you want from me. I'm nonviolent, I don't fight." Then they try to stare you down.

Once, three of them surrounded me in the shower room, but I stood my ground, didn't call for a guard or swear or spit when they twisted my arm up behind my back. My heart was pounding, but I knew it was important not to show fear. "Look," I said, "I can't do anything for you. I'm not holding, and I won't fight back."

"Aw, lay off him," said another, older guy, and they did. If you really mean nonviolence, guys can see it in your eyes, and they leave you alone. But the joint is boring, boredom is the killer; that's why guys fight.

You can't think about anything but the moment. If you keep your life absolutely in the present moment, if you can say I've got this Edgar Snow book here, and I'm going to open it and read it one page at a time, then you'll make it. Meal-times, you just line up and look at your tray and say: All right, I got some creamstyle corn here and some kind of chopped meat patty, some tater tots and a couple pieces of white bread and marge, a lettuce leaf with a half a canned peach on it, no I'm not going to eat the half a maraschino cherry, maybe somebody at my table would like that, it's an opportunity for me to do a little peace education if I give something away and don't ask anything back, and a cup of green Kool-Aid to drink, and what's that up there with the pink and brown sprinkles on it? Why that's probably a square piece cut out of a sheet cake, shit cake some of the guys call it but not me, yes indeed, this is my supper, and I'm just going to see about eating it, then you'll be all right. But a lot of guys can't do that. They can't concentrate.

I never got busted, never got administrative detention, which is what they call the solitary cells. I got along with my cellmates, no matter how crazy. The first was a guy from Wisconsin, a biker speed freak named Dale who drummed constantly on his bedframe, on the washstand, on the walls.

"Please don't do that," I asked Dale the first day. "It's hard for me to concentrate when you're drumming."

"Tough shit," said Dale, and that's the last thing he said. Dale wore shades all the time, never read, not even maga zines, just sat beating out some rapid rhythm on the hollow metal bedframe or the window sill.

I thought to myself, *They put you in here to test me, this is a test of the early warning system. If I can keep my hands to myself, I will be allowed to stay in this nice clean joint, but if I fuck you up they won't keep me here, they'll send me to some much tougher place where I'll have to check my back twenty-five hours a day.*

I would wake up in the night and hear Dale whistling a tuneless rhythm between his teeth. I could just decide that sound is something different, something good, like a dog's breathing or rain on the roof, the sound is neutral, it's what I put onto it that hangs me up. I need to unhook, hang loose.

Dale never got a job, never talked to anyone else as far as I could see, and after about six weeks he (who had been busted for transporting an infinitesimal quantity of angel dust into Iowa) was plucked out of my cell, out of my life. *Goodbye,* I said silently to Dale, *I lived with you and I don't know diddly shit about you, but I survived you.*

Dale's successor was a little plump guy named Torn, a forger and bible thumper. "I want to shake your hand, brother Carl," was the first thing Torn said, and the second was, "And ask you, have you accepted Jesus Christ as your very own personal savior? Because he is waiting for you to do that, he has such divine love in his sacred heart for you no matter what your sins. No matter what you have done or whom you have hurt, our shepherd Jesus Christ stands ready to receive you into his fold of lost lambs, now found."

Every Friday in the prison, you got paid in scrip that could be exchanged for soap, candy, pop, ice cream, shaving cream, magazines, or cigarettes. The balance of your pay went into an account that paid about one percent interest and could be collected when you left. If you left. No, actually, we all expected to get out alive, Sandstone wasn't a dangerous place. The violence was mostly spiritual, it frustrated and deadened you. Torn started a loan agency with fake scrip, so bad it wouldn't fool an idiot, but you have so little to do in the joint that everybody played along. The guards looked the other way, and the guys that worked in the store would take Torn's phony scrip at a rate of five to one.

All the time, Torn was proselytizing everybody, quoting scripture about the parable of the talents and coming on strong with the humility and the salvation. Even at an eighty percent discount, he was making money. He bribed the guards, he bought extra light bulbs, extra pillows, and he passed a lot of money to his sappy-looking partner who came on visiting days. He got colored sheets for his bed; he used a thick towel.

"You could profit by my endeavors, brother Carl," he'd say, "if only you would make a clean breast and come as a humble servant to your master Jesus Christ." I just laughed and concentrated on being a model prisoner with my books and my writing and my little patch of Federal gold.

One of the other politicals, a priest from Milwaukee named Paul Moloney, tried to do some organizing among the prisoners. Paul always talked to you as if you were a huge audience. "We are all political prisoners," he told me right away, with big gestures. "These men are guilty of not conforming, not knuckling under to a government that rewards slavish conformity and punishes independent thought."

The prison chaplain asked Paul to deliver the sermon one Sunday, and he really gave it to them. "This illegal war," he said, "this undeclared war against a civilian population. This war of torturers and corrupt bureaucrats against their own people." The warden and the assistant warden got redder and redder until I thought one of them might have a little cardiac event right there in the chapel. "Jesus denounced hypocrisy and corruption, and He was put to death as a criminal and agitator." Paul pounded the lectern and hollered, and the guys shouted "Yeah!" and "That's the god's truth!" But Paul was good, he calmed them all down with a prayer for peace and forgiveness. That chaplain must have been truly stupid. Or maybe he was a closet pacifist.

The younger politicals looked up to Paul. Most of them were already halfway to radical analysis anyway. I would go and sit with them during evening free time, but I never said anything. The other guys, the ones I thought of as the real prisoners in spite of what Paul said, would come once, and then when Paul got to the part about how the government wants its citizens not to think, to obey without thinking, to work and vote and pay taxes without thinking, they'd say, "Yeah, guess I'm just too smart for the system," and they'd leave. So I didn't think Paul was accomplishing much, but you never know. I do agree, it's better to at least try, to struggle, than to do nothing.

"We can only do what we're called to do," said Paul.

*

I never minded having an outside job in the winter, even during winter storms. I like to be able to smell the air, see the sky. The one thing I miss down here is the big midwestern sky. In the mountains, you only see part of the sky unless you climb all the way up, which I don't tend to do.

Part of my job in prison was checking a series of sewer traps on the east perimeter of the prison, where it butts up against some DNR land. I could see when the buds started swelling on the bushes in late winter, and when the angle of the light grew shorter. After the equinox, snow cover receded a little every day, revealing the green grass that looked as if it had been green all along, sort of like what Mao said about the people preparing for revolution under the old regime.

I managed to make a pretty complete study of China while I was at Sandstone, because Ian sent me all of Agnes Smedley's books about the Red Army. I didn't really see any conflict with my beliefs in nonviolence and the fact that Mao and Chou were military men, and the Red Army had liberated the Chinese people. Paul always said that violence breeds violence, a war of liberation that starts with violence will always end in violence, but I would answer him that nonviolence was my personal choice.

"It's how I choose to live my life, here and now. I can't say how I'd react if things were different. If I'd been a Chinese peasant, for example, I'd probably have joined the Seventh Army."

I thought I'd like to go there after I got out, to see what the Cultural Revolution accomplished. If you made all the teachers live the lives of peasants, wouldn't they become better teachers? And if you put the peasants into the bureaucracy, wouldn't they see what kinds of problems the bureaucrats had—and maybe even figure out better ways to do things? All the objections I could find to Mao's re-education campaign sounded to me like sentimentality and, of course, privilege. No one gives up privilege, you really see that in prison. I thought maybe I could write a *Fanshen* of Sandstone, like that book about a Chinese village.

*

In the summer, Thelma told me Duke was acting up. "What do you mean, acting up, ma? We all acted up."

"No, I mean he don't go to school, he don't have a job, I never know where he is or who he's with."

"He's got a girlfriend, ma. Be happy."

"No," she said, "I don't think he's got a girlfriend." I could see her biting back the words, *He's got* your *girlfriend.*

It ain't your problem, ma, I wanted to tell her, but I couldn't speak the things she didn't want to say. *I'm in here, and I'm fine. Let them be.*

*

In the fall, Ian read me a letter from Selective Service that had come to the MIC. "They call us 'Among the most active draft counseling centers'! Ain't that a hoot? Then they offer to send us:

> Reference copies of comprehensive booklets
> about the draft and military service prepared
> by our organization.

That's *their* organization. Then they say:

> We hope to insure that all young men are intelligently and factually appraised of all the facts relating to the draft, so that they can better plan their futures.... We sincerely hope that you will order this material in the belief that its straightforward and factual contents will be of value to your program and you individual young counselors.

And this—listen to this, Carl:

> If there are additional items which would be of interest to your organization, or if you have suggestions on how we might better improve our relationship with your group, we welcome your comments.

Can you beat it?"

I had some suggestions on how to improve our relationship: First, they should stop drafting people; second, stop prosecuting people who never wanted to be drafted; and third, they can kiss my ass. I told Paul about the letter, and he used it as an example in a talk about cooptation.

The second winter, I didn't see much of Dinah. She was letting everybody else go on the roster. Next time she came, I said to her "So I see where they've abolished the draft."

"Yes," she said.

"So it was all for nothing," I said, just to devil her.

"You don't believe that," she said.

"No, I don't. Do you?"

"Of course not," she said. "We won. Duke says you should take some credit for this. Everybody's saying we won."

"Where are the kids?"

"I thought it would be nice just to be alone."

We were in the visitor room with eighteen or twenty bunches of people laughing and yelling and making out, kids sliding on the floor and hitting the Coke machine. I didn't want to ask her how come she always told me what Duke said, so I just said *Yeah.*

*

Because I trained myself to hide my feelings, after a while I thought maybe I didn't have any. Maybe I'd never had any. Maybe I didn't care if Dinah was getting it on with Duke or whoever, just like I hadn't cared too much if Annie got along better with a woman lover than she had with me. Maybe it was true that you couldn't let sexual things distract you if you were going to do any serious work, political or intellectual.

One of the other politicals was into Zen Buddhist practice, and I borrowed his books. I really liked the stuff about mind examining itself, being its own mirror and its own reflection. Because, however far down you went inside your mind, there was always more, like leaves on a cabbage that turns out to be infinite. I'd noticed with acid and with mescaline that you never got to the bottom of your mind, but with Zen meditation I found it didn't matter, you could stop opening the leaves and just let your mind be, and it will open by itself.

Toward the end of my time, I got to be almost like a monk. I spent most of my time in a meditative state and when a sexual thought entered my mind I would think, *Yes, that's how I could hook onto that again if I wanted to. But I don't want to right now.*

I got so good at keeping myself focused on the present moment that I was almost irritated when the warden called me in for my exit interview after the war officially ended, in the fall of '73. *Now what do they want to kick me out for?* was my thought, *I was getting along so well.*

CHAPTER 9

CARL, AGAIN

On the day I got out of prison, Thelma was waiting in her pickup at the outer gate to take me back to Prairie Farm. It was good to see her smile without a shadow over her face. At first, I was just grateful to go in and out when I wanted, eat what I wanted when I liked, fire up the water heater and take a hot bath in the middle of the night. Then some other parts of me that I had put to sleep started to wake up.

My brother Ian had had his trial and was in the slammer; he only got two years. My sister Holly was teaching school in St. Paul, and she came out to Prairie Farm a couple times a month, and Monette sometimes came out, but Duke never did. I was the only one living at home, and I kept getting into it with Roy, him always with that tight smile on his face so he argued through his teeth, "What the hell you mean, prisons make crim'nals? Ever'body can obey the law, you hear what I say?" smiling so the skin drew tight over his cheeks and his eyes glittered.

After one too many arguments, I asked Thelma to drive me into Menomonie, where I caught the Hound for St. Paul, then hitchhiked over to Dinah's house in south Minneapolis. I knew probably it would make me feel bad to be in her house, but I wanted to see the kids again. I hadn't reckoned on how strong Duke's presence would hang in the air, his wacky projects filling the rooms.

"You guys sure have gotten tall."

"Hi Carl," they said, "When'd you get out? Can you stay for dinner?"

"Yes, stay as long as you like," said Dinah, and she squeezed my arm. She looked good enough to eat, and I almost asked her, *How come you never told me you were leaving me for my baby brother?* but I figured, after all, what could she say.

"Yo bro," said Duke, who was looking bad, red-rimmed eyes, way too thin. I slept on Dinah's living-room floor that night, and I woke up two or three times to hear Duke moving around, talking in a low voice I couldn't quite hear, turning on all the faucets, then running against the wall. *Hzmzhzmz shmzhmzmz whump!* he'd run at the wall head first, then put his hands up against it at the last possible moment. Then he did a handstand.

"Hey Duke, you want to talk?" I asked. Duke turned to look at me, his eyes reflecting light from the streetlamp outside the window.

"No thanks, bro, I don't think so. Can't sleep is all," he said and sat down on the couch whispering some more, and I went back to sleep.

In the morning, the kids went to school and Duke stayed in bed. I sat in the kitchen drinking tea with Dinah, and it felt almost like it did when we lived together, the hum and rattle of the refrigerator, smell of rose hips and her musk oil. She asked me what I was thinking about doing, and I turned it back and asked what *she* was going to do.

"Your friend Duke's in bad shape."

"I know," she said, "but what can I do? I can't make him

get help. Besides, I don't know what would help him, he needs . . . he needs . . . . You're his brother. What does he need?"

"Fucked if I know, Dinah. Everybody needs something. But it can't be real good for the kids, having him around when he's like this."

"They love him so much," she said, "they're so kind to him. I just go from day to day."

Sorta like in the joint, I thought but didn't say.

Then she said, "The war's still going on even though we got out, Cambodia's a mess, things're heating up in Central America, in the Persian Gulf."

"Things're always hot somewhere," I told her. "I think I need to be by myself for a little while." So after breakfast, I went over to the new co-op food warehouse that had grown out of the People's Pantry and said hello to some people I'd known before. One of them, Neil, had been a client at MIC, a tall man with long dishwater blond hair. We helped him get a C.O., and he was so grateful he sent MIC money every month. He remembered me, and he hired me to load trucks that delivered to retail co-ops in Duluth, Redwood Falls, Menomonie.

"How's Miles and Jonathan? And your brother Ian?" Neil wanted to know. I told him Miles was going to law school in Canada, the only one of the original bunch who was still counseling young men. Ian was in prison in Milan, Michigan. I didn't tell him Ian had written to say he was gay, because I didn't think it was any of Neil's business.

"And Jonathan's gone into business—a store where they sell handmade stuff from worker co-ops in the South. It's called Liberty House, downstairs from the old MIC office. Do you know a guy called Norval Wise—old movement type? They run it together. They're getting into social-action stuff."

"Cool," said Neil. "And we're gettin' out of 'Nam. The revolution approaches. Co-ops are the place to be."

Then I went to see Cora, and she told me I could have a

room in their basement for as long as I wanted. You couldn't help noticing Cora's body, she had terrific breasts and legs and that red hair, even though she was nearly as old as my mom—you look at women anyhow.

I always thought Jerry was a lucky guy, having Cora to come home to, and now she's sick. I wonder if she ever got a baby. My friend Karen told me Guatemalan women don't want *estado-unidensas* to adopt their kids, but I didn't write that to Cora because what for.

When my sister Sarah got sick, I almost felt like it was me. It's different with Cora; still, I'm grieving for her, praying she'll get well. You can't help praying when you live with these highland people—with them prayer is as simple as smoking or scratching. I used to give Sister a hard time, now I see how she got into the habit.

Cora and Jerry are really good friends. It made me feel good just to be near them. So, when she said I could stay with them, and she asked *Will it bother you that Dinah visits a lot?* I told her no.

Pretty soon I found I guessed right about the co-op: food was just as interesting as movement organizing. In fact, lots of movement people had gone into food.

"Another name for this place is Mill City," Neil told me. "Food is part of Minneapolis's karma."

I connected with a guy called Mick, who worked at a new co-op bakery called the Mill City Bread Store where the hippies tucked up their long hair into nets and baked real bread, dense and tasty as Thelma's, almost. Half a dozen co-op grocery stores had opened in the Cities, where they sold the bread and also vegetables grown on organic farms.

Mick bragged on the bakery. "We use nothing but whole-grain flour, sea salt, and distilled water in our bread. We trap wild yeast, nothing commercially fermented. A little cold-pressed soy oil to grease the sponge, that's what you call the bread while it's rising, and a little stone-ground *organic* cornmeal on the pan. It's the healthiest thing you can put into your body."

Some of the hippies went rural and became real farmers, raising crops, not just growing their own Minnesota Green dope. I asked my mom if Roy knew about the Twin Cities food co-ops, and she said *You know he never goes to the Cities.* I told her if she had too much garden corn or cucumbers or squash, I could just take them up here to the co-op warehouse, get her a fair price.

Because Thelma always fed the family real food, I hardly ever ate American shitfood until I went to prison. Prison food is really bad, the bread feels and tastes like cotton batting, even when they call it "wheat," it's just tan cotton. Everything tastes of sugar and salt and preservatives. Neil and Mick and some of the others grew up on shitfood, Kraft dinner, Spaghetti-Os, Twinkies, and the rest of it, and they became like proselytes for healthy eating.

After a couple of months, Mick and I decided to go into the organic stone-ground flour business. We borrowed twelve thousand dollars from Jerry and Cora and ordered millstones from a company in West Germany. The stones came on a freighter to the port of Duluth, then on a special reinforced truck to Minneapolis. We rented a loft in an old warehouse near the river, in a building that had reinforced floors and up-to-code 220-volt wiring, and after we got through hassling with customs and with building inspectors and paid overage on the import duty for our incredibly heavy millstones, we started grinding grain for the Bread Store and for People's Peace Bread, a co-op bakery in St. Paul.

I traveled around the region to little towns where college-dropout hippie types were starting other co-op bakeries, places like Northfield and Mankato, Yankton, South Dakota, and Ames, Iowa. I also located organic grain farmers in the U.S. and Canada and contracted for rye, wheat, buckwheat, oats, and corn to grind. It gave me a lot of satisfaction to make a deal with Roy for some of his corn, thoroughly businesslike, no horseshit.

"I can get a better deal from you than from them bandits in Menomonie," he told me.

After six months, my nose was free of the smell of the cellblock and my mouth forgot the taste of the prison bread. My hair was growing long again, and I tied it back in a ponytail, wore Oshkosh B'Gosh overalls with a flannel shirt and a red tie. We started to pay Jerry and Cora their money back, and then I moved out of their basement into a little rented house not far from Dinah, so I could see the boys and kind of keep an eye on Duke.

"He sleeps all day," Dinah said, "or he stays in bed all day. Then he moves around at night, he's like a cat. Sometimes he goes out, and I'm afraid for him. I'm afraid something's going to happen to him."

I'd drop in and act like nothing was wrong. "'Sgoin on, Duke?" I'd say and he would smile at me so affectionately I'd feel nothing really *could* be wrong. But then he'd say something like, *Gotta keep movin', man, the maggots're gnawin' my liver, they want us dead, man.*

And I'd say, *Who, man? Who's after you?* And Duke would smile again and say, *You know, man. The death brigade.*

You had to recognize there was some truth in what he said. There *is* a death brigade, the President and Congress are part of it, and they do want us dead, all us longhaired hippie peace creeps. Those were the Nixon years, but we had a saying, *No matter who you vote for, the same old government gets in.* They want a silent taxpaying citizenry, zoned out on TV and Ho-Hos, that will let them go about their business of commodifying life on the planet, turning everyone, everywhere, into consumers of the poisonous junk America makes—automobiles, Coca-Cola, plastic bags. So how crazy was Duke? Plenty.

"Take a bath, man," I said to him one day. "You're starting to ripen." We were sitting in my kitchen drinking carrot juice from my brand-new, three-hundred-dollar juicer.

"Can't, man, there's shit in the water: brain toxins. You get wet, it puts you in their power."

"Hey, Duke, I take a couple baths a week myself."

"Knew there was something strange about you. Gotta stop immersing, bro, you're turning into one of them."

You couldn't tell when Duke was joking and when he was hallucinating, but then you couldn't tell with a lot of people. I didn't want to think that maybe Duke had blown his circuits with acid, so I always got out of the conversation some way, like making a *boogie-boogie* face and saying, *Man, I soon will be one of them, they're replacing me bit by bit.*

Then Duke would laugh and for a few minutes he'd feel like my baby brother again. We'd talk about the sisters or something until Duke jumped up and said, *Gotta go, man, thanks for the turnip juice.*

Mick and I took out a mortgage and bought our loft. We were working twelve, fourteen hours a day, but I enjoyed every minute except when I thought about Duke or Dinah. I reconnected with my sister Monette who was cleaning people's houses and living a semi-closeted lesbian life. I told her she should tell mom, she would understand.

"I can't. I think about it, and I panic. Don't push me, Carl. I know I'm stuck."

She was in a women's group with Dinah, and I wondered whether that did her any good. But Cora was in the group too, and after all, it was her life.

*

The way the early food co-ops were organized, customers joined by buying a share of stock for a dollar, and they could get a discount if they worked four hours a month at any of the stores or warehouses. Besides our Mill City Mill, and the co-op bakeries which now made crunchy granola breakfast cereal, a very swift seller, there was a produce co-op called Roots and Fruits. There was an herb and tea wholesaler called Red Star Apothecary because the people who ran it were learning about traditional Chinese medicine and how the barefoot doctors combined herbal healing with some Western techniques like immunization; Red Star dealt in dried sea vegetables and herbs with curative and preventive powers, especially ginseng.

I had done my studying about China in the slammer, and I believed in their theories of medicine, the meridians and the reflexes, but some of the guys had this comic-book attitude toward traditional medicine and herbs. They thought ginseng was an aphrodisiac. A Red Star worker told me the collective almost came apart over the question of whether to stock real tea, with caffeine and theine. One faction claimed that caffeine, like tobacco, alcohol, and red meat, made people hostile and aggressive, especially men. Another faction claimed that caffeine had some healing powers, specifically the tea preparation called gunpowder which cleans out your guts in the morning, very wholesome. The question got resolved in favor of maximum profits, as most ethical questions in my experience have yielded to capitalism, and Red Star began to move both tea and coffee.

There was a co-op warehouse for grains and beans, cheese, eggs from a farm where they let the chickens run free, and dairy products from a creamery that only bought from farmers who fed their cattle organically grown feed and refused to give them hormones. It also stocked cleaning supplies from a company that claimed its products were environmentally safe, and healthy, low-ash pet food, because most commercial catfood is just guaranteed to give your kitty kidney stones. The warehouse called itself THUMP, for Trucking and Hauling Upper Midwest Products.

All of these healthful countercultural products cost quite a bit more than you'd pay in a supermarket, but warehousing helped to keep the prices down. And many of the people who shopped at the co-ops used to buy their food in mom'n'pop groceries that cashed their checks. The mom'n'pop is the most expensive form of survival known to humanity. Rich people on Crocus Hill in St. Paul pay less for their food than you pay at the mom'n'pop in the basement of your tenement house, where you share a bathroom with two or three other families.

The co-op community was a place where the younger movement people could discuss the politics of food with elders like Cora and Jerry and Jonathan and Norval Wise, his partner. I could sort of feel myself becoming an elder. My sister Monette put in her volunteer time cleaning the Mill City Mill. Dinah and Cora cut and wrapped cheese one night a week at their neighborhood retail co-op. Every once in a while Jonathan or my old girlfriend Annie or Rebecca turned up on a janitorial detail. Everybody was planning to phase meat out of their diet and replace it with complementary proteins: corn and beans, rice and seeds, nuts, wheat berries, tofu.

People also frowned on coffee, sugar, bananas, coconuts, and pineapple. "United Fruit has turned Central America into a series of one-crop economies," Jonathan told his friends. "The Cuban revolution was about control of sugar markets as much as anything."

"Besides, sugar is bad for you," said Dinah virtuously. "Have you read *Sugar Blues?*"

"Yes. And how about *Killer Salt?*"

As the co-ops took hold and people learned shopkeeping, political differences came out. Mick and I argued all the time about whether the purpose of the co-op movement was to provide healthy food for bourgeois intellectuals like ourselves or whether it was to furnish a base for organizing a revolutionary movement among the workers.

"Beans and grains, they're for people with a lot of leisure time," Mick said. "Hippies and intellectuals, cultural workers, you know, artists. Working people can't eat that kind of food; they don't have the time to cook it. If we really want to serve the working class, we have to sell the food they eat: hot dogs, frozen food, TV dinners."

"But the whole co-op movement is about changing our eating habits," Cora said, when the discussion reached her.

"People can buy shitfood cheaper at chain stores," Monette said. "Let them buy Pop Tarts and Minute Rice at the Red Owl—that's not what the co-ops're about."

"We need to use food co-ops as a base for political organizing," Mick and his buddies would say. "A Black welfare mother with four kids doesn't have time to fucking soak mung beans. But if we can get her in our store to buy baloney and Ka-Boom, maybe we can help her raise her consciousness."

"You are so stupid!" Dinah would yell at them. "Time is exactly what you have when you're a stay-home mom. Money, you don't have. Time, you have in abundance. Jesus Christ, are your brains entirely in your dick?"

Mick's eyes would get shiny and opaque. "Because the co-ops are about political consciousness as much as healthy eating. If we can get working people into the stores, we can educate them."

"You're dreaming," the women jeered. "Working people want to shop fast, in and out, pick up the steak, the frozen french fries, the ice cream, the Hydrox cookies, and out. Or else they shop once a week at a discount store, buy the family pack of pork chops, ten pounds of ground beef, ten half-gallon cartons of milk, twenty-pound sack of dog food. You'll never get working people into a basement to buy granola and little bitty wrinkled organic fruit."

"Maybe I have more respect for working-class people,"

Mick would say. "I believe they'll come to us if we go to them and sell what they want."

I thought the women were basically right, and I said to Mick, "If that's what you want, how come you're working with me?"

"This is a living," Mick answered. "My ideas are evolving. Are you with me?"

"I don't think so."

When his ideas evolved a little further, Mick decided to sell his share in the Mill City Mill. Ian was coming out of the penitentiary, and Monette was sick of cleaning people's houses, so I floated a bank loan and lent them the money, and they each bought half of Mick's share. With his buyout cash, Mick leased an old mom'n'pop storefront with a walk-in cooler in a neighborhood on the border between working-class and boho-bourgeois. Calling his store the Greenery, he said he was going to serve the workers, organize his customers, and spearhead revolutionary consciousness. He hired half a dozen assistants, including my brilliant, crazy baby brother Duke.

After living in Dinah's house like a shadow, hardly moving for days at a time, Duke appeared to change completely. He took a bath, washed his hair and his clothes, and asked Dinah to cut his hair.

Dinah invited me and Monette to dinner to celebrate. "This job'll be really good," Duke told us. "We're going to open at seven a.m. and stay open until nine p.m., so the workers can shop either before they go to work or on their way home. That's fourteen hours. Everybody's going to work an eight-hour shift, with a one-hour overlap."

"I just don't understand how you're going to give your customers a better deal than Red Owl," said Dinah. "Selling lunch meat and TV dinners!"

"You'll see," said Duke mysteriously. "Economies of scale."

The situation with the boys had gotten weirder. I noticed Joel wouldn't look at him, referred to him as the Creep, while Amos acted as if nothing was wrong. "Are you going to sell candy?" he asked. "Or just the yucky stuff like mom's co-op, broccoli and seaweed?"

"No, we're going to have candy. And Ka-Boom and Sugar Smacks and bananas. It's going to be a regular grocery."

"I just don't see it," said Dinah.

Joel left the table. "The Creep was in my room today, mom. Never again." He went into his room and slammed the door.

"I'm really glad you've got this job," Dinah said, "but I do think Mick is a little unreal."

"Yeah," said Monette. "How is he going to do everything he says?"

"Beats me. You know they're planning to sell coffee, bananas, chocolate, meat . . . "

"You just don't understand marketing," said Duke.

*

Mick, who had long silky hair, sad eyes, and a Jesse James moustache, sat on the THUMP board along with eleven others, including Cora and Max, who were long-term financial guarantors. Cora told me that at every meeting for two years, no matter what was on the agenda, Mick managed to introduce a resolution to stock coffee, sugar, and frozen meat in the warehouse, and every time it was voted down. Mick lobbied hard and got Max on his side, but they never mustered more than three votes out of the twelve.

Cora told me Max would lobby her as they drove home. "Look at the elitist bias in the warehouse and most of the stores," she would say, and Cora would answer, "Look, Max, I don't believe in the working class as some kind of rare bird, you put salt on its tail and it eats out of your hand. Working people are like everybody else—some of them want to change to healthier eating habits and some don't. Mick is going to lose his shirt on the Greenery. How's he going to undersell the chain stores? They can buy in huge bulk, and they can afford to advertise and to sell some things below cost as loss leaders. He can't do any of that. And besides, he's going to have to sell all his food for less than it costs him."

"That's just my point," Max would say. "If THUMP would handle the foods working people actually eat, we could match supermarket prices. Last month's volume was up—you heard the treasurer's report. And we're growing."

"But none of the other stores want to carry them—only the Greenery."

"Because they're elitist. You're an elitist, Cory. You're not a pig, but you're not on the side of the workers."

Mick lived with a woman named Joya Rasmussen, whose daughter Kristin went to the same open school as Cora's son Seth and Dinah's son Joel. At school events, Cora and Dinah met Mick on neutral turf. Cora always told me when she'd had a run-in with them, like the time they were eating ginger-snaps and drinking lemonade in the school basement and waiting for the school chorus to begin their concert.

"I don't get it," she said to Mick. "If you're concerned mostly with people on welfare, who are the workers?"

"Workers are people who work for an hourly wage," said Joya.

"Not necessarily," said Mick. "A lot of people who are working class don't have jobs because of the way the economy is fucked up. Lots of single parents, especially Black women, are workers but jobless."

Dinah was always irritated with Mick and Joya because of the way they dressed, like rich hippies in leather pants, long dirty silk scarves, and expensive jewelry. So she always put her oar in.

"Unemployed people don't have a problem with time,"

she said. "They have more time than money. That's a perfect situation for educating them about whole foods."

"You seriously think a Black single mother on ADC is going to take a cooking class from you, to learn how to cook brown rice with miso?" Mick sneered.

"Well if you *don't* think that, what the hell are you doing at the Greenery?"

"We're serving the workers. Once we become a presence in the community, then we can start to organize."

"Organize what? Organize for what?"

"Shh," said Joya. "Here comes the program."

Dinah hates it when you shush her. Personally, I think Mick didn't have an answer.

One Thursday evening at the icy, muddy tail end of winter, the THUMP warehouse was broken into and one of its two ten-ton trucks was stolen. The theft wasn't discovered for twenty-four hours, because a late blizzard came in and hammered us that night and nobody could go anywhere much. The trucks didn't try to make any deliveries because in that kind of a late storm, you see the highways around here littered with jackknifed semis. They look like dinosaurs, huge bodies lying on their sides with their little cabs all twisted up in the air, on the median strip or in the ditch.

After the storm cleared, and they plowed out the warehouse driveway and discovered the truck was gone, Neil said, "Mick. It's got to be Mick."

But it was my baby brother Duke who stole the truck, drove it out to a meatpacking plant a hundred miles away in the storm, ordered a quarter-ton of canned hams and corned beef hash on THUMP's credit, and brought them back to the Greenery's walk-in cooler. Then he sold the truck to a used-car company that sponsored late-night TV movies, all of this while we were hunkered indoors listening to our radios.

Next day, Neil and I and four board members went to the Greenery, and Duke and Mick and two other workers met us at the door with pieces of lath. I got bashed in the head and needed sixteen stitches. The board called an emergency meeting, which was reported to me later by Cora.

"This is no joke," she said to Max on their way to the meeting. "Violence. Meat. I can't believe it."

"I have to agree. They've gone too far."

Mick wasn't at the meeting. Surprise, surprise. The eleven sitting members formally ousted him from the board of directors for conduct injurious to the welfare of other board members.

"Maybe Carl Kjellstrom would take his place," said Neil hopefully.

"Isn't that putting Carl in a helluva spot?" asked a board member named Walker, a Black lawyer. "We're going to have to try to recover the truck his brother stole and possibly prosecute Duke for grand theft and for assault."

"Well, we can ask him."

I accepted. It wasn't possible to recover the truck, even though it clearly had been stolen, because the insurance coverage had lapsed, and the title was unclear anyway. Dean, who agreed to cooperate with the board, said someone had loaned it to the warehouse and then eventually made a gift of it, but he couldn't remember who, and there was no record.

A commitment to nonviolence was strong on the board, and no one wanted to prosecute Mick or Duke. "The courts are a form of violence," said Neil. "I don't want any part of them."

"They are a tool of the capitalist state," said Max. "The people can achieve justice."

"Besides, Duke is sick," said Cora. "He's not really responsible for his actions."

"M'Naghton Rule," said Walker. "Inability to tell right from wrong."

"You gonna pound old Mick?" Joel asked me one spring Saturday a couple weeks later when we rode our bikes out to a state park. "Kristin says he's got it coming. For what him and Duke did to you."

"Nah. No pounding. Think I'll go talk to him, though. What's Kristin like?"

"A fox. Her mom's a fox, too."

We rode along the shore of a small lake, which we could just see through the budding bushes that grew down to the water's edge, red osier, sumac, and nightshade. The blue lake sparkled in the cold sunlight. Once the bushes leaf out, you can't see it at all.

"Say Joel, you know my brother Duke is sick, don't you?"

"I know."

"And he can't help doing that creepy stuff he does."

Joel didn't answer. He was turning his bike wheels in a slalom pattern on the asphalt path.

"Can't be much fun to live with him, though."

"You bet it's no fun. Sometimes I hate him."

"Your mom would help him if she could. So would I."

"Help him to leave my house," said Joel. "That's all the help he needs."

"Wish I knew how."

Over the spring and summer Duke got worse, and finally Dinah kicked him out. The following fall, our big sister Sarah came home on a visit from Central America, and she got him to see a doctor who put him on antipsychotic medication. Then he spent six or eight months in a mental hospital, but they discharged him. He's kind of a street person now. Couple times a year I get a letter from him, typed with a pale ribbon on little scraps of paper. He never writes about people, just his ideas about politics or art. I always answer him.

Dinah started having an affair with Annie Born, my old girlfriend. At first, it gave me kind of a twisted thrill to think of them making love to each other. I still didn't feel ready for a relationship with a woman, and I started to think seriously about going down to Guatemala to work with Sarah on her rural health project, if I could leave the mill in good hands. Ian and Monette were good workers, but they pretty much left the business part of it to me.

The THUMP board presented Mick with a demand for reparations, which he ignored. The Greenery's ideal clientele never showed up, and as soon as Mick's capital was gone, the store closed. Joel heard about their plans first, because Kristin told him she was leaving town, and she wouldn't miss much about Minneapolis.

"You weren't too bad, though," she told him.

"Where you going?"

"My mom and Mick want to move to Oregon. Can't be too much worse than here."

"That's a good place for them," I said when Joel told me. "Lots of workers needing their consciousness raised. Didn't the state of Oregon just put out a notice telling people like Mick not to go there?"

"We won't tell them," said Cora. "We'll let it be a surprise."

Long time ago.

CHAPTER 10

CORA, NOW & THEN

Sleep has become elusive, miragical, like a pool of water in a desert. I lie and long for sleep, and old wrongs rise up and drain the pool so that some nights I hardly rest. I worry that I won't have enough strength later, when Dinah brings me my baby. Serena gives me herb tea. Jerry plays soft music. I watch terrible, boring old movies, but they just make me restless. All the women look like mannequins, I want real women.

Women's voices, women's faces, women's bodies. The women's group. In the late winter of 1971, when Dinah told us she had started sleeping with Duke, we said, *You have to tell Carl.*

"While he's still in slam?" she said, smoking furiously. "Dear Johns are so trite."

At the time I identified with Carl and with his mother, Thelma, whom I had grown to love. What pain it must give her, I thought, this tangle with Dinah. Now I know that our children have their own lives to lead, their own sufferings, but back then I still thought we could shield them with our bodies, our anger, our love.

Dear Johns are only trite, we said, *from a certain point of view.* If you think of yourself as the hometown girl, the high-school sweetheart letting down her man while he's far away, then it's sentimental bullshit—but we think it's a question of ethics.

"You owe him an explanation," said Susan. "And so does Duke."

"Oh, *Duke* won't talk to him."

Why not, we asked. *Aren't they brothers? Don't they share a history, a family?*

"It's not that. Duke *adores* Carl. Hell, he'd give me up rather than hurt Carl."

"But he's *not* giving you up."

"He would if Carl asked him to."

"Well, that's between them. All you can do is clean up whatever's between you and Carl."

Rebecca said, "Lesbians are trying to work out an ethics of non-monogamy. If it works for us, it should work for you."

"What *are* the ethics of—what you said?"

"You know. If people are serious about not owning other people, then probably most men and women will have at least several lovers in their lives. But we need to treat each other ethically."

I said, "Margaret Mead described that—serial relationships. She said it's the next stage of social evolution."

"Well, lesbians are saying it now."

"Gay people have always been the prophets, the oracles," said Carol, in her soft voice. "Tiresias . . . Cassandra . . . "

"Oh, were they gay?" asked Max. "How do you know?"

"There's a tradition," said Rebecca sternly.

"I can dig it," said Dinah. "Tiresias gets to be a man and a woman both. So, what *are* the ethics of non-monogamy?"

"First, you have to tell the truth. Everyone has to tell the truth. I mean, you should always, right? But we have a tendency to lie to our lovers."

"This tendency is not limited to lesbians," said Dinah.

"No," said Susan, "probably all lovers lie. But especially if we're going to trash the old patriarchal notions of chastity and fidelity, we have to replace them with something honorable."

We kept on calling ourselves the women's peace group, but more and more the war we talked about was a sex war, and some of us were combat veterans. I can see us sprawled around my living room, drifts of cigarette smoke hanging on the curtains, posters of Che Guevara, George Jackson, Angela Davis on the walls.

I've never wanted another man than Jerry, what is wrong with me? Oh, movie actors, maybe, in my dreams—Montgomery Clift, Steve McQueen. Am I lying to myself? Something troubled me, vague as a dark shape breaking the surface of water. I told myself this movement will change the world for our children. We will make it possible for them to have deeper, more authentic relationships. People will learn to come clean, to be kind.

Dinah talked with her legs, either she sprawled back and waved them or she got up and paced. "So I have to tell my lover *in prison* that I'm sleeping with his brother? Gimme a break."

"Look, Dinah," said Susan reasonably, "he has to tell you what his truth is, too. Like, did he ask you to be faithful? Or did he just *assume* you would be?"

"Shit, I don't know."

"But see, what I mean is, it's not all your responsibility," said Susan. "That's male thinking, that women have all the power in a relationship. That's the lie that keeps us from seeing that really, men hold most of the power in society. They cloud our minds by treating us like—like—"

"Like sorceresses," Dinah said.

"The python priestess—"

"The hippie witch—"

"La Belle Dame sans Merci."

Did she ever tell him?

&

In 1972, Carl's half-sister Monette joined the group. She had grown into a strong, fair-haired woman like her mother, but with tight muscles and, since graduating from Stout State, she had been cleaning houses for a living.

"I'm a college graduate, and I'm cleaning people's houses because it's the only thing I know how to do," she moaned at her first meeting. "I'm a dyke, and I'm scared shitless to tell my parents, and I'm a fucking housecleaner. I need help."

Then Carl's old girlfriend Annie brought her new lover, Brenda, and asked if they could join our group. They were both nurses, long-legged, high-strung women with clear eyes. Brenda had high cheekbones and straight black hair.

"I think they would be a really fine addition," said Carol. "They're very political."

"We're *all* political," huffed Max. Later she whispered to me, "She just wants them because they're more lesbians."

Dinah asked whether anyone thought there would be issues about Carl.

"Ask Annie," we said.

&

Later that year, Susan broke off with her boyfriend Eli after some final humiliation. I can't remember what it was he did, after years of standing her up, ignoring her in public, and semi-violent sex, but it made us gasp.

"You have to be clear," Dinah told her, "that he went too far."

Dinah worried about Duke, his irrational behavior. "He used to charm me, but the kid stuff is getting old. His art projects have taken over my house. Plus, I'm worried about what happens when Carl comes out of slam."

"What kind of kid stuff?"

"Oh, he competes with the boys. If I have to drive Joel to hockey practice or take Amos to a music lesson, Duke suddenly claims my full attention—he sprains his thumb, or something's in his eye. I mean, it's boring."

"Is he still so good with the boys?"

"Sure. He acts like one of them. Plus he hardly ever wants to play with *me* any more."

Then Susan, having been comforted by her friends for the loss of her abusive lover, decided or discovered that she was a lesbian.

Rebecca told her, "It's not uncommon for straight women to fantasize about lesbian sex. Sometimes they think it's the answer to all their problems."

"Yeah," said Brenda, looking away from Susan. "They're not having orgasms with their boyfriends and they think, 'Now if only I had a nice woman lover who would lick me all over like an ice cream cone, I would be hot stuff.'"

Susan had started to cry, and then she laughed, showing us her shiny wires and rubber bands. "Well, why not? Anything wrong with that?"

"Not a thing." Brenda looked straight at her. "Except lesbian women get exploited."

"Jeez, I don't want to exploit anybody. I just don't want anybody exploiting me."

"I never hear about lesbians snaring straight women and then, after they fall in love, leaving 'em high and dry," said Annie.

"Oh," said Susan. "You mean you think I—"

"Not *you*, sweetheart, nothing personal. But it happens. We've all seen it happen." Monette nodded.

"Besides," said Annie with a glance at Brenda, "you got to do your part. Good sex ain't easy. You bring yourself along, no matter who you go to bed with."

"God knows bad sex is hard."

"If it's a trust issue—"

"You might be thinking it's a man issue—"

"But the real issue could be that you don't trust anybody, man or woman."

Hearing the lesbians give Susan such good advice filled my heart with love for them all and a pang for my Jerry. When we were learning to be lovers, all those years ago, he was so patient, so generous with me, that I've never wanted anyone else. What is wrong with me—what am I afraid of?

Dinah has had more lovers than anyone I know. She talks about them very frankly—this one likes weird positions, cross-wise, backwards, upside down; that one likes her to leave some clothes on so he can tear them off; someone wants her to tie him up; someone else wants to lick her pee—but she does not talk about herself. At first it was hard for me to know so much about her men—Carl, Crater the actor, Miles, Marcus Inchloe, Duke, her ex-husband Reuben, along with many I will never know—but over time I learned to put the lurid images into a memory-drawer that stays shut until she opens it. She never says anything about herself, what *she* likes, and once I asked her, *Where are you while all this is going on?* She looked surprised.

The morning after we discussed Susan's sexuality, Dinah called me. "I felt so horrible last night," she said.

"Why?"

"I just felt like such a hypocrite. Excluded—and dishonest."

"You feel excluded because you don't 'fess up, Dinah. I'll bet whenever you don't say what you're thinking you feel—what's the word? Ostracized."

"Listen, I don't really think it's a neutral choice, Cory."

"What do you mean?"

"I don't think it's just as *good* to be lesbian as to be straight. I mean, it's *okay* to be a lesbian, if you *have to,* if you're *that way.* But Susan's not queer, she's just scared. Eli treated her rotten, but she's not a lesbian."

"How do you know? Did she tell you?" I was really interested. It hadn't occurred to me before.

"No. But I just know."

Scummy glass jars covered my kitchen windowsill and in them reposed Serena's after-dinner gardens, avocado pits with no desire or power for further green activity, desiccating segments of sweet potato, orphan leaves sprouted from grapefruit pips, and pale tangles of ivy and wandering jew. "Tell me more about it. Why do you think that about lesbians? What's the big deal?"

"Because it's not natural. Because you don't get children from licking another woman's pussy, that's why."

"I didn't realize we were such Old Testament moralists around here."

"Hey, I never said it was an abomination before the lord, just that it's a kind of second best."

"Dinah, that's the argument right-wingers use. *Natural* doesn't mean a thing. War's *natural.* Violence is *natural.* Our project here is transforming human possibility, so that we have more choices than the cockroaches."

"You mean you don't feel the same way about sex between women?"

"I never really thought about it."

"I can't believe you," she said. "You are too fucking good to be true."

"I have something to say that's hard," Dinah announced at our next meeting. "You," and she looked at Annie, Brenda, Carol, Monette, and Rebecca, "might not want me to go on meeting with you. But I have to say this. I don't really think homosexuality and heterosexuality are parallel. I mean I don't think—" She stopped and lit a cigarette. We all smoked a lot, it helped us over the hard parts.

Annie said, "Do you think we're *perverts?*"

"That's not what I mean. I want you to know this isn't a social judgment, it's just personal."

"Just personal?"

"I thought the personal is political. I thought that's what we're doing here," said Susan.

"Yes, but—look, Susan, this is about what you were saying last time—about believing you're a lesbian, wanting a lesbian relationship now. I realized the next morning that I don't think this is just something you decide. 'Oh, I'm tired of being straight, think I'll be queer for a while.'"

"I'd appreciate it if you would not use that word, queer," said Rebecca, in her gravelly voice.

"Sorry. You know what I mean."

"All too well."

"Dinah, do you think for one moment that we *choose* to be lesbian?" said Brenda, combing her black hair with her fingers. "I used to pray every night to wake up in the morning and be straight."

"You never told me that," said Annie.

Brenda flushed. "I *used* to. When I was a teenager. I was so lonely. I thought, if I could just feel the way about a boy that I felt about girls—"

"I felt real sorry for myself in high school," said Monette. "But I didn't think about it too much."

"So when did you change your mind?" Annie went on to Brenda.

"When I had my first romance with a woman." Her cheeks flamed.

Susan said she was confused, and we kept veering off the topic, repeating and contradicting each other and ourselves.

"But what about married couples who have no children?" Max asked Dinah. "Do you have the same objections to them?"

"I never thought about it. I—"

"According to Masters and Johnson," said Annie, "most

women climax with techniques that are part of lesbian love-making. Not with a big old penis."

"I read somewhere that gay men don't suffer from impotence," said Susan.

"By the author of *Ten Nights in a Turkish Bath*," said Brenda.

"So what does that mean?"

"That if you're having sex with a person you *want* to have sex with, you can do it just fine," said Carol softly.

"Don't you really think most people are bisexual?" I said timidly, and drew a storm.

"I most certainly am not bisexual! If I were, I could pass for straight."

"Bisexuality is a cop-out."

"Have you ever had a relationship with a woman?" Monette asked, peering at me.

Goodness, I felt picked on. "No. But I've thought about it."

"Well, jeezus," said Rebecca. "Cory's thought about it. Wanna cookie?"

Serena says that, *Wanna cookie?* When Seth says *You shovel the walk, I took the garbage out and I'm tired*, she says, *Aww. Wanna cookie?*

Dinah opened her big brown eyes so wide, you felt you were going to fall into them, the way she does when she is thinking hard. "I've thought about it, too."

"Oh-oh, look out," said Brenda. "Straight ladies getting turned on."

"The point is, that's all you've done, think about it. Speaking for myself," said Rebecca, her neck blushing in blotches, "even when I was a little girl I was drawn to other girls. I never had fantasies about boys, always about other girls. Or women. And I wasn't some big athlete or anything. I didn't have a crush on my gym teacher. I thought I was a freak, and I was terrified my teachers or my mom would find out. I tried having sex with men, but. . . " She pursed her lips and shook her head. "No good. It just didn't work for me."

"Maybe you never found a good man," said Dinah, turning her lamps on Carol.

"Horseshit," said Annie crisply. Dinah looked startled, then she laughed.

"My family was full of women who loved women," said Brenda, pulling at her hair. *"Italian* women. Not sexually, I don't think, but women were the important people. So I got mixed messages. My mother constantly put my father down, and her sisters made fun of their husbands. I mean, now I see it was really hard for my brothers. One of 'em joined the military and one's a charismatic Christian. Men just didn't matter much. But Annie's family was just the opposite, right?"

"Right," said Annie. "You weren't shit if you weren't a guy. So I wanted to be one."

"I was a tomboy, too," said Susan.

"So was I," said Dinah. "That doesn't mean anything. I signed my oath in blood with the other little boys, we cut our arms with an old single-edge razor blade. I hated *girls.* Nobody wants to be a dumb *girl."*

"That's woman-hating," said Annie. "And queer-bashing, if you'll pardon the expression. It ain't healthy. Now, what are you going to do about it?"

"What should I do?" asked Dinah.

"At least you're admitting it," croaked Rebecca. "Most straight people never even get that far."

"We'll have to take you in hand," said Brenda with a smile.

❧

I had crushes on my gym teachers. I always liked to hold and kiss my women friends, but the feelings never became sexual. In me was a smooth high wall between *love* and *love,* and I drowned any little voice that asked me to climb over.

But I'm curious. I'd like to know, just once, what it's like to make love with a woman.

We kept on meeting at my house. Jerry didn't mind, and it's a comfortable place, easy for everyone. I'd leave the supper dishes for Seth or Serena, make sure the walk was shoveled in winter, sweep the old issues of *Ramparts* and *The New Republic* off the sofa, put ashtrays out, and our clubhouse was ready.

Susan started going around with Ian. Carl came out of prison and lived in our basement room. "Will this be awkward for you?" I asked him, "Dinah comes over a lot."

"I've seen her," he said. "It's all right."

We never talked about him in the women's group. Looking back, we never called Dinah on her slimy stuff with men, as long as she was honest with us. But goodness, it's exhausting to change *everything*. You can only work on one place at a time. You clean up your pond, but the underground spring that feeds it is still polluted. You dig a new septic tank and put in filters, you change your detergent, you recycle your liquid wastes, and your pond water's still contaminated from sources you can't control.

❧

Once we trusted each other not to mock or blab, we talked about sex a lot. Dinah wanted us to have a self-examination session, so we could see our cervixes. Carol and Rebecca and Max said no.

"We can get disposable speculums," said Annie, looking at Brenda who nodded and said, "All you need to bring is pocket mirrors."

"Come on," Dinah urged. "It'll be good for us."

But they were firm. My curiosity was awakened, and I asked Jerry to bring a speculum home. "Your insides are gorgeous, baby," he told me but I couldn't take his word for it, so I propped myself up on pillows, stuck the thing in my vagina, pumped it open, and after some yawing and craning I got a look at a great red fleshy flower. *That,* inside of me! I found myself thinking about it when Jerry and I made love, imagining how its lobes would pout or draw in.

"Okay, okay," said Rebecca, when I told about it at our next meeting. "Whoopee. Now can we talk about something else."

Monette followed me into the kitchen when I went to get cups. "Something tells me Becky and Carol don't want to talk about their private parts."

"Max doesn't either."

"You don't always realize how lucky you are, Cory. Privileged and lucky—you have brains and looks and health and a husband who makes enough to support you and your kids. And you're a *happy het.*"

"I know. But I'm confused. Things are changing pretty fast."

"Right. I don't exactly know how to say this, but—your changes are coming out of *our lives.* . . ."

*

One night we were talking about our first sexual experiences.

"The guy next door used to expose himself to me," said Dinah. "I kind of dug it. He was about my father's age, but *big*—thick neck, big muscles. His wife hardly ever went out of the house. He used to do all the shopping, I remember."

"You—*liked* it?" said Max.

"Well, yeah. It excited me."

"Weren't you scared?" asked Susan. "I'd have been scared. It only happened to me once, on a bus with a million other people around, and I was *scared.*"

I was scared when things like that happened to me.

"Dirtballs," said Rebecca. Carol looked sullen and ill.

"Is that all he did?" asked Max. "Expose himself?"

Dinah got up and started to pace, smoking hard. "I haven't thought about him in years. He liked to open his bathroom window when I was in my bedroom. Our houses were pretty close together. This was before my parents moved to Whitefish Bay, when we still lived around Sherman Park. He probably started it when he saw my light go on. And he'd wiggle his dick. Sort of jerking off. He wouldn't look at me." She laughed.

"He was ashamed, I guess. They had kids that were older, the boy went to college, the girl was married and lived in Oshkosh. I can hardly remember the wife, pale, scrawny but flabby, you know? No makeup. I must have been in their house, but all I can remember is him in the window, big hairy belly, little pink dick."

"Ever tell your parents?" asked Annie.

"Hell, no. After a while I tried to get him to look at me. A couple of times I stood in my window with no clothes on. This would be like *before dinner.* I'd pose for him. Like I said, it excited me. I'm getting excited now just talking about it."

"Holy cow, Dinah, you are?" said Susan.

"There sure is no accounting for tastes," said Max.

"I'd see him on the street, and he'd say 'Hello there, Dinah,' and I'd say 'Hi, Mr. Miller, how're you?' and then we'd go inside and put on our little private show. I think of him as— I don't know, almost my first lover."

We told each other about the babysitters who want to look between your legs, the big boys who get you in the basement, the newspaper stories about murderers who cut up children. Max and Brenda went on and on. What a relief, to unpack that filthy old trunk that's been moldering for years in memory's basement, open it up and pull our shames out like torn undershirts, here in my living room where the lamplight falls bright and warm.

Whenever I start on those horrors, I get hung up in the sex-and-violence loop: is sex violent or is violence sexualized?

Which comes first? Could you have sex without violence? What can we do with the violence that dwells inside all of us, each of us? We all feel rage, we all know what it's like to want to hurt someone. Can that desire to hurt be unhooked from pleasure, so men stop thinking of their penises as guns and knives? I don't want to know Jerry's fantasies.

But I want my children to have pleasure without shame or guilt, pleasure without thoughts of pain or violence. And whenever I come close to putting this wish in words, I feel like a mama doll with a painted-on smile.

Over the years we grew able to say things to each other that none of us had ever said. We tried to get down to it, down to the wound through the layers of scarring, the thick blank tissue of forgetfulness. My heart would quicken and I would feel seared, purified by pain. At least, I could let some of my drowned voices speak because Dinah and Annie and Carol disclosed themselves to me. I recognized them; I trusted them.

So that night, the night Dinah told us about her neighbor, I remember I went to the kitchen to make tea. By now we were drinking herb tea instead of wine. The wine lowered our inhibitions, all right; too much. Dinah would laugh hysterically, Rebecca would swear and spit, Max would lecture us, Susan would cry. I acquired a contraption that let you make your own teabags out of a strainer and filter paper, and I would brew up potions of camomile or rose hips and hibiscus, from the Red Star Apothecary co-op.

When I came back with the tray of mugs, Carol was talking, her words falling out in clumps.

"I couldn't do anything because he was my uncle. He had this collection of magazines that he kept in the garage. He worked on cars. They had pictures of children, girls and boys, babies, really, doing—doing sexual things.... Adults in the pictures, too, adult men and the babies licking their, their, or even men putting their, putting their, their... One picture of a little boy with his whole arm inside, inside a woman's—And my uncle Lloyd, he, starting with when I was five or six, I can hardly remember, he'd get me in the garage and close the door and, and lock it and then he'd show me the pictures and say, and say—"

She gasped for breath and Rebecca stroked the back of her neck. "He'd say *Doesn't that look like fun?* and then, and then he'd make me go in a car with him and he would— dirty fingers— I can still smell his hands— "

Carol shook her head, tears falling into her lap. Rebecca rubbed her shoulders. "He, he said he'd kill me if I told anyone, and I believed him. I saw him kill our cat's, our cat's kittens. Lloyd belonged to a club. Young men, old men—He brought me there, I don't know, maybe half a dozen times— other children— "

We sat in silence. The surface of my mind did not want to accept her words; I did not want to know these things.

"How many men were there?" asked Annie softly.

She shook her head. "I don't know." Ash from her cigarette fell to the floor.

I found myself thinking, *Poor little Lloyd, how scared and miserable he must have been, how threatened. What happened to him to make him crazy?* Then I pulled myself up. *Wait a minute. He's not the victim here. Nothing gives him the right to rape a little girl.*

I heard the rasp of Susan's breath. Dinah cleared her throat. "Were they old?"

"Except for Lloyd, I thought they were all really old. One of them looked, he looked kind of like our school custodian. I don't think it was him, though. They would take you into a little dark room and make you take, make you take your clothes off, then they would take your picture and tell you how now you couldn't tell anybody because they had your picture on file. And then they, then they did stuff to you. One of them used to put on a rubber glove and stick his fingers inside me, two fingers, one in my—and one in my—"

Max looked stunned, shook her head and muttered, "Oh how terrible, how terrible. Can something be done?"

"Then they made us play with each other, we had to, we had to do stuff, the other little girl had a bad smell in her, in her vagina, I think now she must have had some infection—"

"Stop. I can't bear it," said Susan. "I'm sorry. It's just so awful. Oh, Carol, I would give anything to make it so that all that never happened to you. I never heard such awful things in my whole life."

"You go on if you want to," said Rebecca. "Anybody who needs to can leave."

"No, I guess, I guess that's probably all I needed to say. Except they had this poem they'd recite: 'Sex before three, definite-lee. Sex before four, they'll always want more. Sex before five—' don't remember. 'Sex before six, you'll get your kicks. Sex before seven, you'll think you're in heaven. Sex before eight, or it's too late. Sex before nine, is really fine.' They would chant it all together and I'd feel so *trapped*, I'd feel trapped like, they'll never let me stop, I'll never get free."

She lay her head back against Rebecca's shoulder. She looked exhausted, her fair hair dark with sweat. "Can I have another cigarette?"

Rebecca put a lit one into her hand, and from deep inside the house I heard Serena's radio, the familiar chords of "Stairway to Heaven." My darling Serena, did any loathesome creep ever menace her? I remember her tears when she was six, and the little boy next door traded looks and told the other kids. Carol, poor Carol.

Her Uncle Lloyd must have filled every day with terror for her: terror in the morning, the birds outside her window calling, *He-will-kill-you-if-you-tell.* Terror for breakfast, pouring into her bowl along with the cereal, eating terror with a spoon. Terror braided into her hair, stuck in her throat, terror in the mirror, in the sunlight, terror growing stronger every time she got close to the garage, so strong she would have to scream or faint. Or go numb.

We sat still. "Oh, Carol, how terrible." "How awful." "Couldn't you tell your parents?"

"But you survived, Carol. That's the amazing part."

"My god," said Max. "My god, can't anything be done?"

"So, how did you get free?" Dinah wanted to know.

"Gosh sakes, Dinah!" said Monette.

"It was sixteen, seventeen years ago," snarled Rebecca. "But you know stuff like it is going on all around us all the time. Kids being abused and threatened."

"No, it's okay." Carol's face crumpled. "I ran away when I was, I think ten, and it was pretty horrible. The police caught me, and I told this social worker that my uncle was doing stuff to me, only I didn't tell her exactly what, because I believed he would kill me. But I almost didn't care. I told her he had these magazines—and then! Like an answer to a prayer, Lloyd got crashed up in a car, he was in this whole-body cast for about six months. And I got up the nerve to tell my mom, a little bit. I think it was having him helpless that gave me the courage. It's sort of a blur now, but he moved out, moved away. I don't even know where he is."

"Oh, Carol, you are so brave."

She opened her eyes. "I don't feel brave. Just tired."

"We can't just let this be," said Dinah. "We have to figure out some kind of resolution. For Carol and for ourselves."

"How about honoring Carol for her survival?" suggested Susan. So we joined hands and stood in silence, then everyone said one thing to honor Carol, and then we gave her a group hug, all of us pressing in with widened arms to surround her with warm women's bodies.

Carol and Rebecca left, but the others lingered. "I don't want to be alone with this," Susan said.

"Neither do I," said Max. "My god, it makes me so *mad*."

"I hope Carol gets mad one of these days," said Brenda.

"Jeez, she only just got in touch with this shit," said Annie. "You could give her five minutes."

"It's been simmering for—what'd Rebecca say, sixteen years?"

"Kid's got a lot of guts," said Monette.

"What happens when stuff simmers?" Annie asked rhetorically. "Either it concentrates, or it comes to the boil. Maybe she can start to get rid of it now."

"Or use it," said Brenda. "Somehow. Do something."

Dinah hung around after the others left. "Quite a night."

"Poor Carol, living with this."

"I know." She stretched her legs in front of her and yawned, pushing her hair back. "This is really an amazing group. Amazing."

Jean Harlow padded back into the room, switching her tail. Our smoke usually drove her into the kitchen. "You know," Dinah went on, "I don't think I was accurate about Mr. Miller. I don't think I ever really saw his dick."

"Unlike Carol and her uncle Lloyd."

"Jesus, no wonder she's a lesbian, with a past like that."

"Dinah!"

The hot-water pipes rattled. Jean Harlow raised her head, then laid it down again.

"I mean, I think I imagined most of Mr. Miller, you know? I'd get off on thinking about him thinking about me. He never met my eyes, but I used to masturbate, and I could make myself come by thinking about him jacking *him*self off thinking about my body. And I might never have actually seen his prick. I think it was more like shadow tennis. Like the game they play in *Blow-Up* with an imaginary ball." She laughed. "*His* balls—imaginary. What do you know? All these years I had it wrong."

PART 3

CHAPTER 11

DINAH'S MEMOIR

When we were together, Carl used to read to me from his sister Sarah's letters. Being an only child, I was curious about all the brothers and sisters in his life.

> Four years of high-school Spanish and a six-week refresher course, and I still can't understand what people are saying. . . . A woman and a man from our orientation group are with me here in San Onofrio Milpas Altas. We get together sometimes to drink beer and speak English. Most of the people speak an Indian language, Cakchikel. Except for the Bible, it's not a written language.

What is she doing there? I ask Carl, and he tells me she is a nurse-midwife in the Peace Corps. I feel jealous of her, off in the highlands of Central America. We're the same age, but I never delivered any babies but my own.

The early mornings are the best, when the roosters start to crow and the air smells of wood smoke. Dawn breaks in long cracks on the eastern sky, light green and then pinkish gold. Then the dogs start to bark, a goat goes ma-a-a, and you hear the women going for water. Then you smell coffee and you hear the trucks on the road. Another day in the highlands.

"I'd really like to meet her," I say, and he says, "Oh you'd get along. Sister gets along with everyone."

The people are very poor and their health is not good. They eat mostly corn, beans, and squash, not enough, and the children don't get enough milk. I've seen rickets, TB, and *parásitos,* which is their name for everything from hookworm to amoebic dysentery. Half the kids die before they are one year old and the ones that survive are sickly. Their mothers are old women at thirty. The other American woman is a dentist, and brother! does she have her work cut out.

"Sounds depressing," I say.

"Sister doesn't get depressed," he says.

No one ever said that about me, I bet.

In 1973, when Carl was in prison and Duke was living with me and the boys, Sister came home for Christmas. She had finished two two-year stints and was planning to go back and live there on her own.

I never exactly told Carl about Duke and me, but he knew. He knew in the way you know things about the people you love, you can smell change on their skin. I knew he knew because I smelled the knowledge on him.

So I went off the visitors' roster. I felt bad sometimes, but it's like Duke put a mojo on me. He needed me so much; his need was stronger than I was. When he strained his long young body up against me and wound his hands in my hair, I felt rooted like a tree in his need, his desire. He flowed around me like water.

Duke is incredibly intelligent, he really is, but out of control. Like water, he scatters; like water, he has no skin. He got suspended from teaching at Zeke and Berry's alternative school because he took his math class down to the river to count the different kinds of river traffic—applied mathematics—and a couple of the boys fell in. He fished them out right away, but one kid panicked and had an asthma attack and his parents pulled him from the school.

"It's mostly just barges anyway," he shrugged.

I was in love with Zeke and Berry. Zeke wore long smocks and caftans and Berry practiced every known domestic art and some I'd never dreamed of. Not only did she make all her own clothes and Zeke's—including their sandals and their rudimentary underwear; if she could she'd have cobbled their boots—but she cooked from scratch every spoonful of food that passed either of their lips and made nutritious veggie lunches for the entire school. She sun-dried fruits and vegetables from their garden, spun hair shed by their fluffy cats into yarn and then knitted the yarn into sweaters, and treated the children's mild illnesses with herbs.

"Doctors give you antihistamines or tranquilizers, but really all most people need is some massage and a few essential oils," she would say, her long cool fingers rubbing the tight muscles in your neck.

Zeke and Berry believed you could live abundantly on what offers itself to you without killing your fellow creatures. They ate mostly nuts and fruits. Cora was funny about them:

she said because they lived in a city, they were forced to hire their food instead of waiting for it to volunteer.

Pupils from their school provided free labor unloading trucks and sorting and bagging the beans, grains, and root vegetables for a food co-op called the Peoples' Pantry. I had a crush on Berry, with her lovely bones and fine curly hair, but nothing could persuade Reuben to send our sons to her school, which was not cheap.

"A good private school, maybe. But why would you want to pay for an inferior education?"

"Cora and Jerry send their kids. Max and Einar send their kids. Cora thinks they do a great job on geography. And history. They teach the kids the real story about how this country was settled, not some sentimental shit about Squanto and Pocahontas. This was not an empty territory, Reuben, there were people here."

"While our forebears groaned under the tsarist yoke. What does this have to do with our children's history? Besides, *you* can tell them the truth."

Of course I could, except that when faced with a choice between my version of the world and his beloved Mrs. Anderson's, Joel went with hers every time. "But honey, the soldiers at Fort Snelling killed people, Indian people. Our government sent them out here to fight the Indians and make sure they didn't get in the way of the businessmen."

"Uh-unh, mom. The Indians did bad stuff. Mrs. Anderson told us."

I called Cora, and she suggested we have Thanksgiving dinner together and invite Tommy Yellow Feather and any other Indian people we knew. We didn't know any others except Arlette and Hazel Thibodeau, the sisters who cleaned our houses, and they always spent holidays with their families up north at Red Lake.

Hazel taught us to say Anishinabe instead of Ojibway or Chippewa. "It means 'the people,'" she said. "All Indian names mean that. That's all we ever called ourselves—the people. 'Course, we all had names for the other peoples, and they were sometimes not so nice."

Tommy Yellow Feather was an Indian activist, and when I invited him for Thanksgiving he said he was going to two or three other white people's houses for dinner.

"Could you squeeze us in?" I asked, and he laughed and said no, but he'd be happy to talk to my kids about Fort Snelling some other time.

Seth and Serena adored the school, and they adored Berry and Zeke, who sheltered them with the generic umbrella of love they held over the world. When they suspended Duke, Cora and I had one of our few disagreements. I was grousing to her on the phone about how poor we were, now that he wasn't bringing in any money at all, and she said well, would I want Zeke and Berry to endanger their students for Duke's sake?

"He wasn't endangering anybody, Cory, he's not a dangerous person. A little wild, maybe, but I trust him with my kids."

There was a silence at the other end of the phone. "I have to tell you, Dinah, I don't trust him with mine. He's got a good heart, but he isn't careful enough with them. And they're precious."

I got huffy with her, and we didn't have Thanksgiving together that year. The boys had dinner with Reuben and Cynthia, and Duke and I went to Zeke and Berry's with twenty-eight other people and ate wild rice and mushrooms, squash-and-apple soup, a salad with avocados and pomegranate seeds, and pumpkin pie with whipped tofu.

On Christmas Day, we drove out to Wisconsin in my old VW bug to meet Sister and have dinner with the family. I was eager to meet her and a little anxious; what's she going to think of me? From everything I know about her, she is strong and good, the sort of person who would never let herself get sidetracked with her lover's little brother.

"Everybody loves our sister Sarah," Duke tells us. "You guys better."

My parents always go on a cruise at Christmas time, but first my mother sends the boys a box of expensive Hanukkah presents. We have packed some of these in an industrial-strength plastic garbage bag and lashed it to the roof rack along with a Jim Beam carton full of pajamas, bathrobes, and toothbrushes, and an Almadén box with our gifts for all the Kjellstroms—clay ashtrays and woven potholders made by the boys, found objects embellished by Duke, and a big bag of hashish fudge, my contribution.

Duke's idea of a nice gift starts with a piece of second-hand bric-a-brac or occasional furniture too ugly to look at. He glues some functional objects onto it, like pencil sharpeners or towel rollers, lacquers it in a color he likes at the moment, studs it with glass jewels, sequins and paillettes, winds it with fringe or rickrack, sometimes découpages it with cutouts from magazines, glazes it with hair spray or clear nail polish, and presents it as a whatnot. *It's a footstool,* he says, or *A portable reading desk.* Or *See?* he says after fixing half-a-dozen partly melted candles to its stressed surface, *It's a candleholder!* My house is filled with them.

He found a broken set of plaster garden gnomes at Lutheran Salvage and is giving them to his lucky brothers and sisters. He has enameled them in shades of mauve, taupe, and khaki and the gnomes look like relics of ancient cultures if you squint a little. They are wrapped in tissue tied with spangled elastic ribbon from a theatrical notions clearance sale. Not all of them fit in the Almadén box, so we have carefully tucked the rest into the back-back, the well behind the back seat where Amos used to ride when he was a baby.

Joel and Amos love to help Duke make presents, though

they are less interested in the result than in the process. They melt down their old crayons to make the candles, and they don't mind taking apart the expensive toys their grandparents send them. Amos especially likes to go and scavenge with him through Goodwill and Salvation Army stores.

The mood in the car is pretty good as we scud through the winter landscape. There isn't much snow yet, just a dusting on the frozen brown ridges of the land. Sun sparkles through the coppery leaves of oak trees. In winter, you get a new appreciation for shades of tan—the parchment color of cornstalks left in the fields, the pale stripes of mowed stubble against the dark earth. Going through some of the little towns that are just a strip on each side of the road I feel the loneliness of the farm people waiting out the winter. Carl and I used to drink beer in these roadside taverns and pretend to search for his father.

A light wind sways bare branches and wires. On the road shoulders, the county crews have strewn a bright buff sand. Once or twice we see a ground squirrel sitting up and sticking its little pointed nose out into the wind.

"Can we sing the chickmunks, mom?" asks Amos, and I say they can.

*

Duke's big sister Holly sits alone in the chilly parlor leafing through a magazine and looking lovely in a bright green dress.

"Going to have to turn on a light pretty soon," she says when we come in. "Gets dark early." In the far corner from the woodstove a big trimmed pine tree looks sadly over-dressed, the way Christmas trees do in daylight.

"Please turn on the tree, it smells so good," says Joel, wrinkling his little face. Amos stands up close to the tree, rustling tinsel. "Cut it out, Ame," says his brother, giving him a shove.

"You don't have to push him, Jojo."

"Oh yes, I do," he says very seriously.

"Fire up the woodstove, too," says Duke. "Where's Monette?"

"Taking a nap," says Holly. "Mom and Sister are in the kitchen fussing around. Dad'll fire up the stove when he gets back. You know how he is about his wood, I wouldn't want to spoil his show."

"Ian get here yet?"

"He went with Dad to get Gramma. Hi you doing, Duke, Dinah? Hi there, boys. Remember me? I'm Holly, the teacher." Amos buries his face in the back of my thigh but Joel sticks out his hand.

"I remember you, you told me about how the Indians gave tobacco to the white guys. Are you going to turn on the tree?"

"Let's take a walk, Dine." Duke is restless as usual, but I want to grab this opportunity to meet Sarah with just Thelma there—dear Thelma, who made room for me when I burst into her life—so I let him take the boys for a chilly ramble, and I go into the kitchen.

I don't know what I expected Sarah to be—someone beautiful, an Amazon, golden like Carl and the other sisters, or at least gracious and womanly like Thelma—but she is tall and scrawny, her hair, skin, and eyes the same dry, tan color as the stubble in the fields. She wears baggy wool pants and a short-sleeved sweater.

"I've heard a lot about you," she says, "and about your boys." She reaches out to finger my earrings. "African?"

"Indian." I embrace Thelma. "We've got a wild rice casserole in the car, and a jug of wine. You want me to bring them in?"

"Later will do. Sister's just telling about her village."

Roast-turkey smell fills the sparkling kitchen, and I pull out one of Thelma's high-backed chairs. I hope Duke doesn't get up to trouble with the boys. How could they, he grew up here. My senses feel dull after the drive and the kitchen warmth makes me drowsy. I want to be alert for Sarah, I want her to like me. One of Thelma's house cats rubs my leg. "Mind if I listen?"

"I don't know how much you know about Guatemala. . . ."

"Really just from your letters, your family's shared them with me. . . ."

Dear, tactful Thelma starts to mince the giblets, strips the meat from the turkey's enormous J-shaped neck. Sarah sits down at the table with me.

"Well, the guerrillas are active near us, and the men go off with them, so the women are left behind with their children. They work in the fields as much as they can—oh, mom, you wouldn't believe what you can grow on a strip no bigger than this table. I'm serious: two dozen cornstalks and a patch of beans. And the kids work, and the old people—old! They're old at forty, *really* old at fifty. All the cultivation is by hand, and they keep seed from crop to crop, you get two, some-times three crops a year where we are. But you know all the land in the whole country is owned by these twenty-four families."

"You wrote us all that, Sister. I thought it was twenty-three. How's the woman who had to have her tooth pulled?" Thelma covers the minced meat to protect it from her cats, who pretend not to notice.

"Oh, Gregoria. Well, you remember she was pregnant? We did what we could but Gregoria had an abscess. So she went to a *curandero* after the extraction, and he gave her herbs for the pain and fever, but they brought on a miscar-riage. She's okay now. But mom, the women count the babies they lose. It's the weirdest thing. She had a little funeral for the miscarriage. Everyone, if you ask them how many kids they have, they'll tell you, 'Six living children and seven that were taken from us before their time.'"

I don't want to imagine a world where having children still carries the risk of death, dealing with that every day, so that dead children are as real to you as live ones. My god, I had an abortion in college without a backward glance, what if I had to remember its name, its saint's day?

"Eighteen years ago they started getting together in agricultural co-ops, when Arbenz was president and started land reform. . . . "

"Oh Sister, I can't keep all that in my head. . . . "

"Just listen, mom. There was a military coup—probably paid for by our government—and the Army installed a dictator. Everyone's frightened of the Army, because it works for the twenty-four families. The people just want to feed themselves and market their surplus, but the landowners took back the farms and they—"

"Speaking of food," Thelma blinks, "we need to get this show on the road. You can scrub some spuds, Dinah. Sister, how about the sweets, we want sweets this year?"

"You bet we want sweets," says Roy, coming in with a rush of cold air, pushing his ancient mother-in-law in front of him.

"Quit *shoving* me, Roy, I can't move so fast."

"Happy Turkey Day, Dinah. Hello, sweetheart," and he kisses Sarah hard on the mouth.

"Hi you doing, Dinah?" says Ian, helping his grandmother off with her coat and pushing-pulling her into the parlor. I'm so glad to see Susan with them, I hug her.

"Where're the kids?"

"Duke took 'em for a walk," Thelma answers for me. "Get that crap off your shoes before you come into the kitchen, why not. Then we need some help around here. Roy, you and Ingvar put the leaves in the table."

"Got to fire up the stove, too."

Holly comes in and ties an apron over her bright mini-dress. "What can I do, mom?"

"Well, you made the raw cranberry relish last night. Want to make the sauce?"

Thelma punches down the dough for the rolls. Big bodies mill through kitchen and dining room. I peel a dozen potatoes. "There's twelve of us, right? That going to be enough?"

"With all we have to eat, I should think so. Just Roy don't think it's a meal without mashed potatoes."

"You know they eat turkeys in the highlands, little scrawny things, you have to cook 'em all day. Then they put a thick sauce on 'em. This would be a real feast."

"Well, it is a real feast, Sister. No one eats like this all the time. Susie, what do you need to do to them Brussels sprouts?"

"I just wish I could bring my whole village here today. Or you there. Somehow."

"You were telling about the land reform," I say under the bustle.

"Later, Dinah. Thanks for asking."

Monette comes downstairs, and the flat light fades, and we start to worry about Duke and the boys. Roy and I put on our coats and go out to look for them. The wind has stiffened. I raise my gloved hands to my mouth and yell "Amos! Joel! Duke!" into the wind. But the river bluff rises over us, already dark, and the fields stretch empty toward the horizon. Across the road, the dark vacant farmhouse poises under her firs and leafless elms like the wreck of an old beauty.

"Looky," says Roy, catching my arm. I peer into the gathering darkness and in a couple of seconds a family of deer take shape out of the dusk, ambling across his stubbled cornfield, stately and slow. Then they scent us and begin to run with a rocking rhythm like children's toys, a young stag with what Roy whispers are pretty good points, a couple of does, and two yearlings. Their hooves thunder on the frozen field, and they yip like dogs as they canter past us.

We go back inside the house, and, of course, my sons and

my lover are there. They crawled up the riverbank on the far side of the house. The boys are wet and shivering and streaked with hard mud.

"Shoo!" Thelma keeps saying. "Go on up and wash yourselves."

I take the boys upstairs and stand them in the big claw-footed family tub and strip them to the skin, my pearly babes goose-bumped and giggling in the dim bathroom. "What were you guys up to?"

"We wanted to see if we could get any freshwater clams, mom. Duke said the river was full of them. Ow, not my hair!"

"You can dry *my* hair, mom. Do I like clams?"

"How was the garden?" I ask them, looping their fine wrists and ankles with the soapy washcloth.

"Icky," says Joel, "all dead."

"Kinda funky," says Amos.

"Mr. Roy and I went out to look for you, and we saw a family of deer. That was cool. Now you dry yourselves and I'm going to go get your peejays from the car."

"Aw, do we have to eat in our peejays?"

"You want to get your wild rice," Thelma reminds me as I head outside through the kitchen, "and your jug a wine."

The boys look very sweet in their flannel pajamas and plaid bathrobes, their hair still a little matted but their faces shining pink.

"What the *hell* did you do to those kids, Donald?" his sister Monette says loudly, and I tell her they're all right.

"Rice got mushrooms in it," complains Roy.

"You'll have enough to eat without it," says Thelma.

When everything has been done that can be done—Thelma's grandmother's embroidered tablecloth and napkins that she brought from Norway found and ironed; the table set with every last piece of porcelain and silverware in the house, whether it matches or not; watermelon-rind pickle, applesauce, and pickled peaches fetched from the cellar; rolls baked brown and perfect; giblets stirred into the gravy and the gravy whisked smooth; the casserole heated, the mashed potatoes, sweet potatoes, sprouts, and squash all cooked and buttered, two kinds of cranberry relish and three fruit sauces heaped into cut-glass dishes, pies stacked in a warming oven and ice cream removed from the freezer to soften in the fridge—we pour wine for the grown-ups except Sister ("I'm on those birth-control pills, and alcohol makes me sick") and apple cider for the children and sit down to dinner.

"Do I like everything?" Amos whispers, and I tell him he does.

"I'm just so glad to be here with you all," says Sister. "I know we never say grace. I know. But I want to say something."

The dance of arms passing plates slows its tempo. "Not grace," says Ian. "You know we don't believe in any old god around here."

"Who don't believe in god, Ingvar? You should speak for yourself, you heathen," says his grandmother.

"Not grace," says Sister. "But thanks. I—"

"We're real glad you're here, Sister," says Monette. "Who didn't get any raw relish?"

"We should all drink to Carl," says Sister, and we raise our glasses. Out of nervousness, I gulp my wine.

"I remember Carl," says Joel. "When's he coming back?"

"I just wish I could say what's in my heart—but I know we'd all rather eat. Please pass the wild rice."

❧

Last Christmas Day, Thelma and I drove all the way to Sandstone Federal Penitentiary to sit with Carl for two hours. My boys were in Oaxaca with Reuben and Cynthia, and Roy's sister made dinner for the rest of the Kjellstroms. We fought snow part of the way, flakes blowing horizontally against the windshield of Thelma's pickup.

"You want to be careful," she warned, "you can't see the ditch in this weather," and she drove down the middle of the road with her brights on. We sang carols, then we sang peace songs.

> *Ain't gonna let nobody turn me round,*
> *turn me round, turn me round,*
> *Ain't gonna let nobody turn me round,*
> *I'm gonna keep on a-walkin', keep on a-*
> *   talkin',*
> *walkin' up to freedom land.*

"I thought you were coming but I wasn't sure," said Carl, after we passed through the security checks. It always shocked me to see him shaven and shorn, like the man who loved the maiden all forlorn. His eyes were red with dope or crying. "Christmas in prison is pretty rugged."

"I didn't know what to get you. . . . "

"It's good just to see you. Anyway, they make you hand it over."

"You mean you can't get presents on *Christmas?*"

"Ma. Think about it."

We cuddled and Thelma chattered, then she cuddled with him and chattered some more. Carl seemed depressed.

"Last year Christmas you were a free man," Thelma said jokingly, and then she started to tear up.

"Next Christmas I'll still be here," he said, "barring a miracle."

"Oh, you know, we still hope for an amnesty."

On the way back in the dark, she and I bought a six-pack of 3.2 beer at a gas station near Sandstone and toked up a few times as we nipped from it. The kid at the register wore a wool hunting cap and never took his eyes off a little old black-and-white TV. He just nodded when we said "Merry Christmas."

We agreed that even if the highway patrol stopped us, they wouldn't ticket us. "What the hell, it's Christmas, right? We'll give 'em a Christmas beer, right?"

"Right. And a teentsy toke, just because."

But they never stopped us, and we ate takeout fried chicken for Christmas dinner, and Thelma spent the night at my house, in Joel's bed. I kissed her goodnight and called her mom.

*

"You know, Dinah," says Thelma under the buzz and chomp, "I can't help thinking about last year. I should be peeved with you for jilting my boy the way you did. Even though it was for my other boy. That's a bad thing to do to a man."

Thelma and Sister are looking at me, but no one else pays attention. I feel a little giddy with wine. "That's life, Thelma. I wouldn't have chosen it this way, but this is how it happened."

"I know he needs you," she says in a low voice, "but Carl does too."

"Say, when are we going to get some grandkids round this table?" Roy pours more wine. "Sister? Holly? Monette? Ingvar, how about you and Susie?"

"Pass the sprouts," says Ian. "Susie and I are just good friends."

"Now, Roy."

"I'm thinking about adopting a kid from the village, Dad. There're so many orphans."

"One a them Indian kids in a blanket? I want some grandkids a my own. Come on, Monette, Holly, you're goodlooking heifers. When're you going to breed?"

"Now, Roy. I think we need more a that bird carved."

"Don't answer him," I say, the wine spreading through me. "Come on, women, don't let a man control your fertility."

"Shut up, Dinah," says Roy.

"Squash, boys? Wild rice? Gravy?" Amos wants more apple cider.

"I want to hear this," Sister says. "We need more of this kind of thinking in this family."

"We got too much already, if you ask me."

"Nobody's askin' you, Roy."

Frail lightweights, we perch on the prairie and stubbornly perform our rituals of food and kinship. We stole this land from the French, who stole it from the Indians, who shared it with the deer. Tremendous gusts of wind whistle around the corner of the house.

"Find me a stud as good as you, dad," says Monette. "They don't make 'em like that any more."

"Watch your mouth, girl."

"That's disgusting," says Holly. "I'm saving myself for a guy with some class."

"You fillies have no respect," roars Roy. I'm pretty sure he's mocking, and his daughters too.

"Who wants pie?" says Thelma, rising with a dirty plate in each hand. "The sooner we finish, the sooner we can open presents, and I know a couple of guys who've really earned their Christmas."

"Actually, Mrs. Thelma, we've been having our presents all week. You know about Hanukkah?"

"Not as much as you, Joel, honey. Why don't you tell us the story?" and she begins to clear the table.

Thelma's mother says she's never known any Jewish people that weren't sharp, look at the Weisses that own the department store in Turtle Lake.

"Hush, now, Gramma, he's going to broaden our minds."

"Okay. There was this family of fighters called Maccabees and this tyrant called Antiochus."

"What's a tyrant?" says Amos, "I forget."

"Someone like my dad, who tells you what to do," says Holly. "Just kidding."

"Shut up, Ame," says Joel, and he tells us about the bloody struggle of the Jews against the Syrians. I feel proud of my little kid, his sleek dark head among all these fair Kjellstroms. I can see Reuben in him, the feistiness I liked.

"And so they went into the temple, and there was a terrible fight, and the Brothers Maccabee were the bravest of all. They killed the most Syrians, pow, pow. And after they smote the Syrians and killed them all, and drove them from the land, they found they only had enough lamp oil to keep the Eternal Flame going for one more day. And, so, they sent their fastest runners to go get some more oil, but the nearest place to get the oil, so the priests could bless it, was eight days' journey, and they knew the Eternal Flame was going to go out. But it didn't! It burned for all the eight days, until the runners got back with the lamp oil. And that's why we celebrate Hanukkah, because of the victory over the Syrian tyrant, and the Miracle of the Eternal Light."

"Whoa," says Ian. "Could this be a liberation story? A little bit like the Vietnamese? Without Thieu, of course."

"And before carpet-bombing," says Susie. "They had to smite each other by hand."

"Sounds like a Jewish Western to me," says Holly.

"There they go," yells Duke. "The grownups're gonna run with your ball, Joel!"

"Is this really a liberation story?" Sarah asks. "I feel so ignorant about Jewish history, but it sounds to me like the Syrians might have been forcibly converting them. Sounds more like what the Spanish did to the indigenous peoples in the New World."

"Except the Jews got to do a lot of the smiting," says Monette, "where the Vietnamese and the indigenous people mostly just got smote, right?"

"I'm a little unhappy about the smiting part. Can we transform this story?" I reach in to clear the serving dishes.

"But mom, the Brothers Maccabee *had* to fight," says Joel, "or they would have been killed."

"I know that's part of the story," says Susie, smiling so her braces shine in the warm light. "But maybe there were some resisters who wanted to persuade the Syrians without fighting."

"You know Carl's in prison because he said he wouldn't fight in this war, don't you?"

"But this is different. Isn't it, mom? The Maccabees *had* to fight."

"The story would be different if the Maccabees had been conscientious objectors," says Duke. "That's all. We'd still give presents."

"Presents!" says Joel in disgust. "It's not about presents. Mostly Jewish people give presents on Hanukkah, so their kids won't feel bad about Christmas."

"Smart-mouth," says Duke.

Sarah says, "I know we're nonviolent in this house—"

"Damn right!" Roy bangs the table.

"—but look. In my village, the people are helping the guerrillas because they believe they're fighting for justice. If I were in their shoes, I don't know what I'd do."

"Right," says Monette. "Like Ingvar says, it could be about the Vietnamese. They're just fighting to get rid of the colonialist oppressors."

"Oh-oh, they're at it again," Duke stage-whispers to Joel.

Mock-wise, mock-weary, Joel nods his head. "Ain't it the truth."

Thelma brings in the apple and pumpkin pies, and Holly brings the ice cream in the cut-glass bowl, hastily washed and dried, that held the squash. We eat dessert, the women languidly, the men stolidly, and drink our coffee with real cream, seeing as it's Christmas. Then Ian and Duke volunteer for dish duty ("Not me," says Roy. "You don't pussywhip me into—" and Thelma snaps his backside with a dish towel), and

Susie puts on a Creedence Clearwater tape ("Not 'Rolling on the River' again!" exclaims Joel, capsizing his eyes as I have asked him not to do), and we open our presents.

The potholders and ashtrays are much admired. "Did you really make this all by yourself?" Thelma coos, and Roy tousles my boys' already messy hair. "By golly, you're some smart fellers."

The family gives each other sweaters and mittens, and we get beautiful long scarves hand-knitted by Thelma from natural-colored yarn spun by their sheep-farming neighbors. "So dad, you learn to knit yet?"

"Hell yes, I know how to knit. I did about half them scarfs, didn't I Thel?"

"Who's counting? He did help, though."

The boys and I drape our new scarves around our necks, although the room is plenty warm with the fire glowing in the old black iron woodstove. They open their last presents from their grandparents, a set of Creepy Crawlies for Amos and a little camouflage fatigue outfit for Joel. "Cool!"

"Honey, we can't have those. They're soldier clothes. Come on, Joel. We don't wear soldier stuff."

"Jeez, Dinah, you'll have to train your parents better," says Monette.

"Let's not fight about it now. We'll talk this over when we get home."

"Ta-daah!" says Duke. "Time for my presents."

"Ta-daah!" says Amos. "I helped make 'em."

"We both did, stupid."

Gingerly, everybody unwinds the elastic ribbon and opens the tissue. Their features clogged with paint, the gnomes emerge transmogrified. Metal coathangers have been thrust over the arms and hands of one. "It's a kids' coat rack," says Joel. "My idea!"

Another has little plastic flowerpots sticking all over him at peculiar angles. "Plantstand?" asks Susie, and Amos nods.

The phallic hat of another has been wired for electricity.

"Plug him in," says Joel excitedly.

"He's a lamp," says Roy. "Ain't that a pisser."

The others aren't so easy to identify. "Duke!" Monette yells into the kitchen. "You get crazier every year! What the hell is this supposed to be?"

"Duke, you gave me one of these for my birthday last year," says Holly. "I don't s'pose you remember. Another year and I'll have a matched set. What are they, anyhow?"

"More durn trash," mutters the grandmother.

"They're *what*nots," squeaks Amos. I can tell he's almost ready to fold.

"Mine matches yours."

"Mine doesn't match anybody's."

"If we ever break up," says Susie, "Ian has to take the whatnots."

"It's easy for you to say that, he's in the kitchen."

"Thelma, you do too," says Roy. "You have to take 'em if we break up."

"Gives me one reason to stay married to you a while longer, you dirty old man."

I've never heard her talk to him like that before. She's flushed with wine and happiness, and having Sarah home, and maybe me.

"Take off that rock music and put on something Christmassy, okay Susie?" We hear loud male noises from the kitchen, followed by crashes.

"'M I going to have any dishes left, Ingvar? Donald?" Thelma calls.

"We're just gettin' 'em *really clean*, ma."

"Don't worry, ma, I can use the pieces in my whatnots."

"Dinah, do you think he's breaking stuff on purpose?"

I smile and shake my head, but that is really the question about Duke: How much control does he have over the craziness? Could he have stopped those kids falling in the water?

Did he have to cover Joel and Amos in mud from head to foot on the riverbank? Are the whatnots his idea of a joke, or does he really think they are useful, pleasant things?

"I wouldn't know," I say. "But I do know it's time for a couple of boys to go to sleep," and I haul them upstairs and put them to bed, with very little protest, in Ian and Duke's old room.

"He *snores,* mom," says Joel. "Don't blame me if I hit him in my sleep."

"You don't have to hit him, honey. If we decide to go back home tonight, we'll warm up the car before we put you in." I kiss them and tell Joel the crack of light under the door is his night light, and he's so blitzed he buys it, practically asleep before I leave the room.

Everybody's sitting around in the lamplight, admiring the tree and saying how glad they are that Sister's home, and how they miss Carl, and when will everybody be together again.

"Sister's going out to Sandstone tomorrow, ain't you, Sister?"

"Think Nixon'll end the war?"

"Sure, like Eisenhower did with Korea."

"Draft's going to end next year. We'll be out of a job."

"Will he declare an amnesty?"

"Pretty much got to, you'd think."

I say, "Here's my present for us all, to help us meditate and to let go of questions we can't answer," and I open the bag of hashish fudge. I made an uncooked candy with butter and sugar and ground almonds, herbs and spices and as much hash as I could afford, and I dusted it with toasted weed that I carefully cleansed of seeds and stems.

"Vision candy," says Duke, taking a big piece.

"Who wants candy after all that food?" croaks the grandma.

"I might try a piece," says Thelma. "What is it?"

"Careful, ma. She puts hash in it."

I never thought Thelma minded cannabis, but she drops the piece she had in her hand. "Hash-ish?"

"Dinah, you could get us all arrested."

"C'mon, Roy, who's going to arrest us?"

"None for me, thanks," says Holly.

"I'll give it a pass," says Monette. "But thanks, Dinah."

Ian and Susie each take a piece, and Duke and I. Then Sister says, "Gosh, I haven't done any dope in so long!" and reaches into the bag.

"Way to go," says Duke.

"Glad you waited till the boys were in bed."

"Now, looky here, I don't like you using drugs in my house."

"It ain't hard stuff, Roy," says Thelma reasonably. "You know, I have smoked it with 'em."

"I still don't like it."

"It's no worse than the wine we were lappin' up at dinner, dad," says Duke. "Fact is, it's better for you—gives spiritual vision, helps you with your quest."

"My quest, right now, is to stay on the right side of the law."

"Now who's going to bust us?" says Ian. "I'm under indictment at this time, dad, ma. No one's going to come here on Christmas night."

"Remember the deer, Roy?" I say. "If they felt safe enough to come so close, we should feel safe."

"I don't care about no goddamn deer, I'm talkin' about drugs."

"It's really good," says Susie. "You really did it this time, Dinah." She slides down onto the braided rug that covers the painted parlor floor and leans her head back on Ian's knee. "Believe I'll cool out here."

"Anybody hear me? I don't want you using drugs in my house!"

"But you smoke tobacco, dad. And you drink alcohol."

"It ain't the same. We pay taxes on them substances, they're legal."

"What about Jorgensons' dandelion wine? What about home brew when you were a kid, you're always telling me about? Smokin' cornsilk?"

"Godblast it, Donald, don't talk back to me. I don't want it, you hear?"

"Every head of household has the right to manufacture up to two hundred gallons of wine or home brew, not to exceed 24 proof, for domestic consumption," says Duke in a toneless gabble. "Beyond this quantity, home fermentation of beverages is subject to taxation and confiscation by agents of the Treasury Department attached to the Bureau of Tobacco, Alcohol, and Firearms. Those responsible are subject to imprisonment for a term—"

"Shut up, Donald. Now I don't want this to turn ugly. Sister, I'm surprised at you eatin' that stuff, that's narcotics. Fun is fun, but dammit, someone always goes too far around here." Roy rises and reaches for the plastic bag full of fudge. He opens the door of the wood stove and tries to swing the bag inside, but as soon as the plastic film hits the hot metal it melts.

"Ow, goddammit!" yells Roy, his hand covered with melting film. Then he grabs a poker and tries to force the swollen bag of candy into the firebox, but the poker stabs holes in the bag and melting fudge runs down front of the stove. The melt drips across the floor, reaching the edge of the rug. Holding his burnt hand to his mouth, Roy picks up a chunk of wood and tries to force the molten mass of candy and plastic inside the firebox.

The smell of scorched sugar fills the room. "I'll get some ice," says Monette. "Dad's hand is burned."

"Bless my sister," says Sister dreamily. "I should have thought of that myself." The five of us candyheads watch.

You know how hash expands a moment of time, blowing it wide like a soap bubble. The cats prowl into the parlor.

"Cannabis is cannabis," says Duke with a laugh. "Smells like catnip to 'em, I bet."

"Specially burning," says Ian and he starts to giggle. Then we all start to giggle at the thought of the nice hash candy burning up inside the stove and sending its perfume into the cold night, luring the cats away from their wonderful pile of turkey bones.

"That candy's going to burn right onto your stove," says Thelma. "It'll coat the firebox just like creosote, that stuff don't burn off."

Roy grunts, holding his hand in the bowl of ice and scowling at us.

Gramma starts to squawk. "Roy, you're a fool, what kinda mess you makin'?" Thelma and Holly fuss over the floor, getting a pan for the melt and a bowl of detergent to scrub at the edge of the rug.

"Jesus, I'm sorry," I say to Thelma. "I didn't know it was going to be such a big deal."

"Oh, you know how he goes off sometimes. Everything's going along fine and Roy gets a burr up his—you know."

"Maybe we should go back tonight?"

"Maybe so, Dinah. He's real tender."

Suddenly, I'm so lonesome for Carl, I could howl. Instead, I go and start the car, collect all our dishes and boxes and clothes, then Duke and I bundle up the boys and array them on blankets in the back seat with their snowsuit jackets over them. We drive home in the teeth of a howling wind that swirls the light snow across the road. As we cross the St. Croix River from Wisconsin to Minnesota, Duke starts laughing, and he doesn't stop until we're nearly home.

CHAPTER 12

Cora, Then & Now

The women's group put Max and me on the spot about not earning our own money, living off Jerry and Einar; it was fashionable to call marriage "legalized prostitution."

"That's what Harriet Martineau wrote," Max told me. "Haven't women learned anything in the last century?"

"We should think seriously about how much work we do," I told her, and I gave a little talk on housework, wearing a housedress from the Goodwill. In a perfect world, couples would share all the work of running a household and raising children, but Jerry's job didn't leave him time to cook or clean. At least that's what I told them.

Now I wonder whether we might have lived our life differently. Last spring, when I first had the desire for a new baby, my idea was for Jerry to share the work. We'll see. At the moment, he and Serena are my high-priced nursing staff. Hazel comes and cleans, but nobody makes the house dirty.

I'd rather remember Dinah talking to us about women in the theater, dressed for the part of a lecturer in a tweed skirt and horn-rimmed glasses. She told us all the great roles were either whores or martyrs. "Or both, like the Duchess of Malfi."

She said all Shakespeare's heroines were played by boys.

"Drag queens!" said Annie and Brenda, yipping with glee.

"It hasn't changed much. Look at Elizabeth Taylor," said Dinah, and we laughed so hard Serena came in, fisting her eyes, to tell us we were making too much noise.

"What's your favorite movie?" Dinah asked Annie.

"*Rebecca.* It's the great closet lesbian love story."

"Who are the lovers?" I asked.

"Rebecca and Danny, of course!" said Annie, Brenda, and Dinah.

"Who's Danny?"

"The housekeeper, Judith Anderson."

"But she's the villain," I said.

"*Exactly.*"

"Think about it, Cory—whose word do you have for her? Only Joan Fontaine, the new wife. And she is wholly owned by the patriarchy."

"Danny loved Rebecca, she tells you that over and over. She loved to watch Rebecca manipulating men."

"I'm not understanding this exactly," said Susan. "You mean, manipulating men is, like, a joke between women? Between lesbians?"

I can see on Dinah's face that she remembers our long-ago conversation.

"Maybe. Sometimes. It could be."

"In a story like that," says Brenda, "where a lesbian choice is impossible, you're grateful for crumbs."

"Gimme a break," says Annie. "Judith Anderson's a lot more than crumbs."

Monette says, "Shit, crumbs: that's the story of my life at the movies. Doris Day. Paula Prentiss."

"Remember Mercedes McCambridge?"

"Ann Miller?"

We talked about the news, too. Funny, awful secrets began to leak out of the Nixon White House: a squad of Plumbers, a bugged psychiatrist's office, our sweaty, shifty president barricading himself behind his squareheaded aides.

"Pat is an absolute zombie. Don't you believe she has to take drugs to endure life with that man?"

"She chose him."

"I'd sure like to know what her other choices were."

The memory unrolls like film. I can watch these scenes from our life, rough memories toss me and then I come to a smoother place. Susan gave us an evening on women poets, Sappho to Sylvia Plath, and the more she talked the more confident and firm her manner became. She ended it with Ruth Hershberger's *Adam's Rib* and her own doggerel:

> *Call me heteroclite or isogamous*
> *If I protect old Ishtar from young Tammuz*
> *Though thick against her foes may crowd*
>   *the field*
> *At times the pen is stronger than the shield.*

Susan had begun to raise her eyes instead of hiding them, and her skin was clearing up. *Goodness,* I thought, *it's actually working.* "Ian's good for her," I remember saying to Dinah.

"Yeah," she said, "they're cute together. But some day he's gonna wake up and discover he's gay."

At one of our meetings Susan said, "There's a group in Boston called Redstockings, and I've brought their manifesto with me. We might want to consider doing something like it."

"That's too organized for me," said Annie, and we all sort of agreed. But we loved the Redstockings.

Rebecca had friends in Chicago who had broken away from SDS and formed a Women's Liberation group. Max knew women in New York. We felt we were part of a national movement, a great tide of change. A book called *The Total Woman* came out, about how feminism was anti-family and women should act like sex kittens around their husbands.

"Look at this!" Dinah brandished the book at a meeting. "We've got them on the run, and they found a woman to rat us out!"

Dinah's style changed. She dropped the beads and fringe, cut her hair, and started to wear tailored jackets and trousers and little gold rings in her ears. Sometimes she wore ties. Then Brenda dropped out of the group.

"Are you having an affair with Annie?" I asked Dinah one day on the phone.

"You know me too well," she said after a pause.

The shadow poked out of the water, and I felt jealous and lonely. Seth was at an age when he had to push me away. Maybe I was easily bruised, but I felt jilted.

"How does Reuben feel about this? He giving you any trouble?"

"You bet," she said. "He wants to take the boys away. Frankly, I'm thinking it might be a good idea. Joel hates Annie worse than he hated Duke. He goes into his room and stays there, he won't even say hello. If he sees her in the morning, he won't eat breakfast, bolts out the door on an empty stomach."

You're a lesbian now, I thought, and so you don't care if your son eats breakfast? "Dinah, how about going easy on the passion. Your house is Joel's house, too."

"I don't care, Cory. My kids have got to live with my choices. This is the sanest relationship I've ever had. I really love this woman. And yes, I've changed my mind about being gay."

"How about Amos?"

"Oh . . . you know Ame, he talks baby talk to her and sits on her lap. That's not so great either. I'm thinking, maybe they should live with Reuben and Cynthia for a while. Find out how good they have it with me."

"Dinah, Dinah, this is serious. Reuben can take them permanently if he drags you to court."

"It won't happen, sweetie. I'll go quietly. Let him have them. I'll get weekly visitation, or something."

Morning sun slashed across the windowsill over the toaster, and I smelled burnt crumbs. No woman ever made a pass at *me*.

"I have something to tell you," Rebecca said at our next meeting. "Carol and I have decided to end our relationship."

"Carol and I have been seeing each other," said Monette with a blush.

"I'm thinking about being celibate for a while," Rebecca said. "And I want to start a women's bookstore."

After a while Max said, "It's just you and me and Susie left in our camp, Cory. I must say I like their openness. No jealousy. No backbiting."

"Oh, that comes later," said Rebecca, and we all laughed immoderately at her first joke ever.

Dinah and Annie shot a glance at each other. "It's not always like this," said Annie. "Sometimes dykes make scenes."

I thought of lively Brenda. Did Annie become distant, unresponsive, then merely polite? Maybe Brenda raged. Annie admitted her attraction to Dinah. Brenda packed in a frenzy, fled in darkness, leaving a trail of bitterness and pain.

"That wasn't exactly how it was," Dinah told me later. "Brenda's got this old lover in Seattle that calls her all the time. She wanted Annie to go out there, but Annie didn't want to go. Because of me, partly, and her job and other things. So it wasn't what you'd call a bitter parting."

*

What consolation, to think of those days! Sydney wants me to try a new kind of chemotherapy, and Serena and Jerry are doubtful. I don't want to do that again, to feel poisoned. I need to save my strength, bank the good days. He says it might make all the difference—but it might not. I don't think I can take the chance.

"We want our baby before the snow comes," I tell Dinah. "Get on that lawyer."

She says she will.

The world has shrunk to my body; can this be what the old philosophers meant by hell? My only escape is memory.

It probably didn't happen as neatly as I remember it now, but right around that time was when our group gave birth to the idea of Isis House. Susan went to work at the Capitol, first as a lowly assistant, then inching up the ladder as a legislative aide, and she also wrote pamphlets and political poems. Rebecca opened her women's bookstore—just a half-store-front at first, hardly wider than a bookshelf, but gradually, as more women's presses began publishing more women's work, she expanded into the other half.

We really need a women's building, someone said, and we all said *Yes, of course!*

*

"You're different," Jerry told me that summer when we went up to our cabin.

"How different?" We were untacking the plastic storm covers from the insides of the windows. I felt good, the shadows gone from my heart, but then I always used to feel good up North, smelling the pines and seeing the sun span-gling the scales of the water like some glamorous serpent's skin.

"I'm not sure," he said. "You've firmed up a little, kid. You say *I think,* more, instead of asking questions, *Don't you think?*"

When Seth was little, Serena used to tease him by saying, "What are you, a woman?" until he cried.

Don't do it, I'd tell her. *Woman's not a bad thing, don't use the word to mean something you don't like. I'm a woman. You're going to be a woman some day.*

And now Serena is a woman: how did that happen? The rush of life carries her past me but some memories rise from the flood, like the year she broke her collarbone, falling out of a tree. She was so interested in how the surgeon set it, she forgot to cry. She had to wear a dressing that went under her arm and she couldn't take a shower for six weeks. I gave her tub baths, gingerly, and the plaster bandage got grayer and grayer. She liked to say, *My bones are knitting.*

Serena loved to help at Isis House, poking in the clinic wastebaskets, when Dinah and Thelma and I cleaned. She got her period right around that time, was she looking for evidence?

The past sits with me vividly, more present than the present, even though I can't put it together exactly. The contaminated pond. Sometimes I don't recognize Dinah. Who is this gray woman, and what has she done with Dinah's long black hair? For years Dinah was my disgraceful younger sister, the one I never had, who dared to make mistakes. Now she is my *comadre.* "If I don't get stronger," I tell her, "you'll have to help raise our *niñita.*"

"I intend to," she says.

"Well, I hope you do better than you did with Serena."

"What do you mean?" she says indignantly. "I did fine with her."

At Isis House, she told Serena, "You can use sponges for your period, especially at your age. Why use up paper products, kill trees? You boil the sponges once a month, it's a breeze."

Later, I told Serena that might not be such a hot idea, but of course she ignored me, and she and Dinah both got itchy yeast infections.

Maybe Persimmon will help, too. Who is this roundlimbed girl, my almost-daughter, flirting with my son? Monette brought her to an organizing meeting when our group began to raise the money for Isis House. She was a dancer then, and her name was Jodi Ann. She was looking for studio space. All the women in Minneapolis wanted to claim room in our women's center.

"Isis House must be all things to all women," Dinah said. "Our needs are great."

Jodi Ann and her friends put on a dance concert that raised a little money. Thelma drove in every week from Wisconsin with jars of preserves and loaves of homemade bread; they raised a lot. Dinah and I did the shitwork, phone calling, printing flyers.

How right we were to do it. Most of us had never thought of asking for our own spaces; women lived in family houses. I had my kitchen, my half of a bedroom; I shared my life with my beloveds, and I never missed what I didn't have.

"You've never really felt your own needs," Carol told me in the flush of her counseling-psychology degree. "None of us has."

Look what happened when we did.

My needs are shrinking, now, like my reproductive organs—maybe that's how it works, as your capacity for increase wanes, you take up less space. Those horrible map drawings that show people crowding the earth, vertical mobs crushed together in Manhattan, Calcutta, then you can see space between them in Siberia, Montana. Those schematics are racist propaganda; the problem isn't population, it's mal-distribution. Women know the planet is abundant, it could provide for us all, if a few humans didn't take a million times more than they need.

Us, too. Me, too. Living in this big house, although my space has shrunk to the bed, the sofa, the toilet, the chair. I resisted the chair, but it lets me go outside. On sunny days, Dinah or Persimmon takes me for a walk. Persimmon wheels it pretty well; Dinah's too impatient, she doesn't take the corners right, bangs my foot. I'll be able to leave the chair when the baby comes, I know I will. Besides, wheelchair women have babies, and mother them.

"Lesbians are no different," Annie told us. "Just because I'm not married doesn't mean I'm any clearer about my space, my rights, my wants."

"But once the idea starts to percolate," said Dinah, "being gay does give you a little head start."

Right around that time, Roy Kjellstrom left Thelma for a younger woman. When Thelma drove in every week to see Duke in the state hospital, she stayed over at our house. Between Roy and Duke she had a lot of sorrow. Sometimes she would cry after seeing Duke, and I would get to hold her solid body. She cried hard and deep, and then she stopped. "He hardly knew me today," she said once. Then next time, "He's more in touch, but he seems even crazier."

Duke got better and talked about getting out, and Thelma registered him for Medical Assistance and helped him find a furnished room. "I done what I could," she said. "Now I got to let go of that one." How I loved her sprigged nightgowns, her calming presence at the breakfast table.

"It's different on the farm," she told us. "You got too much space, too much time alone. Farm women need a place to be with other women."

"We all need that," Annie said.

What did we want to put in our women's building? Rebecca's Aphra Behn Bookstore, of course; and Susan and Carol voted for a women's therapy collective; and Dinah and Jodi Ann said a women's theater or dance troupe. Jodi Ann had a dream and told me I was Kore and she was Persephone, only that name was too funky, she'd rather be Persimmon. Her pregnant belly gave her weight among us.

"I hope I'm carrying a woman baby. Do you think we'll ever have space for a women's clinic?"

Annie looked thoughtful. "I don't think we can get an M.D. to help. But we could do women's self-help and health advising; we could do that with nurses and lay people if we didn't call it medicine."

"Just, you know, massage and herbs, maybe?" asked Persimmon, and Annie said cautiously she thought that might go.

Monette said a women's cafe, where we could have poetry readings and women-only dances.

"You can count me out of that one," said Max. "Do you like that women's music stuff?" and I said no, not really, and she said she couldn't stand it, give her the Weavers or Ewan MacColl and Peggy Seeger any day.

Me, too, I told her, but I could understand the others wanting a safe place to hang out in the evenings. And the new women musicians are writing songs about loving women, they fill a big gap.

She sighed. "I guess we don't have to love everything about this project." She and Einar gave the building fund a couple thousand dollars.

"This is where we came in," Dinah said to me. "Only now we're doing it for ourselves." She found the perfect building, an old Minneapolis library, built around 1910 out of limestone that looked like marble, a little Italianate palazzo that only cost eighty-five thousand dollars.

Once we started to raise money seriously, we called up the radio and TV stations and newspapers and gave interviews. Susan turned out to be wonderfully articulate, her braces gone, her face clear. She had a new haircut, a new authority. Dinah looked so beautiful on TV that people called the station asking for her phone number.

Carl hated the project. "I don't understand," I said. "What's not to like?" He couldn't explain, just said it gave him the creeps.

Jerry understood. "Poor guy, here's one brother in the funny farm and one just out of slam, his stepfather's gone, and all the women in his life aren't taking care of him any more. They're doing some goddamn women's thing. Look—two of his old girlfriends are sleeping together, and his mom's hanging out with them. I get it."

I didn't get it. "You're on our side, aren't you?" I asked Jerry.

"Baby, I'm always on your side. But you're going awfully fast here. I don't know if I can keep up."

Our old MIC buddy, Jonathan, supported the project, and so did his partner Norval Wise; in fact, we hired Norv as a fundraiser. He hit up some of the big food companies in town, Pillsbury and General Mills, pointing out that women had made them into multi-million-dollar corporations, and it was time to give something back to us—to women as a whole.

The corporations ponied up: a couple thousand here for remodeling, a couple there for operating costs, and we had our capital. But while we were breathing dust and shopping for restaurant stoves, a reaction had set in against us in Minneapolis. People wrote vicious letters to the editor attacking us, saying we were hostile to men and what we were doing undermined the structure of the family. What women needed, said our critics, was to be better wives and mothers, not frustrated old maids holding endless hen parties.

"Hen parties!" Dinah exploded. "Can you believe it? "

"At least they're not saying all we need is a good screw," said Annie.

"No, but they're thinking it," said Dinah.

"What's a hen party?" asked Persimmon.

Some of those scenes, words, moments are so vivid, they could have happened yesterday, but most have sunk below the water, they are lost in the past, and it was just a few years ago.

Persimmon's lover, Kevin, was a Vietnam vet, I

remember, and he beat her. We didn't know he beat her until her daughter Shawana was born, an exquisite light-brown baby with curly black hair and long eyelashes. Kevin was White, he knew he was not Shawana's father, but when he saw she was a mixed-race baby, he went berserk and punched Persimmon in the eye right there in the hospital.

"Oh, yes," she told us, "he's out of control a lot. He has nightmares, flashbacks—he hit me once before. Poor guy, I really feel sorry for him, but I'm going to have to get a court order now to keep him away from us. Can't have him around this little honey." I remember her light hair falling over the peaceful sucking baby. "I really hope he gets help."

"Good for you," said Susan. "I had a violent lover, and I just took it. I wasn't as smart as you."

Was it then we got the idea for a shelter? All these fragments rush past on the flood, like tree branches and old tires streaming down the street when a swollen river overflows its banks. We felt so strong, so proud. Yes, we were going to do everything for ourselves. We took out a mortgage and bought the building, and Susan set up a corporation, Isis House, Inc. Carol and another woman started a practice in feminist psychotherapy. We argued endlessly over how much rent to charge them, how low their fees could be set; we wanted to help all women, poor women, wanted to spread our pride and strength around to all our sisters.

Push brooms, sweeping compound, sheetrock dust . . . my bones ache to remember how hard we worked. The bookstore opened up in front, in the old children's library. Susan held a law clinic once a week, sitting behind the old circulation desk, bolted to the floor, I remember that. We made a women's health center out of the old closed stacks in the back of the building, where Annie and another nurse held a little health advice clinic two evenings a week. They taught self-examination, yogurt for vaginal infections, herb tea for clearing up urinary tract infections, healthy diets for pregnancy.

Isis was such beautiful space. We decorated it carefully, too, with Georgia O'Keeffe wall posters and Danish shelf units. Persimmon and I made wall hangings to hide the raw partitions, and Norv and Jonathan put in new lighting fixtures, fluorescent but soft.

We wanted to make an example of our building, to show that we didn't have to waste gas or electricity. Jonathan built solar panels for the roof; he told us Minnesota had enough sun to heat most of our water. We turned the water heater way down, we cleaned with vinegar and baking soda.

The therapy practice made money right from the beginning, so Carol and her partner earned a living, and the bookstore and coffeehouse helped with the mortgage payments, even though the coffee was terrible. "That's not what people come here for," Dinah laughed at me. "Drink tea."

I went once and drank lukewarm spring water and watched the women dancing to taped music. They held each other close and sexy, rubbing their breasts against each other's shirts, or they pranced and swung their hips. They looked warm and happy.

"Not your scene," said Dinah kindly.

We scrubbed the place clean every week. I'd bring my kids, Persimmon would have the baby on her back. "Can't wait till I'm a woman," Serena would say. "I'll have other people's moms and kids working for me."

The smells come back: we never got rid of the thick mustiness of old books. Vinegar, ammonia, furniture polish, patchouli oil, diapers, coffee, camomile, steam in old pipes.

Shoveling snow off the broad steps in winter—how did we do it?—keeping the thermostat as low as we could, the money crunch in our second year when the bookstore and the cafe weren't paying expenses. We argued passionately again about raising the fees for therapy, for legal advice, for health advice. We were all still volunteers, except for the therapists, Rebecca in Aphra Behn Books, and Monette in the Womyncup Cafe.

Then the health department gave the cafe a citation because the hot water wasn't hot enough and the fridge wasn't cold enough, such an insult to everything we were trying to do. Monette cried, I remember, sobbing, "We want to live lightly on the earth and here are these dorks telling us You Must Waste Energy. They say they're worried about salmonella. I think they're worried about Northern States Power and Minnegasco."

She was right, I'm sure. The utility companies don't want us to live lightly. Their wealth comes from leaving heavy prints on our fragile planet. My illness is energy-intensive, the radiation therapy, the equipment. Nowadays they throw everything away in hospitals, everything is disposable. When I had babies, hospitals sterilized equipment and reused it, but not any more. "When did that happen?" I ask Jerry, "where are the autoclaves?" But I don't listen to his answer, I have drifted off on another flood of memory.

I remember that we didn't always know how many women are beaten by their lovers and husbands, even with Persimmon's evidence in front of us. Susan's clients often came with bruised faces or on crutches or with their arms in slings.

"Bastard did it again," the woman would say. "I gotta get a writ."

We learned fast. Everything we did at Isis House, it seems to me now, pointed us in that direction—the therapy, the health clinic, the bookstore.

"This is where militarism leads," Susan would say. "You train men to fight, to smash each other, to hit and shoot and kill, and then that becomes the only thing they know how to do."

"It's more than that," Dinah said. "They're brought up to

think they should control women. Then, when women show any kind of independence or initiative—*pow.*"

Near the end of the seventies, a law was passed in the state legislature that made woman-battering a crime, and that meant there was money for battered women's shelters. Susan and Dinah and I wrote a formal request for funds, and we got a grant for twenty thousand dollars. Isis House had found its true identity, and Persimmon celebrated by getting pregnant again.

*

I live one day at a time, trying to stay sane, to anticipate the baby without thinking too hard about her. I'm learning to let go, and I'm amazed how easy it is. I just don't think about the future, about whether Seth and Persimmon will really get together, or whether Serena will find a partner and have kids, even about whether Max wins a seat on the school board, or Congress votes more aid to the Contra. This body, this day, this moment.

CHAPTER 13

MAUREEN

I came back to Minnesota in the early 1980s. It was hard getting used to the winters after living in Central America for so many years, but I soon limbered up my snow-shoveling muscles. I lived with two other sisters, and we shared the dream of opening a shelter for women and their children. We found a beautiful old building in a perfect location—Isis House, a women's center that was struggling to stay open. Cora, that bright spirit, and Dinah and others poured their energy into the place, but it was a common story: the people whose endeavors paid the bills, the therapists and lawyers, left the center after a while because they could make so much money elsewhere. Then the women who were left couldn't get funding for the center.

So we negotiated to buy Isis House. I know it hurt our new friends when we changed the name to St. Savior's, but we urged them to think of all sacred beings as aspects of the One. I've had my difficulties with the Church, yet I believe it is the greatest force for good that I can join myself to. My friends are secular, but they are also truly good, especially Cora, who touches my heart. She is brave in her sickness, even though I believe she is misguided in wanting to adopt a child. It is a response to her mutilation, I fear, and not a real call to devote herself to the wretched of the earth.

For a year or two, we busied ourselves raising money for the shelter—from the archdiocese, the city, and private donors. It was exhausting, but the committed life involves such efforts. Then, as soon as we moved in, we had to replace the roof. There was plenty to occupy us, running the house in a neighborhood where many families are scarred by poverty and shocked by drugs. But once we got that under our belts—the new roof, then a complete remodeling, building rooms in the open spaces, buying beds and refrigerators, and taking out a second mortgage—we opened our doors.

Cora and Dinah and some others, Norval Wise among them, decided to focus attention on the Gladdwin Corporation, an old Minneapolis company that made temperature regulators for home furnaces. Its name was stamped on many homes, on the furnace or thermostat: *Minne-Gladdwin Regulator Co.* Over the years the company changed: it makes computers, now, and missile guidance systems, and bombs.

Thanks to microprocessor technology, the makers of weapons can now design and launch them from a console like a typewriter or an organ keyboard. And thanks to its pact with the devil, father of lies, Gladdwin has grown from the harmless name on everyone's wall into the state's largest military contractor. In the heart of our city, where so many of us struggle to live according to Jesus' prophetic words, this corporation grows fat on the blood of innocent victims.

This is what Norval and Cora and I thought: as citizens, our taxes pay for weapons of violence instead of milk, schools, or safe housing. And because Gladdwin headquarters sits just twenty city blocks from the Bookbinders' home and twenty-five in the other direction from St. Savior's, its business is a neighborhood issue.

The Gladdwin Corporation doesn't make the bombs and the missile guidance systems right here in the middle of the city, of course. For that purpose it has built factories beyond the suburbs, chopping down the big shade trees that used to shelter little towns among the soybean fields and hog wallows and apple orchards. They bulldoze the land flat, and then they throw up cheap industrial buildings. Harder for us to reach, with our banners and leaflets, although we used to go out twice a week: once to the ordnance plant where they make cluster bombs and once to the terrible one-story shed where women workers assemble the microcircuits that go into the nose cones of guided missiles. The building is long and low and it has no windows. I cannot imagine working in that building with any joy, regardless of what is made there. To do the work of destruction in such a place seems doubly terrible to me.

The workers belong to a union, a local of the Teamsters, and they treat us with hostility. We visited their workplace regularly until they made it clear we angered them; they felt we wanted to rob them of their jobs. We tried to tell them, *We believe in worker and community control of Gladdwin Corporation,* but our words were not heard. On bright late summer days with prairie wind flattening the grass around the wire fence surrounding their building, they told us they didn't want our leaflets, and if we tried to stand in front of their cars they would run us over.

The corporate headquarters is right in the city, in a handsome old red brick building, and that is where we have decided to direct our work and our prayer. It's the symbol of the company; the older I get, the more I care about symbols.

When Norval and Cora and Jerry and Dinah first had the idea for the Project, they held a demonstration in the spring, during the annual shareholders' meeting. Two hundred people marched outside the building with signs that called for Gladdwin to stop making weapons. Inside the meeting, a group called the Interfaith Council for Corporate Responsibility used its little bloc of Gladdwin shares to introduce a motion directing the board to convert from weapons production to more socially useful work—housing or mass transit. And, as it was every year, the resolution was voted down by the massive blocs of shares controlled by the Gladdwin board of directors.

Then the Bookbinders and other friends bought individual shares of Gladdwin stock and gave their voting proxies to Project activists, so we could pack the annual meetings. We put on middle-class clothes, stockings and blazers and pleated skirts. Men wore jackets and ties. At first, we were excited by the notion, as though we were going to a party. Beware of any enterprise that requires new clothes, Thoreau warned, and he was right. They were a sad travesty of real meetings. All conclusions had been reached long ago.

Then we began to have large demonstrations in the fall as well as the spring, and some of us held vigils weekly at the headquarters. We brought votive candles, and bread to share, and when the headquarters staff, the executives and their assistants, turned up for work, we were there to greet them and ask them to change their ways.

Norval had marched with the Southern Christian Leadership Conference and the Student Non-Violent Coordinating Committee, and he was in touch with peace activists all over the globe. He would receive reports of Gladdwin weapons being used in El Salvador and Guatemala, Soweto, Belfast, or Beirut. We always focused our vigil on the latest report. If we had the names of victims, we would read them. Friends in El Salvador were still sending me names of those who fell to the death squads, and we read them aloud: Heriberto Molina, *presente,* Ana Maria Vasconcelos, *presente,* and on and on.

Sometimes we hung a banner over the freeway bridge near the corporation headquarters. *Stop Making Bombs* it said on one side, and on the other, *No More War Toys.* We

238

bannered on Friday mornings for nearly a year, along with the Tuesday morning vigils. Then the Gladdwin security guards started to hassle us. They would come over the bridge with their walkie-talkies and their shiny boots and say, "You're distracting motorists. You want to cause a pile-up on the freeway? We thought you people believed in life, not reckless endangerment. We're going to call the cops."

"This is public property," we told them. "We can stand here."

"Well, then, we can stand here, too."

Cora always gave them a cheery *Good morning* with a smile, and she offered them coffee from a huge thermos jug. One of the young, angry guards would say, "You'll have to come down. You're obstructing visibility. Criminal nuisance."

The first time he said that was in November, after All Souls'. I remember being up there on the bridge in gray dawnlight, with the wind whipping through our hair, hearing this young kid say *Obstructing visibility* and feeling the metal tremble under our feet when the trucks went under us on the freeway. I always liked that feeling. I miss it.

But then we began to think, what if he's right? What if we do cause drivers to take their eyes off the road? Cars are so terrible—driving is so dangerous—if we're increasing the danger in any way, we should stop. So we stopped.

Then we held vigils at headquarters on martyrs' days—on Holy Innocents' Day, and on Dorothy Day's and Gandhi's birthdays, early in the morning. "Listen, Sisters," said Cora, "I don't like all the blood and holes in your religion, but I'll vigil with you."

We brought candles and flowers, made a circle, held hands, sang, and then prayed in silence. We didn't do it for the TV cameras or for the passing cars, we did it for ourselves. Then we would go to a coffee shop and break bread together.

I found Norval a good friend and a true brother in struggle, but the other men in the Gladdwin Project couldn't seem to get along with him, especially the young men who had been active against the Vietnam War. They drifted away, and we found that at the core of the project, those of us who were willing to commit ourselves to the work of rectification were mostly women, except for a few supporters like Jerry Bookbinder.

So, we got the idea of committing civil disobedience, deliberately trespassing on Gladdwin property, risking arrest. We saw that our brothers and sisters in other parts of the country were doing this. The Clamshell Alliance in New Hampshire was preventing the opening of a nuclear power plant. The Plowshares Collective in Pennsylvania disabled some missiles. Good people deliberately broke laws, trespassing, destroying government property.

The four of us, with many others, trespassed on Gladdwin property several times a year. Norval made it a point always to speak with the company's representatives, telling them what we were planning to do and why. "It's a holdover from my SNCC days," he said. "You always had to let the sheriff know when you were in his territory, and let him know that the feds knew, too."

We made leaflets and sent them to Gladdwin, asking them politely to tell their employees why we would be blocking the doors on a certain day, and we called the newspapers and the radio and TV stations. The first few years, we were news. Then the media stopped publishing our press releases, although they always came with their cameras to watch us being arrested. I prayed for the strength not to perform for the camera.

It is perilously easy to become a media victim, a plaster saint, as you are pushed and pulled into a paddy wagon or squad car. The temptation to care whether Channel 4 or Channel 5 gives you the longer segment is insidious, and I found myself succumbing, Norval as well. We gave interviews. We spoke in the name of the Project. I remember the

feeling of excitement when I would holler into a micro-
phone, "Management will not hear us! We ask for peace
conversion with no loss of jobs!" as the cops led me away.
Cora was blunt, she called us *starfuckers*. Some marvelous
young people like Persimmon joined us, though, and I won't
say it wasn't because of the publicity.

Cora and Dinah and I had the idea to do a women's action
at headquarters, to bring ladders and go over the fence into
the corporate courtyard that was filled with fancy modern
sculptures. No cars were allowed in there, and no foot traffic;
it was like an outdoor museum, but really just another symbol
of corporate power, with large dangerous-looking sculptures
in aluminum, stone, and stainless steel. This company is so
powerful, that courtyard speaks, that we can even give our
workers art.

We met on the bridge, the freeway overpass, at four in
the morning on a Monday in October. It was misty and cold,
you could see your breath and not much else. The city's lights
burned as if they had scarves wrapped around them. I rode
my bicycle over to Gladdwin. I usually do, when we risk
arrest; you can always park a bike. My stomach was acting up,
and half the night I had been driving the porcelain bus, as the
kids say.

There was a holy lot of us, Christians and not, a few men
but mostly women. We didn't know what to expect. Black
figures kept coming, streaming over the bridge, cars, too, and
the van from Persimmon's collective with the ladder. All the
red lights turned to green at the same time. You could hypno-
tize yourself watching them.

Some people brought candles, some brought fruit to
share. Cora led us in song, then Persimmon and her friends
positioned the ladder. Dinah handed me the bullhorn. I raised
it and waved it in the direction I thought we should go.
"Good morning," I said into it. "May the spirit be with you."

"And also with you!" came the answer, loud and strong. I

forgot to be cold, and my stomach felt fine. We said some prayers and did some witness, then it was time.

Indian people say, *No one of us can speak alone, and no one can finish the witness.* The parley is always open-ended, waiting for the next speaker. I think of that every time I speak among our people, peace people—that I'm just the next one, adding my voice to all that has been spoken before.

In the eastern sky, a dark misty blue began to be split with lines of pale, pale green. Such freshness in the air made me think of the first morning of the world, before coal was burned or oil, before cities or money or the established Church, just the holiness of creation and the dewy chill. We were in the right place, doing the right thing.

"All right, everybody, let's go," I shouted into the bull-horn, and we surged across the street to the cyclone fence that stood around the bomb factory, Gladdwin headquarters. Persimmon and her friends opened the ladder and steadied it.

"Maureen!" called Persimmon. "Wanna be the first one over?"

"No, thank you," I hollered back, and then the women started swarming over, dark in the early light, a mass of down jackets and woolly hats. They put their signs aside and climbed into the belly of the beast. You are living prayers, I blessed them, folk of good will acting on faith. Others fanned out and blocked the doors.

Against the fence stood all our homemade signs: *Bread Not Bombs; Gladdwin Out of Central America; Peace Conversion with No Job Loss; Jobs with Peace & Justice; Let the Workers Decide; Gladdwin = Sore Losers.* Then the cops came down—city cops, not Gladdwin security.

We never saw them until they were on us. I always thought they wanted you to see them, that was part of the terror: they look fearsome, inhuman, in riot gear with their gas masks and visors and sticks. But these cops must have been hiding inside the building until enough of us were over the fence, or until we had blocked enough doors. They came pouring out of a security door that was usually locked, and they came out swinging, hitting at our legs, our heads, wherever they could reach.

Our people were good. We didn't scream, just tucked our heads down like we had been taught in the nonviolence training, curled up into balls so you protect your soft parts and leave your hard shell exposed to the stick and the boot. I hunched over the bullhorn, putting one arm over my head. The cops were inside and outside the fence, hitting on us. They didn't speak, we didn't scream. All you could hear was the thuds of them hitting us.

Then their big guy said through his bullhorn, "You have broken the law by entering this property and every second you remain you are continuing to be in violation of city ordinance number 2310.3. Leave the property now or be subject to arrest."

Now how could we leave? We didn't dare even straighten up for fear one of these assholes would break our heads. I sneaked a peek out from under my arm, and there they were, poised. "Don't move!" I yelled and got myself a hit on the back.

One woman started to weep. I could hear teeth chattering. My back ached where the riot stick came down, but I'm sure there were people hurting worse. They let up on hitting us for maybe fifty seconds, and then they started to arrest us, one by one.

Two cops to every person: one to hoist you to your feet and jerk your shoulder up so you're off balance while the other puts a pair of plastic handcuffs on your wrists and yanks them tight. The handcuffs have little teeth like the twist-ties you put on a garbage bag, only we are not garbage, we are the precious bodies of this community of conscience. Some of us were fighting for breath, I heard some rattles of asthma along with the sound of teeth chattering. Some of the older people gasped from the shock of the threats and the beatings.

Then Cora started to sing, in her high, sweet voice:

We do not care that we go to jail,
it is for freedom that we gladly go.
We do not care that we go to jail,
it is for freedom that we gladly go.
A heavy load, a heavy load,
and it will take some real strength.
A heavy load, a heavy load,
and it will take some real strength.

The rest of us joined in. Singing can be wonderful for asthma, it can open the airways. Blessed Cora always brings music. Since her illness, our voices sound harsh, cacophonous. I pray for her return among us, and I know that her healing will require more miracles.

I was still curled up, but more and more of us were standing as the pairs of cops got us trussed and ready. When all the women inside the fence had been handcuffed, the cops pushed them into a line of yellow school buses that appeared in the driveway. They must have been parked on the other side of the block. As the buses filled, they drove out of the courtyard.

You can't move well when you've been curled up into a ball on a chilly autumn morning to avoid getting hit with a riot stick, and then you've been handcuffed too tightly with your shoulders out of kilter. People stumbled and fell getting onto the buses, and the cops just threw them in on top of one another. Still, we were true; no one yelled or kicked, though I saw some people crying. By this time, broad daylight spread the sky, but it was cloudy and gray, thick as apple butter. The street was full of traffic, people going to work. Could they see what was happening to us, or were we just a blur in the street? You never know.

All the prisoners from inside the fence were on the buses now, and the cops started to come around outside to get the ladder. But we moved too fast for them, all of us on the outside. We threw ourselves up the ladder and over the fence, tumbling down on the other side, landing on one another, squashy and squirmy in our down coats. The ground was muddy from the scuffling. I flew up and over, landing on an older woman and a young student who got my mitten in her face. "Hi," I said, "I'm Maureen."

"It's a good morning," she said and smiled.

Then the four women who had been holding the ladder tried to come over, but the cops grabbed the ladder and started beating them with their sticks and yelling, "Fucking bitches! Dykes! Diesel dykes!"

I stood up the best I could and raised the bullhorn. I prayed I had left it on, and there was power in the batteries still.

"Stop!" I called to the police. "You are using unnecessary brutality! This is seriously wrong! Stop beating our sisters!"

The cops looked up at me in their pighead helmets like a line of terrible dolls, and I saw they all had tape over their shields, so we couldn't identify them.

🖋

What do you do with your anger? To be bound with plastic handcuffs, jerked around and flung into a police van like a sack of garbage made me angry. It roused my righteous anger, and I was thankful for the hours I had spent on nonviolence training, praying and learning to hoist my thinking up to a level where anger does not rule me. The cops are also oppressed by the system that casts them as brutes. They are robbed of their full humanity, worse than we are. But that analysis just pushes my anger to one side, it doesn't heal it or transform it to something else, to love or forgiveness.

This is the great question of our movement, what to do with the rage bred in us by an unjust world. Our Black brothers and sisters in the South, in the great desegregation marches and confrontations when they were reviled and spat upon, bitten by dogs, struck and shot at and wounded and killed, they found a way to deflect the rage they must have felt against those who tried to victimize them. Blessed Martin Luther King taught that rage can be purified to a love that transforms injustice. But there was a difference, for them. To be Black and to live in this country must be to come early upon your anger, your righteous anger, and Black people who fight for justice learn to channel it, so that it doesn't drown them. Richard Wright remembered his mother beating him so cruelly that he was ill for days, when he was only a small boy, after the first time he sassed a White person. *I thank her for that,* he wrote. *She saved my life.*

In Salvador, in Nicaragua, I knew simple people of strong faith, whose anger slept deeply. Their brothers, sons, husbands, lovers were killed by soldiers, by death squads, and the people swallowed their anger: they understood well that to feel angry put them in danger. But the deep injustice in those countries produced revolutionary leaders of miraculous simplicity, and the priests in Christian base communities gently woke the sleeping anger of their flocks and transformed it first into righteous wrath and then into action that could liberate them, reconcile them. The danger is great, the blessing also.

Here in this northern place, where our peace community struggles to be born, we are mostly White, mostly middle-class, and mostly women. We don't know what it is to have our children's hands or heads cut off and left on our doorstep. We don't see our dead, we don't have the empty belly, the naked child. Most of us have been taught it is unwomanly to feel rage, so we turn our anger against ourselves, stuffing it down our own compliant throats. We write our anger on our bodies. Some of us grow fat on our anger, feeding it with sticky buns and tuna-noodle hot dish, eating anger until it puffs up our bellies and we swell like dirigibles, and some of us grow bitterly thin. We try to starve our anger and it carves us out and eats us. We sink into a deep hole dug by the unfed jaws of our rage. Or we drown our rage in alcohol or drug it with pills. We abandon our children. Sometimes we kill ourselves, or we find men who slap and punch us and kick us with their studded, rubber-soled shoes.

But we're never angry back at them. Goodness no, sweet Jesus! A woman who expresses anger is a bitch. In the convent, many women grow thin. At St. Savior's, I have learned what we women do to our bodies, the sadness and the anger we carve out of our flesh—or cover with it. I have learned about beatings, too. You work with these women, open yourself to them, and you come to understand how it is that they stay with the people who harm them—who punch and kick them, feed them drugs and liquor, steal their children, take their money, break open the wells of their self-respect and self-love, and drain them dry.

Most of the women who come to the shelter have nothing but the spark of hope that gets them to us. We aim to fan that spark, help them to fan each other until each one blazes up in righteous anger. We want them to lift their anger, brandish it, and witness our deep intention to salvage the stolen wealth of our people and turn it to peaceful uses. But most of the women cannot. They are too caught in webs of damage and poverty and fear, and they go back to their lives. Our hearts are broken every day. I pray to live among furious women, burning with the injustice of what has been done to them and their children. It is for them I turn out at Gladdwin on the cold mornings, for them I'm beaten and cuffed and thrown into a paddywagon, for them I celebrate and give thanks for goodness.

And then a beautiful soul like Cora's struggles with evil, and I am tempted to despair. I believe she is in error with her desire for a Guatemalan child, but the greater evil is the cancer that attacks her body and drains her energy. Each day I pray for acceptance of God's will, and each day I think I achieve it; and then, once again, I am tempted to despair. Good and evil are greater than I can grasp; I can only surrender.

CHAPTER 14

PERSIMMON

By the time I helped to organize the ladder action, I was a seasoned Gladdwin veteran. The first time I got busted, we were closing down the bomb factory, blocking Gladdwin's workers from coming to business as usual. "No more business as usual!" we yelled, and we formed a human chain around corporate headquarters while the others sat down in front of the doors. And when the police began to arrest them, pulling them away from the doors and loading them into big yellow school buses, I lay down in the street to help some of the nuns who were blocking the buses.

The cold came up from the asphalt, and I remembered playing in the street when I was little, sitting on the asphalt pretending an old throw rug of my mom's was a magic carpet. Then, four young policemen dragged us out of the way of the bus, yelling, *Don't do that! You'll get hurt!* as if they were there to protect us.

I kept asking them why they weren't with us. "We're doing this for you, too, you know," I said as they carried me to a paddywagon. "Your taxes pay for cluster bombs too. You don't really need any more weapons, do you?"

They were rough, but Kevin handled me much rougher. While I was with him, my life hung by the chains of his rage. After he hurt me, he would cry. When he cried, I felt sorry for him, for everything he went through in 'Nam. But I'm so glad the Goddess made sure I broke those chains when Shawana was born.

This one nun and I were the only ones in the completely dark wagon and we groped our fingers toward each other, giggling with excitement.

"My first bust," she said.

"Mine, too."

Holding hands on the hard benches, like schoolkids, we told each other everything we'd seen that morning: the Pax Christi people with their banners, the Jewish students, the Socialist Workers Party people selling the *Militant,* the guy in the skeleton suit—pretty creepy, huh?—and the Native people in their blankets.

I wondered what the police thought about my friend Momo and her drum, white people trying to respect Native American culture while Gladdwin mines for uranium in their sacred burial grounds.

"Jesus," murmured the nun, "I knew about them mining in South Dakota, but I didn't know they were digging in *sacred burial grounds.*"

"Oh yes," I told her. "Many, many places on the northern plains are sacred to tribal people."

"And the Vets for Life, beautiful guys," she said.

"And I love you nuns, you're so fierce," I said. "But that priest from St. Kilda's, he's kind of an asshole."

"Lots of cops," she said. "Funny how you can always tell the undercover cops."

"Yeah," I said, "the female cops always wear blue eyeshadow. Why do they go undercover—what are they afraid of?"

"They're afraid of us," she told me.

"But we're nonviolent," I said.

"They don't know what that means," she said. "And anything they don't know scares them."

"Oh, wow," I said, "do you think they'll get crazy? I left my kids with Momo and her kids. She wasn't going to risk arrest. If they bust her, what'll happen to them? If there was decent day care, I could have left them at a nursery."

She put her arms around me and smoothed my hair, all rough from the wind and the street.

"Day care for demonstrators?" she said.

I got excited and started to yell, "Day care for everybody! For everybody! But no—" I got quieter. "It costs too much. We gotta have another effing *bomb.* Oh, those kids. It's nearly lunchtime. What's going to happen to them?"

"Did you hear Maureen's speech through the bullhorn?" she asked. "When she told the cops about how the world's wealth is squandered? We keep increasing our defense budgets while fourteen million children starve to death each year. Did you hear her?"

"You bet," I said. "I heard her say, *That's one child dying every two seconds, officer. While we have been talking, thirty little children have died on the planet.*"

"That's good, Persimmon, you have a wonderful memory."

Then the paddywagon doors opened and two more bodies tumbled into our darkness. In the brief light I saw Momo, and I started to scream. "Where are the kids? What happened to the kids?"

Momo started crying, too. "They took them to Juvy, some policeperson in a dress. I tried to stop them, but—"

"We should have had a better plan," I sobbed. "Oh, jeez, Momo, what's gonna happen to them?"

Momo still had her goatskin drum. The person with her, a tall man in Oshkosh overalls with a wreath of daisies in his hair, said in a deep voice that they'd probably be all right.

"They just take them to, like, a nursery, give 'em teddy bears and ice cream. It's where they take kids for foster placement, not juvenile criminals."

"I hope so. My kids don't eat ice cream."

"They will today," said Momo. "By the way, this is Jonathan." We all shook hands in the darkness, recognizing each other like animals because we could touch and smell but not see. I was crazy with worry but also spiritually high on our action.

Early that morning, Momo and I and four other women had danced and chanted and then sat for two hours in front of a pair of glass doors that we symbolically wove shut with strands of red and purple yarn, because those are the Tantric colors of love.

Our sisters and brothers were sitting in front of the doors, blocking entrance into corporate headquarters. When the police began to carry some of them away and put them into school buses, we got angry enough to risk our own selves and we sang

We are a gentle, angry people
and we are singing, singing for our li-i-i-ives

and then we joined hands and lay down on the blacktop in front of the bus, believing they wouldn't run us over.

Four or five more people were thrown into our paddy-wagon, and it was very hot, and then they drove off. Of course we couldn't see anything, but deep-voiced Jonathan said he thought we were headed downtown to the police garage underneath City Hall. Finally they spat us out into the hands of waiting police officers, men and women who searched us, snapped our pictures, and took our fingerprints.

"Sure are a lot of you this morning, ain't they?" said the policewoman at the entrance to city jail. "Supervisor hauled us back from vacation early, they're giving us overtime. How many of you's they gonna be, anyhow?"

Hundreds, we said proudly, and while they were hustling us through their procedures we tried to tell them about our action. *We don't want our taxes to pay for making weapons,* we said. *Our wealth is stolen from us and turned into engines of destruction.*

"Uh-huh. Just press here, stand there, that's right," they said. "Turn to the side. Walk this way, arms at your sides. No, not that way, this way. Empty your pockets, any medication? Any weapons? You'll get it all back, and your I.D. too, no, this way, no, you can't go to the restroom right now, no, you can wash the ink off your hands later, no, that way, no, this way. No. No. In here." *Clang.*

We spent the rest of the morning in a holding cell along with Cora, Dinah, Maureen, and fifteen or twenty other women. "Kore," I said, "here we are in the underworld," and she laughed, and then I told her about my kids and I broke down, and she hugged me so I could cry against her shoulder.

Besides us protesters, there were some shoplifters, bad-check passers, and massage-parlor employees in the holding cell, and one of the other women told me, "It ain't so bad. My kids've been in Juvy a couple times."

"Mine have too," said another woman.

"Both times it was a mistake, see, but they didn't mind. It was okay, just like a weird new daycare."

"But how do you get 'em back?" I wailed.

"That... sometimes that's not so easy," said the first woman, vaguely. "My husband got 'em out, and he still has 'em. They're all right, it's just I can't get 'em."

"You just have to go down and prove their custody is not contested."

I was really grateful for Kore that day. "They will be all right," she said, hugging me to her firm, warm body. "They are precious spirits, and they can survive this little encounter with bureaucratic brutality. You stay right here, don't let yourself scatter."

253

She has been a lighthouse to me. Please, Goddess, let her disease yield to her goodness. I don't trust the chemo, but herbs and vitamins might cure her. In that jail cell she just shone.

"None of us is in here because we harmed anyone," she said. "We're all in here because we threaten men's property arrangements."

"Right," said one of the masseuses. "Men want to control who hauls their ashes. They hate it that I'm makin' a living. Charge me with *procuring,* I ain't no pimp. Anybody got a cigarette?"

"What is it you-all done?" asked one of the women I thought of as the Real Prisoners. "You lay down in the road?"

"We were trying to close down Gladdwin headquarters," Cora told her. "So we climbed over the fence."

"Men's property," said Maureen, nodding. "You know what happens at Gladdwin? They make bombs and missile systems. Not just thermostats, honey, no way! They make and sell weapons, and they hire people to lobby the Pentagon to buy the things they make. We were trying to close them down for even one day, even a few hours."

The holding cell had no outside windows, and the tile floor felt damp. I hugged Kore because we were so cold, but pretty soon the cell got hot with all of us breathing, sweating, laughing women. "Whew!" said Dinah, and she started to take off her clothes, and one by one the rest of us did too, until we were peeled down to T-shirts and panties, sitting on the floor and singing.

"You women stop that singing," said the young cop who patrolled the corridor.

"We have a right to sing," Maureen told him.

"It's disturbing the other prisoners," he lied. "Now you stop it or I'll say no talking. You're in jail, you know, not on the street."

Some men just hate it when a woman says *I have a right.*

Once when I was in Kevin's apartment alone late at night, the super knocked on the door to tell me the painters or the plumbers were coming the next day. I said to him, "My friend doesn't want his apartment painted."

"Well, he has to," said the super.

"No he doesn't," I said. "I don't have to let them in," I said. "He has a right not to have his apartment painted, and I have a right not to let them in."

"O-ho," he said, "you have a right, do you? What are you—a Commonist?"

"Creep," said Maureen. "They can't shut us up."

"You tell 'em, honey."

"What's he mean, you not on the street?"

"They should have the rules over the washstand, you know, like in a hotel. 'No singing,' or whatever."

"Except in a hotel, they're on the door."

"Yeah, but did you notice? There's no door."

"Right."

"Funny."

"No door."

"You're in jail, you know."

"Maybe not knowing the rules is part of the punishment."

"Yeah. They keep you off-balance."

"This ain't no hotel, girl."

"They ain't going to tell you what not to do. They going to let you find out for your own self."

"It's part of the total experience. The jailhouse experience."

"Like not having a door."

"Like having to pee in front of twenty–thirty people."

Jailhouse air and jailhouse light are not the same as light or air anywhere else, and the water is different, too—lukewarm and slimy if you drink it, but cold when you try to wash. The air is clammy. The light is too dim, but harsh.

Momo and I did a little breathing and chanting together,

trying to stay present and not to let worry for our kids distract us from our first moments in jail as prisoners of conscience. We felt so strong not even the food could bring us down, the stale baloney sandwiches and terrible coffee.

"Law say they have to feed you, but it don't say what."

"This ain't a hotel, you know."

"In South Africa, they can keep you like this for months."

"In South Africa, they can beat you to death, too."

"That's been known to happen closer to home."

"Shit, they can beat you to death in Georgia. New York."

"Glad I live in Minnesota."

"Sure is cold, though."

"Not in here."

"Now there's a good reason to get busted. *Spend a warm winter in Minnesota—come to jail.*"

"Think we'll ever get out?"

"You going to be arraigned in afternoon court," one of the shoplifters told us. "About two o'clock."

"How are we going to plead?" asked Dinah.

"I don't know."

"What's the difference?"

"You plead guilty, you get a fine. You plead not guilty, you got to come back."

"Can we get a jury trial?"

"Absolutely," said Maureen. "Even for a misdemeanor. They're going to charge us with trespass. If you plead not guilty and ask for a jury trial, they have to give you one, a jury of six persons. That's how we get the word out. I think we ought to ask for a mass trial, something the media would want to cover. There were more than a hundred of us busted today."

"I thought a jury had twelve people," said Dinah.

"Not for civil cases," said Cora. "Sue me, I don't know why."

"I thought you all got busted for disturbing the peace."

"Nah," said Maureen. "Trespass. We're chickenshit. Disturbing the peace you can get hurt."

"Anyway," said Cora, "we're pacifists. We do nonviolent resistance. You have to piss them off before they'll charge you with disturbing the peace. And I figure we're in this for the sake of peace, if we can't behave peacefully, what's the use? So I sat in peace until they dragged me away."

"If we plead guilty," explained a woman named Barbara, who had been through this before, like Maureen and Cora, "we'll probably be released without bail."

"Yeah, they call it RPR, release on personal recognizance. That means you promise to come back."

"Seems to me you women got it backward—like, you *want* to go to jail. The usual idea is to stay out, as far out as possible," said one of the massage-parlor employees, a tired-looking woman in toreador pants.

"Yup," said Maureen. "We want to stand trial, and we're not afraid to go to jail. Of course—" she hurried to say, as though she'd forgotten something important, "—there's a lot less at stake for most of us than for you. This is chickenshit, this is a petty misdemeanor. None of us has ever gotten more than a couple of weeks, and we can usually get work-release, too."

"What's that?"

"Huber Law, they call it. There's a special part of the workhouse for prisoners who have a regular job. They take you downtown in a van, pick you up after work. It's not too bad."

"I got a regular job," said one of the massage-parlor women, "but I doubt they'd release me from jail to go do it."

"Honey, you just have to switch to the day shift," said her friend.

*

The courtroom was clean, with bright lights and thick carpets. I hoped wherever the kids were looked more like this. The judge and a woman from the city attorney's office talked in low voices about complaints and procedures. As soon as we entered, I felt a wall go up between us mostly White, mostly middle-class protesters and the other women, a wall that wasn't there in the holding cell.

Lots of Gladdwin Project supporters came to court, some of them people from the demonstration who were arraigned in morning court. Norval Wise got arrested in the morning, arraigned, and released, and went back to sit in front of the door at Gladdwin Headquarters. They arrested him again in the afternoon, but they held him in jail; they didn't let him be arraigned again with us. Cora's husband, Jerry, was there, and dozens of others sitting in the comfortable seats like an audience at a play.

The judge mispronounced all our names; he must have been nervous. His bailiff had one of those oak-thick torsos you see on law-enforcement people and on bikers, hung with deadly weapons. I wonder how people get to look like that. I mean, when you think about it, little kids are more or less all shaped alike.

The massage-parlor women had a lawyer, a soft-spoken man in a silvery silk suit who said things to the judge we couldn't hear. The judge had his clerk riffle through the large pages of her calendar until she found an open date for a preliminary hearing. Then he asked if the city wanted bond, and the city attorney said fifteen thousand dollars, and their lawyer agreed to post it, and they all left. The tired-looking woman turned and made a thumbs-up sign to us on the way out.

The shoplifters pled guilty and got fined. One of them said she couldn't pay the fine, and the judge said she had to go back to the holding cell. It was so close, the jail part to the courtroom part. The bailiff just took her arm and walked her through a door at the side of the witness stand, no mingling with members of the public. A matron in a brown suit took her on the other side of the door. I thought of her going back to jail, and I hoped the holding cell held some of our presence for her.

The bad-check woman pled not guilty. The judge gave her a date for a hearing, then released her on her own recognizance.

"RPR," Cora leaned forward and whispered into my ear.

Some of us pled guilty and were fined, but refused the fines. Instead of sending the refusers back behind bars, the judge said we could work off a fifty-dollar fine with five days of community service. He spoke to us very respectfully. I found out later that Barbara's husband plays squash with him.

Most of the women accepted the community service, but not Maureen. As near as I can remember, Maureen said, "I consider what I did this morning my service to the community. I am a religious of the order of St. Joseph, and until recently I was a teacher of young children. I'm now a worker in a shelter for women and their children, many of whom are victims of domestic violence. I spend my life in service to my fellow creatures, and I resent you, Judge Thorp, sentencing me as though I have done something wrong." She was scared, I could tell by the way her eyes bugged. I was so proud to be a woman at that moment. *Crazy Maureen,* I thought, *kick out the jams!*

Catching a deep breath she said, "I can't really accept the jurisdiction of this court. Some call what we did this morning civil disobedience, but I believe what we did should be called *holy obedience.* I went to Gladdwin Headquarters this morning out of obedience to a higher command than the laws of the state of Minnesota that tell me I must not trespass on private property. And when I trespassed upon the property of the bomb-makers, I was doing my duty to God and to my human brothers and sisters.

"God didn't want me to move, Judge Thorp. The Gladdwin executives did, and the company security, and the

Minneapolis police, but God didn't. The police did just what the corporate executives wanted. We both know that. But God wants that company to stop making weapons and to stop making plans to use them, and to stop subverting the democratic legislative process with their lobbyists and their technical advisors. And God wanted me to stay there. So I guess you're just going to have to send me back to jail."

"I guess so," said the judge tiredly. I could hear him because I was sitting in the front row, but everybody else was clapping for Maureen, so he had to bang his gavel for quiet. Then everybody raised their hands up to their shoulders and waved their fingers in silent applause, like we'd learned to do. They don't call it *Quiet* in court, they call it *Order.* We were very orderly, it just happened to be a kind of order the bailiffs weren't too familiar with.

Judge Thorp sent Maureen back through the door, and we all waved and blew kisses until the brown figure of the matron blocked her from us. Now she and the shoplifting woman could keep each other company. The next six of us all pled not guilty, only Cora said, "Innocent!" with a shining face.

"Not guilty," said the judge out of the corner of his mouth to his clerk. We felt so *free!* The judge and his clerk, the bailiff, and the city attorney all seemed like part of a huge wind-up toy.

Barbara got on her feet and said, "Could we have a mass trial, please, your honor, all of us who plead Not Guilty to this charge?" And the judge conferred with his clerk and the woman from the city attorney's office, and they all shook their heads and mumbled, and when the huddle finally broke, the city attorney said, "No, your honor," and Judge Thorp said, "I'm afraid we have to refuse your request. But if you form yourselves into smaller groups, the court will do its best to accommodate you."

So Cora and Barbara and Dinah and Momo and I said yes, we wanted to stand trial together, and the clerk found another date in her big thick book and wrote down the date on carbon flimsies and gave us each a copy, and then we were set free to walk out onto the pavements of the city. Except that it took Momo and me two weeks of screaming and crying and going downtown every day to beat our heads against their walls before we got our kids back.

As soon as we were released, we went straight to Juvenile Detention but none of the clerks would give either of us a straight answer or even tell us if our children were there. *Come back tomorrow,* they said. I started yelling, and they threatened me, the big thick cop standing next to the clerk moved in on me. So Momo took me back to the commune, and we made tea and rubbed each other's backs. We did eventually get to sleep that night, but we were awake at five the next morning and downtown by seven-forty-five when the office opened. We brought their birth certificates and all our I.D., but we got the runaround again.

We found out later that Shaman and Shawana and Momo's daughters Dawn and Renée were placed with foster families some time on that second day, but none of the clerks would tell us where they were. They did say that the families had been kept together, so we could comfort ourselves with that, but the clerks wouldn't even let us pass along any clothes or toys.

"Shawana's big enough to care about what she wears. I hope they don't make her wear pedal pushers, she hates them."

"Dawn, too. She won't wear any pants."

The clerks were all young women with stony faces who chewed gum. Two of them had frizzy perms, one blonde and one light brown, and two had straight hair flipped at the ends. Their names were Karen, Karen, Kim, and Lisa.

"Don't any of you have kids?" Momo asked, but they just ignored her. "How can you be so cruel?" she said softly, and they went on filing.

Finally Lisa said, "Look, ma'am, we can't tell you anything. You'll have to go through the court placement officer."

One of the lawyers who does pro bono work for the Project talked to people he knew at City Hall, and they got through to the juvenile-placement office. In two weeks, the foster families let go of Shaman and Shawana, Dawn and Renée. We both had to fill out a mountain of papers about how many square feet of living space in our house and did our kids share a bedroom and had they had their shots, did their fathers have visitation rights, how many days were they absent from school.

"I wish you cared as much about the world they are going to grow up into," I said when I gave them back their mountain. "You know, if we don't stop the warmongers, we will all die."

"Then there's not much we can do, is there?" said the dumb placement officer, a young guy in a blazer with blow-combed hair.

We could hear the children's voices, and then they ran down the corridor and threw themselves at us, Shawana almost up to my shoulder. "Why didn't you come get us?" the kids asked, of course, and I broke down weeping and crying and told them how hard we had tried.

"Was it bad?" I kept asking them. "Was your foster family okay, did they give you enough to eat, they didn't paddle you, did they?"

"They were okay," Shawana finally said, "only they gave me this doofy polka-dot dress to wear to school, and I hated going to a new school. Mama, whyn't you come get us sooner?"

"I don't like instant pudding," said Shaman, "and I want my own bed back. Mama, don't get busted again, 'cause we'd have to go to jail."

CHAPTER 15

SERENA

It's a pretty weird world here on the far side of 1984. My mother is dying, and I am taking care of her, which is like a tape running backward from when she gave me life. She clings to this crazed idea about adopting a baby. My dad and I think she might have brain metastases.

Then there's Dinah. She comes to see my mom, and I have known this woman all my life, practically, and it's like she's a different person. She is totally in denial around this phantom baby thing. My mom asks her these pathetic questions, and she just says *yes, yes.*

When I was a little kid, she was a hippie and a rock-and-roll mama. Then when I was a teenager, she was a lesbian intellectual in a necktie. Then she married this snake of a guy and tried gracious living. Now she's like a beautiful piece of driftwood, smooth and silvery. And washed up.

She's sad about my mom, of course, and about her kids—two boys, younger than me. Joel is a total yuppie, and Amos, the musician, is incredibly handsome but a user, a manipulator. A friend of mine had a crush on him, and he used her, tried to get her to make these creepy phone calls to his other girls. She was a total groupie for about three weeks, but then the magic stopped.

My brother Seth tried to be friends with Amos. Amos has this wild, lost quality. Like while he's telling you about something rotten he did to some woman, he's laughing and showing his beautiful teeth, and all of a sudden it's like he's the victim, he's the one who got humiliated. He completely becomes a little lost boy. Where Joel has gone incredibly straight, he's a management intern, Ame is still flopping around with his band, trying to get a life. My mom would probably say I'm being too hard on them. Dinah can't stand them, I know. I've heard her say *My sons are real assholes.* But it seems to me, you can't just blow them off, I mean if your kids really do happen to *be* assholes.

It's a mystery, how people's kids turn out. I thought our neighbors' kids, Ilya and Kaia, would grow up to be total creeps, because I never liked their parents. Ilya was a little bully, he used to pinch my brother Seth until he howled. I did too, of course, but that's different. Ilya was a sneak. And Kaia had these spindly legs and stuck her finger in her mouth. When she was a little kid, she whined and she wore thick glasses, but she could hit a fly ball out of the back yard. I think if you can do something like that, you give up your whining rights. But they've turned out okay—Kaia's in law school and Ilya works for some union.

Joel and Amos, I don't know. Maybe they got their dad's values. We were practically raised with them when we were little. Then their dad wouldn't let them go to Zeke and Berry's school, this terrific experimental school where we studied ecology in the woods, along with history and economics and botany, and art and social history in museums, and learned Spanish and Swedish and Lakota from native speakers. Berry used to practice herbal medicine on us. That's when I got interested in healing. I went to their school for five years and

Seth for six. Maybe that's why we're so neat, and they're such jerks.

Because they *are* jerks. I remember a seder at Dinah's house when she was married to this greasy guy, King. He was an art teacher at Amos's school, and terrifically boring, although he was handsome if you didn't listen to him. Joel and Amos's dad is this big psychiatrist, president of a temple, Dr. Reuben Berns. King was not Jewish, he belonged to some weird cult. He used to go to these weird cult meetings—sometimes they lasted a whole weekend—and Dinah would be over at our house bitching to my mom. But she said he was always after her to express her Jewishness. I once heard her telling my mom, who isn't even Jewish herself, about how King wanted her to light candles on Shabbat, put a napkin on her head and wave her hands. She said it was because he was a very spiritual person, and then another time I heard her go, "Oh Cory, I've made a terrible mistake."

This particular seder I'm thinking of, I must have been in college and home for spring break. We almost always had these hard-line liberation seders with Kaia and Ilya's parents, Max and Einar. Seth always got to ask the Questions, we never said *Next year in Jerusalem* without saying *And to dwell in peace with our Muslim sisters and brothers.* Max and my dad were the only real Jews, but everybody got into it. They let us drink wine and the discussion always got really loud. It was fun. I liked it.

So I didn't want to go to Dinah's, but she had really bugged my mom. King wanted her to invite Reuben and his new family, but she wouldn't, and he was only satisfied when she got my mom to promise to bring our family. So there we are—I'm a student at the University of Chicago, my brother Seth would have been sixteen, Joel fifteen, Amos thirteen. Seth never was bar mitzvah, because our parents didn't push it and he didn't care. I think he would have liked the presents but he is not, repeat, *not,* a religious person. Neither am I.

Joel and Amos went to Hebrew school because of their dad and stepmother, who threw huge bashes for them, according to Seth.

"Please, please, come with us. This will be a cultural experience," said my mom. "You remember seders at grandma and grandpa's, don't you?"

I just barely did. Maybe twice in my life, we drove down to Florida to have Passover with my dad's parents and his sisters. I totally hated the whole thing, sticky hot Miami, my bratty New York cousins, my grandparents were way old, and my dad's sisters are complete witches, long pointy nails, voices like seagulls. So I said I hoped it would be a different kind of cultural experience.

Was it ever. King opened the door looking incredibly handsome in a shirt with full sleeves, black velvet trousers, and a black velvet yarmulke embroidered in gold. Dinah was gorgeous also, in a long velvet dress the color of amber. They looked like Fleetwood Mac. I just remember walking into her little house on a cold wet spring day, and they had a fire going and a white cloth on the dining-room table with all these glasses gleaming on it, reflecting the firelight. This guy, Norval Wise, was there that my parents know from the peace movement, standing by the table holding on to a glass of red wine for dear life.

While she was married to King, Dinah's house looked really good. She packed away some of her more doofy posters, Dorothy Day and Sojourner Truth, Dodo and Sojo, she called them, and hung a few of King's drawings on her walls. Her furniture was just these slender pieces in dark wood. There was a fluffy white rug on the living room floor, and we all sat on it, except for my dad because of his back.

Then we sat around the beautiful table. My mom brought gefilte fish and chopped liver, but before we could eat we had to get through the amazingly boring service, drinking a few drops of sweet wine and eating totally tasteless matzoh and reading stuff. Norval was the only one who could read the Hebrew, my dad has forgotten how. Amos read the Four Questions like he was on "The Price Is Right," and Joel and Seth got the giggles. I wished I had stayed home.

After the ceremony we ate a huge dinner and drank a lot of wine, and when the parents had coffee, the four of us went upstairs. I actually missed Ilya and Kaia. We went into Joel's room and watched something on TV, a "M.A.S.H." rerun. Joel kept getting off the bed to press his weights. He had this bulky musclebound body, his neck was too big for his head. We were all four on the bed for a while, then Amos slid onto the floor. Then he asked Seth if he wanted to play Atari. I looked through Joel's books, but there was nothing I wanted to read, just Nathaniel Branden, Erich von Daniken. I thought I'd go down and talk to the 'rents.

Joel grunted, and I had to ask him what he said. "Want to try something?"

"Like what?" I asked.

"I've got some coke. You ever do coke?"

"Come on, Joel," I said. "It's Passover." I was freaked.

"I know what it is," he said. "You want to do a few lines or not?"

I mean, I was curious. Kids in my dorm talked about it, especially these two girls from New York. One of them claimed to know another girl on the fourth floor, Jeanne the Cocaine Queen, who scored for everybody; she had a connection. But I never did it. In my experience, doctors' kids don't do a lot of drugs. Maybe because our parents tend to be such straight arrows. But I could be wrong. I mean, here was Joel, definitely a doctor's kid.

"Does your mom know about this?"

"Of course not, stupid."

I love it when people call me stupid. *Not,* as Amos would say.

"Or your dad?"

"What do *you* think? Be real."

"Where'd you get it?"

"You must be kidding." He looked straight at me. "Don't they have it in Illinois?"

"Of course they *have* it in Illinois. But you're still in *high* school."

"Didn't you guys do drugs in high school?"

"Dope. Mushrooms. Not much else. A little acid, maybe. Nothing hard."

"Times change." He went into the teensy bathroom he shared with Amos and came out with an amber plastic bottle like prescription drugs come in. He opened the child-proof cap.

"That's so no little kiddies get at this." He flashed me a fakey grin and took out a twist of paper. "Gimme your mirror."

"I don't have a mirror."

"Come on. Girls always have a mirror."

"Not me."

He looked disgusted and took a plaque off the wall, brown plastic, grained on one side to look like wood but totally smooth on the back. "We'll use my Junior Achievement Award."

He did the whole number, shook some powder out in a little pile, cut the pile into four lines with a razor blade, rolled up a ten-dollar bill and snorted a line up each nostril. Then he held it out to me, and I did, too—although I turned the bill around, not wanting to stick the same end in my nostril. Perhaps the word *snot-nosed* rings a bell.

"What would King say? Or Norv?"

"Norv is a fucking derelict. Seriously. He never has any money. And King Nerd Artiste had better keep his mouth shut. Seriously. I don't know how much more of him I can take."

"Your mom's okay, though. I really love Dinah."

268

Cocaine makes you very mellow very quickly, and then you get silly and charming, and then you get uptight.

"Dinah's a slut." He didn't sound charming, he sounded pissed.

"Come on, Joel. She's your mom."

"She better stay out of my life." He rocked back on the bed and seized his ankles, then did a backflip onto the floor. He opened his arms and took a little bow, and I could swear I heard a trombone go *Da-daa!*

"When the Angel of the Lord passes over Minneapolis tonight, there'll be a little dab of coke on your door to fool Herod's soldiers."

"We forgot to leave a line for the prophet Elijah."

"Joel! We should give some to everyone, my mom, your mom, my dad, Norv, King, Seth, Amos—and then leave a line for the proph'."

He went into the bathroom and knocked on Amos' door. "You guys better get in here." And when they came in sort of sheepish, Joel shook out another little pile and cut some more lines like a big man and said, "Here, you want a snort?"

Seth shook his head. After Amos did his little lines he blotted up some stray grains and rubbed them on his upper gum. Thirteen years old, and it wasn't his first time, either. He was beautiful even at that awkward age, and he gave me a lovely smile when he snorted the cocaine, his little white satin yarmulke still bobbypinned to his thick dark hair.

Everything was silly and wonderful for a few minutes. We played Crazy Eights and then Strip Crazy Eights, and then Joel said, "Anybody want some smoke?"

"I'm thirsty," said Amos, and Seth, who was straight, went down and brought up some cans of Pepsi, kosher for Passover. Meanwhile, Joel rolled some reefer. I mean, here are my mom's best friend's children doing crimes upstairs from a family holiday party, while their stepdad is some kind of fundamentalist.

Seth and I didn't smoke any reefer, but Joel and Amos did.

"They're just killing brain cells downstairs with their drug of choice," said Joel. He had been losing and was stripped down to his underwear, that sexy Calvin Klein stuff.

"Does your dad let you do this?" asked Seth, and Amos said of course not, Reuben was even more of a straight arrow than King. He and Cynthia didn't let them drink wine with their meals or anything. So Seth goes, "Well, where'd you get it?"

"You must be kidding," Joel said. "It's all over my school."

"Yeah," Amos said. "I'm in the middle school, and it's even all over us, like a cheap suit."

"How much does it cost?" asked Seth, who is very practical.

"The blow? A hundred for a quarter gram," said Joel. "It's a really frivolous drug." The way he said that, I knew he'd heard someone else say it, maybe the older kid who sold it to him.

"Not a good old-fashioned, hard-working drug," I said. "Like penicillin or pot."

"That's right," Joel said. "Except my dad says they used to allow coke to be used medicinally. And they haven't even begun to learn about the medical potential of pot. You know THC, tetrahydrocannabinol, that's the active principle of marijuana? They've synthesized it, and it's being used in clinical trials, my dad says. It controls nausea in cancer patients on chemotherapy."

"My brother knows so much," Amos said. "How much does my brother know? He knows so much that—"

"Shut up," Joel said, "or I'll paste you in the mouth."

I lost the next hand, and I had to take my sweater off. And this is really sick, except I guess I was still stoned: I was kind of flirting with Amos, this funny, beautiful little kid. I thought Joel was flirting with me because he wanted to get over on my brother Seth, but he was totally repulsive to me. You know how some guys get big muscles and body hair sort of before they're ready for it? Most boys go through puberty later than most girls, but some get it really early, like Joel. But I was feeling really warm about his little brother.

So of course, as soon as I'm sitting in my bra, Joel says he wants to arm-wrestle. And then leg-wrestle. And he beat Ame and Seth both, pushed them off the bed and onto the floor. "You have to get out now," he said, "while I wrestle Serena," and he hustles them out and locks his room door.

It was really warm in Joel's room, which was all decorated in browns and dark reds. When Joel was leg-wrestling, I could smell the talcum powder his mom makes him put in his crotch. "Oh no you don't," I said and I got off the bed.

"Oh yes I do," he said, and he pushed me back down. "Goddamn it, Serena, you can't sit around in your bra and expect to get away with it. Guys get aroused, you know," and he's got this boner and he's trying to get on top of me.

I can hear Seth and Ame giggling at the keyhole, and I start to giggle too. "Joel, you are such a weenie. You think I'm going to let some little high-school kid into my pants for a couple of lines?" And I try to push him away, but I'm weak with laughter. He heaves himself on top of me and jerks his body a couple of times, and I think he must have come in his Calvin Kleins. Next thing I know, he's rolling off me, and I can't see his face, but the back of his neck is bright red under the royal blue satin yarmulke.

"What's going on up there?" King calls in this Brady Bunch voice. "You young people are awfully quiet," and Seth and Amos sing out, "Oh nothing, we're playing cards," and our dad calls up, "We're planning to split in ten or fifteen minutes, that suit you?" and Seth goes, "Fine" and Amos goes, "Aw, can't you stay overnight?" and that starts me giggling again, and Joel has been fighting his way into his trousers, and he finally gets one leg into each trouser leg and zips up his fly.

"Slut," he hisses.

I ignore him while I try to find my clothes, but I am getting totally annoyed. He snatches away pieces of my clothing until I grab his hand.

"Just what are you doing?"

He pulls me over and kisses me hard somewhere between my nose and chin, but I can tell he has never done this before, because his teeth get in the way. I pull away from him, and he snarls *Slut* one more time. I find my sweater and unlock the door, and our little brothers tumble into the room, screaming, "We saw! We saw!"

"Act your age," I say to Seth, and I go into Dinah's room to straighten my hair. Her bedroom has walls the color of cinnamon drops and a big white comforter on a king-size bed—not bad, King-size—and I try to chase the last of the cocaine giggles, but Joel's dumbness has brought me down totally. The little weenie tried to rape me.

By the time I go downstairs, no one can tell I've taken anything. We say goodbye, and on the way home my dad goes "Absolutely the last time," and my mom goes, "Somehow I don't think it's going to be a problem," and I go, "Are they going to get divorced?" and Seth goes, "Ame really can't stand King."

I couldn't sleep that night. That was the only time I ever did coke, but I think Dinah's boys still do it—a lot, from what I hear. Joel is pretty successful. He lives in Chicago, but some of my friends see him when he comes up to Minneapolis. Seth was friendly with Amos for a while; after Ame graduated from high school, he didn't know what he wanted to do next, and Seth suggested they should go to Israel and work for a while picking grapefruit or avocados. But it didn't work out. I've never heard his band, but Seth says it's pretty primitive.

I told my mom what happened, more or less, and she told me that after we went upstairs that night, they broke out the brandy and liqueurs, this stuff called Sabra, and King said how much he always admired Jewish people because of their strong family values, and Dinah cut her a look.

Norval laughed at him and said, "Me, too. It's always nice for a Jewish bachelor like me to have some Jewish friends, some place to spend the holidays."

A couple months later, when I made a flying visit home, Dinah had kicked him and his drawings out of her house, and Dodo and Sojo were back up on the walls. But she changed: she stopped coloring her hair and started looking like this sculptural object or some tragic heroine.

"You're not into cocaine, are you, darling?" asked my mom, and I could tell her *No* with a clear conscience.

CHAPTER 16

DINAH

I bob like a fishing lure at Cory's doorstep, trying to catch health for her, or I go in and read magazines and pet the ancient dog. About once a day, I get up the nerve to go into her room, and she always says she's glad to see me, but Jesus, she looks like she's wearing an age mask, collodion and rubber cement. I want to get out the solvent, rip her wrinkles off, pull the fake grayish wisps off her scalp and comb out her glorious hair. I want to kill her for dying.

"Hiya, kiddo," she croaks. "How's life with Leaf?" She gets a kick out of that.

"Limited," I say, and she involves me in some insane discussion, like whether I think she should start taking five thousand milligrams of acerola vitamin C at the same time as her multivitamins.

"I don't know, what does Sydney say? What does Jerry say?"

She lifts one bony little claw from the bedspread and says, "You know doctors don't know shit about health, they just understand disease. We're talking wellness here."

Besides the wheelchair, she has a hoist for her bath. Once

I make myself help Serena bathe her. She tells me to run the water just a little warmer than room temp, tepid, really, the idea is to avoid extremes. I have to turn off all my feelings, tenderness and disgust, make myself blank. Cory helps by not talking while we literally get her ass in the sling, crank up the hoist, and roll her over to the bathroom, then I spread a plastic bath sheet in the tub and Serena cranks her down into it and gently soaps her arms and legs. They have gone all flat, the strong arms, the long legs; her muscles have atrophied in spite of the physiotherapy exercises.

Her frail chest sports an x-ray tan and the big diagonal scar. She has lost so much weight that her right breast hangs like a collapsing balloon. Her freckled back looks like a turtle's shell because the ridge of her spine is so prominent. Her curly golden pubic hair is all gone except for a couple of colorless threads, and the skin of her belly droops.

"Now help me pat her dry," says Serena, and I can't help thinking she is hollow, fragile as an eggshell, and if I pat too hard I could crack her. I pull a fresh nightgown from her drawer. We're awkward getting it over her head, and she says, "Ow, you guys."

When we crank her back into bed she's exhausted, but she says, "Like the duds?" with an old lift to her eyebrow. Her sisters-in-law have sent her beautiful nightgowns, silky Swiss batiste, handkerchief linen, and elegant dressing gowns in her colors: deep blues and greens, rose and purple and gold.

I can't talk to Jerry. I'm too choked up. But when I get back home, I bitch at Leaf.

*

She still talks about her baby, but even *I* know she is dying. It's as though the baby fantasy is her grab-handle onto life. I haven't been able to tell her the truth.

Jerry is furious with me. Right after I got back from Guatemala, he asked me what was going on, and I eased out of the question. I gave him back seven thousand dollars, and I said, "We made some progress. This lawyer's keeping an eye out."

"Jesus Christ, Dinah. *Look at her.* This is loco, dingaling. She can't take care of a baby. It's not about money, but you've got to tell her no. You're not doing her any favor."

But I couldn't.

⬗

After her last course of chemo, Cora says she wants to go out and see Thelma. She doesn't say *one last time,* but she doesn't have to. So we drive to Wisconsin on a blue November day, the kind that's an upper Midwest specialty: the air tight as a clean pillow, sky blue as a movie, gold stubble in the fields, smoky smell of autumn. A day that brings to mind pheasants and deer, winy apples, black coffee from a thermos. Most of the birds are flown and October frost has killed the mosquitoes and midges, and for a few days the sun lays kisses on the land, bedtime kisses before mama goes south and tucks us up for winter.

I drive because Cory needs to sleep at unpredictable times. I almost miss the exit off the Interstate; my Toyota doesn't know the way to Prairie Farm the way my cars did in the sixties and seventies, before the freeway. I haven't been out there in years, but I try to keep track of the Kjellstroms.

Right around the time Duke was diagnosed as a schizophrenic, Roy left Thelma for some younger woman. Thelma used to come up to the Cities all the time while Duke was in the hospital, but once they discharged him I only saw her at demos. I haven't seen her at all since Cory got sick.

I see Monette and her girlfriend sometimes. She told me the old farmhouse blew down in a tornado last summer. Holly got married and moved to Davenport, Iowa. Ian came out as a gay man and lives the life of a full-time movement organizer in northern Wisconsin. Duke lives on the streets, now, I think, or in a room somewhere. Every once in a while, someone tells me they've seen him.

Carl, of course, lives in Guatemala, where he went to work with Sister, who died of leukemia last summer before I went down to try to get the baby for Cory. Sister flew home last winter and was diagnosed, then went back to die in San Onofrio, the village where she worked. Carl was with her when she died.

I figure Cory wants to talk about her illness with Thelma, so I don't bring it up on the drive down. Like not mentioning there's a warthog on the hood. I ask her how Seth is.

"Great."

"What about the thing with Persimmon?"

"I don't know, honey. It's their life." After a minute she adds, "He's probably my favorite man in the world, right now."

"Oh, Cory, I wish I felt that way about one of my sons! Joel's a cold fish. And Ame is such a sleaze. He's still playing us off against each other. He doesn't make any money with that awful band, and he bounces checks and borrows from me, and if I don't give it to him, he hits up Reuben."

"You're hard on them, Dinah. Reuben can afford it."

"He can afford it a lot better than I can. But he's mean, you know. Or maybe he's just smart. Anyway he doesn't often lend him the dough. So then he hits up Joel. Joel's still a soft touch, thank the Goddess. Ame is probably the only person who can get to him."

"How's Joel doing?"

"He's fine, he's a success. I just don't like to be around him."

"He got a girl?"

"Guess so. He doesn't tell me much, but Reuben drops hints that reach me in devious ways."

I have to slow down for one of those large frail rigs you see on country roads at haying time. They travel about fifteen miles an hour, but they're never on the road long. I don't

mind. They give me a chance to look at the familiar landscape, today throbbing with *last time, last time.*

"Maybe you'll get some grandkids out of him."

"I doubt it. It's a hoot, really, how the news gets to me—
Reuben tells Amos that Joel's seeing some woman who's a
commodities trader, and Amos tells me. Or Joel tells Amos
that they're going away on vacation together, and Ame tells
Reuben, who tells Cynthia, and then I run into her someplace
and she tells me."

The rig turns off onto a gravel road, the driver waving
gaily.

"I just think I really blew it with them."

"You are one crazy dame, Dinah. They're healthy, they're
grown. You were not the only person in the world for them,
you know?"

"I know. But still."

She sighs. "I'd like some grandchildren for the baby to
play with." Then she slips into a doze, snoring softly. We
drive in silence for a couple of miles, around the right-angle
curve on County Road V that passes a tall windmill whose
blades are choked with vines. A lot of the old farms in Burnett
County have a windmill standing somewhere, but I've never
seen one working.

I've adopted that particular one, planted where the road
turns and the land dips below the grade and you can see a
patchwork of field and meadow, woods and yard, sloping
down on one side to a line of deep green woods and up on
the other to gentle hills, tan and golden and dark red. My
windmill stands close to the road between a couple of weath-
ered empty sheds, and now that the leaves have fallen off the
wild pumpkin vines that run from the ground up to the frozen
blades, they look like the strings of a bass. That stilled wheel
is one of my images for Prairie Farm.

Cory jerks forward a little with her mouth open, squinting
in the sunlight. We're on the hairpin-curve part of V where

the road switches back under the bluffs. The locals take those curves at high speed, but Cory and I always slow down for them, past the mulberry tree with a trunk thick as a silo, past the muddy Holsteins in their feedlot. The husband of the young widow Roy Kjellstrom left Thelma for crashed up on one of those curves.

I was living with Annie at the time. Duke finally left my house after Joel attacked him with a pair of scissors. It was a pretty awful scene, Duke, thin as a scarecrow, flapping around the dining-room table, trying to get away from red-faced Joel.

"Okay, okay, man, you bet I'm splittin', you are the anti-Duke, man, one look at you and I shoulda known–"

From Joel's point of view, I did everything wrong. He was the wrong age when I left Reuben; he never really bonded with a man. He treated Carl and Duke both like they were big brothers who got to sleep with mom. He ignored Annie when I was with her, never talked to her, looked past her at dinner or ate with his head down. And he hated King. So now he gets back at me by growing up to be just like his dad. At least he's not a doctor, but otherwise he's exactly like Reuben, down to the way he snickers in the back of his nose.

I'm an expert, by now, at unfolding the wheelchair and holding it so Cory can slide in, but Thelma's house has little flights of stairs up to both doors, front and back. "No, no," Cory brushes away my helping hands. "I can manage."

She pulls herself up the four steps to the back door while Thelma holds it open, then they fall into a big hug. I fold the chair and lean it against the side of the steps because I think she'll need it when we leave, even to save her a dozen steps to the car door. A few brown leaves scud through the sere grass in Thelma's neatly raked yard.

Her kitchen looks as clean as ever and smells of oilcloth and buttermilk.

"Goodness, Thelma, I haven't been out here since—since—"

"Since before Duke went crazy. I know. It's good to see you."

We unwrap the sticky buns we bought at Bark's Bakery in Baldwin ("Biggest Little Town in Wisconsin") while Thelma puts up a pot of coffee. I feel split, watching myself play the role of Dinah. *Are you going to tell her the treatment's not going well?* I ask Cory silently. *You can't not mention it. You've got to say something.*

"How's it going?" Thelma asks. "The therapy and all. Hope they got all the cancer." She shakes her head in commiseration.

"Me, too."

"We had a letter from Ingvar after Sister died. Says them power lines could a gave her the leukemia."

We nod. Ian works with a grassroots organization trying to get the U.S. Navy to remove the Extremely Low Frequency power line it has strung across the northern face of our country. The ELF line carries impulses so faint you'd think they were useless, but Ian's group knows they can send and receive signals to nuclear submarines. Much higher rates of birth defects and cancers come to families living along the power lines. Ian and his people collect information on cows' miscarriages, crop failures, human diseases, and everything else they suspect might be influenced by ELF's magnetic field.

"So th'other girls might get it too. Or me. Or the boys."

The coffee drips and the clock ticks. "Well," says Cora, "everybody has to die of something."

Thelma bursts out laughing. "Ain't you the cheerful one!"

"I mean it, Thelma. Having cancer gives you a whole new perspective. But I'm going to beat this one. Did I tell you I'm adopting a baby?"

"No! Are you?"

"Yup. A Guatemalan child. Dinah's helping me."

Thelma darts her eyes at me, but I look down. "I did go there last summer, but we couldn't work it out. There's a lawyer working on it."

"Soon as I get my strength up," smiles Cora.

Thelma looks embarrassed. "Say, you didn't get to visit Carl, did you? Down there?"

"I couldn't. I thought about it, but I couldn't."

She nods, then shuts that topic and turns back to Cora. "So, tell me what them vets got in mind for you now."

Cory sketches the details of chemotherapy. "And this one ghastly surgeon told me if I was his wife he'd advise me to lose the other breast, to cut down the chance of tumor there. Can you believe it?"

"Ah, them vets don't know nothing, do they? Unless they're like Jerry and *know* they don't know. Mostly they get so puffed up they don't ever tell you what they can't understand."

She gets up to fetch the coffeepot. "You both take cream, don't you?"

Cory says not any more, the vets told her fat was bad for her. *This is really happening. I am sitting here with my two best friends talking about disease and death, here in this kitchen.* Thelma could make me feel like a horrible hypocrite, a randy slut prancing around with a lead fastened to my clit. But then she'd do some dumb, generous thing, and I'd fall in love with her all over again.

"So, Dinah, cat got your tongue?"

"Yup."

"You still with the Project?"

"Maureen and Persimmon have pretty much taken it over," says Cora. "That's the way it should be, bless 'em."

"Bless you too, Cory. All these years. It's hard for me to get to the Cities, but I still watch for you on TV."

I miss my lovers: Crater, Carl, Duke, Cora, Annie, Thelma, King. One by one, they leave me.

"Ever hear from Duke?" I finally ask, and I get a mean thrill of pleasure when Thelma's face falls. She has been keeping it up for us, a cheerful facade. She must get lonely, living alone. She looks old, her fine skin lined and gathered, her blue eyes watering.

"He calls ever' once in a while," she says, "usually about four in the morning, you know how he is, how he got to be. He only calls when he's on the upswing, tells me ever'thing's great. Sister explained all about his sickness, how his brain don't make the right chemicals and that, but he does all right with the meds. I ask him does he take his meds and he tells me he has a handle on that."

She laughs her old laugh but her eyes stay sad. "Say, my real problem's Gramma. You mind if I talk about her?"

We say of course not.

"It ain't that I don't like my mother," she says, and her face colors. "I love her a lot. I go to see her couple-three times a week, now that she's in the Pioneer Home over to Boyceville. But see, Gramma's from another generation. Sometimes she'll say things—like about Monette she'll say, 'I don't see no grandkids coming out of that one,' and I'll say, 'No, you know, mama, she don't love men. She likes 'em, but she lives with a woman, and she likes it that way,' and Gramma says, 'It's against nature,' and I says, 'Well I don't know about that so much, you see a lot of things in nature, bulls and roosters too, mount anything holds still for 'em,' and Gramma says, 'You got such a mouth on you, got a answer for ever'thing, that's your whole trouble.' And I come away feeling bad."

Cory gazes raptly at her and nods in sympathy.

"Gramma never forgets, she always brings up how Donald ain't right in the head. 'Why ain't he gone to college like the rest?' she hollers, and I tell her it's because he's *too* smart, places round here couldn't teach him nothing and he can't afford to go noplace that can. 'If he was that smart they'd pay him to come,' she says. 'They'd pay him to come.' She gets all agitated, and they have to give her a pill.

"Now I hate it when they drug her, but what are they going to do? She's a ornery old lady and they're understaffed. They got some high-school kids working as aides after school, helping the residents wash their hair or reading to 'em, but during the day it's just the one nurse and the housekeeping staff and a couple of LPNs, they have their hands full changing the incontinent ones, making beds and giving baths. They keep her clean, I'll give the Pioneer Home credit for that, but I wish they could do something for her so she didn't get so cranky. It's boring, being in a home.

"I guess I'd rather have her ornery than drugged up, but it ain't my choice to make. And then she starts in on Roy. 'Course, I do think Roy did a very foolish thing takin' up with Jaylene Gilbertson over to Rice Lake, she's young enough to be his daughter, but never mind. You remember—it was right around the time Donald went into the hospital, and just after Monette come out to us that she was gay—though I suspected before that she was not the marrying kind—and I think maybe he needed some more reassurance in the man department than he could get from me. We been together a long time."

She wiped her eyes and drank her coffee. "Jaylene was working part-time in the feed store that Stan Gilbertson left her when he hit that iced-up curve on County Road V three years ago, and she's a big, good-looking woman. So, even though he had no reason to go to no feed store, Roy was driving over to Rice Lake couple-three times a week. And you think Gramma ever lets me forget that?

"'He's no good,' she says, forgetting that he's supported these six kids and two of 'em not his, forgetting that he's a real good man, don't drink to excess, never hit me, or the kids beyond what was normal, a loving father and always welcomed 'em home when they had to come home. Proud of Carl and Ingvar both, although both of them was in prison at different times for their beliefs, proud as a peacock when Holly got her teaching certificate.

"Proud of Sister going to Guatemala, even though he always said he couldn't pronounce the name of the country where she was, guacamole or something, and always good to me. Even when he was sneaking off to drive eighty miles round-trip to see Jaylene Gilbertson, he was good to me, so I can't stand for Gramma to call him no good, and then I kind of get into it with her. 'He just follows his pecker round the country,' she says, 'before you was married, he was after everything in skirts in five counties and all the way up to Tomahawk.'

"'How come you know so much?' I says, and then I feel bad to be yelling at a old woman that can't even leave the grounds of the Pioneer Home by herself. She carried me and nursed me and sewed my good dresses when I was in high school, taught me to cook and can and crochet, clean fish, darn socks, and make head cheese though I haven't done too much of that in twenty years or more."

Cory nods and smiles. I'm grateful that Thelma is doing all the talking.

"When I married Sister and Carl's dad, she never said a word, though anyone could see it wasn't going to work. He was a good-looking man but kind of a starter he'd start one job, then start another, never finished anything. We was not a good match. He left me the first time after Sister was born, then he run off for good after Carl come. Gramma surely loved Carl, though, said he'd grow up to be a senator or president. Everything he did just tickled her—rolling over, sitting up, peeing in his little potty. The first year I was alone with them two kids, she was always coming over with a quart of stringbeans or a apple pie, and when they slaughtered a cow she wrapped up some of the meat and kept it out of their locker, brought it over so we'd have food.

"It's true, she never liked Roy, especially the organic

farming part. 'I don't hold with his ideas,' she'd say. But that's all she ever said until lately. She wasn't so thrilled about my other kids, but I just thought maybe the novelty wore off. Only one can ever be your first grandson.

"She's my mother, and she done a lot for me, but I just hate for her to go after Roy like that. I'm kinda tender on the subject myself, but I try to keep quiet and let her have her say. I think of what it's like for her to be there in the Pioneer Home day in day out, year after year, with no one to talk to but the ones that are even older and worse off than her. 'Salisbury steak tonight,' she'll say when I get up to go, or 'Chicken pot pie. They let the bottom crust get all soggy, they don't know to brush it with shortnin' before the fillin' goes in, and when you try to tell 'em how to do it right they just don't listen.'"

She fell silent, gazing into the distance.

"That's how it is," says Cora. "Sometimes you trade places. Serena's changing my diapers now. Soon I'll be changing our new baby."

"I could take the stuff about Roy if she'd stay off of Donald."

"Oh Thel, it must be so hard," says Cora, "Especially now Sarah has died. But you have four other beautiful people. Poor Duke."

"Poor Duke. Never could get used to that name."

"Poor Duke," I say. "He was like Tammuz, you know—a young corn god, all golden silk, swaying in the wind."

Thelma wipes her eyes again, pours more coffee. "Wherever he's gone, it's beyond me now."

He doesn't call me, but I won't tell her that. I plunge into my loss, chewing over ancient sexual triumphs. I'm glad I can get at Thelma with her clean counters, her tall sons and daughters, her healthy breasts.

Cora's eyes are hot. "See, Thel, I want another chance. That's why I'm going to get this Central American baby."

Thelma flushes. "It's a beautiful dream," she says. "You really think you're going to get strong enough? I don't know that *I* could take care of a baby these days." She laughs uncomfortably.

"Yes. Yes, I do. I have to. One more crack at it."

"The kids you have are terrific," Thelma says.

"I know. I know they are. We should have had six, like you. I can taste how much I want her."

"Gotta be a heifer, huh?"

Cory looks confused. I can't stand it. "Cory, I didn't tell you the truth. There isn't going to be any baby. I wasted your money, threw away three thousand dollars. The lawyer is a creep. The baby he found for me died. I can't go back. I fucked up. I couldn't tell you. I thought—"

But I'm shaking too hard to say *I thought you'd realize how impossible this whole scheme was.*

Thelma's jaw drops, then she shuts her mouth. Cory slumps forward at the table. I'm gasping for breath. It gets so quiet I can hear the hum of the freezer down in Thelma's basement.

After a while Cory lifts her head, and her face looks old, beige. "I don't believe you, Dinah. Why would you do that?"

My teeth are chattering.

"This was my last delusion," she says, her eyes gone dull

She sleeps all the way back to Minneapolis, and when I help her out of the car, she says, "Poor Dinah. Poor silly bitch."

I wheel her up the walk and then up the ramp Jerry had poured next to their front steps, being careful not to bang her foot. Inside, I help her off with her jacket and scarf, keeping my eyes down. This is the worst moment of my life. I want to die.

Her eyes have sunk deep into her head, somewhere behind her face. "Why?" she says. "Why did you let me drivel on if you knew all the time there wasn't going to be any baby?"

I can't answer. I look at her and start to cry. I put my arms around her waist and bury my head in her lap and sob and sob. After a minute her hot dry hand smooths my hair. "Poor silly bitch," she says. "Poor Dinah."

Then I stop crying. "I couldn't tell you because I wanted so much for you to get well, and I thought if I told you there wasn't going to be a baby it would be—it would be like giving in. I don't want you to be as sick as you are. I want you to be well. I thought it would help you, help you to fight, help you to get well."

Her hand trembles like a bird. "I trusted you, kiddo. And you raked me over."

The phone rings. "Let it ring," she says. "The machine will pick it up."

I help her to the sofa and turn on the lamps. "Do you want me to go?"

"No. I want to know things. Was there ever a baby, really? Or a lawyer? What did you *do* down there? What happened to the money?" She speaks slowly and carefully. So I tell her the whole shitty story: Guate, the rain, Basket, the scabby baby, the Earmanns and O'Donnells, the traffic in children, the bright red gums, the open sewers.

"I was ashamed, darling, scared and ashamed. I'm not good at fear and shame. I couldn't—I couldn't—"

"You couldn't deal. Poor, poor fucked-up Dinah."

"Ah, Jesus, Cory!"

"Stay with me now, honey. I need you, warts and all."

"Warts! Cory, I'm a hideous monster."

"Don't flatter yourself, kiddo."

So I take her in my arms, and she falls asleep, her breath hot against my shoulder. The furnace clicks on and Jean Harlow pads in, whining. Jerry finds us there when he comes home.

Next morning, I have nothing to do, nowhere to go. Before she goes to work, Leaf asks me what happened, and I tell her. "Listen, don't let your shit keep you from being with her," she says. "Cora needs you. You go on over there, and have a good day. Cora, too."

"She'll never have another good day," I grump, "or me either. She's dying, Leaf, and I let her down, and it fucking bugs me."

"Well, I hope she has a good death. Don't you?"

"I don't want to let her go."

"It isn't up to you."

Then I yell at her not to talk to me like that, she's only thirty-seven, and she opens her arms and hugs me tenderly.

"Anyone you love, I love," she says, which has got to be bullshit. Leaf is one of these good people, like Serena or Shawana. I don't know. Maybe the shit in the milk, strontium, or the fluoride or something, made our kids good. Maybe, if it doesn't kill you or drive you nuts, like Sister or Duke, it sanctifies you.

I don't hang out at the Bookbinders' all the time. I still do the Friday-morning picket with Persimmon and Maureen and sometimes Barbara. I still go to meetings of the peace-and-justice coalition, and I write press releases and help to plan actions. Max wins her school-board seat. "Just in time," I grouse to Leaf, "since none of us has kids in school any more."

"Hey," says my insufferable, precious love, whose pink tongue is slick and eager as a puppy's, *"someone's* got kids in school."

Then the weather turns cold, and the president announces he is sending National Guard units to Central America for maneuvers. "We know what he has in mind,"

Maureen says. She explains that our fresh-faced national guards will be teaching the latest techniques of counter-insurgency to boys with downy upper lips in Guatemala, Salvador, and Honduras, dewy novices who have already been supplied with weapons by some of the president's friends.

We pressure our governor to file suit against the federal government, to stop them from sending any Minnesota National Guard units. A federal court judge appointed by Nixon refuses to grant the injunction, and in January, we get word that a unit will be taking off on the nineteenth from the Air National Guard base at Fort Snelling, out near the airport.

Cory has had another course of radiation, and after feeling very sick she rallies and tells Jerry she's going to go to this demo. "He didn't even argue," she tells me, sitting on her living-room sofa in an azalea-pink velour caftan from Bloomingdale's, her head wrapped in a silk turban of rose, violet, and blue. "That's a bad sign, right? Well, if I'm going to die, it might as well be at an action."

"I love the idea, but maybe it's a little messy for the rest of us."

"I didn't even think of that. Sure, you don't want to have to pack a stiff along. Although—"

"Although—" and we chime the words together, "—if we're packing a stiff, maybe we won't get busted!"

The coalition plans the demo. I go to meetings, but my mind wanders. I can't stop my thoughts jogging along the old circular track: Cory's dying. It's not fair. We've done nothing, succeeded at nothing; we can't even keep her alive. All our jumping up and down has been useless. The winter sunlight is old. The world is old. I feel old. Old and worthless. Nothing I've ever done has come to anything—my marriages were disasters, my kids are assholes, I betrayed the people I love. I've poured my energy into experimental theater and the peace movement, futile pursuits if there ever were any. Then what's the point—why do we keep on going through the motions? Because it's better than not. But Cory's dying, and it's not fair.

*

A week before the demo, Jerry calls to ask if I'll drive. "I think we should have two cars, just in case," he says. "You never know."

When I call her to arrange pickup times, Persimmon says, "She's dying of the treatment, don't you think? They give her chemo. It destroys her immunity. They give her radiation, that they don't really even know *what* it does, except make her nauseous—"

"So, doctor, what would *you* do?"

She sighs. "It's complicated, you know? I mean, you have to believe in the treatment, or it won't work. Might not work anyway, but if you don't believe in it on a really deep level, it certainly won't."

"So what? What?"

"Oh, Dinah, you know. I'd have her eat macrobiotically, and I'd give her megavitamins. She'd do a lot of meditating and focusing. I'd get help from other healers. But none of that would do any good if she didn't believe in it."

"I don't think she believes in the stuff she's getting now."

"Well, that's the problem. I mean, Cory's pretty much of a wholistic person."

"She lives the best life of anyone I know. And she does a lot of meditating and focusing."

"Sure. She's really integrated, she's just attached to all that Western medicine."

"Her husband's a doctor, for Christ's sake."

Now I know who gave her the idea of the daily five thousand milligrams of vitamin C. We all want to be in her death.

January nineteenth, the night of the action, is clear and very cold, a typical Minnesota winter night. Lots of snow fell in December, and now the roads are rutted ice. Maureen brings a muskrat coat with a torn lining that someone donated to St. Savior's.

"Cory would never wear fur if she was well," she says, "but this is a special time, don't you think?"

At the Bookbinders', Maureen and I get to wrap Cory in the coat, then we put a knitted cap on her skull and drape a cashmere scarf over it. Layers of socks and gloves with astro-nautical insulation to protect her precious extremities, rugs and shawls for tucking in around her. Then Jerry carries her down the neatly shoveled walk and out to their van, and I bring the folding wheelchair. We form a convoy and set off to pick up Persimmon and Shawana. Serena is on hospital duty. Shaman is babysitting Abdul-Aziz. "His first real babysitting job, you don't think he's too young, do you?"

"No, of course not, Joel babysat with Amos when he was ten."

Shawana is so excited to be going out with the grownups at ten o'clock on a winter night that energy radiates from her little body in its down jacket and moon boots. At Fort Snelling, the airfield looks like a sea of frozen mud stretching off into the darkness beyond the reach of lights. Jerry and I unload the others, then we have to cruise for miles to find parking space.

"Good omen," he says as we stride back toward the airfield. "Should be lotsa folks out."

"Cold enough."

"Those bastards. They never jerk our chains in good weather."

"'Course, good weather here is rainy season down there. I mean, I suppose right now is ideal weather for whatever they have in mind."

"Bastards."

I have too much to say to Jerry ever to want to talk with him.

When we get back to the airfield, more folks are massing.

Cars keep pulling up and thickly wadded bodies keep emerging, clumsy mittens lofting signs: *U.S. Out of North America, No Taxes for War, Contras* with the diagonal line through. I can't see beyond the lights, but in the lurid space defined by the road, the hangar, and the chain-link fence separating us from the runways, I estimate we are a couple hundred peaceful, angry souls. Maureen has taken charge of Cora's chair, maneuvering it over the bumpy frozen ground. Persimmon and Shawana wear coverings made out of giant black plastic garbage bags.

"What are those supposed to be?" asks Maureen.

"Mostly they keep us warm," laughs Persimmon, but Shawana says, "And they're supposed to remind you of body bags."

"Because I don't like to see people wrapped up like garbage," Maureen says. "We're not garbage."

Shawana can't contain herself. "Say, Maureen, did you know Dow Chemical makes these? And that's the same company that made that napalm they used in Vietnam?"

*

There's a lot of confused milling around in the cold and dark. Norval Wise is the designated coordinator for this action, so I feel like we're safe. Norv doesn't do crazy things. A couple of black-and-whites have pulled up across the highway with their motors running, so the cops inside can stay warm. I watch the hydrocarbons belching out of their tailpipes into the black crystal of the night. They'll blame us for the extra pollution. And there's the inevitable school bus churning out destruction of the ozone. They'll put anyone they arrest into the bus and take them wherever they're going to book them. Some of us intend to go over that chain-link fence onto the runways and block the transport planes with our bodies.

"Don't you think I could do it if you all lifted?" says Cory.

"I mean once you get me to the top, I can just roll down the other side. It would make such good TV. 'Minnesota National Guard Runs Over Protester in Wheelchair.'"

Maureen and I cackle. A couple of people around us look offended. Through its PA system, the police car tells us to disperse. It tells us we're on U.S. government property (we yell back, "We *are* the U.S. government! It's *our* property!"), and then it tells us we have been warned. If we don't heed the warning, we will be subject to arrest. I never cease to marvel at how bureaucratic these dudes are. If they can say it in fourteen words, they'll never say it in six. Not— *Leave or we will arrest you,* but: *All who do not obey our warning to disperse will be subject to arrest.*

Our faces are livid in the bright lights, and for ten or fifteen minutes we march, chant, pray, and visit with each other, not dispersing but stamping our feet and admiring our blown-out breath. It's very cold, a deadly deep-freeze cold that seems to bloom from the darkness, the way a lump of coal will bloom if you put salt on it. Deep cold, the cold of dead stars. Cora's face is pale, but in their shadowed hollows her eyes sparkle. I have to grit my teeth to keep from fussing at her, straightening her shawls.

Norv says something into the bullhorn, and the crowd moves down the ice-rutted field toward the fence. We group for a brief solidarity service, holding hands—tonight gripping mittens. *We are a gentle, angry people, and all we are saying is give peace a chance.* Each of us hugs the person on our right, but lots of people come over to hug Cory. Then Norval gives the signal, and twenty or thirty people rush the fence.

Most of them look familiar, the dear knockabout peaceniks I've been getting busted with for years. In front—in the vanguard, as Carl used to say—there's a tall thin man with flowing hair who reminds me of Duke. Of course, it can't be him. The last time I heard anything about him, he was putting down the peace movement as *a bunch of ego-tripping masochists.* They're scrambling for the top of the fifteen-foot fence when a fire department truck rumbles out from behind the hangar and turns a thick stream of water on them, knocking most of the climbers to the ground.

"Those bastards!" yells Jerry. "It's twenty below!"

People are screaming and the swish of the water sounds horribly loud. Another truck rolls out, a flatbed with a spotlight turned on the fence, where half a dozen people have stuck, clinging to the mesh. "O my god, Cory! Can you see? I think they're freezing to the fence. How horrible!"

The people who have fallen off are mostly still on the ground, and the cops bend over them, twisting their wrists together with plastic handcuffs. The long-haired man in sneakers hasn't let go, in fact he's climbed higher, even though the hose is still soaking him with a considerable water pressure. Harder to see in the glare are two figures swathed in something dark and shiny. Plastic, could it be? Like plastic garbage bags?

"Goodness, Dinah, look at Persimmon and Shawana! What if they make it?"

"I know. Wouldn't it be great? Cory, can you see the long-haired guy who's—oops, there he goes! He got over!"

"I saw him. I saw him. He looks like Duke."

"I know, I thought the same thing. But it can't be."

"Who else would be crazy enough to come out in January wearing sneakers?"

Just then the airfield lights go out. The only illumination is the rented spotlight in its truck bed, focused rigidly on the fence where now nothing moves. "Cory, they got over! The three of them got over!"

"I hope you're right. Do you think they killed the light?"

In the black sky shines a high Minnesota moon, aloof and pristine. After a moment our eyes adjust, and the moon gives enough light for us to see each other.

"What about the people who were knocked off?" she asks. "Can you see anything?"

"No. I think Jerry went over to help."

"I hope he remembers not to get busted. That would make a good headline: 'Doctor Arrested for Giving Succor.'"

I wheel her chair as far as I can toward the confused knot of people around the cops arresting the protesters who were knocked off the fence. The ones who can walk are being bundled onto the school bus. Some can't get up.

"Help us," says Jerry peremptorily. "Norv has a broken ankle." Maureen gives him her broad shoulder.

Cory slumps forward. I bend over to hear her murmur, *I'm really tired, darling. I hate to leave, but I've got to. Can you tear yourself away?*

So I turn her chair and, after some jockeying around the police, I make pretty good time over the ice ruts. Weak lights come on as we retreat. "They must have an emergency generator," I say, but she is too exhausted to talk.

I wheeled her all the way to my car, trusting that Jerry would bring Maureen back, and that the support people wouldn't strand Persimmon and Shawana. She was limp with fatigue and cold. Once we were in the car with the heater on, she revived enough to say, "Thanks, darling, that was truly great." It was the last thing she ever said to me.

CODA

CORA

My job now is reconciliation. There is no hope, in any sense of the word I understand. Even Jerry and Serena don't urge me to focus any more, to keep up the exhausting effort. The task is to live sanely without hope. I want to tell Dinah I love her, and I'm glad she didn't get me a baby.

"It's okay to be angry," Jerry whispers, rocking me in his arms like a sick child. "It's okay. Life's fucking unfair, but you've done pretty well, you're gonna finish ahead of the game."

"Do you think it was the bubbling place?" I ask him. "Did that chain reaction get to me?"

"Nah. Could be the general level of shit—the increase in background radiation, pollution of the air and water. You know, though—there's a couple of different things going on. People are living longer, so we're seeing more diseases of old age, like cancer. It's hard to tell how much of the increase is from the yoomin race filling up the world with filth and how much is from the fact we don't die of infectious diseases any more."

Education is such a comfort.

Things will go on, there'll be struggle and resistance. No hope doesn't mean no joy, I try to tell my friends, but they can't hear.

My temper is much better than last summer, when I still had hope. Jerry and I can even laugh. He is my rock, but he breaks down sometimes, and I love that too.

Serena looks very drawn. *We gave it a run, mom. You're a world-class patient, a champion.*

I know they both feel failure because they're doctors, and part of what sustains a doctor through cruel and unusual training is the fantasy that they can save lives. Even Serena, who knows perfectly well that clean water and vaccines save more lives than pediatric reconstructive surgery, has her fantasies of heroism. She found her vocation when she went down to Nicaragua to work with a group of Cuban surgeons patching up kids who were injured in Contra attacks.

Her unit here at University Hospital flies in kids from all over the world, she tells us, though not from Nicaragua, of course. The ones from Thailand are the most wrenching—refugee children blown up by land mines in Laos and Cambodia that date back to when the U.S. Army bombed and mined the Ho Chih Minh Trail. When was it? Fourteen years ago.... Bombs and land mines made in Minnesota, some of them, cluster bombs made by Gladdwin....

She is repairing the world we broke, trimming the missing limbs, grafting skin, smoothing the hideous wounds.

"Yes, we're repairing the world," she says, "but I just hope we can hold onto some of the gains you made."

"What do you mean?"

"Feminism! Do you realize, Mom, how *hard* it is to be a feminist in medicine? It's im*poss*ible. Everything we do totally perpetuates the status quo. We don't see patients, we see arms, legs, abdomens, chests, brains. When you do your ob-gyn rotation you see breasts and pelvises. They make you tell the patients to call you Doctor, and they don't want you to take the time to warm up the speculum or anything, forget listening to what the patient has to say. They really teach you to mistrust your patients, so how are your patients ever going to trust you? And civil rights—you know, affirmative action— every medical school dean I've ever seen completely does everything they can to get around it. They don't even *apolo*gize. And the students nod like sheep and become total little doctor clones."

Ten years ago she was in high school, volunteering at Isis House. She learned her politics by doing, and now she tries desperately to engage me, but I'm slipping out of the web. I don't really care.

If Dinah had pulled off the Guatemalan caper and come back with a baby, what a mess we'd be in. That hunger for a child. . . that was my body mourning. Jerry was right all along. I was grieving for my breast, the poor sick breast, the bad breast. What did she do that was so bad they had to cut her away?

We are gentle with one another, even Jerry with his big paws and his rough, mocking voice. I know he won't let me suffer. I wish I could return the favor.

🌿

I'm glad I did one more demo. Goodness is strong, it shines from us like a line of beacons showing the way.

One image glows in memory: I see Dinah naked at Marcus Inchloe's induction refusal, all those years ago. Six o'clock in the morning on the steps of the old Federal building, another cold demo, the air was blue with cold. She wore a cape, a long, dark cloak with a hood, and she held a pumpkin, or was it a squash? I don't remember, but it was big and full, a voluptuous vegetable. She held it in both her hands and raised it silently to the sky while someone drummed, one of the Icehouse people, and you could see she was naked under the cape. Her breasts glowed in the dim light. I remember thinking, she doesn't look like a woman who's had two children, and then she lowered her arms and laid the squash on the top step.

Inchloe stared at her. We all stared at her, our heads thick with the early hour and the sound of the drum. Quite a few of us were gathered there, we made a point of supporting the draft refusers, Jerry and I, and we always loved the Icehouse people. Icehouse to Isis House. From somewhere under her cape she pulled out a big knife in a leather sheath, drew it forth, raised it in both hands, a graceful gesture with the folds of the cape falling softly around her lovely naked body, and she stabbed deeply into the flesh of that round live thing. She murdered that squash. Drove the knife into it again and again. All you could hear was drumming and the squish of cut flesh. The squash began to lose its shape, and the seeds ran out on the steps. Someone burst into tears, I don't remember who. Someone blew their nose.

She kept stabbing the squash, and the tempo of the drumming increased, and finally it was just a mash on the steps. Ceremoniously, with both hands, she raised the knife and lifted her eyes to heaven, and for a moment I thought she was going to stab it into her own beautiful body. Her breasts and belly looked perfect framed by the dark cape, soft and pearly in the morning mist, but she held the pose while the drum got faster and louder, and then at the climax of the drumming she dropped her head to her chest. The knife gleamed in the dawning light. I turned around to see, and there was a ridge of gold in the east, below the heavy curtain of blue. Then she slid the knife into its sheath and stepped back. Inchloe made a speech about refusing to kill. I hold her image always.

Martha Roth is founding editor of *Hurricane Alice: A Feminist Quarterly*. She is a co-editor of *Mother Journeys: Feminists Write About Mothering* (Spinsters Ink, 1994) and a co-editor of *Transforming a Rape Culture* (Milkweed Editions, 1993). Ms. Roth lives with her family in Minneapolis, MN.

Other Titles Available From Spinsters Ink

All the Muscle You Need, Diana McRae $8.95
Amazon Story Bones, Ellen Frye $10.95
As You Desire, Madeline Moore $9.95
Being Someone, Ann MacLeod $9.95
Cancer in Two Voices, Butler & Rosenblum. $12.95
Child of Her People, Anne Cameron. $8.95
Common Murder, Val McDermid $9.95
Considering Parenthood, Cheri Pies $12.95
Desert Years, Cynthia Rich $7.95
Elise, Claire Kensington $7.95
Fat Girl Dances with Rocks, Susan Stinson $10.95
Final Rest, Mary Morell $9.95
Final Session, Mary Morell. $9.95
Give Me Your Good Ear, 2nd Ed., Maureen Brady. $9.95
Goodness, Martha Roth $10.95
The Hangdog Hustle, Elizabeth Pincus $9.95
High and Outside, Linnea A. Due $8.95
The Journey, Anne Cameron $9.95
The Lesbian Erotic Dance, JoAnn Loulan. $12.95
Lesbian Passion, JoAnn Loulan $12.95
Lesbian Sex, JoAnn Loulan $12.95
Lesbians at Midlife, ed. by Sang, Warshow & Smith $12.95
The Lessons, Melanie McAllester $9.95
Life Savings, Linnea Due. $10.95
Look Me in the Eye, 2nd Ed., Macdonald & Rich $8.95
Love and Memory, Amy Oleson $9.95
Martha Moody, Susan Stinson. $10.95
Modern Daughters and the Outlaw West, Melissa Kwasny $9.95
Mother Journeys: Feminists Write About Mothering, Sheldon, Reddy, Roth. .$15.95
No Matter What, Mary Saracino $9.95
Ransacking the Closet, Yvonne Zipter $9.95
Roberts' Rules of Lesbian Living, Shelly Roberts $5.95
The Other Side of Silence, Joan M. Drury $9.95
The Solitary Twist, Elizabeth Pincus $9.95
Thirteen Steps, Bonita L. Swan $8.95
Trees Call for What They Need, Melissa Kwasny $9.95
The Two-Bit Tango, Elizabeth Pincus $9.95
Vital Ties, Karen Kringle. $10.95
Why Can't Sharon Kowalski Come Home? Thompson & Andrzejewski $10.95

Spinsters titles are available at your local booksellers or by mail order through Spinsters Ink. A free catalog is available upon request. Please include $2.00 for the first title
ordered and 50¢ for every title thereafter. Visa and Mastercard accepted.

Spinsters Ink
32 E. First St., #330
Duluth, MN 55802-2002

218-727-3222 (phone)   (fax) 218-727-3119

Spinsters Ink was founded in 1978 to produce vital books for diverse women's communities. In 1986 we merged with Aunt Lute Books to become Spinsters/Aunt Lute. In 1990, the Aunt Lute Foundation became an independent nonprofit publishing program. In 1992, Spinsters moved to Minnesota.

Spinsters Ink publishes novels and nonfiction that deal with significant issues in women's lives from a feminist perspective: books that not only name these crucial issues, but—more important—encourage change and growth. We are committed to publishing works by women writing from the periphery: fat women, Jewish women, lesbians, old women, poor women, rural women, women examining classism, women of color, women with disabilities, women who are writing books that help make the best in our lives more possible.